Praise for Anna Lee Huber's Verity Kent Mysteries:

Penny for Your Secrets

"Readers looking for atmospheric mystery set in the period following the Great War will savor the intricate plotting and captivating details of the era." —*Library Journal* (**Starred Review**)

"Action-filled . . . Huber offers a well-researched historical and a fascinating look at the lingering aftermath of war."
—*Publishers Weekly*

"No sooner are Verity Kent and her dashing but troubled husband, Sidney, back from solving a mystery in Belgium (*Treacherous Is the Night*, 2018) than they are confronted with one at home in London . . . Touching details of the Kents' struggle to overcome Sidney's anguish add to the stellar mystery here, making this a great read for fans of the series and for all who enjoy Downton Abbey–era fiction." —*Booklist*

"Huber's historical mysteries are always multilayered, complex stories, and *Penny* is an especially satisfying one as she interweaves social commentary and righteous feminist rage into the post-War period. With a perfect blend of murder, mystery, history, romance, and powerful heroines, Huber has yet to disappoint." —*Criminal Element*

"This is a fine historical mystery series that will not disappoint."
—*Historical Novel Society*

Treacherous Is the Night

"A thrilling mystery that supplies its gutsy heroine with plenty of angst-ridden romance." —*Kirkus Reviews*

"[A] splendid sequel. . . . Huber combines intricate puzzles with affecting human drama." —*Publishers Weekly*

"Masterful. . . . Just when you think the plot will zig, it zags. Regardless of how well-versed you may be in the genre, you'll be hard-pressed to predict this climax. . . . Deeply enjoyable . . . just the thing if you're looking for relatable heroines, meatier drama, and smart characters with rich inner lives."
—*Criminal Element*

"Huber is an excellent historical mystery writer, and Verity is her best heroine. Sidney and Verity are a formidable couple when they work together, but they are also very real. They don't leap straight back into life before the war but instead face many obstacles and struggles as they readjust to married life and post-war life. Nonetheless, the love between Sidney and Verity is real and true, and the way that Huber creates their re-blossoming love is genuine. Topped off with a gripping mystery, this will not disappoint." —*Historical Novel Society*

This Side of Murder

"Huber paints a compelling portrait of the aftermath of World War I, and shows the readers how devastating the war was for everyone in England . . . I am looking forward to reading many more of Verity Kent's adventures." —*Historical Novel Society*

"I loved *This Side of Murder*, a richly textured mystery filled with period detail and social mores, whose plot twists and character revelations kept me up way past my bedtime. Can't wait for the next Verity Kent adventure!"
—**Shelley Noble, *New York Times* bestselling author of *The Beach at Painters' Cove* and *Ask Me No Questions***

"A smashing and engrossing tale of deceit, murder and betrayal set just after World War I. . . . Anna Lee Huber has crafted a truly captivating mystery here." —*All About Romance*

"The new Verity Kent Mystery series is rich in detail without being overwhelming and is abundant with murder, mystery, and a bit of romance. The plot is fast-moving with twists and turns aplenty. Huber knows what it takes to write a great mystery."
—*RT Book Reviews*

"A captivating murder mystery told with flair and panache!"
—**Fresh Fiction**

"Sure to please fans of classic whodunits and lovers of historical fiction alike."
—**Jessica Estevao, author of *Whispers Beyond the Veil***

Novels by Anna Lee Huber

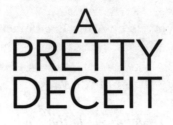

A
PRETTY
DECEIT

A PRETTY DECEIT

A Verity Kent Mystery

ANNA LEE HUBER

KENSINGTON BOOKS
www.kensingtonbooks.com

KENSINGTON BOOKS are published by

Kensington Publishing Corp.
119 West 40th Street
New York, NY 10018

All Kensington titles, imprints, and distributed lines are available at special quantity discounts for bulk purchases for sales promotion, premiums, fund-raising, educational, or institutional use.

Special book excerpts or customized printings can also be created to fit specific needs. For details, write or phone the office of the Kensington Sales Manager: Kensington Publishing Corp., 119 West 40th Street, New York, NY 10018. Attn. Sales Department. Phone: 1-800-221-2647.

Kensington and the K logo Reg. U.S. Pat. & TM Off.

ISBN-13: 978-1-4967-2847-0
ISBN-10: 1-4967-2847-5
First Kensington Trade Paperback Printing: October 2020

ISBN-13: 978-1-4967-2848-7 (ebook)
ISBN-10: 1-4967-2848-3 (ebook)

10 9 8 7 6 5 4 3 2 1

Printed in the United States of America

For my brother Jeff,
who has always been big-hearted, dedicated, and
determined. Thank you for always being there, whether
the chips are up or down! You have always jumped
wholeheartedly into fun, and your kindness and generosity
of spirit is inspiring to all, especially your students.
I'm so proud of you!

ACKNOWLEDGMENTS

Heaps of thanks and gratitude go to . . .

My spectacular editor, Wendy McCurdy, and the entire team at Kensington, including, but not limited to: Elizabeth Trout, Ann Pryor, Larissa Ackerman, Kristin McLaughlin, Michelle Addo, Carly Sommerstein, Lauren Jernigan, and Alexandra Nicolajsen.

My agent-extraordinaire, Kevan Lyon, and everyone at Marsal Lyon Literary Agency.

My writing group partners—Jackie Musser, Stacie Roth Miller, and Jackie Adams—whose care and feedback is always invaluable.

My husband, whose love and encouragement mean more than anything, and who is (almost) always willing to listen to me ramble and help me plot.

My daughters, for their snuggles and laughter, and for showing me how to view the world through different eyes.

My family, for all their love and support, especially my mom.

And most importantly God, for all His blessings, guidance, inspiration, and strength.

PROLOGUE

And, after all, what is a lie? 'Tis but the truth
in masquerade.
—Lord Byron

April 1918
Bailleul, France

Mud. Muck. Miles and miles of it. As far as the eye could see. Though the rain had stopped two nights' past, the constant churning of feet, hooves, and wheels kept the condition of the roads soft and ever mutable. Perhaps tonight's chill would freeze it solid, albeit into rutted tracks and ridges.

Except a spell of dry weather meant the renewal of the Germans' advance. As the second day of brilliant blue skies stretched toward nightfall, I could sense the tension palpably running through everyone I passed. Be it the French refugees fleeing from their homes with their most precious possessions strapped to their backs in the onslaught of this latest German assault, the ambulances carting away the groaning wounded, or the fresh troops marching up the line to relieve their exhausted allies. It was only a matter of time before the next wave of attack began.

With that clock ticking down in my head, I pressed on, ignoring the sharp pains in my feet and the stitch in my side, as well as the curious looks I received from some of the soldiers marching alongside me in long columns. Their boots and putties already flecked with mud, and their drab wool uniforms stiff with sweat, few of them paid me more than a passing interest. Their thoughts were too centered on what was to come. After all, only a week before, Haig had issued his "backs to the wall" order, and our boys were taking it seriously. They hadn't bled and suffered for three and a half long years to go down now.

In all candor, that bloody-mindedness was one of the reasons I'd made it this far up the line. Normally, I would have been halted and repelled miles back, sent packing with the other refugees. Two officers had tried, but I'd double-backed and circumvented them, keeping a wary eye out for their companies. In the chaos and confusion of the swift retreat, a sympathetic soldier might buy my story of having lost track of my young brother during my family's flight from our home in Bailleul, but they would grow suspicious if they caught me again.

I pulled the dingy, frayed coat tighter around my frame, keeping my head down, as I bustled past the officers at the head of the latest column. Battered and broken buildings lined this stretch of the road. The once-prosperous farm reduced to rubble and ashes, much like the newly budding trees that resembled little more than charred stumps and splinters of wood. The air smelled not of spring—new growth and freshly turned earth—but fetid decay, smoke, and desperation.

The Germans had already penetrated nearly fifty miles into the Somme sector of the Western Front, and now their troops to the north were pushing westward toward Ypres and beyond. Towns that had been safely tucked behind the Allies' lines since late 1914 were now cowering from German shells or escaping their advance. And so the war of attrition had begun to move, simply not in the direction we wished it to.

I spared a glance toward the west and the setting sun as brilliant oranges, mauves, and purples tinted the sky—a poignant reminder that even the hellishness of this war, and its utter destruction to the landscape, could not blot out beauty completely. I blinked hard, choking down a sudden swell of emotion. *Don't think of him now*, I ordered myself. *After. Once the message is delivered. Once the job is done, you can collapse in a shell hole and consign yourself to his fate, if you wish. But you have to finish this one last thing first.*

At the sight of the wrecked rail track stretched across the landscape in front of me, I quickened my pace. I'd been able to inveigle out of a second lieutenant I'd spoken to near Saint-Jans-Cappel that Brigadier General Bishop had created a temporary command post in a crude shelter by the side of the road a short distance from the remnants of a farm and a shattered rail track. Though I'd seen several damaged farms, this was the first one I'd spied next to a rail line.

This had to be it, and I might have made it with just moments to spare. For the chill dark of night often meant only the beginning of the days' true hostilities. I had to reach the general before the Germans renewed their bombardment or fog rolled in to obscure another of their advances.

I spied the shelter, light gleaming through a few of the rough slats, and the sight of my objective perhaps made me a bit reckless. Rather than pause to consider the best possible method of gaining access, and give the sentries posted outside the warped door time to take an interest in me, I charged forward, attempting to obscure my approach as best I could behind the lines of marching soldiers. But eventually there was nothing between me and them, and I had to rely on the element of surprise to slide between them as they turned to stop me with a shout of protest. By then, I was already throwing open the slatted door and stumbling down the three steps into the partially submerged single-room shelter.

I stopped short of the rickety wooden table set near the center of the room, maps and papers strewn across it, dimly lit by the lanterns swinging from hooks in the ceiling above.

In the yellow glow, I met the eyes of the man I'd traveled so far and through such precarious territory to reach. And I held his gaze even as I heard the click of at least three Webley revolvers being cocked as they were drawn from the holsters of the commander's subordinates and aimed at me.

The general assessed me with a swift perusal of my person. "Young woman, what do you think you are doing?" he demanded of me in French, mistaking me for the refugee I appeared to be.

"Brigadier General Bishop," I replied, my crisp upper-class British accent making his pupils widen and the gentleman holding the revolver to my left waiver. "I have a dispatch for you from London."

The commander scrutinized me with new eyes, displaying enough intelligence not to ask stupid questions. Evidently, he recognized that if a young lady had been sent under disguise all the way from London with a message for him, then it must be of utmost importance.

"Lower your weapons," he ordered his young officers. Then his gaze shifted to the sentries standing at my back. One of them had grasped my elbow. "We will discuss this breach later," he promised them, and then dismissed them with a nod of his head.

Extending his hand, he snapped his fingers, beckoning me forward. I pulled the letter from the inner pocket of my coat and passed it to him across the broad expanse of the table. His eyes continued to inspect me even as he broke the seal and unfolded the paper.

What precisely it said, I didn't know. Only that I'd been charged with the task of delivering it by C, the chief, himself. As an agent working for the British Secret Service, the foreign division of Military Intelligence, I'd spent a number of weeks behind enemy lines in the German-occupied territories of Belgium and northeastern France, liaising with members of our intelligence-gathering networks, but I'd never been this close to the front line. The rare times I'd been sent on a mission behind British lines, they had been well in the rear of the trenches. It was too difficult for a woman to approach the battle zone unnoticed, and the army's own military intelligence officers handled most matters that might require our attention there.

In the normal course of matters, they would have handled this as well. Except we'd long suspected someone along this stretch of front was intercepting Bishop's reports and forwarding the information to the enemy, and we'd recently begun to realize that person was among the brigadier general's staff. Army intelligence had been charged with investigating the matter, but now that the Germans' big push had begun and was concentrating in this sector, while army intelligence had yet to do anything to root out the traitor, C had decided it was imperative that Bishop be warned. Especially if the spy turned out to be one of his intelligence officers.

When Bishop had finished reading, his sharp eyes again met mine, clearly apprehending I was far more than the messenger I seemed. I had no choice but to trust he would keep this insight to himself.

"Captain Scott," he snapped, calling forward a man with cool, crystalline-blue eyes. "Please escort the mademoiselle to safety at the rear of the latest train of refugees on the road to Hazebrouck."

That he'd been tasked with this assignment undoubtedly must have displeased him, but the captain did not show it by even a flicker of an eyelash. For my part, relief at having completed my assignment was swiftly giving way to exhaustion and malaise, and I felt almost as if I was sleepwalking as I turned to proceed the captain through the door. The sentries were both scowling at me as I strode past, but I hadn't an ounce of energy or sympathy to spare for them. Not when the fact of the matter was they hadn't been doing their jobs very well, or else they would have stopped me.

The never-ending columns of supply lorries and troops continued to march past into the twilight, and in the distance I could hear the rumbling prelude to the evening's salvo of artillery fire. All of these sights and sounds should have been a shock to my system, but instead a haze of numbness seemed to have settled over me. I was striding down the verge of a muddy road outside Bailleul, but I was also locked somewhere inside myself. Somewhere where the full impact of the telegram informing me of my husband's death, which had been delivered some four weeks past, was hammering away at what little will I had left.

I'd forced myself to keep working, to keep moving, to keep doing my bit for all that Sidney had fought and died for. And at night, when the pain and grief became too much, I did my best to drown it out with gin and whisky. But it was such a strain to carry this weight around day after day, to bear up under it all as if I hadn't completely crumbled to pieces inside. There were moments when it would suddenly all come crashing into me, and I would find myself barely able to breathe. There were some nights I couldn't even pray, my pluck and spirit all gone. And sometimes I wanted nothing more than to lie down and consign myself to the dust around me. Perhaps then I could rejoin Sidney on the other side. Perhaps then we could be together as we'd never truly been allowed to be here on earth with the war constantly tearing us apart.

The captain walked lightly beside me, his hand gripping my elbow, completely oblivious to the turmoil inside me. I wanted to tell him to let me lie down in the shelter created by the fallen branches of a shelled tree to our right and leave me to my fate. When we veered in that direction, I began to wonder if I'd actually spoken those words aloud. But then he yanked me behind a smaller structure, shielding us from the road, and slammed me against the rough wooden boards.

"What are you doing here?" he snarled at me, inches from my face. "What did you give the general?" When I didn't answer quickly enough, he grasped my upper arms, slamming me back against the wall a second time, this time knocking my head against the planks. "Why are you here?"

I closed my eyes, my head whirling from the impact, and tried to gather my scattered thoughts. "You saw . . ." I stammered, endeavoring to force my sluggish mind into action even as the back of my skull pounded. "I delivered . . ."

He shook me. "Tell me!"

The look in his eyes when I opened them told me he would not spare me in finding out what he wanted to know. I'd seen the same expression on the face of a member of the German Secret Police ruthlessly interrogating an old Belgian man at a checkpoint before he'd broken his arm. My nerves tightened in awareness, recognizing I needed to get away—that this might be the very man we'd been warning Bishop about—but my mind was still struggling to catch up, my vision blurry.

Had Bishop known who the spy in his camp was? Had he deliberately sent him away with me? But if so, why hadn't he warned me? Or had he, and in my grief-stricken haze I hadn't noticed?

I tried to remember my training, to recall which limb I should strike out with, or whether I should slump against his grip and allow the dead weight of my body to pull him off balance. Before I could decide, the choice was made for me, as suddenly the whole world was upended.

A terrific explosion ripped through my ear drums even as I was being tossed through the air, landing with a painful thud against the earth. For a moment, it was all I could do but to lie there utterly stunned. Struggling to draw breath, I worried my lungs had been punctured, but then I realized the wind had simply been knocked out of me. Something pressed against my back, holding me down. I shifted my knees up beneath me, trying to leverage it off of me, but it wouldn't budge.

I must have cried out, for hands were soon pulling me

out of the rubble. Soldiers from the road had rushed to my aid. I blinked against the brightness of the sudden inferno before me. The entire temporary headquarters had gone up in flames. No doubt killing everyone inside, including the brigadier general I had journeyed all this way to deliver that message to. Of all the rotten misbegotten luck, for his HQ to suffer a direct hit from a shell when everyone knew the artillery's aim was rubbish. Sometimes they couldn't target an entire bloody town, let alone a single house, though the Germans were admittedly far more accurate than we were. A few minutes earlier and I would have been killed, as well.

Such a realization made my knees feel soft, particularly given my morose ponderings as I'd left that shelter.

A face loomed before me. My ears still ringing from the impact, I couldn't hear the words the man was saying, even though he was screaming them directly into my face. Finally, he just grabbed hold of my arm and began pulling me away from the debris. As another shell landed some several hundred yards away, sending dirt and debris in a plume up into the air, I grasped what he was trying to communicate. Take cover!

We ran in the direction of the wrecked rail line, pausing only long enough for him to grab the helmet from a fallen soldier, his vacant eyes staring up at the night sky as one by one the stars began to wink into existence. To our left, I noted the man being attended to by another pair of soldiers. It was the captain who had attacked me. We'd been thrown apart, and apparently he'd suffered greater wounds than I had, for his head was bloodied, his eyes closed in unconsciousness.

I had only a moment to spare a thought for what to do about him before the soldier and I were running again and then diving into a makeshift trench that had been dug to the west of the road. The soldier crammed the scavenged helmet onto my head, and I slumped down beside him, cowering as the shells continued to fall and the world quaked and trembled around us.

CHAPTER 1

October 1919
Wiltshire, England

There are few things more wonderful than seeing the face of someone you love lit with pure joy. Particularly someone who has faced so much darkness, so much horror and grief. It makes your breath catch in your throat, and turns your heart inside out and then right-side out again at the realization you would do anything to preserve that happiness, that delight.

Anything but die, that is.

"Darling, I'm glad you're enjoying your new roadster," I called, raising my voice to be heard over the roar of the engine and the cool rush of the wind past my cheeks. "But if it's all the same to you, I would like to make it to my aunt's house in one piece."

Sidney's eyes gleamed with exhilaration. "Isn't she a beauty?" he exclaimed, his hands caressing the driving wheel much as he had caressed me the night before.

"She is," I agreed, and I meant it. Though not as zealous a motorist as my husband, I could certainly appreciate the fine craftsmanship and performance of a magnificent motorcar. Just as I could appreciate his enthusiasm. After all, his previous Pierce-Arrow had been destroyed during a dangerous investigation we'd undertaken in war-ravaged Belgium, and

Sidney had waited three long months for this replacement to arrive from America. Even I had felt a surge of elation at my first sight of her, all sleek lines and glossy deep carmine-red paint. Which only made my desire not to collide with a tree, or worse, another motorcar, even greater—for the roadster's sake and mine.

The motorcar soared over a slight rise in the road and then raced downward, fast approaching a sharp curve. My fingers gripped the seat beneath me until I felt Sidney apply the brakes and ease around the turn with precision handling, only for the car to spring forward again, like a young horse pulling against its traces.

Not that I minded the speed, in general. I relished the thrill of the world whipping past and the raw power of a good engine driving beneath me as much as anyone. But the roads in this part of Berkshire were narrow and lined with tall hedges and dense coppices, making it impossible to see what was around the next bend until you were already upon it. So the use of this new Pierce-Arrow's extra surge of speed was perhaps a trifle reckless. But reckless always had been Sidney's driving style.

He threw me a disarming smile as we approached another curve, and I felt some of my tension ease. After all, four months ago I'd still believed him dead, and here he was, returned to me, to the life he'd lived before that fateful day in August 1914 when war was declared. The last thing I wanted to do was crush his enjoyment. But nonetheless, he seemed to recognize from my clenched fingers and tight jaw that perhaps I wasn't enjoying myself as much as he was. As he straightened out of the turn, he trod more gently on the accelerator, hurling us forward at a slightly less hell-for-leather pace.

"Tell me about your aunt," he urged me as he scraped a hand back through his dark wind-rifled hair. He'd long since discarded his hat in the seat behind us. "She's your father's sister?"

"Yes, or else I doubt my father would have bestirred himself to interrupt my mother." I turned to gaze through an opening in the hedge line through which I could see the rolling hills of the North Wessex Downs and the winding blue ribbon of the River Kennet.

I thought back to my mother's telephone call the day before. It had been at least a fortnight since I'd last heard from her, and she rarely let a period of such length pass without calling to harangue me about one infraction or another, or to complain about my sister or one of my brothers. But the reason for this call had been something of a shock. Even more so when my father had pried the mouthpiece from her fingers to add his voice to her request.

"What your mother's trying to say, Ver, is that your aunt's had a rough time of it since the war," he had told me in his warm, gravelly voice. "Losing Sir James and Thomas almost one right after the other nearly broke her. And then for Reginald to have come home the way he did, well, she's done in."

"I'm sorry for Aunt Ernestine, I truly am," I had replied. "But Mother said she needed my help, and I honestly don't know what I can do. Have they tried one of those specialty hospitals I've read about, the ones that are supposed to treat returning soldiers in situations like Reg?"

"Aye, yes. They've tried all that. In fact, he's just returned from one. But this is nothing to do with your cousin."

"What do you mean?"

Father had exhaled a long, weary breath, letting me know Mother had already talked circles around him on this subject, and all for naught. For once my father made up his mind about something, it would take a force greater than a whirlwind to move him from it. And my mother was very nearly that. "As I understand it, the manor is in shambles thanks

to the airmen who billeted there from the neighboring aerodrome during the war. And now your aunt has discovered
she hasn't the coffers to pay for it. Apparently everything is
already mortgaged to the hilt, and a number of the estate's
priceless heirlooms have gone missing from storage, so she
can't even sell her most portable property to raise some of
the funds."

I had felt a pang of empathy for my aunt. And my father.
Aunt Ernestine had always been a woman enamored with her
own consequence, and never content enough until everyone
knew it. This situation must be extremely lowering for her.
While my mother must be silently crowing with delight—
evidence that the vain and mighty shall fall, and the meek
and humble shall flourish. At least, when the vain and mighty
were her enemies.

"But surely this is an issue for the War Office to sort out, if
there are damages and theft to be reported?" I had countered.

"Yes, but your aunt has watched her orderly world crumble around her, and I'm not certain she's thinking clearly."

"You think she's lying?" I had said in surprise.

"Not lying. Just . . . confused. To hear her speak, Littlemote House is practically crumbling to pieces around them,
and yet I find it difficult to believe the Royal Air Force would
ever have allowed it to get to such a state." My mother's
voice mumbled in the background, and my father turned to
speak to her before heaving another aggrieved sigh. "She was
also rambling on about a missing servant and a ghost, of all
things. Yes, yes, Sarah," he shushed my mother. "I admit it
sounded all a little mad. Certainly unlike Ernestine."

"Yes, very odd," I had acknowledged hesitantly, already
conscious of where this was going.

"Can you and Sidney pay her a visit at Littlemote? Find out
exactly what the situation is there? I would ask your cousin
Reginald, but he's in no state to deal with all of this."

I wasn't certain I agreed with his final statement. After all,

Reg was the new baronet, and blinded or not, he would have to confront the concerns of his baronetcy at some point.

But there was another reason I was reluctant to go to Littlemote, though I would never have voiced it aloud. Not to my father, in any case. Moreover, he didn't give me a chance.

"Please, Verity. You are the closest, and your husband undoubtedly has the most clout to get something done should your aunt's claims prove true. After all, they did just pin a Victoria Cross to his chest for valor. We're dashed proud of him, by the way."

I had smiled tightly into the mirror that hung above the bureau where our telephone rested in our London flat, refusing to examine the unsettling jumble of emotions that mention of Sidney's medal always threatened to dredge up. Instead I focused on my father's voice, on the evident worry and uncertainty that tainted his normally stoical tones. When, if ever, had my father asked me for anything? It seemed churlish to say no. But still I resisted.

"I'll speak with Sidney. If he has no objections, we'll drive out to Littlemote tomorrow," I had promised, privately hoping my husband would nix such a plan, though I'd known he wouldn't. We were bound for Falmouth anyway, and a stop in northeastern Wiltshire was virtually along the way.

So here we were, slowing to motor through yet another of the tiny villages that dotted the English countryside in counties as fertile as Berkshire and neighboring Wiltshire. "Aunt Ernestine is father's younger sister," I explained to Sidney. "He's always been a bit protective of her, to Mother's everlasting annoyance."

His lips quirked in amusement.

I lifted my hand to return the excited wave of a little girl perched on her stone house's front step. "Sadly, her husband, Sir James Popham, died two years ago. A heart attack, from the strain of losing their eldest son, Thomas, the doctor said."

"Thomas served during the war?"

I nodded. "Part of the Irish Guards. Killed at Loos."

There was no need to reply. His heavy silence said more than enough. Simply the name of some battles told the entire story in and of themselves, imbued forever with the death and destruction that had happened there. Loos. Verdun. Passchendaele. The Somme.

I took a deep breath, forcing myself to continue in a light voice as the Pierce-Arrow reached the edge of the village and again began gathering speed. "By comparison, their younger son, Reginald, seemed to live a charmed war. Ostensibly." For I understood, as Sidney certainly did, that no soldier had survived the horrors of trench warfare without some sort of scars, invisible though they might be to the eye.

"Until he didn't," he surmised.

"He was blinded at Ypres in 1917."

"Poor bloke."

"Yes, well, don't let him hear you say that." I turned to peer out over the countryside to the north at the sound of the familiar buzzing rumble. "Last I saw him, he was already feeling sorry enough for himself, and he won't thank you for it."

"Noted." His eyes darted between the road and the same patch of sky I was monitoring.

When finally the aeroplane soared into sight, passing over the copse of oak trees just beginning to burst into autumn color, and the welcome roundel insignia could be seen painted on the underside of the wings, we both seemed to inhale a breath of relief. I wondered how long it would take before the sound of approaching aircraft no longer filled me with dread. How long until the instinct to duck and cover was no longer my first impulse?

Sidney's hands tightened and then relaxed their grip on the driving wheel. "We must be close."

"Yes," was all I could manage, my heart still racing from the instinct of prey. After all, during my time working behind enemy lines in the German-occupied territories of Belgium and northeastern France, that had been very much what I was.

Sidney rested his hand on my leg and offered me a consoling smile, letting me know that I hadn't hidden my alarm as well as I'd hoped. But his attention was soon reclaimed by the aeroplane as it wheeled about, returning toward us. I shielded my eyes to gaze up at its metal frame glinting in the crystalline-blue sky. Rather than fly off in the direction of the aerodrome, from which it had come, the light bomber seemed to swerve back and forth over top of us. Something I was none too comfortable with.

"I'd wager that pilot is a bit of motor enthusiast," Sidney proclaimed with pride. His eyes glinted with challenge. "Shall we give him a show?"

No sooner had the words left his mouth than the Pierce-Arrow surged forward, its engine revving as it gained speed over a relatively straight stretch of open road. I pressed my Napoleon blue cloche hat down tighter on my head, my stomach fluttering as the wind whipped past my cheeks. However, I wasn't unmoved by the exhilaration of such speed, and a breathless laugh escaped from my mouth, belying my trepidation.

The bomber kept pace with us, more or less straightening out his flight path. Though, of course, had the pilot wished, he could have left us in a trail of his fumes.

"Sidney," I gasped. "Tell me you are not trying to race that aeroplane."

The widening of his grin was my only answer.

I shook my head and clutched the seat beneath me, my fingernails biting into the leather even through my kid gloves. "I'm all for a bit of fun," I shouted over the wind. "But I cannot promise your prized car's upholstery won't have claw marks in it when it's over."

He glanced over at me, perhaps recognizing for the first

time the uneasiness underlying my banter, and eased up on the accelerator. And not a moment too soon. For the motorcar whipped around a bend and into the outskirts of another village, where a man and woman stood yelling at each other in the middle of the road.

Sidney stomped on the brakes, fighting to bring the Pierce-Arrow to a safe stop while I braced myself against the dashboard. When the motorcar shuddered to a stop, dust from the road billowing up around us, the couple stood but inches from our front fender.

The man appeared frozen with shock, while the woman seemed to teeter and then stagger backward a few steps, her face contorted in a grimace as she blinked rapidly. For a moment, I feared we *had* struck her. But once she'd righted herself, she swayed back toward the man, her head bobbling on her shoulders as she raised her finger to resume whatever tirade she had been delivering. The man ignored her words in favor of scowling at us. And rightfully so. Though what had he expected, standing in the middle of the road, and a rather well-traveled thoroughfare at that?

I heard the metallic squeal of a lorry's brakes as it rumbled up behind us and then the blast of its klaxon, clearly impatient to be on his way. I suspected that was all that saved us from a blistering rebuke from the fellow in the road. He grasped the woman's elbow and pulled her from the thoroughfare, and all the while her stream of words never stopped.

Sidney eased past the couple and their neighbors, who were watching while I struggled to steady my breath. Once we were beyond the village of quaint stone and brick buildings, he increased his speed, but to nothing close to the pace he had been driving before. I looked overhead, noticing his aerial competitor had flown on to wherever his destination was.

"Sorry about that," Sidney murmured, shifting gears. "I suppose this isn't the most ideal place to be putting her through her paces. But on the bright side, at least we now know her brakes are tip-top."

I glared at him in mild annoyance that he could be so blasé about the matter.

His eyes cut to me before returning to the road, and then he reached over to press his hand over mine where it rested in my lap. "I didn't mean to unsettle you. I shall take more care from here on out."

I arched a single eyebrow at him. "Is that out of concern for me, or because you'd rather not see your new Pierce-Arrow come to rack and ruin like the last one?"

His deep blue eyes flashed with humor. "You, of course."

"Uh-huh," I replied, unconvinced.

He squeezed my hand before releasing it, gripping the driving wheel with both hands to navigate around a sharp curve. Once the road straightened, a sign on the side of the road proclaimed we were entering Wiltshire.

"The turn for Littlemote House is just up here," I directed, pointing off to the right.

Sidney followed my directives, turning the motorcar onto the rutted single track. Here he kept the roadster at a slow speed, lest the rough, pockmarked lane damage it.

"So what do you think that row in the road was all about?" he asked, nodding his head back in the direction we'd come as we bumped and trundled down the track. Perhaps using the eastern entrance had not been the wisest choice. I could only hope the main drive farther along the road, leading away from the house to the south, was in better condition.

"I don't know. But it seemed obvious she was three sheets to the wind, and I have to wonder if he was at least a trifle zozzled himself. I'm simply glad we didn't hit them," I added in a softer voice.

Soon enough, we caught sight of the squat guard house, which now stood abandoned, ivy and creeping vines overgrowing its pocked stone walls. Beyond this point, the lane widened and, happily, smoothed out, being better maintained than the rest of the approach. Passing a copse of poplar trees, Littlemote House sprang into view, its sprawling flint, limestone ashlar, and brick edifice dominating the highest elevation for miles in either direction. Though not to my taste, my aunt had reason to be proud of the Elizabethan manor, particularly the extensive gardens, which had always been her pride and joy. Though I had to wonder if any of it had been planted over with vegetables when the government had begun urging citizens to utilize any arable land for crops.

We rounded the circular drive, pulling to a stop at the arched portico standing over the heavy wooden double doors. My eyes scanned the structure for signs of the damage my aunt had eluded to, but other than a broken and patched window, and a general air of unkemptness, I couldn't say it looked much different from what I remembered. But once I stepped out onto the crushed-stone, I began to note the things I'd missed from a distance. Smashed and broken shrubbery, a few fallen roof tiles, and pits in some of the brick, as if someone had fired a gun at it. The trellised greenery covering the exterior, which had always been so lovingly maintained, and was even now bursting into bright red in the autumn chill, had quite obviously been the victim of some airmen's prank. Why they had taken it upon themselves to climb the structure, I didn't know, but it was fortunate the iron brackets fastening it in place had held, otherwise the entire wooden lattice might have come crashing down along with its foliage. As it was, there were broken and splintered rungs, as well as some badly bruised ivy.

So absorbed was I in taking inventory that I didn't notice the doors had opened until I heard my aunt's voice.

"Oh, Verity, thank heavens you've come," she exclaimed as she hurried across the portico to wrap me in her lavender-scented embrace. "They've ruined everything!"

CHAPTER 2

"Hullo, Aunt Ernestine," I replied, hugging her back as she continued to heave aggrieved sighs. "Who's ruined everything? Our flyboys?"

"Pack of savages!" she exclaimed with vehemence. "Why on earth Sir James ever allowed them to use Littlemote, I'll never understand."

Her husband likely had no choice, but I refrained from saying so.

She shook her head. "Oh, I should never have allowed him to convince me to stay in London. I should have insisted on keeping a corner of the manor to myself." Her dark eyes flashed martially and her spine stiffened. "I should have kept those young men in line." She sniffed through her dainty nose—the daintiest part of her matronly form swathed in blond silk and tweed wool—and turned toward Sidney, her demeanor softening. "Lovely to see you, Sidney. The family is all quite proud of you, my dear boy."

"Thank you, Lady Popham," he replied, taking her proffered hand as he bowed over it. He'd quickly learned it was the only response he could make. Demurring the honor bestowed upon him and his own actions only seemed to somehow disparage the sacrifices made by other men and their families, so rather than convey an unintentional slight, he simply said very little about it.

She patted his hand where he held hers. "Please, dear. Call me Aunt Ernestine. We are family, after all." Then she pulled him forward, lacing her arm through his. "Now, let me show you what else those savages have done."

I smiled at my aunt's ancient butler standing by the doors and then followed in their wake. There was no doubt from whom I'd inherited my figure. All the women in my father's family, including Aunt Ernestine, were pleasantly rounded, while my mother was whipcord lean. Being young and inclined toward sport, no one could accuse my form of running to fat, but I looked nothing like the thin, boyish figures beginning to grace the covers of the fashion magazines.

Stepping out of the bright sunlight and into the entry and then through to the great hall, where the majority of the walls were covered in dark wooden paneling, it took a moment for my eyes to adjust. But once they did, I recognized what had so dismayed my aunt. The airmen had evidently put the large open space with high ceilings to good use as some sort of recreation area, though what precisely they had been playing, I could not say. There were gouges in the walls and paneling from some sort of ball or other projectile, and a number of window panes in the large latticed windows had been replaced by new glass of uneven quality. Even the flagstone floor sported its share of scuffs, cuts, and dents.

"You were wise to put the weaponry in storage," Sidney remarked as he gazed up at one rather impressive broad sword now reaffixed to its position on the wall.

"I should say so," my aunt proclaimed, fairly quivering with outrage. "I shudder to think what state this house would have been in had I left them and our best furnishings to those *scoundrels'* uses."

I tilted my head to study the pair of mismatched wall sconces that had been hung to replace their eighteenth-century predecessors. That they'd been switched rather than repaired indicated the condition they must have been in.

"We were told officers would be residing here, but that is *obviously* not the case." She sniffed. "For I cannot believe gently raised men would treat an ancestral home so shabbily."

Sidney's head turned, his gaze meeting mine in silent communication. Yes, but what is an Elizabethan manor but wood and stone when a man was faced with the very real possibility of his death—and a horrendous fiery one at that—not to mention the deaths of his friends and the pilots under his command every time he took to the skies for their bombing runs. There was a reason the casualty rate for the Royal Flying Corps, and its successor, the Royal Air Force, was so high.

"You can't tell me your brother would have behaved so appallingly."

I should have expected it. I should have been prepared for my aunt to invoke Rob's name and dredge his memory into the matter purely because he had been an airman. But I wasn't. And it cut me to the quick. As if someone had slipped a stiletto under my rib cage and extracted it before I could even flinch. The pain radiated outward, and it was all I could do simply to draw breath.

That Sidney's eyes happened to be locked with mine at that moment was both troubling and reassuring. For I could tell he'd witnessed the hurt I struggled to hide and even deny. Rob had been dead for over four years. I knew this, and yet part of me, perhaps foolishly, still wished to pretend it wasn't true. That he was merely far away, and next week or month or year I would see him again.

Sidney measuredly crossed the room toward me as I inhaled a steadying breath and turned to face my aunt. "Is there more damage?"

"Oh, yes," she assured me as my husband pressed a supportive hand to the small of my back. Her eyes flickered toward him, observing our allied front. "But for the moment, that can wait. At least until you've had some fortification."

She pivoted on her heel, moving toward the entry to the Elizabethan Room, where her butler stood waiting to open the door, having anticipated her wishes.

In that room, the blue silk wallpaper and gold drapes had largely survived the flyboy invasion intact, save for a few stains, but the paper and plaster chandelier had clearly seen better days. Aunt Ernestine swiveled to face us before the gold chintz settee arranged before a low table, catching my gaze directed at the ceiling. Her mouth pursed into a moue of displeasure. "Yes, needless to say, Lady Elizabeth is not best pleased."

As always, when that ancestor was mentioned, the chandelier lightly swayed and trembled. But then it had already been doing so.

My aunt nodded at it, as if in proof. "See."

I smiled tightly and then shook my head at Sidney before he could voice his evident confusion. I had no desire to rehash the sad tale of Lady Elizabeth Popham, or debate whether her ghost roamed Littlemote House, shaking chandeliers to indicate her ire.

So instead I introduced a subject certain to distract my aunt as we settled on the settee opposite hers. "What of Reg? Will he be joining us?"

She sighed, her normally indomitable energy deflating. "I think not." Her eyes dipped to a spot on the bare wooden floor—the carpet being another casualty, I suspected. "Today has not been one of his good days." Her eyes lifted to meet mine, heavy with grief. "But you may visit him later, if you like. He's normally out on the terrace, when the weather allows."

I nodded in acceptance, intensely curious about the state in which I would find my cousin. Though I had spoken with Reg since he was evacuated home, it had been half a year since my last visit.

"Father said matters have been a bit chaotic since you reclaimed the house," I said, turning back to the reason we were there. "That some heirlooms have gone missing."

"Not just missing, my dear Verity. I've reason to believe a number of our paintings and other objets d'art have been replaced by *forgeries*." Her voice was aghast as she sank deeper into the cushions. "Why, I was never so humiliated in all my life than when the appraiser I invited here told me nearly everything of value I'd thought to sell was, in fact, worth almost nothing!"

Sidney and I shared a look of surprise. "And these were objects that were placed in storage before the airmen arrived?"

"Of course. I oversaw their removal to the attics myself. The doors were secured, and I gave Miles the keys." She dipped her head toward the door through which we'd entered and the butler had since slipped away. "But that doesn't mean some unscrupulous person didn't pick the locks." Her hands fluttered before her until she clasped them together in her lap. "It's all quite distressing."

If what Father had said was true, and I could only imagine it was—for my aunt would never have admitted how low their coffers were unless the estate was in dire straits indeed—then Aunt Ernestine must have been relying on those sales to help keep them afloat. Upon reflection, I'd realized their circumstances were not all that surprising. Uncle James had never been the frugal sort, and I had heard Father bemoan his brother-in-law's horrid choice in investments in the past. Add to that the inflation, income taxes, and heavy death duties owed not only from the passing of Uncle James, but also Thomas, and any estate not on a healthy footing before the war would now be crippled. Sadly, it was an all-too-familiar story among the landed elite, and but another indication of how the world was changing.

However, the discovery that a number of heirlooms had not just been stolen, as my father had indicated, but replaced with forgeries, was troubling in a different way. Such maneuvering required a level of calculation and prolonged access to the house that I had not expected. Particularly when one considered that some of the objects were paintings, and possibly large ones at that.

"Can you show us later which heirlooms are forgeries?" I asked.

"Of course. After our tea."

As if awaiting just such a pronouncement, Miles slipped into the room, carrying the tea tray. That he was waiting on us thusly told me more than I'm sure my aunt wished, for in the past she'd always been quite the stickler about the separation of duties, and carrying the tea tray was not the butler's job. Which could only mean that my aunt was short of staff. I didn't know whether that was because she couldn't pay them, or they simply weren't available. Since the war, there was a shortage of people willing to go into or return to service, particularly young women. I suspected it was a bit of both.

Once we were settled with our tea and the dry biscuits my aunt preferred—for her digestion—Sidney took it upon himself to broach another crisis my father had mentioned. "I understand you've also had a servant go missing?"

"Oh, yes. It's quite vexing. The girl apparently packed her bags and took off for parts unknown," she declared with a bob of her head as she lifted her teacup. "For her family in the village has no knowledge of her whereabouts either. But they were certain to collect her owed wages."

I frowned. "I doubt that whatever the maid's motive was, it was to inconvenience you, Aunt Ernestine. How long ago was this? Has no one seen her since?"

Her eyebrows snapped together. "About two weeks, and I honestly wouldn't know. My mind *has* been preoccupied by more pressing matters, Verity, than an absent maid."

"Then why mention her to Father?"

She huffed in annoyance. "Because I didn't know then that

her absence wasn't truly troubling. Her family isn't worried about her, so why should I be?"

She had a fair point. Surely if there was some cause for concern, her family would be the ones to raise it. Maybe they knew more than they were saying. In any case, whatever she'd told my father and mother, she evidently wasn't anxious about the maid's fate, merely the loss of a staff member. She'd probably mentioned it only as additional evidence of her strife to elicit sympathy from my parents.

I set my cup and the mostly uneaten biscuit on its saucer on the low table. "Father said you were keen to have us visit when he suggested it. But what is it you wish us to do?"

Her gaze slid toward Sidney, her next words confirming precisely what we'd surmised. "Well, with your husband's recent honors, your father thought he might know the right people to apply to in order to have the damage to my house rectified. And to see to it that this matter of theft and forgery is properly investigated."

Having been put on the spot, there was nothing for it but for him to nod and assure her, "I'll do what I can."

"Thank you."

Though Sidney didn't display any uneasiness with this request, I knew him well enough to recognize he was not comfortable with it either. Consequently, I was irritated on his behalf. He was already struggling with guilt over his survival when so many millions of other soldiers had died, and the added weight of being given a medal for his valor in doing what he believed simply to be his duty. He didn't need an extra helping of expectations heaped upon him. Particularly when my aunt had a son, who while blinded by the war, was still perfectly capable of petitioning the government about these issues himself. In any case, we had other matters of more pressing importance, and we'd already interrupted our pursuit of them to assist her.

Eager to view her evidence and whatever else she intended us to see so that we might move on in the morning, I pushed to my feet the moment my aunt set her cup aside. "Shall we examine these forgeries, then?"

My aunt rose somewhat reluctantly to begin her tour of the "devastated country," as she called it with a wry chuckle. Sidney and I, having both spent time in the war-ravaged regions of Belgium and northeastern France, which had earned that sobriquet, did not find this comment to be particularly amusing. Wine-stained drapes and a charred section of the rug in the library could hardly be compared with the utter destruction of the Western Front and the swathe of country burned and ravaged by the invading Germans. However, once my aunt gained her momentum, she could not be stopped. Each room we entered was narrated by a long list of even the minutest of damages.

In truth, after a time, I stopped listening, knowing I would never remember it all, nor did I wish to. I was far more interested in the paintings and objects she pointed out as being forgeries, or in a few instances the patches of faded wallpaper indicating where a portrait used to hang or tables devoid of decor. In most cases, the forgeries were skillfully done, so much so that I couldn't tell. But I trusted the appraiser was correct. My aunt hired only the best.

Nonetheless, I did note one curiosity. Most of the forged items were large, cumbersome, or intricate; but without fail, the items that were missing altogether were small and compact. In a word, portable. Had the thief thought the smaller items would not be noticed if they went missing? Or were we dealing with two different culprits?

I was contemplating this as we passed through the long gallery on our way to another strip of damage my aunt was anxious to show us, when I chanced to look to the left. Peering through the windows out onto the terrace, I could see a solitary figure seated near one of the columns. His back was to me, but I recognized his silhouette all the same, for it had always reminded me of someone even dearer to me. Even the slight tinge of red in his brown hair, which I could see now, glinting in the sun, brought forth a bittersweet pang of memory.

I glanced in the direction my aunt and Sidney had disappeared, hoping my husband would forgive me for abandoning him, and then inhaled a steadying breath before I stepped out through one of the French doors. I moved forward slowly, not wishing to startle him, but also to allow myself time to absorb the shock of his appearance.

Not that he was in any way disfigured. In truth, beyond the series of tiny scars near one of his eyes, Reg still appeared unscathed. The other wounds caused by the shrapnel had all healed neatly, and whatever concussive force had rendered him totally blind had left no other visible trace. But time and age had altered his face slightly, so that he looked even more like my brother. In some ways, it felt like looking at a ghost.

He hadn't given any indication that he'd heard my approach, his head facing resolutely forward to gaze sightlessly out at the gardens, until he spoke. "Well, are you going to come say hullo, Verity, or are you going to just stand there staring at me all day?"

I laughed as lightly as I could, forcing my feet forward again. "How did you know it was me?" I asked, leaning down to buss his cheek.

"Your shoes. Nobody else I know prefers those clackety pumps. Certainly nobody around here." He grasped my arm when I would have straightened, his voice softening. "And you always did prefer something dainty and floral rather than one of those musky French perfumes that are so popular."

I smiled. "You're right." I searched his familiar face. Though he couldn't see me doing so, I figured he could sense it. "It's good to see you, Reg."

The corners of his mouth curled upward in an all-too-brief smile. "Did your war hero husband come with you?" he asked as I pulled a wicker chair closer to him and sat down. Though I couldn't detect any bitterness in his voice, I tread forward carefully nonetheless.

"Yes, he's inside with your mother, being given a complete tour of the damage the airmen wrought to your home."

Reg heaved an exasperated breath. "That again. Tell me, how extensive is it, truly? I cannot see it myself, but I've asked Hatter to describe it to me in detail, and it doesn't seem as bad as all that."

"There's certainly damage," I replied, tucking my arms tighter to my sides inside my woolen scarf coat against the chill breeze. Something Reg didn't seem to notice in his gray flannel suit, though it stirred the hair at his brow. "And some of it is rather severe. The carpet in the library, for instance, will have to entirely be replaced. And the floorboards in the corner where the fire was located might have to be repaired, as well. But the house isn't in shambles or near to crumbling over your heads."

He nodded, as if this confirmed his thinking. "I told her to have everything typed out and submit it to the RAF for repayment, but she insists the matter is worse than I could possibly know and that she'll handle it in her own way." He scowled. "However, I didn't realize that would involve calling Uncle Frederick and dragging you into the matter."

"Your mother didn't tell you I was coming?"

He chuckled wryly. "Of course not." He turned his head to the side before adding in a tight voice, "But I overheard her telling Miles. She forgets that although I cannot see I can still hear."

I couldn't blame him for his anger. It sounded as if Aunt Ernestine was doing everything in her power *not* to trouble him. Except, in truth, the estate was *his. He* was the new baronet, and so the managing of it should fall on his shoulders. She might be trying to protect him, but by refusing him the ability to shoulder his responsibilities, she was also rendering him useless.

He turned toward me, his brow furrowed and his jaw hard, though his hazel eyes were blank. "As did you, apparently," he said accusingly. "Why didn't you come forward immediately? You were staring at me."

I grimaced in shame at the hurt I'd caused him. "I was, wasn't I?" I admitted softly.

His pursed mouth slackened as he attempted a jest. "Do I truly look so awful?"

"No," I replied. "No, not at all. It's just . . ." I swallowed and then forced the words out. "You remind me of Rob." Little as I'd wanted to admit the truth, to speak my brother's name, I couldn't let him go on thinking I was disgusted or horrified by him. Everything was awkward enough without that added strain.

His brow smoothed in understanding, and he stretched his hand out toward me as I sat silently battling the dark well of emotion I'd kept tapped down for so long, refusing to draw from it. I lifted my hand to meet his, focusing on the warmth of his skin as I choked it all back.

"Sometimes, when I'm in a crowd, I'll hear a voice and think it's Tom. I'll even turn to look for him, forgetting I can't see. And then I'll remember." His voice was hollow like the wind. "It can't be him."

I blinked back the stinging wetness in my eyes, grateful the breeze was there to dry any tears before they fell.

He tilted his head in my direction. "Do you ever do that?"

"Yes," I replied simply.

We sat side by side, quietly acknowledging our shared pain at losing a brother. The longing that they could be there with us now, listening to the wind rustle through the yew trees, and smelling the freshly turned earth in one of the flower gardens that had been given over to vegetables. One of them would cajole us to play a game of tennis on the court in the southeast corner of the garden, or race to the large, rectangular fishpond. But it couldn't be. Just as Reg could never see the blue sky or the perfect white fluffy clouds dotting its expanse ever again.

I frowned. Or the massive hole in the brick wall of the gazebo down near the river, where it looked as if something— be it a motorbike or an aeroplane—had crashed into it. Good heavens, what *had* the airmen been doing?

From the far corner of the terrace, I heard Aunt Ernestine's voice ring out, and turned to find her and Sidney bustling toward us.

Reg squeezed my hand, pulling my attention back to him as he spoke hastily. "Verity, can you do something for me?"

"Of course."

"Find out what the deuce is going on with mother's bed-chamber door."

"Her door?"

"Yes." He leaned nearer, recognizing they were drawing closer, and lowered his voice. "It's been locking or sticking or some such thing. Trapped her inside once. She tells me it's nothing to bother myself over, but I've since learned she's started sleeping in another room." His eyebrows arched. "That doesn't sound like something that's not a bother."

"That *is* odd," I conceded, already contemplating what the cause could be. "I'll see to it."

"Good."

CHAPTER 3

"Verity, we wondered where you'd gone," my aunt exclaimed as she huffed forward. "You missed half the tour."

"Yes, well, I saw Reg out here and thought he could use some company," I replied.

"I see." Her voice and her eyebrows raised with suspicion. "And just what have you two been conspiring about?" She wagged her finger between us. "They always were, you know," she told Sidney in an undertone, as if we couldn't hear her. "The lot of them. Verity and the boys. Her mother despaired of her ever learning to behave like a lady."

I laughed. "I can't help it that all my cousins are boys, and my only sister so many years younger. You didn't expect me to be able to convince them to have tea and play with dolls, did you?"

"No, but a young lady might have balked at wading barefoot into the river to catch tadpoles or climbing trees and tearing her dress."

Reg let out a crack of laughter. "I'd forgotten about that. Ripped it clear up the back. I thought your mother was going to have an apoplexy when she saw you running toward the house in nothing but your shift."

Sidney, who had been observing us all in amusement, his hands tucked in the pockets of his trousers, chose that moment to disabuse my aunt that she had any ally in this argument. "I think I would have liked to see that."

My aunt scowled while Reg nearly doubled over with merriment.

It was painful, yet also somehow comforting to talk about old times, like using a muscle that's grown weak from disuse. "I do believe you witnessed me doing enough foolish things to try to impress you the first time you came home with Freddy from school," I reminded Sidney. "And none of those were cherished memories to your sixteen-year-old self."

"Darling, you underestimate your eleven-year-old charm," he teased.

I screwed up my nose. "No, I do not. I was a perfect pest, as you've admitted."

He chuckled. "True enough. Who knew how much I would find you changed in six years' time?"

"Not so much changed as aware that men do not like apples thrown at their heads or secret admirer notes doused in pilfered perfume tucked under their doors."

"Good Lord, Verity," Reg cried, clutching his side in hilarity. "How have I never heard this before?"

"Reginald, don't hurt yourself, dear," his mother cautioned.

His brow creased in annoyance, and Sidney stepped forward to clasp his shoulder. "Good to see you, Popham."

"Likewise, Kent. Hope you didn't travel all this way just to pay us a visit." That this comment had been calculated to irritate his mother, there was no doubt, for his jaw clenched, as if prepared for her answering rebuke. And she gave it to him.

"What an absurd thing to say, Reginald. It's not as if we live in deepest Cornwall or, heaven forbid, Scotland. In any case, it's a lovely day for a jaunt out to the country, and I'm very grateful to have their company." Her gimlet stare fell on me. "Though I hope your cousin hasn't been saying anything untoward to upset you."

There was a topic she clearly hadn't wanted me to broach with him, and I had a strong suspicion of what it was.

"Of course not. What an absurd thing to say," he responded with biting mockery. "We were merely reminiscing and discussing my still-stunning good looks." His head turned vaguely in the direction of where Sidney stood. "You understand, old chap. One can hardly trust one's own mother for confirmation of this fact. She'd likely call me an Adonis even if I looked like a gargoyle."

"What nonsense," Aunt Ernestine huffed. "Come with me, Verity. There's something I wish to show you."

More likely she wished to scold me. But before I could object, she'd already turned to stride off, expecting me to follow.

"Now you've done it," I teased, rising from my chair and turning with a swish of my blue skirt. "She'll never let me come back out and play."

"Fortunately, she retires early," Reg called after me. "And we have a full sideboard stocked with gin."

I laughed as I lifted my skirts to better hasten after my aunt, who could move with surprising swiftness when she was working herself into high dudgeon. I caught up with her just as she turned into the corridor, which led to the grand staircase, her chin arched upward imperiously.

"I hope you haven't said anything to Reginald about my troubling discoveries," she proclaimed in a sharp voice calculated so that it could not be heard beyond a few feet away above the echo of her footfalls. "His health is delicate, and I've no wish to upset him more than absolutely necessary."

"His health doesn't *seem* delicate," I replied, matching her tone. "If anything, he seems frustrated and listless. And in any case, *shouldn't* you be conferring with him on the matter of these forgeries and thefts? He is the baronet, after all. Perhaps he has some insight."

She pulled up short to glare at me just as we reached the base of the staircase. "I forbid you to speak of them."

I frowned at the vehemence in her tone.

Swiveling abruptly, she began to march up the stairs. "Just because I called you here for your help, does not mean I will brook any interference. I should think I know better than you what my son needs."

"I meant no insult, Aunt Ernestine, but don't you think . . ."

"*You* were not here when he came home from the hospital that first time," she continued in a brittle voice. "*You* didn't see the scars beneath his bandages, or hear his cries of terror when he couldn't tell whether he'd woken from his nightmares or was still trapped inside them because he could no longer see."

My steps faltered on the landing though she continued on. I'd forgotten Reg had been buried under a collapsed trench wall when they pulled him out after the shell explosion.

"*You* weren't here begging him to return to the hospital out of fear he would put a pistol in his mouth if he did not." She paused to glower down at me from halfway up the flight, her face pale and haggard in the light of the window at my back. "So don't presume to tell me what I should or should not do in regards to *my own son*."

I nodded and she turned to carry on. I hesitated before following her, realizing I'd clumsily trampled over a chasm of grief, dread, and insecurity. She was right. I hadn't been here when my cousin had been at his lowest, and it was callous and presumptuous of me to think I understood all of what he had been through or what he was thinking simply from one short conversation. But that didn't mean I was entirely wrong about Reg's frustration or his capabilities either.

However, I would obey my aunt's wishes for now. At least until I'd confirmed my suspicions about the forgeries via a different angle.

"I've placed you in the laurel-green chamber." My aunt continued speaking, as if our confrontation had never occurred, and I hastened after her. "I know it was one of your mother's favorites, and honestly it's one of the least damaged. The officer who stayed in that room was more conscientious than his fellow airmen." She opened a door a short distance from the landing and allowed me to proceed her into the chamber.

My eyes swept over the warm oak furniture and laurel-green walls, and I could well imagine why my mother had liked it. The gleaming furnishings were at least two hundred years old, and the color palette, while understated, was still pleasing to the eye. "Thank you. It's lovely." My gaze fell on the painting of a bay laurel tree hanging above the bed in an ornate swirling frame, and a thought occurred to me. "What a charming picture." Then feigning sudden inspiration, I turned toward my aunt. "I seem to recall a portrait hanging in your bedchamber. One of you reading under a willow tree. Please tell me that isn't one of the forgeries."

She gave a soft laugh. "No, child. That wasn't me. It was naught but a pretty picture I found at a shop in London and took a fancy to."

This I well recalled, but I figured it would deflect some of the pointedness of my sudden interest.

"Then it's still there? In your room?"

"Yes, above my writing desk, where it's always been," she said with a gentle smirk.

"May I see it?"

She didn't respond, and I had difficulty interpreting the look on her face. It was pained in some way, though I couldn't tell if that was because she suspected my subterfuge or for another reason entirely.

"Maybe that seems an odd request . . ." I continued, trying to gauge her reaction.

"Oh, no," she replied. "It's simply . . ." She broke off, shaking her head before she offered me a determined smile. "Come with me."

I followed her down the corridor, its runner scuffed and

worn beneath our feet, and around the corner toward the grand master bedchambers. A gold-haired maid who had been walking toward us down the main corridor turned to watch us with interest as we approached the suite of rooms, and then she hurried on.

"I should warn you, the door may not open."

Relieved that she'd broached the matter Reg had wanted me to look into herself, I regarded her quizzically. "What do you mean?"

"We've had some issues with doors in this part of the house sticking and the locks jamming." She spoke evenly, as if the matter was not of great concern, but I could hear the consternation beneath her words.

"That sounds unsettling."

"Yes, well, apparently a leak was found on the roof in the upper story, and it's seeped down into the walls along this corridor, causing the wood to swell. Or at least, that's how our man-of-all-work explained it."

My eyes trailed up the walls to the ceiling, searching for any evident signs of water damage. "Can the problem not be fixed?"

"Yes, but at some expense." She reached for the door to the lady's chamber and paused, as if bracing herself, before turning the handle to push it open. Contrary to what I'd expected after what she'd just told me, it swung open with ease. "Sometimes it's like that," she explained. "While other times it seems nothing will force it open save the hand of God Himself."

"Is it safe for you to stay here, then?" I asked, following her inside. I wondered if she would confirm what Reg had already told me.

If the wood was truly that warped, that temperamental, then was this part of the house even structurally sound? And heaven forbid, if there was a fire and she needed to escape.

"I've moved to a room down the hall. Temporarily," she

stressed, anxious to make some point, though I wasn't certain precisely the aim. If they were as strapped for funds as they seemed to be, then they hadn't the money available to make such extensive repairs. But of course, maybe my aunt didn't want me to know that. Though surely if my father knew, she must have anticipated he would tell me.

A quick perusal of the lavish rose and gold decorated chamber showed that much of the chamber's contents were still present. From the ornate walnut furnishings to the thick Aubusson carpet to the paintings and artwork gracing the walls, it appeared more or less as I remembered it. I crossed toward the writing desk to gaze up at the painting I had asked to see, while all the while my mind was sifting through everything she'd just told me. "You said the locks on the doors sometimes jam?" I turned my head to look at her where she stood next to an ormolu table, fiddling with the items resting on top. "Isn't that . . . peculiar?"

"Apparently not. I, of course, have no experience with such things, but Mr. Green says it happens more often than one would realize."

I assumed she was speaking of the estate's man-of-all-work, and I couldn't help but wonder at his credentials. Was he qualified to make assessments of such matters? I had no more experience than my aunt, but while I had witnessed wood in houses swelling and doors sticking, I failed to comprehend how that could cause a lock to engage on its own and jam. The scenario seemed all too improbable, if not impossible.

I wondered if perhaps Sidney would have a better grasp of the mechanics of the matter than I did, and so I asked him later that evening when we had a moment to ourselves after dinner.

He paused in loosening his tie to cast me an incredulous look. "I would say that's worse than improbable. It sounds suspicious."

"I had the same misgiving," I admitted as I removed the bracelets dangling from my wrists and stacked them in my jewelry case. "But I can't comprehend the motive for impelling my aunt to leave her bedchamber. From what I could tell, nothing was missing except her more personal property, and she undoubtedly moved that to the bedroom she's currently occupying."

He shrugged out of his black evening coat and tossed it over the back of the chaise lounge. "Still, I think it would behoove us to find out more about this Mr. Green."

"I'll speak to Miles tomorrow," I replied, pulling the bejeweled headband from my hair and raking my hands through my auburn castle-bobbed tresses to remove the indentation. "There are a few other things I'd also like to ask him."

He lifted his head as he bent over to remove his shoes, casting me a knowing look. "The forgeries?"

"Among other things." I sank down beside him on the chaise, removing my black T-strap pumps. "What did you and Reg discuss after Aunt Ernestine summoned me away?"

"Nothing of interest," he remarked before flicking open the top two buttons of his crisp white shirt and draping his arm over the rounded back of the chaise behind my shoulders.

I arched my eyebrows, letting him know I was well aware that "nothing of interest" was man-code for "something of great interest," but whatever it was, he wouldn't share it. Whether that was because Reg had asked him not to, it was inappropriate for a lady's ears, or more likely, that it had to do with the war and that curious realm of comradery shared only by fellow soldiers, I couldn't tell. While I had witnessed more than most British citizens and endured my share of ghastly experiences during my time as an intelligence agent, I had not fought in the trenches. I had not slept in muddy dugouts knee-deep in water, or made tea in a bully beef tin, or singed lice hidden in the seams of my clothes with matches. I had not witnessed my friends being mowed down by a machine gun's bullets, or torn apart by shrapnel, or choked by gas. I knew full well that there was a limit to what I could understand, and what any returning soldier would share beyond that. Even my husband. Especially him.

"Then he didn't confide in you his frustration at his mother for involving you in the complaints about the damages to the estate?" I asked.

"No, but that much is obvious." His voice was droll. "Otherwise, what reason would your aunt have had for deliberately excluding him from our conversations on the matter?"

So he had noticed that as well. Whatever the truth about Reg's health, or his good and bad days, as baronet, he still should have been consulted.

I sank my head back against his arm. "One thing is certain. While the house is undoubtedly damaged, it is *not* crumbling down around them." I rolled my head to the side. "Though I suppose one could argue that the roof over the master bedchambers is in danger of doing so. But I don't think my aunt can lay the blame for that at the airmen's feet. Not if the roof has been leaking for some time."

"And that's supposing that the information this Mr. Green gave your aunt is correct. Did you see any evidence of this water damage?"

"Well, no. But I didn't precisely peer behind all the doors along the corridor looking for it."

Sidney reached over to idly run his finger over the black seed pearls decorating the skirt of my gown. "Whatever the case, all your aunt can do for now about the damages done during the war is submit a claim to the government. Reg and I can do our best to exert pressure on them to take care of the matter swiftly, but that doesn't mean we'll be successful. This is the government we're talking about, and there's already a long line of petitioners for war reparations."

"And even if they do pay for the damages, it doesn't mean it will fix their dilemma. Not if they are as empty in the pockets as Father suggested. They'll have to sell off part of the estate, if not the house. That is, if it's not entailed."

Sidney's brow furrowed. "Bloody feudal regulations. I hope they change the laws or one of the men in my family finds a way to break the entailment before I stand to inherit. Otherwise we shall be strapped with the Treborough monstrosity of an estate. One I have never been fond of, and that will bleed us dry if we try to fix it."

I was somewhat startled by this pronouncement. As the only surviving grandson of the fifth Marquess of Treborough, I knew Sidney eventually stood to inherit the title currently held by his oldest uncle, but I'd never visited Treborough Castle. "Is it truly as bad as all that?"

"Worse," he stated glumly. "My grandfather may have been rather progressive in distributing his unentailed wealth among his three sons evenly. But in doing so, he failed to anticipate the changes in Britain's economy, and so saddled Uncle Oswald with an estate he couldn't hope to maintain on the income it generated alone."

Sidney's father, the youngest of the brothers, had compounded his inherited wealth through sound investments and by marrying an heiress, though not for purely mercenary reasons. They'd fallen in love, and from all indications were still as enamored with each other today as the day they'd wed, sometimes to the exclusion of everything else, including their own children. Given what I knew about his father's wealth, and the more than generous annual stipend Sidney received, the notion of Treborough Castle and its estate being in such a state as to cause bankruptcy was shocking indeed.

"Well, let's not think on that now. Not when it will be many years before it is your father's or our problem." I curled my stockinged feet up on the chaise and nestled in closer to Sidney's side. "We have more pressing matters to consider."

"Indeed." He shifted his broad shoulders so he could gaze down at me more easily.

"I know there's nothing we can do about the damages, but I would like to take a closer look into these forgeries and thefts, as well as the matter of my aunt's mysterious locking door. I think I should ask the staff about the missing maid as well, just to be sure there genuinely is no cause for concern." I frowned. "For all my aunt's professed eagerness for our assistance, she's not being very forthcoming."

"Only when she thinks the information is relevant to her wishes," he agreed, having noticed the same diversionary tactics I had.

"Moreover, it seems rather rude to rush off less than twenty-four hours after my arrival. I'm sure my father expected more from me." I turned to gaze up into his deep blue expectant eyes. "However, there's no need for us both to stay."

"Are you suggesting we divide and conquer?"

"I don't expect there's much more to discover here, so there's really no reason why you shouldn't keep our appointment in Falmouth and then return to collect me on your way back to London." I searched his face. "Unless you'd rather remain?"

But I already knew his answer. I could sense his desire to be off. Part of it was an eagerness to be back behind the wheel of his new Pierce-Arrow, but part of it was something else. A restlessness that stemmed from the war, particularly when he was confronted with a situation that dredged up fraught memories. There were plenty of potential sources for that here at Littlemote.

"No, I suspect you're right. And such a tactic might work in our favor, for I'd wondered how comfortable the employees at Lord Rockham's import-export business would feel speaking to a woman about the questions we intend to ask them."

I understood what he meant. For all my annoyance at men who considered women incapable of understanding business matters or were shocked that they should even take an interest, in my intelligence work I'd learned the importance of accepting reality and adapting to work within others' limitations and prejudices if I hoped to achieve results. The men at the shipping yards in Falmouth would share far more with Sidney than me, just as the employees at a London milliner might be more forthcoming with me than they would be with my husband.

"You should have said something to me sooner," I told him, wondering if he would have if I hadn't unwittingly introduced the subject myself. "We have to be smart about this. Lord Ardmore is almost certainly already aware of our gathering further information on him, as well as Rockham's and Flossie's murders. So we may only get one chance to ask our questions before he interferes."

We'd tangled with the calculating and elusive Lord Ardmore several weeks earlier while trying to solve two seemingly unrelated murders. And while we'd unmasked the perpetrators responsible for pulling the triggers, both literally and figuratively, we were also convinced Ardmore had been the ultimate architect of the killings, as well as a number of related deaths. However, Ardmore was far too clever to be connected easily to the crimes. His ongoing role with Naval Intelligence was shadowy, the details unavailable even to my former chief, C, at the foreign division of Military Intelligence—the Secret Service. But one thing was certain, C didn't trust him, so neither did I.

So we'd begun clandestinely collecting information about Ardmore, trying to piece together the components of the previous investigations we hadn't possessed, hoping one of them would lead us to the proof we needed to convince Ardmore's highly placed friends of his guilt. The trouble was, Ardmore was much too good at covering his tracks, or eliminating the people who could make those connections. Even the details we could confirm seemed to lead to a dead end, either by Ardmore's design or because he'd destroyed the evidence.

"You're thinking of that girl at the orthopedic foot appliance store," he deduced.

"Of course, I am." I crossed my arms over my chest, still struggling to control my temper days later. "She was perfectly friendly and talkative the first time I visited the shop, and happy to tell me all about her former coworker. How Flossie began stepping out with a customer she met there. A gentleman who claimed to be writing a book about some of the unresolved mysteries from the war. A man who claimed aloud he'd worked for the intelligence service and spoke about all the information he often uncovered from reading people's mail." I arched my eyebrows in emphasis. "How Flossie had seemed to devour his tales, even though the shop girl had maintained a healthy skepticism. Which might have simply been her effort to mask her jealousy that Flossie had snagged such a beau and not her, but either way, the connection seems obvious."

"You said the description she gave you of the man didn't match Ardmore."

"No, but I imagine it matches one of his underlings. And I'm certain it was Ardmore who sent him to that store to scrape up an acquaintance with Flossie. To charm her, and somehow inveigle her into stealing her housemate Esther's correspondence." That Esther had then caught Flossie doing so, and Flossie had accidentally killed her trying to escape seemed pure chance, though one that had benefitted Ardmore. Until Sidney and I had stuck our noses into the matter.

I scowled ferociously, wrinkling my nose. "I'm also certain it was Ardmore, or another of his henchmen, who convinced that shop girl to refuse to speak with me when I tried to follow up with her a few days later."

Sidney pulled me closer, tipping my chin upward so that he could look into my eyes. "Don't let him vex you," he reminded me. "You know that's exactly what he wants. For you to stew in frustration." His thumb brushed a wayward strand of hair away from my cheek. "It's doubtful you would have gotten anything else useful from that shop girl anyway. And now at least you have a description of one of the men working for him."

I exhaled a long breath, conceding he was right. "But you understand this means Ardmore must be aware we haven't stopped investigating. And that means he's anticipated our making a trek west to Falmouth." My gaze trailed over the bronzed skin of his square jaw and high cheekbones before staring intently into his eyes. "Be careful. Watch your back in Falmouth." My lips quirked upward at one corner. "And perhaps lay off the accelerator just a bit."

He heaved a sigh of long suffering. "Because you asked, I will."

The glitter in his eyes told me he was only teasing, but I emphasized the point anyway. "I mean it, Sidney."

"I know, Ver," he assured me, his face softening with sincerity, though the twinkle never left his eyes. "I'll be back by Monday. I wouldn't want to miss your birthday." His voice lowered. "Not when I have a special present planned for you."

"Do you?" I murmured back playfully, draping my arms over his shoulders.

He smiled secretively.

"What is it? Can you give me a hint?"

He tilted his head in consideration. "No."

I pouted my lips and his gaze fastened on them.

"But I can offer you a preview of the other festivities," he proposed as his mouth captured mine.

What exactly he had planned for my twenty-third birthday in three days' time, I didn't know, but the preview assured me it would be more than spectacular.

CHAPTER 4

After seeing Sidney off the following morning, I went in search of my aunt's butler and found him emerging from the breakfast parlor. "Miles, just the person I need."

"Yes, madam." His wrinkled face was fixed in lines of mild inquiry. "I thought you might be wishing to speak to me."

I smiled. "My mother always said you were the perfect butler, aware of everything one needed before one even realized it oneself."

"Mrs. Townsend is an astute and discerning woman."

"Yes, she is." When she wished to be.

I stepped back. "Shall we step into the study?" Entering the room, I crossed toward my uncle's massive oak desk, but remained standing as I knew Miles would never be convinced to sit in my presence. Though the window drapes had been drawn, what sunlight penetrated through the thick, old glass was soon swallowed up by the dark wooden paneling and bookshelves that dominated much of the chamber.

I tilted my head, studying his stalwart visage and sparsely threaded gray hair. "You must be aware of the forgeries and thefts my aunt has told us about," I began, leaning against the edge of the desk as I assessed his demeanor, having already deduced that his body language would tell me more than his words.

His back remained rigid; his hands clasped behind his back. "I am."

"When the house was requisitioned for use by the military during the middle of the war, did you remain here or go to London with Sir James and Lady Popham?"

"London."

I nodded, narrowing my eyes in thought. "Did any of the staff remain?"

"Not from the house, madam. Those who were still employed here were sent off to various posts or acquired positions helping with the war effort."

I'd suspected as much, the Royal Flying Corps and then the RAF after them wanting to hire their own staff, but it was always good to verify. Because much of the gardens had been turned over to vegetables and other crops, I wondered if they'd retained any of the groundskeeping servants. That is, those who hadn't volunteered or been conscripted into the war. But my aunt's old stablemaster would be the person to ask about that.

"You supervised the storage of the more precious items and heirlooms in the attics?"

"Yes, madam."

"And you supervised the restoration of them and the rest of the house—what could be salvaged, that is—upon the RAF vacating the estate?"

His expression was pained. "Yes, madam. It was in a state I should not like to see ever again."

"Had it appeared like anything had been moved or shifted in the attics? Had the items seemed tampered with in any way?"

Miles's dark eyes were shrewd with intelligence. "No, nothing appeared altered from when I'd locked the doors three years prior."

"Then, it didn't appear as if anything had been removed and later replaced?"

"Allow me to clarify. There is every indication that the items we stored in that room in 1916 were exactly the same as the ones we removed from it in April of this year."

If that were true—and I had no reason not to believe it, for I could see no reason for Miles to lie—then that meant that the forgeries had been created before they were placed in storage.

I studied the butler's expectant expression. "Did Sir James ever send off any of his paintings or heirlooms to be . . . cleaned, or reframed, or refurbished? Appraised, even?"

His eyes gleamed with satisfaction that I'd hit upon this question. "He did, indeed, madam. Quite often, in fact, during the years before the war."

I turned toward the window as I digested this bit of news. So my uncle was responsible for replacing his objets d'art with fakes, not the airmen. This wasn't truly surprising. In fact, I'd suspected as much. For the estate to be in such a state now meant it must have been bleeding assets for some time. Nor was it surprising he'd not told my aunt. Their marriage had been molded in the old pattern, in which my aunt didn't ask and my uncle didn't tell.

But I was surprised she hadn't suspected it. Or perhaps she did, and instead had chosen to ignore the likelihood of such an unpleasantness and instead blame our flyboys. If so, it angered me that she'd carried this blind pigheadedness so far as to share her accusations with me and Sidney, and push for us to do something about them. It also explained why she was so adamant I not share the matter with Reg. Perhaps he was already aware of what his father had done. Or if not, more likely to recognize the truth and its harsh reality than his mother.

Of course, the forgeries weren't the only items of interest.

"What of the thefts?"

His bushy eyebrows furrowed the barest bit. "Those are more concerning."

"Then I take it they occurred after they were removed from storage."

"Yes. Or in some cases, they weren't stored at all, but taken to London with Sir James and Lady Popham."

"And these items are more portable?"

He nodded. "A small vase or figurine. A box of old coins. A gold letter opener. A calling card case fashioned from ivory."

"When did these items start disappearing?"

"About six months ago. Not long after we returned to Littlemote."

I hated to think it, but I couldn't help but question whether my aunt was behind these "thefts." After all, she'd already contacted an appraiser to evaluate her paintings and larger pieces of art, presumably intending to sell them until she discovered many of them were forgeries. What if she'd begun with the smaller objects that were missing?

But then, why mention them at all? She could have just as easily said nothing about them and I would have been none the wiser. Why cast aspersions when she could pretend they'd never existed?

There was one other possibility that had occurred to me. "What of this maid who vanished two weeks ago? What was her name?"

"Minnie Spanswick."

"Could she have anything to do with it?"

He lowered his head, frowning at the rug at his feet. "I admit, when she didn't turn up I deliberated over the same thing. She did begin working here a short time before the thefts began. But so did much of the staff." His eyes narrowed in contemplation. "In all honesty, she wasn't well-suited to life as a servant. Oh, she was a hard worker and well-liked among the rest of the staff. But she wasn't . . . content, if you understand what I mean."

I nodded, grasping that he meant she wasn't satisfied with such a lot in life, but few young women were nowadays. The war had given them a taste of freedom, many of them having taken up jobs at the munition factories, the land army taking care of the agricultural work, with the "whacks"—the Women's Army Auxiliary Corps (WAACs), and other various positions. I could hardly fault them their desire for something more, for even though I was from a higher social class, my aspirations had also been heightened by the war.

"And she had a rather excessive fondness for those lowbrow film periodicals she was always reading in her spare time," Miles added with a sniff.

"You mean like *Photoplay* and *Motion Picture News*?"

"Yes, and others. She was a cinema enthusiast. Visited the one in Hungerford whenever she had a day or afternoon off."

Considering the fact that many household servants received a day off every other week and an afternoon off in the week between, while many Londoners visited the cinema two or three times a week, this did not seem particularly obsessive. After all, what else was there for a young woman to do in a country village?

I gripped the edge of the desk, recalling what my aunt had told me. "Lady Popham said her family lived in the village. That they hadn't been concerned by her disappearance."

"I didn't speak with them myself, but that's what I've been given to understand. You might speak with the other maids. Naturally, they were more in her confidence than I, and they might be persuaded to be more forthcoming with a lady of your reputation."

I stifled a smile, recognizing by the tautness at the edge of his voice that he didn't precisely approve of this reputation, though he strove to hide it. But it wasn't my fault all the society papers stalked me and Sidney, printing our photographs and exploits about London. We tried to avoid it when we could.

Regardless, his suggestion that I speak to the other maids was a sound one. They *were* more likely to confide in me, and the timing of this Minnie Spanswick's departure was suspicious. It wasn't proof of any wrongdoing. Far from it. But it merited further scrutiny.

"Will that be all?" Miles asked, recalling me to the fact that he still had many things to attend to today besides answering my queries.

"Just one more question. Lady Popham told me she's started sleeping in another room because the door of her bedchamber keeps sticking and even locking. She said the man-of-all-work suggested the cause is swelling wood from water damage. Is that correct?"

"I believe that's the crux of the matter. It's unfortunate. I know Lady Popham dislikes this alteration to her circumstances exceedingly."

I imagined this was the old retainer's polite way of saying that my aunt had been testy, out of sorts, and generally difficult to deal with. She was nothing if not enamored with her position as the wife of a baronet, and all the trappings therein. Being forced to give up her sumptuous bedchamber must have been a sore point.

Though, if I were being fair, I had to admit I might also be testy if I'd been forced to vacate the surroundings I most found comforting for an indefinite period of time. During the war, I'd been forced to sleep in places as lowly as barns, and dusty hiding spaces in attics and cellars, and on one rather memorable occasion beneath the abandoned hulk of a splintered cart with two cracked wheels. However, no matter how mean and uncomfortable my circumstances, I'd always known I had the sanctuary of my Berkeley Square flat to return to.

Not that a guest bedchamber in a manor such as Littlemote House was in any way comparable to a bed of squelching, muddy ground and the chill night air of Flanders, but war had a way of testing your limits and making the things you would never have believed possible seem practicable.

"What do you know of this Mr. Green?" I asked. "Is he qualified to be making such judgments?"

"Mr. Green grew up in Hungerford, and he worked here as a gardener before the war. He was called up when conscription began, and served quite honorably, though he'd no great desire to soldier. He was pushing forty when the war began, with a large family to support. It's a blessing for them he returned. So many did not."

We both fell silent for a moment, acknowledging that fact.

When he spoke again, he surprised me by admitting, "As to his being qualified, he would be the first to tell you he's not. That's why he urged Lady Popham to hire an expert to assess the damage, but in the meantime, to ensure her own safety, she should vacate the rooms before some accident occurred. He was quite conscientious in his duty."

"It sounds like it," I agreed, mulling over this discovery. It certainly cast a favorable light on this Mr. Green. "Has Lady Popham taken his advice and contacted an expert?"

The butler's voice was solemn. "She has not."

I nodded. "Thank you, Miles."

"Of course." He bowed and exited the study, leaving me much to think about.

I crossed to the window, staring down over the neglected and overgrown west garden. Yet more evidence of my aunt's reduced staff. Before the war, there had been a dozen or more gardeners and groundsmen, not to mention carpenters, gamekeepers, river keepers, woodsmen, farmhands, and other various members of the estate staff charged with upkeep. How many of those positions were currently filled? As her man-of-all-work, how much was Mr. Green responsible for?

There was one person, I knew, who would know the answers to these questions and more. He was also just as likely to have a bottle of his scrumpy set aside to warm him on a day like today.

Heavy gray clouds had been threatening rain all morning,

and not trusting they would withhold their bounty until I returned to the house, I dashed upstairs to don my dowdy mackintosh before exiting the manor through the east door. The packed earth of the estate yard was riddled with grooves and divots, and in desperate need of maintenance. It forced me to mind where I stepped, lest I twist my ankle.

The stables were warm when I slipped inside, and smelled of fresh hay and oats. A single gray mare stood in the nearest stall, her head bowed with age—the last of the nearly two dozen fine horses that had once filled the boxes. Though there was hardly a stable left to manage, I knew the old stablemaster, Mr. Plank, well enough to understand he would never abandon his post until *all* the horses were gone. And perhaps not even then.

In truth, he should have been pensioned off ages ago. My uncle had attempted it once, but Mr. Plank had only laughed and continued about his work, heedless of anything his employer said. I expected he would keep doing so until the day he dropped dead.

As such, I strongly suspected he'd gone on working here even when the estate was under the control of the Royal Flying Corps and then the RAF. In a match between the cantankerous Wiltshire man and military bureaucracy, I would wager on the stablemaster every time. They might have told him not to return, but when faced with his stubborn persistence, I imagined they'd eventually given in, recognizing him for the harmless codger he was. Particularly if he'd shared his stash of scrumpy with their lot.

The mare lifted her head as I approached her stall, sidling over to press her muzzle to my proffered hand as I crooned to her. "There's a good girl. You poor dear. It must be lonely with only that crotchety old fellow for company."

"Who ye callin' crotchety?" Mr. Plank demanded behind me in his gravelly voice.

I leaned closer to the horse to hide my smile, rubbing

my hands up and down her neck. The stablemaster was as predictable as ever. Concealing my amusement, I turned to watch as he hobbled closer, his legs bowed and even thinner than I remembered. His scraggly brows lowered in a fierce scowl, but I knew better than to be intimidated.

"I suppose you're going to tell me you're as meek as a lamb?" I challenged.

"O' course, I am."

I arched a single eyebrow in skepticism.

His lips curled into an impish smile, revealing several gaps in his teeth. "An' twice as bandy-legged." At this, he made a shuffling hop to the side, one that was far sprightlier than I'd imagined him capable of.

I couldn't help but grin at his antics. "It's good to see you haven't changed, Mr. Plank." My voice softened as I glanced down the row of empty stalls. "Even when so much else has."

"Aye, well, it'd take more than a few rowdy airmen to overset me." He scanned my features through narrowed eyes. "But I know you're not here to talk about an old gaffer like me. Best come with me."

I followed him into the harness room, which also doubled as a sort of office or lounge. He offered me the single chair—I knew better than to decline the hospitality, lest he be affronted—and then poured me a glass from the bottle of cloudy, golden scrumpy perched on the table.

"Did you remain here through the war, then?" I remarked, accepting the drink from him.

"Aye," he replied, turning to pour himself a glass as I sipped the dry, fermented apple cider. Experience had taught me it was best to drink it slowly. Many an unsuspecting visitor had found themselves scrooched on this West Country beverage.

"Someone 'ad to care for the horses. That nincompoop the major brought with 'im certainly didn't know what 'e was about. Now, Miss Townsend . . ." he declared as he sank down on a battered old trunk. "But I 'spose it's Mrs. Kent, now, isn't it?" He arched his eyebrows not so much in question, but as if to say his memory wasn't faulty. "What can I do for ye?"

"You've heard about the troubles up at the house?"

"I don't concern myself much wi' what goes on inside. But aye, I heard about the jumble those lads left the place in." He snorted. "T'would be difficult not to, what with that hole in the gazebo in the garden, and how her ladyship's been carryin' on about it night and day." Mr. Plank had never cowed to his employers, saying whatever he thought about them, and I supposed it was too late now to expect that to change.

"What of the forgeries and thefts?" I asked, curious whether he could confirm anything the butler had told me.

"I heard about those, too. Not that I know anythin' about 'em. When they were smuggled out o' here, must've been by a motorcar." He wrinkled his nose, expressing his well-known aversion to the vehicles. "An' I got nothin' to do wi' those."

I took another drink of the scrumpy to mask my chuckle, able to guess what Mr. Plank would think of Sidney's prized Pierce-Arrow. "What are the other servants saying? I imagine they have their own ideas."

"Aye," he confirmed, scratching the scraggly beard on his chin as he nodded. "Not that I listen much to 'em, mind. But 'tis hard to ignore the maids when they're shriekin' and carryin' on."

I lowered my drink in surprise. "Shrieking?"

"Aye. One o' 'em swears she saw a ghost."

I sat blinking at him, struggling to accept this assertion, or connect it to anything I'd yet learned.

Mr. Plank's face split into a wide grin. "Don't know about that yet, I see. Aye, there are some 'at say that airfield"— he dipped his head in its general direction—"be constructed on an ancient burial ground. That they plowed through an

ancient barrow and disturbed whatever souls were restin'
there."

I scowled. There were barrows—Neolithic and Bronze
Age burial mounds—dotted all over the Wiltshire countryside, the largest and most famous being West Kennet Long
Barrow, a short distance to the west of here. Many of the
smaller barrows had never been excavated and were barely
notated, so I supposed the plowing over of one was possible.
But that did not mean that something superstitious need follow. "Are you trying to tell me it's haunted?"

He shrugged one shoulder. "Maybe. Maybe not." His dark
eyes gleamed as he leaned forward, enjoying the tale. "But
that airfield has seen a number o' crashes, and there are some
that say it's the work o' the spirits."

I thought it more likely the fault of the foggy conditions
in this part of the country, and the fact that RAF Froxfield
also served as a training base. Inexperienced pilots plus misty
weather seemed a recipe for mishaps.

"Has anyone else seen this . . . ghost?" I asked skeptically.

Mr. Plank sat back, suddenly sobering. "Not that'll admit
to it."

"What do you mean?"

His gaze dipped to the floor; his brow furrowed with some
troubling thought. For a moment he seemed to debate with
himself whether to answer, and when he did, it was in a low,
unsettling voice. "Mr. Green—he's our odd-job man. He re-
fuses to do any work in the west garden or beyond once the
light begins to fade. Says it plays tricks with him." His eyes
lifted as if to gauge whether I understood what he was trying
to say without putting it into so many words. "He served in
the war, ye know. With great distinction."

I thought of the other veterans I'd met, men like my husband, who struggled to leave the war behind. Men who
sometimes saw shades of their fallen comrades when the man

walking toward them on the pavement or standing in front of them in the queue resembled them, or when the angle of the sunlight was just right and their eyes were tired from yet another night spent tossing and turning from bad dreams. Had Mr. Green seen things in the west garden? Had he feared it was his mind playing tricks on him—conjuring the friends and fellow soldiers he'd lost?

I nodded solemnly. "I can't help but notice how reduced the number of staff is. This Mr. Green. How much is he responsible for?"

Mr. Plank inhaled a deep breath. "A fair bit. There's one gardener still helps out however 'e can, but he's as old as I am, and his back's as crooked as a lightning bolt from spendin' his life bent over with his hands in the dirt."

"Then the rest of the staff is gone?"

"Aye, either lost to the war, pensioned off, or moved on to other posts."

I allowed that sobering discovery to sink in before pressing my chief concern. "What do you think of Mr. Green?"

He leaned back, scratching his chin again. "Well, 'e was in the war, ye know?"

I nodded, for we'd already established this.

"And 'e came back a changed man, that's for sure. Quiet, resigned, mostly keeps to himself. Can't blame 'im for that. But 'e works hard. His jobs are never endin'." He tipped his head to the side. "Though I suspect that's part o' the appeal. I gather his home life isn't so peaceful."

What exactly he meant by this, I didn't have the chance to ask, for his eyes clouded with distrust.

"Why are ye askin'?"

I took one last sip of the scrumpy before setting it aside. "He gave my aunt some advice on something up at the house, and I suppose I just wanted to gauge his credibility."

"Aye, 'bout the wood rot." He harrumphed. "Told her ladyship to bring in an expert. It's no' his fault she hasn't."

"Yes, I understand that." I sighed. "But you understand what my aunt is like."

He harrumphed again, probably a nobler course than voicing whatever words were curdling his tongue into a grimace. He downed the rest of his glass before offering me a bit of advice. "Before ye go takin' her ladyship's word for anythin', ye should try talkin' to her maid. Miss Musselwhite knows what's what, and what's merely her ladyship's haughty imaginings."

"Then she sounds like the person I should speak to next."

CHAPTER 5

Unfortunately, corralling Miss Musselwhite proved easier said than done. My aunt seemed to have constant need of her, particularly on a day like today, when she declared her nerves to be frazzled, her constitution unsettled by the previous day's revelations. Whether her health was actually poor or this was merely meant to elicit my sympathy, I didn't know, but when I visited as a child I remembered my aunt had forever been taking to her bed whenever anyone did something to overset her.

Regardless, I was not going to waste the day seated by her bedside when there were other things I could do to ease her mind. That is, if she truly wanted it eased and this wasn't all a colossal bid for attention. If that was the case, I would rather she'd simply invited us to visit.

The housekeeper allowed me to use her parlor bursting with pillows and samplers embroidered with improving verses to speak with the two other maids remaining on the staff. These girls had been closest to the missing maid, Minnie Spanswick, and I hoped they might share with me everything they knew or suspected. Though it took a bit of coaxing, the butler's supposition proved correct. They were eager to talk to me. But interestingly, they disagreed on what Minnie's fate had been.

"Minnie wanted to be an actress," the apple-cheeked maid

named Agnes stated with disapproval. "She was forever yammering on and on. Hardly ever shut her gob about it."

Her slighter friend with chocolate-brown tresses frowned. "Don't pretend it isn't true, Opal. How many times did you and I have to redo her sloppy work just so Mr. Miles wouldn't dock us all?"

Opal's expression seemed to acknowledge the truth of this.

Agnes crossed her arms over her chest. "Seems obvious she simply up and went to London. She'd been saving her blunt for just such a scamper." She shrugged a shoulder. "Maybe that officer she met from the airfield offered to help her." Her lips curled derisively. "For a price."

Opal seemed less certain of this, shifting back and forth on her heels.

"You look like you might think differently?" I asked carefully, curious what she thought, but not wanting to offend Agnes, lest she refuse to say more.

Agnes glowered at her friend, but under my steady gaze, Opal arched her chin. "No, I don't think she scampered. Not without telling us that's what she meant to do."

"Then what happened?" I pressed.

"Well, it's true. She *was* steppin' out with a flyboy." She bit her lip, casting a look at Agnes out of the corner of her eye. "Used to meet him at the edge of the estate, where it borders the airfield."

A righteous gleam lit Agnes's eyes, as if this confirmed her suspicions about Minnie and her virtue.

"She . . . she asked me to come with her once, but I had to finish dustin' Sir Reginald's room and she wouldn't wait for me. So I followed after her when I finished."

Agnes planted her hands on her hips. "Opal!"

The petite maid scowled. "Oh, stuff it, Agnes. I didn't do anything wrong. I didn't even make it to the edge of the estate." Her indignation swiftly faded. "Because that's when . . ." She swallowed. "When I saw the ghost."

So this was the origin of the tale Mr. Plank had alluded to.

"You told us you saw it when you were out for a walk," Agnes accused.

"I *was* out for a walk," Opal insisted. "I just didn't tell you where I was going."

"This ghost," I queried, trying to keep my skepticism out of my tone. "Where exactly did you see it? What did it look like?"

"In the west park, near the river." Her eyes were wide in her pale face. "I didn't get a good look at it, but it was tall and wore some sort of long gray robe."

"Why do you think it was a ghost?"

"Because no one around here wears clothes like that. And its eyes." She shivered. "They . . . they were like two black holes." Her voice lowered to a whisper. "I'm not even sure it had eyes."

I struggled to maintain my patience with her. A ghost, indeed. And one without eyes. I wondered where on earth she'd dreamed up such a being. Given the fact her current employer was blind, it wasn't difficult to guess.

"And you think this ghost has something to do with Minnie's disappearance?"

"Isn't it obvious?" She glanced at Agnes as if for support. "The ghost must have done something to her."

But Agnes just shook her head. "That's nonsense. Minnie ran off to London. You told me yourself her parents believe the same thing."

Opal flushed. "Aye, but you know Minnie never got along with her stepmother. So she was certain to think the worst of her."

"For good reason."

The two young women glared at each other, clearly never going to share the same opinion of their errant fellow maid.

"Has anyone heard from her since she left?" I interjected before they could dissolve into outright squabbling.

"No," Agnes replied scornfully. "But then, none o' us expected to."

I studied Opal to discover if this was true. The manner in which she'd lapsed into a surly silence rather than defend her friend implied she agreed, however begrudgingly.

I was inclined to believe Agnes had the right of it, especially since Minnie's family also assumed she'd run off to London. For one, there was no evidence anything untoward had happened to her. For another, her possessions had been packed and removed, something I doubted a ghost—if such things even existed—would bother to do. Her love of the cinema and desire to be an actress seemed to be well-known, and she wouldn't be the first girl to have been seduced by a man's promises, false or otherwise.

The question that remained was whether Minnie had helped herself to a few of my aunt's trinkets to fund her new life. Short of tracking her down in London and retracing her every step, I doubted we would ever know the truth, and I was not about to invest the energy in such a pursuit. Not when there were much larger concerns to occupy my time.

As for the idea that a ghost haunted the airfield and west park, and had abducted Minnie, well, I'd never heard anything more ridiculous. But I did find the fact that the Littlemote estate actually bordered the airfield to be interesting. I wondered whether any of these supposed sightings of spirits were actually airmen wandering onto the estate. After all, the flight suits and mechanic coveralls they wore would not look so very different from the long gray garment Opal had described seeing in the distance.

If so, I was curious whether they had permission to do so. Not that I begrudged their enjoying the peace and beauty of the park, but perhaps if the staff was aware of the potential of their presence it might prevent such outlandish imaginings from taking hold. And relieve Mr. Green's mind.

I dressed early for dinner in a sage-green evening frock with a draped V neck and then wandered downstairs to the Elizabethan Room, where we'd gathered before dinner the previous evening. A chill had settled over the manor with the fall of night, and rain rapped against the windows. I was relieved to discover the fire in the room's hearth was a roaring one, and I crossed eagerly toward it, spying my cousin seated in one of the leather wingback chairs, a book opened in his lap. His fingers appeared to dance over the page, and I realized he was reading Braille. Having learned my lesson the previous day, and knowing Reg was already aware of my presence from the tapping of my heels against the bare wood floor, I greeted him immediately.

"Good evening, Reg."

He lifted his head, though he didn't turn my way. "Hullo, Ver."

I paused to gaze over his shoulder. "What has you so engrossed?"

He closed the book so that I could read the words on the cover printed above the Braille markings.

"*The Hunchback of Notre-Dame.*" I couldn't help but arch my eyebrows at his reading selection. "I applaud your choice of Hugo, but I much prefer *Les Misérables*," I declared, settling into the chair opposite him. "It's a shade less . . . chastening."

"Yes, well, it's the only book Mother said she could find on her last trip to London."

I felt a stab of guilt that I hadn't even paused to consider this part of my cousin's life. Aunt Ernestine possessed a number of wonderful qualities, but patience was not one of them. I imagined she'd visited one bookstore and purchased the first book in Braille that was presented to her.

"Well, I shall send you a stack of them when I return to London," I replied breezily, hoping to gloss over the matter before he could object. "So, is this what they taught you at that special rehabilitation hospital?"

His lips curled into a sneer. "Well, it wasn't as if they were going to teach a baronet how to chicken farm or make shoes."

"Can you type?"

"Oh, yes. I'm cracking good at that."

"You needn't be so derisive," I said softly. "Simply tell me if I've overstepped."

His brow furrowed as if he intended to argue with me, but then he closed his eyes and heaved a weary sigh. "Sorry, Ver. I suppose I've gotten so used to being treated like a doddering imbecile that I've forgotten not everyone sees me that way."

"Surely that's not true. I know your mother is a trifle . . . overprotective, but surely the staff wouldn't dare be so disrespectful."

He made a noise at the back of his throat that fell somewhere between a grunt of agreement and a snort of disdain, a sound that was wholly noncommittal, before turning the subject. "You know you didn't have to give in to Mother's demands and remain here. You must have a dozen places you'd rather be."

"Oh, it was my idea."

His face registered genuine surprise. "It was?"

"Oh, yes. I didn't really want to tag along on Sidney's errand in Cornwall." This was an exaggeration, but easier stated than explaining why it was better if I didn't go. "And you know I can't resist a good mystery."

He grimaced ruefully. "My backside remembers."

This startled a laugh out of me for I hadn't been thinking of the time I'd decided to uncover who'd stolen the last of Uncle James's vintage Madeira wine, only to land Reg in a heap of trouble when he was proved to be the culprit. He'd received a rather sound thrashing.

His grimace softened into a genuine smile—clearly having

enjoyed making me laugh—and it transformed his face from something hard and bitter into the handsome, good-natured young man I'd known before the war had beaten him down and stolen his vision. It was a welcome, but sobering sight. A reminder of everything we'd lost, and the other things we'd willingly given up because of it.

Even though Reg couldn't see me, I found I couldn't look into his face as I spoke again with forced lightness. "Besides, I've been avoiding some things for too long simply because they're painful." I traced my finger over the fabric at the edge of the chair. "And I suppose it's time I stop."

Silence fell between us, broken by the crackling of the fire in the hearth, and then the crinkle of Reg's clothes as he shifted to set the book in his lap on the table beside him.

"Mother said you hadn't been back to Brock House since '15. Since . . ." He didn't need to complete that sentence, for we both knew what had happened in July 1915. My brother Rob had died.

It was true. I'd been avoiding my parents' home—the place of so many memories that could not easily be shut away. And not just of my brother, though his loss was the chief splinter in my chest now that I knew Sidney was alive, but also the other boys of Upper Wensleydale. Boys I had known since I began toddling around the nursery, many of whom had not returned. And yet, the war had ended almost a year ago. I couldn't stay away forever.

"Quite." I inhaled a deep breath, determined not to let us devolve into morose ponderings. "Well, enough of that. I have a question for you." Marking the wariness that hunched his shoulders, I added in a low voice, "One that your mother doesn't wish me to."

His expression turned inquisitive, just as I'd known it would. "Really? And what is that?"

I looked toward the door, trusting the room was large

enough that my voice would not carry to someone standing outside. "You know about the forgeries, don't you? The ones she's so determined you not hear about. You've known about them for some time."

His mouth curled upward at one corner in cynicism. "As I said, doddering imbecile. She forgets my hearing is remarkably keen."

I clasped my hands in my lap, tilting my head. "Your mother seems determined to blame the airmen for them."

Reg's mouth drooped.

"In fact, I believe she means for Sidney to intervene on her behalf to have the matter investigated."

His head dropped back against the chair as he lifted his face to stare sightlessly up toward the paper and plaster chandelier overhead. "Mother!" he cursed under his breath.

"But you already know who is responsible, don't you? And it's not the airmen."

He scowled and then relented. "No, it's not the airmen. Father ran into some financial trouble a few years before the war. So, he sold some of the estate's more precious artwork and sculptures, and replaced them with forgeries. *Not* that he told me, mind you," he remarked bitterly. "I wasn't his heir then. And I doubt he would have even told Thomas had he not been required to get his heir's written permission since the art was part of the entailment."

"Then how did you find out?"

"By paying attention," he muttered dryly. "Father wasn't exactly stealthy about it. I guessed what he was about, and when I asked Thomas he confirmed it."

"Did your mother know?"

"I'm sure Father didn't tell her, but she must know the truth. She can't be that willfully blind."

I arched my eyebrows. "Are you certain about that?"

His mouth pressed into a thin line as he seemed to give this some consideration. "Yes! I know she discovered some of the gems in her jewelry are fake. I heard her say so. So she must at least *suspect* the truth about the rest."

And yet she was still prepared to blame the airmen.

This fact did not endear my aunt to me. From the look on his face, neither did it please her son.

"What of the smaller portable items that have gone missing?" I asked.

"Which items?"

"When I asked Miles, he mentioned things like a vase, figurines, a box of old coins, and an ivory calling card case."

His fingers tapped the arm of his chair in agitation. "Yes, I did know about a few of those things. Mother asked me about the coins and I heard her complaining about a Dresden shepherdess. But I didn't know there were others."

"Miles also mentioned that they started going missing after the airmen departed and the family resumed habitation of Littlemote."

"So Mother can't pass the blame onto the flyboys for those."

"No." I hesitated to voice my next question even though he obviously held no illusions about his mother's rectitude. "But do you think she might have had anything to do with them? Could she have sold them and then lied about it to save face?"

His brow lowered as he mulled over this possibility, but then he shook his head rather forcefully. "No, I don't. Simply because of the fact that she was so upset when she discovered the coins and the figurine were missing. She even went so far as to accuse me of having done something with the coins when much of the time she treats me like I'm incapable of even crossing a room."

"What type of coins were they?"

"Just ones that have been found about the estate in centuries past, by the family or the gardeners. Thomas and I dug one out of the riverbank when we were boys." The corners of his mouth briefly lifted in a small smile at the happy memory. "Father dropped it in the box with the others that he kept on a shelf in his study." He tilted his head. "As I recall, another coin was found just last year, and I imagine it was tossed in with all the rest. There are at least a few Roman and Anglo-Saxon coins among the lot—scuffed and worn from time— so I imagine they're worth something to the right buyer."

I turned the matter over in my mind, wondering if there might be a way we could trace the coins in reverse by finding those right buyers.

"What about the door to my mother's bedchamber?" he interjected. "Have you uncovered anything there?"

I explained what I'd learned about the possible water damage and Mr. Green's suggestion they hire an expert to assess the problem.

"And yet Mother hasn't done so?"

I started to shake my head, but then realized he couldn't see me. "No. I'm not sure . . ." I broke off, deciding to rephrase the matter. "The repairs could be quite dear."

"No need to tiptoe around the matter with me, Ver. I know my pockets are practically to let." His good humor at the situation abruptly faded. "Mother might like to pretend that decades of mismanagement hasn't left us in a bit of a pickle, but I refuse to harbor any illusions. After spending three years in the trenches, I've had enough of that to last a lifetime," he added wryly.

I smiled tightly in commiseration and opened my mouth to ask him what he intended to do about it, when Aunt Ernestine chose that moment to finally make her appearance.

"Here you are," she announced as if she'd had to search the entire house for us rather than finding us exactly where we were supposed to be. She eyed our cozy tête-à-tête before the fire with misgiving. "Well, my, aren't we both punctual. I apologize for my lateness, but my nerves, you know."

Given the fact she'd been indisposed the entire day, I'd

wondered if she might bow out of dinner. Instead, it appeared she'd chosen to play the martyr-card. Indeed, all evening she never missed a chance to remind us of her overtaxed nerves, even as in the same breath she assured me that, as hostess, she couldn't leave me to fend for myself my entire visit. Never mind the fact that Reg and I had been rubbing along just fine without her. I felt it more likely she didn't wish to leave us alone for too long, lest I share something she didn't wish me to. Too late for that.

Given Reg's antagonistic behavior toward his mother, I half expected him to demand answers to the revelations I'd made at dinner, but he held his tongue. Obviously, he knew her well, and had probably already guessed she'd forbidden me to speak of it. Given that, I was grateful for his discretion. But seeing the look on his face as I excused myself for the evening, I would not have wagered on his willingness to hold his tongue for longer than it would take for me to pass out of earshot.

CHAPTER 6

The following day dawned crisp and cool, with the rays of the rising sun sparkling off the drops of dew coating the lawn and gardens. Though bundled in my Prussian blue velvet coat with roll collar, I was grateful for the rugs the chauffeur had provided my aunt and I in the rear seat of their Rolls-Royce. Especially as my aunt's frigid silence cast an added chill over our drive to the church in Hungerford—a building built of Bath stone during the Regency Gothic Revival in the early nineteenth century, complete with castellations and pinnacles.

Given the content of the vicar's sermon about charity and forgiveness and our position in the front pew as the first family of the area, I thought she might thaw toward me. But when she snatched away the arm Reg had offered to me, insisting he walk beside her as we exited the church, I realized she was as furious as ever. Her terse explanation of who I was to the vicar caused him to raise his eyebrows, and I had to set about charming him so that he wouldn't remark too finely upon it. Just as I had to charm the few parishioners who dared approach us in the churchyard when it fell to Reg to introduce me because my aunt was largely ignoring me.

It became a struggle to mask my irritation with my aunt, for her behavior was not only petty, but it was also making a spectacle out of us when my celebrity and Reg's blindness already garnered us enough attention. For all that Aunt

Ernestine would be horrified at such conduct in others, she was remarkably oblivious to the fault in herself. So when a couple began to argue at the edge of the churchyard nearest the Kennet and Avon Canal, which flowed lazily past, I was almost grateful to them for drawing everyone's avid gazes away from us.

That is, until I realized they were the same couple Sidney had almost run over with his motorcar two days earlier. We were too far away to hear most of what was being said, but from the looks on the other villagers' faces this was not an uncommon occurrence. Yet no one tried to intervene, not even the vicar. That is, not until the golden-haired maid I'd seen in the upper corridor of Littlemote House stepped tentatively forward. I'd since learned this was Miss Musselwhite, my aunt's maid. She spoke to the woman, who was doing a large part of the yelling.

At this, my aunt was galvanized into action, even going so far as to forget she was not speaking to me. "That woman is a disgrace," she pronounced crisply, never removing her contemptuous gaze from the couple. "Mr. Green needs to get a better handle on his wife before she does something he cannot undo."

I scrutinized the couple with greater interest, assessing the man with new eyes. I noted how he seemed to restrain himself, even when his wife lashed out at him, causing a gasp of disapproval to rise up from the congregation watching. He caught her hand before it could connect with his face, holding it firmly for a few seconds before letting go.

"Come. We are leaving," my aunt announced as she strode down the path overarched by trees in burnished autumn colors toward the lychgate, leaving Reg and I to follow in her wake. I looped my arm with his and walked steadily forward as fallen leaves crunched beneath our feet. Though I couldn't resist stealing another glance toward the Greens. Miss Musselwhite had managed to pull the woman to the side and was speaking to her as the vicar moved forward to address her husband.

Once we were settled in the motorcar, I couldn't withhold the question bubbling up behind my lips, not even with the chauffeur listening. "That was Mr. Green? Your man-of-all-work?"

Aunt Ernestine's mouth opened and then shut again, as if remembering her decision to ignore me. Her mouth firmed into a prim line.

Fortunately, Reg was not cross with me, nor willing to take part in such childish maneuvering. "Yes, he's a good man. Served with the Second Wiltshire Battalion."

At his mention of the Wiltshire Battalions I cringed, knowing the First and Second had been decimated during the German's Spring Offensive of 1918. The same offensive in which Sidney had been wounded by and reported dead by a fellow officer.

"And his wife?"

"Is a drunk," Reg stated, his voice devoid of any sympathy. "And has been for over three years. Or so I'm told."

My aunt exhaled an exasperated breath. "Reginald, mind your tongue. We may not approve of Mrs. Green's behavior, but we will speak respectfully of her." Her gaze flicked toward the chauffeur, who wisely kept his eyes trained on the road. "She is Miss Musselwhite's sister, after all. A regretful connection, to be sure. But nonetheless, we shall not gossip about her."

Not in front of the servants anyway.

Nevertheless, she had unwittingly provided me with the answer to my next question. So that had been why Miss Musselwhite had intervened. They were family.

I turned to gaze out at the passing scenery—the brilliant colored trees and sun-soaked fields. Such a stark contrast to the grim place I'd gone to in my mind. Reg had derided Mrs. Green as a drunk, but had I really been much better?

Certainly during the months after Sidney's supposed death when I still worked for the Secret Service I'd known the limit to how much I could drink in any evening to forget the pain and still be able to perform my job the next day. While behind enemy lines the imminent danger of detection by the Germans had been enough to distract me. Most of the time. But what about the months following my demobilization? Then there had seemed to be nothing worth sobering up for, and I'd felt myself falling further under gin's sway. If not for that letter accusing Sidney of treason, if not for his return from the dead, who knew what shape I would have been in by now?

So I couldn't help but feel empathy for Mrs. Green. Men often dismissed how hard the war had also been for the women. Waiting, wondering, dreading—every hour of every day, for four long years. Trying to carry on with life, shouldering the burdens of both husband and wife, mother and father, and pretend it all couldn't end in an instant. Scouring the Rolls of Honor listed in the newspapers every morning for the names of loved ones. Fearing the sight of the messenger boys on their red bicycles pedaling up the drive to deliver a telegram from the War Office. It strained the nerves past endurance.

If you were one of the lucky ones and your husband did come home, this wasn't an end to it. For once you'd lived with such fear, such horror for so long, it could never be forgotten. Nor could the emotions and resentments and frustrations that had been festering be brushed aside. In most cases, the returning soldiers and their wives were both the walking wounded, whether they were still suffering from injuries inflicted directly in battle or not. And those people whose husbands and loved ones had not returned were far too quick to dismiss their pain out of hand, jealous of their good fortune.

Given the injuries Reg had suffered and his resulting blindness, I could understand his scorn for Mrs. Green, but that did not mean he was right. Compassion need not be a restricted commodity, especially not during a time when *everyone* was still struggling to right themselves after the topsy-turvy years of the war.

Having had enough of my aunt's chilly treatment, upon our return to Littlemote I attempted to speak to her privately and apologize for speaking to Reg about the forgeries when she'd expressly forbidden me to do so. It didn't matter that I'd been right—that Reg had already known about them and so had not collapsed at their discovery—I had still disobeyed her order, and I knew she would never forgive me unless I offered my apologies first. But she would have none of it, deliberately rebuffing me and pleading a headache. I couldn't resist rolling my eyes as she suddenly demanded the footman's assistance in climbing the stairs to her bedchamber, despite the fact she'd been perfectly fine moments earlier.

Reg, it seemed, was also not in the mood for company. So left to my own devices, I enjoyed a delicious solitary luncheon and wandered the battered and overgrown gardens. From my point of view, my work here was done. I had looked into the matters my father had asked me to and had answered them to my satisfaction.

The airmen had undoubtedly damaged Littlemote, but the manor was far from falling down over their heads. Except perhaps the master bedchambers, but that was the fault of neglect, not the RAF officers. The majority of the "thefts" had been perpetuated by my uncle in order to replenish his dwindling accounts, and the smaller items that had disappeared might be impossible to recover. I could try to trace the old coins, but only if Reg or Aunt Ernestine wished me to pursue it. And that would have to be done in London anyway.

As far as the missing maid, she had more than likely taken off for London to follow her dream of becoming an actress, just as Agnes and her parents believed. There was no evidence of anything else. I'd learned she'd departed on a Sunday morning while everyone was at church, slipping away quietly. There was no sign of a struggle, and her possessions had been taken with her. Her decision to leave without collecting all her wages did seem somewhat odd, but perhaps if there was an officer from the airfield acting as her benefactor, or she'd taken some of the smaller portable items that were missing, then she'd thought she wouldn't need the small amount of pay still owed to her.

And I wasn't about to speculate on the ghosts. That was merely so much nonsense.

I'd intended to ask Reg about the airmen's possible use of the grounds, but had not yet had the chance. But even if they weren't expressly allowed, that didn't stop them from doing so. Especially when there was a bridge spanning the river that directly connected the properties as it had during the war for the officers' convenience. They were the likeliest explanation for what Opal had seen.

So, there was really no need for me to stay any longer. I paused at the edge of the gardens before it sloped downward to stare across the River Kennet at the wide fields beyond, toying with the idea of taking the train back to London that afternoon. But I quickly discarded the notion. Leaving my aunt on such terms would only widen the fissure of enmity between us to a chasm and anger my parents when they learned of it. They were already upset at me for refusing to return to Upper Wensleydale these past four years, and for not behaving with the circumspection my mother thought I should. The last thing I wanted to do was exasperate them further.

In any case, Sidney would be returning for me later that evening or early the next day, for tomorrow was my birthday, and I trusted his word that he would be back in time. I only hoped he didn't drive through the night in order to do so.

When I woke the next morning, I half expected to find

him lying beside me—having arrived in the wee hours of the night—but the space beside me was empty. I stared at the pillow where his head would have left a dent in the smooth surface, feeling a pang at his absence. Though we'd spent the majority of the five years of our marriage apart, in the four months since his return to the living apparently I'd grown accustomed to having him near. While I'd been refusing to acknowledge it since his departure forty-eight hours earlier, the truth was, I was missing him. Terribly. I only hoped he arrived sooner rather than later, for if my aunt and Reg continued their vigils of silence, I would go mad with the need for distraction.

Happily, when I arrived in the breakfast room they were both already seated, and Reg at least appeared to have restored his good spirits.

"Morning, Ver."

"Good morning, Reg," I declared as Miles held my chair for me. "You look quite dapper in that brown suit. Is it whipcord?" I leaned over to feel the fabric of his sleeve, ignoring the reproachful look my aunt threw my way. As if any comments that might remind him he couldn't see were forbidden. As if he could forget.

"Do I? I'll have to remember that. You always did have an eye for fashion. Or so the papers claim." He grinned.

I laughed. "Yes, well, I can't help that the society pages feel the need to describe and comment on every item of clothing I choose to wear."

"If you ask me, it's a shameful waste of ink," my aunt declared as her eyes raked up and down my appearance.

It being my birthday, I'd chosen to wear one of my favorite gowns—a myrtle-green wrap dress with a sheer overlay. The color accentuated the green in my eyes, and the shape played up my curvier than was strictly fashionable figure. It was a trifle more daring than most of my other daytime apparel, but I knew I looked smashing in it. Sidney certainly couldn't take his eyes off of me. As such, I wasn't about to let my aunt shame me.

"Well, someone must be reading it, or else they wouldn't print it." I lifted the silver coffee urn from the center of the table and poured the dark brew into my cup. Giving a little toss of my head to move the tendril of curls that had fallen over my eyes, I lifted my cup to take a drink, addressing my aunt over the rim. "How is your headache? Did a day's rest help?"

Her eyes narrowed at the corners as she tried to decide whether I was being facetious. I stared back at her guilelessly, waiting to hear how she would respond. But before she could do so, a scream shattered the silence.

I lowered my cup and turned toward the door. The shriek had come from the direction of the entry hall, and yet it sounded farther away.

"Good heavens," my aunt gasped, pressing a hand to her chest. "What is going on? Who is that?" she demanded as the woman continued to shout.

"Allow me to ascertain, my lady," Miles pronounced as he crossed toward the door, only to stop short as it was pulled open from without. The footman who had done so appeared to be all of seventeen. He staggered forward another step before glancing around the room with wide eyes.

"Robert, what is the meaning of this?" my aunt demanded of the young man. "Who is that shrieking like a banshee?"

The footman's throat bobbed up and down as he swallowed. "It's Opal, milady. Sh-she found Mr. Green out in the park west of the gardens. He—" He broke off to swallow again. "He's dead."

"What?!" Reg demanded, slapping the table with his hand, which made us all jump.

But the footman could say no more. He shook his head, and Miles ushered him out.

"Oh, oh, my!" Aunt Ernestine exhaled, slumping in her chair as if she might faint.

Somewhere toward the rear of the house I could hear the maid wailing. Whatever she had seen had upset her. The hairs along my arms and the back of my neck stood on end. Something was not right. And though I had not yet seen the body or the place he'd died, I already knew what needed to be done.

When Miles returned to the room, I turned toward my aunt and Reg, who both stared unseeing at the table before them. Although while my aunt's gaze was stupefied, Reg's face burned with ferocity.

"You have to send for the police," I told them in no uncertain terms.

Reg's shoulders dipped at this pronouncement, as if he'd recognized the same thing I had and was relieved to hear it.

"The police?" my aunt stammered, her eyes blinking rapidly. "Oh! Oh, my. Are you sure that's really necessary?"

"Yes," Reg and I replied in unison. Then he turned to Miles. "Do as Mrs. Kent suggests."

"Yes, sir," Miles answered without hesitation, hurrying out into the hall.

Aunt Ernestine draped her hand over her forehead. "Oh, goodness. Oh, how horrid."

But her son only seemed to have attention to spare for me. "I assume you intend to be taken to the body?"

Seeing the determined expression on his face, I nodded. "I do."

"I'm coming with you."

"Of course," I replied, having already deduced this would be his next statement.

His mother saw things differently. "What?! You cannot do that. Reginald, be reasonable."

He pushed to his feet, rounding the table with gentle touches to guide him.

"What do you expect to be able to do? You cannot *see* anything."

I halted in the middle of rising from my chair, shocked by her callous words. But one look at my cousin's face showed his jaw had hardened with resolve. He reached for my arm and threaded it through his.

"Reginald, sit down! I absolutely forbid you to go," Aunt Ernestine snapped.

His arm flexed, quivering with restrained fury as he turned his head to address her in a voice pitched dangerously low. "You forbid me? I fought in a war, Mother. I was in command of hundreds of men. I saw, and smelled, and touched, and did things you cannot even *begin* to imagine. You cannot forbid me from doing anything!"

He abruptly turned away, urging me forward. But not before I saw the daggered glare my aunt had aimed at me. It was obvious she blamed me for her son's sudden display of defiance. However, I didn't think I could take credit for any of it, other than the fact I refused to treat him like he was helpless.

Whatever the impetus, I was relieved to see my cousin showing some backbone. Though I didn't dare tell him that. Not unless I wanted him to direct the simmering rage he'd suddenly tapped into toward me.

We donned coats, hats, and walking boots and set off across the gardens with an older footman. Opal had been too agitated to relay more than the barest of details. Apparently, the warming oven in the butler's pantry had been acting up, and with the footmen busy attending the breakfast table, Opal had been sent in search of Mr. Green. The chauffeur had suggested she check the west gardens, where Mr. Green had been making repairs on the ha-ha that separated the gardens surrounding the house from the park. The ha-ha functioned as a sunken fence, which formed a vertical barrier to any livestock grazing in the park but preserved an uninterrupted view from the gardens out over the estate. Opal said she didn't know what had made her think he might be out in the park when she didn't find him at the ha-ha, except she thought she'd seen someone walking in the distance.

Standing at the edge of the ha-ha, one could see a fair distance to the west over the park despite the number of tall trees dotting the landscape. It was easy to see how she might have caught the barest glimpse of someone, and yet they not hear her when she called out. That is, if they'd wanted to hear. Perhaps that person had been Mr. Green, or perhaps it had been someone else who hadn't wanted to be seen.

We descended into the park and set off down a path worn through the grasses, past towering beech and yew trees. To the right of us, I could hear the burbling of the river, though it was shielded from our sight by a thicker band of trees. The air was crisp with the scents of decaying leaves and sun-warmed dew.

I noticed that Reg had fallen silent, but perhaps that was because he was concentrating on his other senses, trying to orient himself to where we were. Though he utilized a walking stick to tap the ground in front of him, for the most part he trusted me to guide him around any ruts or roots. Only once did he balk at my tug on his arm, having recognized before I had that the earth grew boggy on that side of the path, and I swiftly corrected.

"How much farther is it?" I turned to ask the footman walking behind us. Opal had said she'd found Mr. Green a few yards to the right of the path, near a copse of hawthorn trees.

"I'm not sure, ma'am," he replied uncertainly.

I nodded, recognizing the fact that most of the household servants would have little reason to venture in this direction.

"It shouldn't be far," Reg murmured. He lifted his head, closing his eyes against the glare of the sun. "The river turns to the north just before the copse the maid seemed to be speaking of. If you listen, you can hear that it's grown fainter."

I tilted my head. "You're right." Glancing about me, I surveyed the ancient parkland, wondering what, or who, had drawn Mr. Green into this part of the estate. No one was currently doing any hunting here, and this land certainly wasn't cultivated. I was about to ask Reg his opinion of the matter when I spotted him.

"There he is," I murmured, pointing toward a patch of lawn about fifty feet from the path.

Reg's jaw tightened, but other than that there was no discernable reaction to the tension in my voice.

We approached slowly, our footsteps crunching through the leaves strewn across the grass. Mr. Green lay on his side, turned toward the river with his knees drawn up toward his chest. About three feet away from the body, I released Reg's arm and began to circle it. One look at the face told me what had so upset Opal, for his eyes were wide open, seemingly frozen in agony. Though death had stolen his muscles' rigidity, the roundness of his eyes, the position of his legs, even the manner in which his hands seemed to grasp at his chest all seemed to point to the fact that he had died a terrible death.

CHAPTER 7

By the time the local police arrived, the lonely glade had gathered half a dozen spectators. A fact that did not please the local detective inspector when he approached with his constable as Miles led the way. He brushed past the butler, taking but a brief notice of the pair of footmen and the kitchen lad gawking beside them, before scowling at me and Reg, as well as Mr. Plank, who stood just beyond my shoulder.

"Stand back, if you please," he ordered.

I took hold of Reg's arm, as much as to provide a united front as to prevent him from tripping as we backed up half a dozen steps. Apparently, this was not enough to satisfy the inspector, for he scowled.

Miles shook his head as if in disapproval of such a shocking thing happening under his authority, and turned to herd the younger footman and the kitchen lad with a stern word back to the manor.

"We're certain of the identity?" the inspector asked as he knelt to examine the corpse. His constable remained at a distance, taking a notebook and pencil from his pocket.

Never having officially met Mr. Green, I turned to Mr. Plank, who took his cue. "Aye, it's Mr. Green, all right."

"Aye, I recognize him," he replied.

I frowned. Then why had he asked?

From his graying hair and the stern lines at the corners of

his eyes and mouth, I estimated he was about forty-five years of age—which made him a contemporary of Mr. Green. His height combined with his barrel chest easily marked him the largest man present. Something I suspected he was accustomed to.

The inspector swept a precursory glance over the body, and then he pushed to his feet.

"We couldn't find any evident signs of injury, but of course, we didn't move the body," I supplied.

His gaze brushed up and down my frame much as it had the corpse. "And yet you trampled over possible evidence."

I arched a single eyebrow imperiously. "We had to ascertain he was, in fact, dead, did we not?" In truth, the body had been cold to the touch, suggesting he had lain there for at least several hours. "Besides, I stepped carefully." I nodded at his bulky boots and then lifted my daintier one in illustration. "I certainly didn't disturb anything more than you have."

Mr. Plank chuckled under his breath, but it was to Reg that the inspector's eyes snapped. My cousin's pursed lips did almost nothing to hide the smile lingering there.

"Who is this woman?" the inspector demanded, his disregard for Reg apparent.

A vee formed between Reg's brows. "Why, don't you recognize her, Titcomb?" he retorted, making it evident he wasn't going to overlook the fact that the inspector hadn't addressed him correctly by returning the insult. "This is my cousin, Mrs. Verity Kent."

The constable, who until this point had merely given us cursory notice, fumbled the notebook clutched in his hands, nearly dropping it. His cheeks reddened as his gaze riveted on me and then darted away.

The stony expression on Inspector Titcomb's face never wavered. "They might do things differently up in London, but here in Wiltshire we don't need help from the likes of some society darling." With this derisive snarl, he turned his back on me to bark at his constable. "Jones! Search the area."

"About fifty yards west of here, I believe you'll find it significant that the ground is disturbed," I supplied.

Titcomb turned his head to observe me.

"As if someone has been digging." I allowed the implication to hang. A poor attempt to conceal evidence of some kind, perhaps?

"I'm sure we'll come to it in due time," he replied, dismissing me again.

I scowled. "We also noted there is an item clutched in Mr. Green's left hand. Though I didn't dare 'disturb' the body further, so I can't tell you precisely what it is, but it looks to be metal. And it was undoubtedly valuable, at least to him, judging from the fact he held on to it so tightly."

If ever I'd seen someone's hackles visibly rise, it was then. His shoulders hunched and the muscles of his thick neck seemed to ripple with irritation above the collar of his coat.

"You've done it now," Mr. Plank leaned closer to murmur. "More than like, 'e was gonna pocket that trinket. But now 'e can't, cause ye called attention to it in front o' all these witnesses."

I turned to him in shock, particularly astonished that he'd seemed to deliberately pitch his voice low, but not low enough that Titcomb couldn't hear him.

The inspector turned to glare at him, but Mr. Plank merely grinned.

"Sir Reginald," he growled to my cousin. "Kindly remove your cousin and this doddering old man from the glade. This is a police matter." He turned to the footman. "You can stay, if you plan to be of help. Keep a sharp eye out for my police surgeon."

I stiffened in affront at the manner in which he'd spoken of the stablemaster, but Mr. Plank cackled with amusement. "Aye, aye. Keep yer trousers on, Paul. I'm a goin'." Witnessing my evident confusion, he smiled even brighter. "'E's my nephew."

My eyes widened as I compared his shriveled, bow-legged form to that of the burly inspector.

He cackled even louder. "Aye, takes after his da', 'e does." He puffed out his chest. "Though I wasn't always such a scrawny gaffer. Might be more Plank blood in 'im than it seems. He certainly got his brains from his mum."

The corner of Titcomb's mouth twitched upward as he observed his uncle's preening, infinitesimally softening his otherwise steely exterior, but he shook his head in response and turned away.

"Come on, Ver," Reg coaxed. "There's nothing more for us to do here, and Mother's certain to be working herself into a flap waiting for us to return."

I allowed myself to be led away, knowing he was right. From all appearances, this was a natural, if painful death. There were no obvious wounds, no evidence of physical trauma. There was always the possibility such injuries were located on the left side of the corpse, beyond our sight without disturbing the body, but given the lack of blood pool it seemed doubtful, unless he'd suffered a fatal blow to one of his internal organs. The only trace of visible blood was a small smear at the back of his neck, barely visible above his collar, and that seemed more like a nick from shaving than anything else. All other indications were that Mr. Green had simply died of a heart attack or an apoplectic seizure, or perhaps some unknown medical complication from the war—a blood clot or a burrowing piece of shrapnel piercing a vital organ.

Yet, something about the nature of the man's death bothered me, though I couldn't place my finger on the precise reason why. Undeniably, the location was odd. Why had Mr. Green come to the west park in the wee hours of the night? What was he doing? Was he responsible for the disturbed earth we'd found? Had he been digging for something? But then, where was his shovel and lantern?

And what of the position of his body? It seemed a strange way to collapse, whether he was struggling toward help or had simply fallen down dead. It was almost as if his body had slowly frozen into that agonized position.

As such, I'd briefly considered poison as an option, but there was no evidence of vomiting, either on the body or within the twenty-foot radius we had searched. Of course, poison didn't always mean retching, but there were also no other signs—no blisters or strange striations, no swelling or pupil dilations.

Whatever the case, this was a matter for the police. I had no further justification for interfering. No one had requested my assistance in the matter. *If* there was even a matter to pursue. I was heartened by the fact the police seemed to be taking the matter seriously, but perhaps they did so with all suspicious deaths until proven otherwise. So, as long as they proved to be competent, I had no call to interfere.

I studied Mr. Plank out of the corner of my eye as he hobbled along just beyond my right shoulder. "Mr. Plank, you implied your nephew has brains. Does that mean he's a good policeman?"

"Oh, aye," he assured me in his creaky voice. "He's a hard man, 'e is. And I chalk that up to his da'. He was meaner than a weasel in a chicken coop. But me sister—'is mum—raised 'im straight. He's an honest one, and there's no doubt 'e's good at his job. So long as . . ."

I turned my head to regard him as he seemed to waver from what he was about to say.

He lifted his cap, swiping a hand over his forelock as he grimaced. "Well, so long as he doesn't view ye as feeble in some way."

I felt Reg stiffen beside me, recognizing now why Mr. Plank had hesitated to speak.

"There's still enough of a bully in 'im from his da', and a fear o' frailty to make 'im cringe at any show o' weakness."

"What of Mr. Green? Would your nephew have viewed him as feeble?" I asked, turning the conversation away from Reg.

He shook his head. "Nay, not after the war." He frowned. "Unless . . ." He shook his head. "Nay, 'e respected Mr. Green."

"But I bet he didn't approve of him allowing his wife to publicly harangue him," Reg said, wondering aloud the same thing I did.

Mr. Plank remained uncharacteristically silent, but the furrow in his brow answered for him.

Regardless of Titcomb's opinion of the Greens, if the death proved to be murder it was obvious who the main suspect would be. After all, Mrs. Green had been seen shrieking at her husband and attempting to strike him just the day before by several dozen witnesses. I was curious how she would take the news when she learned of her husband's passing. Who would tell her?

It seemed I was to have the answer to those questions sooner rather than later, for Mrs. Green suddenly appeared in the distance at the edge of the ha-ha. She paced left and right, and then gathered her skirts in her hands, preparing to jump down when Miss Musselwhite reached her side. Grabbing her arms, she spun her about to plead with her, but Mrs. Green yanked her arms away, stumbling back a step before righting herself. She pressed a hand to her head and then staggered forward again, half stepping and half falling over the three-foot dip of the ha-ha.

Fumbling upright, Mrs. Green charged toward us, her thin figure swathed in a faded blue gown. The silk flowers in her hat were worn and ragged, much as the face beneath it. I suspected she had been handsome once, but time, worry, and drink had prematurely aged her. "My husband. Have you seen my husband?" she demanded of us, bowling forward as if she meant to knock us down if we stood in her way.

"Tilly, stop," her sister begged, pressing her hand to the white cap covering her golden hair lest it fly away.

Reg stepped forward as she bore nearer, his hands lifting as if to prevent her from plowing into him. "Mrs. Green, please stop. We have news of your husband."

She abruptly halted. "Where is he? W-where's my husband?" Her voice shook and her paper-thin hands trembled as she gripped Reg's sleeves. "Tell me."

Reg's gaze flitted blankly over her head. "Perhaps your sister should—"

"Tell me!" she yelled, her face white with the effort. She panted, scouring his shocked face, and then began to back away, as if unnerved by the fact his gaze couldn't focus on her. Her sunken and hollow eyes darted to her left, and finding me staring directly back at her, she lunged toward me. "Tell me," she entreated.

"Tilly . . ." Miss Musselwhite started to interrupt, but I decided Mrs. Green deserved the truth. Had our situations been reversed, I would have wanted to know. In any case, her response could be revealing.

"Mrs. Green, you husband is dead," I told her as gently as I could.

The dark depths of her eyes quivered with desperation. "No," she rasped, the word sounding ripped from her throat.

"I'm sorry, but I'm afraid it's true."

"No," she repeated a little louder, and then a little louder and a little louder, until she collapsed against her sister with a keening wail.

Miss Musselwhite struggled for a moment to keep her upright, gathering her close and murmuring sounds of sympathy as her sister wept into the crisp collar of her gown. "How?" she asked me, her own tearful eyes stark with grief.

I shook my head, unable to answer her, and unwilling to share my speculations.

How much Miss Musselwhite might have apprehended I didn't know, but her eyes shone with an intelligence that made me suspect she missed very little.

Her sister inhaled a ragged breath, stammering between sobs. "I didn't mean it. I didn't mean any of it."

Miss Musselwhite stared down at her and then back at me, alarm flashing in her eyes. "Tilly, there's no need to . . ."

"I told him I wished he was dead. Last night before he left. It . . . it was the last thing I ever said to him. But I didn't mean it. Oh, God, I didn't mean it!" Her body was wracked by a shuddering sob. "He just wouldn't let go of—"

"Tilly, hush!" Having recovered from her shock, Miss Musselwhite cut her off there. "You are not to say anything more. Not one word," she reiterated, shaking her. "Do you hear me?"

Her sister's stern tone seemed to penetrate through Mrs. Green's haze of grief for she nodded meekly.

Mrs. Green might not recognize what a predicament she was in, but her sister did, and spewing confessions about having wished her husband dead just hours before he expired would only hurt her if the worst should prove true—that her husband was murdered.

"The police have taken charge of the body," Reg told them, which elicited a whimper from Mrs. Green.

Miss Musselwhite nodded. "Then perhaps I should return my sister to her home. The children will need to be told."

"Yes, that's probably for the best," Reg replied reservedly.

She pleaded with the stablemaster. "Mr. Plank, if you wouldn't mind assisting me."

"O' course," he murmured, springing forward. Between the two of them, they managed to bundle Mrs. Green away.

I threaded my arm through Reg's as he stood silently with puckered brow, listening to them depart. "What are you thinking?" I asked him once I could be certain my voice wouldn't carry to them.

He turned his head. "Just that Inspector Titcomb is going to want to speak with her. And how fortuitous it is she made that outburst to us and not him."

"Yes." I contemplated their parting figures. "It doesn't mean she's guilty of anything, of course. But it certainly wasn't complimentary."

"No, it wasn't."

A buzzing noise in the distance made me swivel to look back in the direction where the body lay, scanning the sky for the aeroplane that was making it. A sudden thought occurred to me. "RAF Froxfield borders the estate to the northwest, correct?"

"Yes, along a narrow expanse of the river."

"Hmmm," I hummed distractedly, narrowing my eyes as if I could peer through the canopy of brilliant autumn hues.

"I know that tone of voice," Reg replied. "What notion is wriggling around in that brain of yours?"

"Only that I wonder if it's a coincidence," I said lightly, deciding it wouldn't do to draw too fine a point on it. Especially when I didn't know if it actually mattered. But there were two ways of entering the west park, and Opal had mentioned seeing someone in the distance and, thinking it was Mr. Green, followed them. We now knew that person couldn't have been Mr. Green, for he'd expired hours earlier. So whom had Opal seen?

In any event, I was sure Inspector Titcomb would question her about it. I had no business butting in, regardless of my insatiable curiosity and fluttering instincts.

"Come on, then." I urged Reg forward. "Before your mother forces Miles to shuffle back out here after us."

He scoffed. "True. And she already sends that man shuffling after more than enough."

CHAPTER 8

The moment Reg and I stepped inside off the terrace, we could hear my aunt's wails and moans issuing from the Chinese Drawing Room. I cringed at the strident tone of her voice, briefly considering sneaking past. Until a familiar deep voice responded. Hastening forward, I paused in the doorway to gaze in relief at my husband—whole and seemingly healthy—as he chuffed my aunt's hands.

He looked up, one lock of his dark hair falling forward to curl over his forehead, and offered me a resigned smile. I was sure this was far from the scene he'd hoped for upon his arrival, and wondered how long he'd been sitting there, comforting my aunt as he waited for us to return.

The Chinese Drawing Room was so named because of the four beautiful hand-painted Chinese panels that graced the walls. An elegant fretwork motif decorated their mahogany frames, as well as the doors, the dado rail, and the shutters over the windows, which were thrown open to let in light. The delicate chandelier overhead was fashioned of a similar wood, as was the daintily carved furniture, including the settee where Sidney and Aunt Ernestine perched.

"Oh, thank heavens!" she exclaimed at the sight of us. "When you were gone so long, why, I feared the worst."

"What did you expect to happen to us, Mother?" Reg retorted snidely. "For us to stroll off a cliff? Be eaten by a bear?"

"No, but if there is some madman running about the grounds, shooting people . . ."

"Mr. Green wasn't shot, Aunt Ernestine," I replied before Reg could voice the nasty thought curdling his lips. "Or stabbed," I added for good measure as I sank into a caneback chair upholstered in a pale blue floral. "And he died several hours ago." My gaze met Sidney's, communicating I had a great deal more to tell him later.

"Well . . . I suppose that's a relief. Oh, but poor Tilly Green. For her husband to survive the war, only for this to happen." She stiffened, gazing at me in question. "Unless . . ."

I shook my head. "No, it's not suicide." I frowned. "At least, I don't think so." Though I supposed it was possible. Mr. Green *could* have poisoned himself. But with what? We'd found no vial or drinking vessel. Unless he'd been lying on it.

I looked up at Sidney. We both knew how difficult it was for the soldiers returning from war. How they struggled to put the horrors of those four years behind them. How challenging it was to rekindle their bonds with families and loved ones when the government propaganda had created such an unbridgeable divide between the truth and what had been printed in the newspapers. All one had to do was look at the alarming number of suicides among veterans to understand there was a problem.

My aunt sighed. "Well, I suppose, at least, that can be some relief to her."

I frowned.

"That he didn't *wish* to leave her," she clarified. "Given the circumstances."

Sidney looked to me for clarification, but I decided now was not the time.

"I suppose something will need to be done for the family." She closed her eyes, pressing a hand to her chest as she inhaled a strained breath. "Oh, but I can't think of that now." She scowled at the door. "Where is my maid?"

"Miss Musselwhite is accompanying her sister home." I turned to regard Reg, who still stood at the edge of the rug. "Mrs. Green came here looking for her husband. Apparently he left home last night and never returned. As you can imagine, she was incredibly distraught when she learned of his death."

"Oh, but she never asked my permission to do so," my aunt surprised me by protesting.

"*I* gave her permission," Reg replied. "It was the humane thing to do."

"Well, you shouldn't have done that! I . . . I have need of her." She rubbed circles on her chest, her voice tightening with agitation. "She's the only one who can administer my medication."

"Do you actually need another dose?" His voice was doubtful.

"Yes," she snapped. "This morning has been a great strain for me, and you know how that affects my heart."

"Is that what the medicine is for? Your heart?" I asked.

"It's for her nerves," Reg retorted flatly.

"And my *heart*," she countered. "Dr. Maslen prescribed it for me before the war, and that new young fellow who took his place, Dr. Razey, agreed."

"Could I give it to you?" I offered, trying to keep the peace. "Do you have the dosing instructions?"

"Thank you, Verity, but only Miss Musselwhite understands exactly how it's to be done."

"Of course."

My aunt turned to look at Sidney. "Someone simply must fetch her."

"You are *not* sending Kent, or anyone else for that matter, to collect Miss Musselwhite," Reg protested, clearly having guessed his mother's intentions even without the benefit of his sight. "Her sister's husband just died. Pulling her away would be cruel."

His mother stammered in outrage. "But my medicine!"

"If you have need of your medicine, I'll send one of the servants for Dr. Razey. I'm sure you won't object to *him* administering it."

She glared at her son in impotent fury before pushing to her feet. "Reginald, if you will please escort me to my chamber."

Reg's mouth flattened into a thin line of protest, but then he heaved a sigh of resignation. "Yes, Mother."

Sidney waited only long enough for them to exit through the parlor door before teasing me. "I leave you here alone for two days and already you're stumbling over dead bodies."

I turned to glower at him, and his expression turned more serious as he leaned toward me.

"What's going on, Ver?"

I glanced toward the doorway. "Not here." Taking hold of his hand, I pulled him to his feet, urging him to follow me through the house and up the stairs to our bedchamber. I closed the door to the corridor and the one that led into the adjoining dressing room before turning to speak.

"Wait," Sidney interrupted, abruptly pulling me close. "Before this conversation devolves into mayhem and murder . . ." His hand slid beneath my curls to cup the back of my neck as his lips sealed over mine.

His mouth was supple and sure, and it quickly drove every thought from my head except for him. I pressed against him, raking my fingers through his dark hair. I could smell the wind in his hair and the mild aromatic smoke from his special blend of Turkish cigarettes still clinging to his clothes.

Why his kiss should feel even more potent after two days apart, I didn't know, but I supposed it had something to do with the fact that sometime in the past four months I'd grown accustomed to him being around. After four and a half years of months-long separations and near constant goodbyes—not to mention the fifteen months I'd believed him to be dead—

such a thing had seemed impossible. The very thought that he would ever be around long enough for me to become inured to his presence had seemed unimaginable. And yet, here we were.

He was the one to end the kiss. The deep blue of his irises was almost swallowed by his pupils. "Many happy returns, my darling," he murmured, his voice roughened by desire.

I smiled almost shyly. "Thank you."

His arms circled my waist, anchoring me to him. "You didn't think I'd forgotten your birthday, did you?"

"No, but given the topic of discussion in the parlor, I know it hardly seemed appropriate for you to extend your best wishes there."

"True." His brow ruffled. "Not that your aunt wouldn't have found some way to make the occasion about her."

"She does have a rather self-centered outlook."

He arched his eyebrows at this bit of understatement.

"But enough about her." I anxiously surveyed his face. "You didn't drive all night, did you?"

"No, I stopped at an inn east of Exeter. Though I didn't exactly receive the welcome I was hoping for when I arrived at Littlemote after dragging myself out of bed before sunrise this morning to get back on the road."

I laughed. "No, I suppose not. Not if Aunt Ernestine immediately launched into histrionics."

"And you off 'poking ghoulishly' at a dead body. That sounded like much more fun."

My head reared back in astonishment. "Is that really what she said?"

"You don't think *I* came up with such a theatrical description, did you? She fairly accused you of turning her son against her, as well."

I rolled my eyes. "She's doing that well enough on her own."

He guided me toward the oak settee upholstered in caramel and cream brocade situated near the tallest window. "Yes, well, forget her for a moment and tell me about this Mr. Green."

I relayed everything I knew about Mr. Green's death, including a few of my conjectures on the things I didn't, watching Sidney's face closely as he sifted through all the information.

"Why do you think it's not a natural death?" he queried, as always seeming to see to the heart of the matter whether I wished him to or not.

"I didn't say I didn't."

"No," he granted, clasping his hands behind his head as he sank deeper into the cushions. "But it's obvious you're suspicious."

I frowned at a worn spot in the carpet, trying to put into words the vague sense I had that something about Mr. Green's death seemed abnormal. "I suppose I am. It was just . . . such an odd place to die. And the manner in which he was lying there . . ." I shook my head, trying to dislodge the memory of his tortured expression. The man had been through the hell of war, and yet something about his death had terrified him.

"I imagine a natural death could be just as painful as an unnatural one. And if he were suddenly struck by . . . a heart attack, shall we say, he would hardly be able to choose the moment or location when and where it occurred."

"Yes, I know that."

He tilted his head. "Men do fall dead from a simple heart attack. Even men as relatively young and fit as Mr. Green." Far too much wisdom shimmered in his gaze. "Or don't you wish to hear that?"

I struggled not to fidget, uncomfortable with the realization that he had recognized even before I had how such a notion unsettled me. That just because Sidney had survived the war and returned to me didn't mean he couldn't be snatched away again forever. And not by some traitor's bullet, but something as unassuming as a heart attack, or heaven forbid, another round of that dreaded Spanish influenza.

I inhaled past the tightness in my chest. "Yes, I suppose it's easier when death has a more tangible culprit and cause." Out of the corner of my eye, I could see him watching me with a tenderness I felt too fragile to endure. Summoning the last dregs of my self-possession, I straightened my green skirt primly. "Whatever the reason for Mr. Green's demise, that shall be the police surgeon's duty to decide. Either way, it will still be painful for his wife. Doubly so if it proves to be murder."

"How so? Because someone chose to kill him?"

"Because she will undoubtedly be the chief suspect."

He lowered his arms in interest. "I understand that the spouse is often a suspect in such things, but that doesn't mean it's always so."

I turned to face him more fully. "True. But do you remember the couple arguing in the middle of the road that you almost struck with your motorcar?"

He nodded.

"That was Mr. and Mrs. Green."

His eyes widened.

"Apparently, those public quarrels were not uncommon. About forty villagers and I witnessed another in the churchyard after service yesterday. And there's a great deal of gossip about and disapproval of her drinking. How, more often than not, she's corked."

I expected Sidney to react similarly to Reg, albeit with less disdain. Instead he sat quietly, his gaze fixed across the room, though I could tell his thoughts were somewhere in the past. At first, I thought he was recalling my confession to him some months prior. How I'd admitted to drinking more than a few gin rickeys to get me through each evening late in the war. But then he spoke in an abstract voice.

"I had a sergeant. A tall, wraithlike fellow from somewhere near Leeds. Rather stoic chap. His best mate was in one of the Bantam Battalions." He cracked a smile, using the name the soldiers had bestowed on the special units of men who had enlisted in 1916 after the height requirement for new recruits had been dropped from five feet three inches to five feet tall. "The two of them together made the funniest sight, especially when the bantam one started rambling in his unintelligible dialect while my sergeant merely bobbed his head or answered with crisp 'ayes' and 'nays.'"

Given the very little he ever shared about the war, about the men he'd commanded at the front, I was justifiably stunned to hear my husband volunteer such information. And I struggled not to show it, lest he stop. All I could do was smile in acknowledgment and hope it wasn't too strained, but not too eager either. Fortunately, he wasn't paying me any heed.

"One of the photographers prowling about snapped a picture of them once. I wonder if it ever made it into print anywhere." He shook himself. "Anyway, this sergeant had a wife and a few children back home." He reached into the inner pocket of his coat and extracted his battered silver cigarette case—the one I'd given him as a wedding present before he left for the front. "He didn't talk about them much. At least not to me." His voice deepened. "But I'll never forget when he came to beg me for compassionate leave." He frowned down at the unlit fag in his fingers. "How his wife had been driven to drink out of fear. How he needed to go to her, to help her."

I watched as he lit the cigarette, inhaling a deep drag. "Did you approve his request?"

"I did." He exhaled a stream of smoke. "But HQ denied it." He inhaled again, a greater indication of his agitation than perhaps he knew, for I'd noticed how he smoked more when he was angry or unsettled. When he needed a distraction for his hands and his mouth. "He was killed a few weeks later."

My heart squeezed in answer to the hollow ache in his

voice. I wanted to ask after the sergeant's family, to know what had happened to his wife, but I didn't dare. Not knowing that would only add to the burden Sidney already felt. So instead I leaned closer, resting my head on his shoulder. He continued to smoke in silence for a few moments while the ormolu clock ticked away on the mantel, and then lifted his arm to drape it around me.

"So Mrs. Green is not an isolated case," I finally ventured to say.

"No, she isn't."

I wondered how many more women there were across the country like her, across all the belligerent nations. How many of them were also scorned and derided, chided for their failure to bear up under the strain, for daring to show such weakness?

"I'm sorry, Ver," he murmured, and I lifted my head to look at him. "I don't imagine this was how you wished to celebrate your birthday, is it?"

"Well, no. But it seems churlish to complain. After all, I doubt Mr. Green planned on dying. And now his family must go on without him." It was a lowering thought.

He stubbed out his fag in the dish on the table at his elbow and then gathered me close. "I somehow doubt your aunt and cousin are going to be much help in making merry, and you don't seem to feel much like it either. Justifiably so. So why don't we postpone our celebration until later this week in London."

"I would like that," I replied earnestly, and then attempting to rally for his sake, I draped my arms around his neck. "But do I still get my present today?"

"That depends," he teased. "Tell me first, when *are* we returning to London?"

"Tomorrow, if you like."

He reared back in surprise. "Truly? You're not going to insist we remain here until we know whether Mr. Green's death was caused by fair means or foul?"

"I think the police have matters well in hand. There's little I can do."

"And what of the matters your father asked you to look into for your aunt?"

"The person responsible for all the forgeries is my dearly departed uncle."

"Ahhh," he replied.

"You don't sound surprised."

He shrugged one shoulder. "I figured it was something like that."

I opened my mouth to question how he'd come to such an assumption, but then closed it, deciding the answer was probably obvious. After all, I'd worked it out rather quickly myself. "Mr. Green recommended my aunt hire an expert to examine the roof over the master bedchambers, but since the estate can't afford the repairs, she has not. And the maid who is missing likely took off for London to become an actress, *possibly* with the smaller items missing from the manor in her bag to fund her new life."

His eyes shone with admiration. "You've made quick work, haven't you?"

"Well, it's not as if any of it was difficult to deduce," I demurred, basking in his praise all the same. "And it's not as if I had to drive all the way to Falmouth to gather *my* information. What did you find out? Were any of the employees at Rockham's import-export business willing to speak with you?"

His face transformed into such a fearsome scowl, I was almost sorry I'd asked. "Not a one."

"Truly?"

He nodded. "They clammed up the moment they realized why I was asking questions." His voice was deathly earnest when he spoke next. "Someone got to them, Verity. Someone told them to keep their mouths shut."

There was no need to speak the name of the person responsible, for we both knew it. Lord Ardmore. Once more, he'd beaten us to the punch.

I exhaled in frustration. "We need to get back to London. Maybe Max has uncovered something in his father's papers at his office in Parliament." Even as I said it, I didn't really believe it, for I knew if Max had discovered something, he would have found a way to contact us.

Though our relationship with Max Westfield, the Earl of Ryde, was complicated—because he'd served as Sidney's commanding officer at one point during the war, and because I'd started to develop feelings for him when I'd still believed Sidney to be dead—Sidney and I both acknowledged we could possess no greater friend. Over the past four months, Max had been there whenever we needed him, ready to leap in with his assistance. And when we'd recently uncovered a heinous plot that involved not only Lord Ardmore and Lord Rockham, but also Max's late father, he'd barely flinched before diving in to help us uncover proof. That we now suspected Ardmore of also arranging Max's father's death, and destroying any evidence of their connection, complicated matters. But Max had willingly agreed to search through the remainder of the meticulous records his father left behind to locate whatever information he could find that might help us in our quest to expose Ardmore's treachery and to discover the endgame behind all his machinations.

"Maybe," Sidney replied doubtfully. "But you are right. We do need to return to London."

Despite the unpleasantness of Mr. Green's death, the past four days had served as a welcome distraction from the shadow Ardmore had cast over our lives. And a much-needed reminder that the elusive lord didn't lie around every corner or hang over every mystery. One day we would find the proof we needed, one day we would snare him in his own trap. But in the meantime, life must go on.

"But not before I give you this." Sidney extracted a long, thin box from his coat pocket and handed it to me with a warm gleam in his eyes. "Given our recent exploits, I was tempted to arm you to the teeth instead. A pearl-handled pistol for your clutch, a dagger to strap to your thigh." His voice softened. "But I've had this tucked away since our wedding."

I looked up from the box in shock.

"I meant to give it to you on my first leave. But then, part of me started to think that, if I had this hidden away waiting for me to give it to you, then the fates would have to let me return."

I felt tears burn at the back of my eyes. "Where was it hidden?"

He shook his head, a smile lurking on his lips. "If I tell you that, then where will I hide your Christmas gifts?" He nodded at the box. "Open it."

My hands trembled slightly as I lifted the lid only to gasp at the sight of the diamond and emerald bracelet nestled within—a perfect match to my wedding ring. "Sidney," I breathed in awe, lifting the flashing gems up to the light. "It's beautiful."

He took the bracelet from my fingers and then grasped my hand, turning it over and bringing my wrist up to his lips. His deep blue eyes watched me as he pressed a warm kiss to the delicate skin, making my pulse flutter. Then with a smile that I knew would only ever be just for me, he fastened the bracelet around my wrist. "Happiest birthday, darling. Here's to many more."

CHAPTER 9

I inhaled a deep breath of smoke, gin, and Tabac Blond perfume as the driving rhythm of the music filled my blood. The band at Grafton Galleries—one of the London night clubs Sidney and I frequented—seemed particularly uninhibited tonight. But then, they always seemed freer when my friend Etta Lorraine took to the stage. She stood at the center, gripping the microphone as she belted out "Royal Garden Blues," her fingers and shimmying hips encased in gold silk keeping the tempo driving.

Sidney and I had deliberately arrived at the club later than usual that evening. The day had already been a long one. My aunt had protested our departure, but since she'd taken to her bed again, she hadn't been able to put up much of a fight. Seeing how pale and weak she seemed, I'd felt a moment's qualm about leaving her. But Miss Musselwhite had returned, looking drawn and sad, and promised she'd look after her closely, lest she have a relapse of the illness she'd suffered a few weeks earlier.

In any case, my mind was soon occupied by other worries when I noticed how Sidney winced every time he lifted his left arm. He strove to hide it, but from time to time the muscles in his chest that had been damaged when he was shot nineteen months prior still pained him, particularly when he exerted them more than usual. Between all the driving he'd

done to Falmouth and back, and his thorough efforts the evening before on behalf of my birthday, I wasn't surprised his
old wound ached. So, despite my curiosity being piqued by
the message we'd received from Max asking us to meet him at
Grafton Galleries that night, I'd insisted that Sidney lie down
and rest for a few hours before we set out on the town.

Fortunately, Grafton Street and Piccadilly weren't far from
our flat in Berkeley Square, and within minutes of stepping
into a taxi we found ourselves descending into the club. As
a former art gallery, the club boasted some fine spaces, but
no lavish décor. At least, none like those at the exclusive Em-
bassy Club. But people didn't come to Grafton Galleries to
stare at the walls. They came to dance. As such, it was the
perfect place to meet. Not only was it less conspicuous than
closeting ourselves away in our flat, but the loud music foiled
any would-be eavesdroppers. Given the fact that we were
fairly certain Ardmore was having us surveilled, this was no
small thing.

My friend Daphne twirled by in the arms of a gentleman in
white tie and tails, a red carnation tucked in one button hole,
giggling as she waggled her fingers at me.

"That is one brave fellow," Sidney remarked, pressing a
hand to the small of my back, where the deep vee of my jade-
green gown exposed my skin.

"I thought you'd developed some appreciation for Daphne,"
I protested over my shoulder. Until a few weeks prior, he had
barely tolerated her, while my friend had been determined to
win his approval.

"I'm not talking about Daphne, but that drink of hers."

I turned to see that she cradled a glass of the brilliant pink
concoction called "Turk's Blood," one that came perilously
close to spilling over the sides onto her partner's white coat
with each revolution.

We wound our way through the crush of beautiful bodies, pressing a kiss to a flushed cheek here and shaking the

hand of a grinning chap there as we searched for Max. Finding it impossible to make our way around the edges of the dance floor, Sidney whirled me into his arms as we gave in to the syncopated urges of our bodies and let the music pull us under its sway. My husband had always been a marvelous dancer, though I couldn't help searching his face for any sign of strain.

He dipped his head so that his mouth was next to my ear. "I'm fine, Verity. Stop fretting."

As if to illustrate this, he twirled me out and then pulled me back in, his eyes glinting in challenge. I needed no further encouragement, meeting him step for step as the fringe of my dress swirled about my sheer silk stockings. We danced two rags, and then I spied Max a few feet away from us as the band transitioned into a more traditional waltz.

"Verity, Kent," he declared with delight when he saw us bearing down on him. "I wondered if you would make it." As always, he cut a handsome figure with his butterscotch-blond hair, soft gray eyes, and his easy smile. He led us toward a table a dozen feet away, scattered with empty glasses. Raising his hand, he caught the attention of a passing waiter and ordered a round of our preferred libations.

We settled in the chairs with the walls covered in tissue paper at our backs, and the men each pulled out a cigarette. They lit them and leaned back in their chairs, for all the world as if we were about to discuss the latest film playing at the cinema or plans for a jaunt to the countryside rather than investigating treason.

"Evidently, we received your message," Sidney drawled.

"Yes." Max sighed, exhaling a stream of smoke. "I wish it was to report better news."

My shoulders must have visibly slumped, for Max cast me a chagrinned smile.

"I've scoured the last of my father's papers, and I simply can't find any information linking him to Ardmore or to the

incident with the *Zebrina*." He arched his eyebrows significantly. "And note I say *any*. Not one notation to suggest they
even knew each other."

"But we know they did," I countered. "That they *must*
have had dealings in Parliament and over the war. And we've
already confirmed your father and Lord Rockham, and almost certainly Lord Ardmore were involved with that hack-
neyed plot to smuggle opium to the rebels in Ireland on the
Zebrina."

"Which means *someone* did a thorough job of scrubbing
all mention of Ardmore and any questionable dealings they
were involved in together from the late earl's records." Sidney's expression was forbidding. "Better to remove it all than
risk leaving something incriminating behind."

The fact that the discovery of such a scrupulous removal
would not only confirm our suspicions but also frustrate us
by the lack of tangible proof would merely be a boon to Lord
Ardmore. He loved nothing more than to toy with people.

"Then you haven't found any explanation for your father's
last letter?" I asked, knowing it weighed on Max. The late
earl's missive, sent a year earlier while the war still raged, had
been oddly vague, stating that he wished to discuss something
important with him on his next leave home from the front.
That he was going to do everything in his power to make that
happen sooner rather than later. His failure to make any mention of it in the meticulous notes he had kept about everything
had forced Max to leap to a troubling conclusion.

"None. I still haven't the slightest confirmation what he
wanted to tell me. Or whether his sudden death before he
could speak to me is somehow related."

We could speculate all we wanted about the possibility his
father wished to confide in him about his ridiculous smuggling scheme, and how horribly wrong it had gone—resulting
in the crew of the *Zebrina*, and their illegal cargo, going missing. Or that he'd discovered Ardmore was involved in even

more traitorous activities. But we needed proof. Just as we needed proof that Ardmore was behind the deaths of Lord Rockham, three others, and possibly the late Lord Ryde, all in an effort to cover up the events on the *Zebrina*.

Max took one last drag on his fag before savagely stubbing it out in one of the dishes littering the table. "For all I know, he could have simply wanted to wish me a happy birthday."

I knew he didn't believe that any more than I did, but given the fact his father had died almost exactly a year ago, it did draw my attention to something else. "When is your birthday?"

He cast an uncertain look at me. "Friday."

I laughed. "Mine was yesterday."

He sat taller. "It was?"

"And as it just so happens, it wasn't the most auspicious of celebrations, despite Sidney's stellar efforts," I replied, reaching for his hand with the arm wrapped in his lovely gift.

His mouth quirked upward at the corner. "I can't be held responsible for the dead bodies which seem to appear in your wake."

Max's eyes widened.

"He's teasing," I said, brushing the matter aside. I had no intention of discussing Mr. Green and his untimely demise. "We planned to hold a little impromptu birthday gathering tomorrow at the Savoy, but why don't we make it a joint party. You invite whatever friends you wish and I'll invite mine, and we'll make an evening of it."

"You don't mind?" His gaze darted from me to Sidney, who didn't appear to be the least ruffled by this suggestion.

"No, it'll be fun," I said. "You'll see."

"Well, all right, then." He smiled. "My sister is in town, and she has been pestering me to do something special to celebrate."

"Then this is perfect."

But later, after we exited the club before the playing of

the national anthem that ended every evening, and hurried through a phalanx of photographers hoping to snap a few pictures of the young and wealthy out and about in their glad rags, I asked Sidney how he actually felt about my idea. "I hope I didn't overstep," I told him in a low voice, snuggling close lest the taxi driver overhear us. After all, it wasn't so long ago that the three of us couldn't be in the same room together without feeling the strain of what had occurred, or almost occurred, on Umbersea Island.

"I admit, I was surprised at first. But no, I don't mind." The gleam of the passing streetlamps reflected off the windows, casting his profile in highlight and then shadow as he seemed to choose his next words carefully. "I've accepted that I bear a large part of the responsibility for the fact that any attraction developed between you two. Had you not believed I was dead, you never would have even contemplated it." He pulled my fur-trimmed coat tighter around me against the chill of the night and gazed into my eyes. "But I trust Ryde. And more importantly, I trust you. Whatever was, is no more."

I wouldn't have gone so far as to say that. Attraction didn't simply flicker on and off because you wished it to. But his point was still valid. Neither Max nor I would act upon it. Nor did I wish to. Not with Sidney back in my arms.

"Besides, I like Ryde. I always have." His features twitched in amusement. "Even when I was cursing his orders to shore up a trench wall or lead a raiding party over the top in the pouring rain." His gaze dipped to the diamond tear drop earring dangling from my left ear. "He's an honorable fellow. I'm glad we have him on our side."

"Me too," I replied softly. In more ways than one. For I'd already recognized that I couldn't help Sidney heal from the horrors of the war, or release the guilt he carried like a yoke. Not alone. Max and Sidney understood each other better than I ever could, and I'd hoped their friendship would be beneficial to them both in that regard.

"What did he have to say when Crispin pulled me out on the dance floor?" I asked. Crispin Ballantyne was one of Sidney's oldest friends, and also one of the most gregarious men I knew. Some weeks ago, I'd asked him to keep his ears to the ground and let me know if he heard anything of interest about our current two favorite subjects—Lord Ardmore and the *Zebrina*. Unfortunately, he had nothing to tell me about either.

But he had heard whispers that Lady Rockham had been moved to a more private and secure location since her incarceration for the murder of her husband. I still felt certain that Lord Ardmore had been the catalyst behind the decision made by my former friend, Ada, Lady Rockham, to shoot her husband. That he held something over her, something worth killing to keep. Since her arrest, I had tried multiple times to visit her, and been repeatedly turned away. I felt that if only I could convince her to confide in me, if only she would tell me what she knew, we might be able to gain some traction in our pursuit of proof against Ardmore. But thus far she'd proven unwilling.

I met this news of her transfer with skepticism. Although it was true she'd received intense interest from the press—attention she'd eaten up—and even death threats, which she'd played up to with all the fervor of her theatrical personality, Holloway Prison seemed secure enough to me. It seemed more likely to me that Ardmore had pulled strings and seen her moved to prevent her from speaking to me or anyone else about what she knew.

"Only that Ryde's fairly certain someone broke into his town house three nights ago."

I sat upright in alarm. "What happened?"

Sidney glanced at the driver, who was now watching us in the mirror, and pulled me back against the seat beside him. He lowered his mouth to speak in my ear. "A window in

Ryde's study was left open, one that his butler and a footman both swear was locked. Apparently, he'd cautioned them
about the potential for intruders."

"Was anything taken?" I murmured.

He shook his head.

I felt a tremor of unease run down my spine. "Then this
was Ardmore's way of telling us he can get to us—any of
us—at any time."

His eyes flashed. "He can bloody well try," he growled,
and I suddenly realized how infuriated he was by this revelation.

I lifted my hand to touch my thumb to the cleft in his chin,
drawing his attention back to me. "I'm not concerned for
us," I assured him. "I know you would protect me." My voice
hardened. "And I'm far from a helpless damsel. But what of
Daphne or Etta? Or even George? He spent his war breaking codes, not fighting in the trenches. I'm not sure he even
knows how to throw a punch."

"He survived Eton. He knows," Sidney assured me, revealing more than I wanted to know about the education elite
boys received before university. "But I take your point. Anyone who Ardmore might think is assisting us, anyone connected to us, might be at risk."

My own anger ignited that he should attempt to intimidate
us in such a way. "If the proof we're seeking isn't among
Max's father's papers, then we'll have to find it another way."
I turned to gaze out at the elegant Georgian façades of Mayfair, wondering how many of those buildings were still kept
in good repair, and how many—like Littlemote House—were
rotting from within. "We need to know every potential secret
he might be hiding. And the only way we can do that is to
discover everything we can about him."

Thus far we'd been approaching the problem from the
present, working backward to find the proof of Ardmore's

perfidy. But perhaps if we approached it from a different angle, if we looked to the past, our answer would present itself. Or at least provide us a clue.

"Sun Tzu does say one should 'know thy enemy,'" Sidney ruminated.

I turned to him in surprise. "I don't know about that." Or who Sun Tzu was. "But I do know the perfect person to apply to for such a dossier. Particularly as I'm certain much of it already exists."

The guarded look in his eyes told me he knew I was referring to my contact at the Secret Service. Though officially I'd been demobilized, along with most of the female staff, earlier that year, unofficially I'd been given a new code name and a separate handler who reported my activities directly to C— the chief. "Yes, but will they share it with you?" he asked, acknowledging the difficulty I faced as a covert agent among covert agents.

"I suppose we'll find out."

Though we'd given them less than twenty-four hours' notice of our plans, the Savoy ensured we had everything to our liking for our impromptu soirée that evening. A set of tables was arranged for us near the columns to the right of the entrance, so that we could come and go as we wished to the Thames Foyer, where a floor was laid out for dancing. White roses spilled over the tables, and champagne was already chilling in buckets. The chef had even been convinced to serve us flaming bombe Néro for dessert, at my special request.

For all the annoyances of being hounded by photographers and reporters, and instantly recognizable to much of the London population, there were many advantages to our status as celebrities. Though, I suspected Sidney and Max's status and wealth would have also done the trick.

At the risk of angering some of my wide array of acquaintances, I'd elected to invite only my closest of friends living
in London, and Max, it seemed, had done the same. All told,
there were only fourteen of us, but a merry lot we were. I
laughed more over dinner than I had in months, and I knew I
looked smashing in my new emerald-green drop waist gown,
which Sidney's gift perfectly complemented.

In fact, all the ladies appeared lovely in their silks and
beads, strands of pearls and gem-encrusted corsages, and
headbands sparkling in the light of the chandeliers hanging
from the soaring white paneled ceiling. Max's sister, Livia,
made a particular impression on me. Although we'd yet to
meet, I'd heard Max speak of her and her two children. Her
husband had served with the expeditionary force and had
been killed during the initial disastrous retreat in the autumn
of 1914, leaving her a young and wealthy widow.

In most ways she was a feminine foil for Max, possess-
ing the same soft gray eyes and sharp nose, albeit with more
delicate features. Her pale brown hair was also several shades
darker than her brother's butterscotch blond, which she
hadn't yet dared, or perhaps didn't wish, to bob. However,
beneath her gentle, muted coloring lay a vibrant personality.
The epitome of artless charm, she was never at a loss for a
conversational gambit, and teased her younger brother with
such warmth and ease that it was obvious the pair were close.
It also made me wonder about their mother, for the late Earl
of Ryde had seemed like a rather cold and calculating man.

"Max tells me that you and your delightful husband visited Nettlestone briefly some weeks past," Livia remarked as
we sat sipping champagne, referring to her brother's estate on
the Isle of Wight. "I wish I'd known. I would have motored
over from Newport."

Much as I was enjoying her company now, I was glad she
hadn't. Her presence would have only made an already awk-

ward encounter even more so, as we'd accused their deceased father of the foolish plot of attempting to smuggle drugs to the Irish rebels in an effort to foil their plans for revolution.

"It was a rather spur-of-the-moment decision," I replied with a shrug.

"Well, you must return sometime so we can properly entertain you," she urged with a smile before turning to watch her brother as he finished descending the red carpeted staircase with Daphne on his arm. Both seemed exhilarated from their dance in the foyer above. The sounds of the orchestra playing a lively waltz floated down from above, a soft accompaniment to the clink of crystal and silver, and the rumble of voices as diners enjoyed their meals.

Livia's head tilted to the side as her expression took on a more somber cast. "Max hasn't invited many guests to Nettlestone. Not since the war. I worry about him in that big, rambling manor all alone." She turned to look into my eyes, searching for something I was not willing to give. "I'm glad he's become friends with you and Mr. Kent, however that came about."

I gestured with my glass toward where the two men now conversed as they approached us, Daphne having taken up the offer to dance from Max's friend. "Max was Sidney's commanding officer for a time."

Her lips curled into a smile. "Which still doesn't answer my unspoken query," she murmured, clearly unwilling to be placated with half-truths. "But have no fear, I have no intention of pressing the matter. I recognize well enough when there are things that are best left unsaid. You forget, my father was the holder of a great deal of secrets. Many of which I doubt he needed to hold so close to the vest," she added dryly. She gasped suddenly, holding up her hand. "Which reminds me . . ."

I watched as she rummaged around in her handbag before removing a faded white envelope from within. Then she turned and held it out to her brother, who accepted it with a grin.

"From Lucy?" he asked, naming his young niece.

"No, Father."

Max halted in opening it, glancing up at her in shock.

She nodded. "He gave it to me a few weeks before he passed with strict instructions not to deliver it to you until your twenty-ninth birthday. I know it's absurd," she continued in response to her brother's continued astonishment. "But you know how he was. He never explained anything to us he didn't have to. Anyway, I realize your birthday isn't until Friday, but I figured the date is close enough."

Max stared down at the envelope almost as if it were a cobra about to strike.

Livia frowned, clearly not understanding his reaction. Not like Sidney and I did. We exchanged a look of strange foreboding, but also anticipation.

She stepped forward to touch his arm. "I'm sorry, dearest. Did I do wrong?" She lowered her voice. "Should I have given it to you later?"

Max inhaled a swift breath, seeming to recall himself. "No, Liv, it's fine you gave it to me now. I'm just . . . a little surprised, that's all."

None of us commented on what an understatement this was. Not when we were so curious to discover what was inside that envelope.

Max broke the seal and pulled out the paper within before slowly unfolding it. His brow furrowed as he perused the contents and then separated the first sheet from the second to do the same. When he lifted his gaze, it was to seek out mine. "It's written in some sort of code," he declared in a sort of baffled horror.

CHAPTER 10

I stepped forward hesitantly to peer over Max's shoulder. He was right. It was definitely a code, written in neat blocks of jumbled letters. Which meant only one thing. The late earl hadn't wanted just anyone to read it. Not if he'd given it to his daughter before he died with such strict instructions for its delivery. Not if he was going to such lengths to mask its content.

"Code?" Livia stated in confusion. "Why ever would Father do such a thing?"

Whatever the contents were, they must be important. My heart quickened at the thought that this could be the information we'd been looking for.

My gaze immediately sought out George, who had been listening to this exchange with interest from the neighboring table. As one of the foremost cryptographers working in 40 OB for Naval Intelligence during the war, George would crack the code far quicker than I could. There wasn't a code yet that had defeated him, no matter how canny.

He dipped his head once. "Whatever you need." But when he began to rise to his feet, I urged him to remain seated with a gesture of my hand.

I turned to Max and held out my hand, the look in my eyes encouraging him to trust me. Although he was unaware of the actual role George had undertaken for Naval Intelligence, he did know that I had worked for the foreign division of the Secret Service. I'd been forced to disclose as much during the course of our investigation on Umbersea Island some months past, and he and my husband were still the only people outside of fellow Military Intelligence personnel who knew the true nature of my war work.

Max vacillated for but a moment, the depths of his eyes reflecting uncertainty and even fear, as if he had not yet fully confronted what it might mean if our suspicions proved true. But then his jaw firmed and he passed me the document with a sure hand. I felt the weight of his faith in me settle over my shoulders.

I swiveled to return to the table where my handbag lay, surreptitiously sliding the letter into the front of George's coat as I passed his chair. "Put this in your inner pocket," I instructed him, and then placed the empty envelope inside my beaded reticule, hoping that anyone watching us would think I'd maintained possession of the letter.

Meanwhile, Sidney had beckoned Crispin forward, clasping a hand on his shoulder and speaking into his ear. Like most artillery officers, Crispin had suffered some hearing damage from the repetitive percussive firing of the massive guns used to hurl shells at the enemy miles away. "I need you to escort Bentnick to our flat and stay with him there until we return. Can you do that for me?" The look the two shared was deathly earnest. "I'll make sure Miss Wrexham returns home safely," he assured him, referring to Crispin's fiancée seated a few feet away.

"Aye," he replied. "Just let me explain the situation to Phoebe."

There was no need to caution him about discretion. He would tell her as much of the truth as he could and no more.

One look at George's pale face told me he'd overheard their

exchange. We weren't taking any chances. Not when some-one had broken into Max's town house just a few days ear-lier. Making a show of trying to make it look natural that I was tucking my handbag securely under my arm, I returned to Sidney's side.

Having observed all of this with wide eyes, Livia now stepped closer to her brother. "Max, what is going on?" she hissed. "Why did you give Father's letter to Mr. Bentnick? Why are you all acting like there are spies all around us?" Her eyes blazed with fury. "And don't even think about swinging the lead."

It seemed so incongruous to hear soldiers' slang emerge from her lips that I felt the sudden urge to grin.

It appeared Max felt the same way, for the somber lines of his face softened. "Come on, Liv. I'll take you back to the town house and explain on the way."

She appeared at first as if she would argue, but then agreed. Our parting was somewhat stilted, and while I was sorry to have upset her, especially after such a pleasant evening, I really couldn't fault her for her sudden reserve.

Once Max and Livia and then George and Crispin were sped on their way, Sidney and I circulated among our remain-ing guests, attempting to extricate ourselves without reveal-ing more than necessary. Fortunately, they all seemed to be having a splendid time, and though they protested our depar-ture, I knew they didn't really mind it. Rather than leave with us, Phoebe Wrexham even elected to remain with a group of her friends also dining and dancing at the Savoy.

Etta and her beau, Goldy, decided to depart when we did, for her first set at Grafton Galleries that evening was sched-uled to begin soon anyway. She looped her arm through Sid-ney's as they climbed the stairs toward the foyer, her mink stole dipping low to reveal the smooth mocha skin of her back. Goldy grinned and offered me his left arm before reaching over to secure it with his gloved right hand. Having suffered burns to the right side of his torso during an aeroplane crash, he never removed it in public.

Before he could launch into a discussion of his latest efforts on behalf of his family's aviation company and enthusiasm for the development of passenger air service, I seized the opportunity to ask him something I'd wanted to since Saturday. "Goldy, are you familiar with RAF Froxfield?"

"Sure." He narrowed his eyes in contemplation. "It's on the border of Berkshire and Wiltshire, isn't it? They flew 'Ninak' light bombers out of there during the war." He turned his head to regard me. "Why?"

"Do you know if they had more crashes than average?"

"You mean, in and around the airfield?"

I nodded.

He frowned. "Well, I believe they conducted quite a bit of training there, and crashes sort of come with the territory. Minor ones, that is. But . . . no, I can't recall ever hearing anything particular about the place."

I thanked him and was prepared to drop the matter, especially as we were now crossing the foyer, which echoed with the music of the orchestra, but then another thought seemed to occur to him.

"Wait! Is that the airfield where there are rumors it was built over some ancient barrow or tomb?"

"Yes. What do you know about it?"

He shook his head, but his chuckle of amusement belied his answer. "Not much. But I remember one of my buddies from the Ninety-ninth telling me how some of the locals had worked themselves up into a lather. Some woman claiming she was a druid priestess even tried to gain access to the site so that she could lay the spirits to rest, or so she claimed."

Before I could respond, Etta turned to buss my cheek, and soon we were saying our goodbyes and waving them into the first taxi so that Etta wouldn't be late. I fluffed my collar up against the chill and turned to speak to Sidney, when I felt a sudden sharp tug on my arm.

"Hey!" I shouted as a man in a dark overcoat and hat dashed down the pavement with my handbag.

Sidney turned in alarm, and then realizing what had happened, prepared to set off in pursuit. But I stayed him with my hand.

"Don't bother. He's long gone by now." At this hour, the street would be filled with people bustling to and from their evening entertainments. "Besides, he's going to be disappointed when he discovers the only thing inside is an empty envelope." I sighed, glancing in the direction he'd disappeared. "Though I *was* rather fond of that handbag."

"What about the rest of the contents?"

I shrugged a shoulder. "A lip salve and some face powder can be replaced."

One of the Savoy's doormen stepped forward to apologize about the thief loitering on their pavement, and Sidney assured him we bore them no ill will. It would be all but impossible to spot such a crook when he had been dining in their restaurant, posing as a regular patron. For how else had he known about the envelope stuffed in my handbag? It certainly wasn't a coincidence I'd been targeted.

We climbed into our taxi and set off down the Strand. I wrinkled my nose in aggravation. "I'm more miffed I didn't notice the fellow following us. I allowed myself to be distracted."

"Did you? Or were you actually hoping Ardmore's man would try something?" Sidney ruminated wryly, clearly anticipating the latter.

"Well, I admit the thought did cross my mind." I smoothed my skirt over my lap. "What better way to discover if Ardmore is having us surveilled, and how extensively?"

"Don't you mean, what better way to tweak his nose?"

I shot him a look from under my lashes. "Darling, if he's in any way annoyed by this, it won't be at me." I sat back, crossing my legs at the ankles. "Sadly, I get the impression he enjoys the challenge I present. He's far more likely to be pleased." I frowned at the blur of lights passing outside the cab window. "And determined to heighten the stakes."

Sidney's hand clasped mine. "This isn't a game, Verity," he grumbled into my ear.

"Do you think I don't know that?" I snapped. "But Ardmore seems determined to make it so. It's not as if I can refuse to play. Not with the death toll already this high, and the ending stakes, I fear, even higher."

He scrutinized my face, seeming to try to study every square inch of it as shadows flitted in the depths of his eyes. "Well, then, perhaps Ryde's letter will be our ace."

"Maybe," I murmured, unable to shake the uneasiness that had settled over me. "But somehow I fear we're not playing at something as simple as pontoon or twenty-one. I don't know if it's possible to best him by simply holding the better hand."

Sidney's neck straightened, seeming to be much struck by this metaphor. "You think he's playing something more like brag."

I nodded slowly. "I'm not sure it's possible to best him without drawing him out into the open. If we charge at him with all the information we possess, then he'll fold and wait for a better hand. Unless there is irrefutable proof somewhere, something he cannot twist or deny . . ." I rubbed my brow wearily. "And the longer I contemplate all this, the less convinced I am that such a thing exists. Then I don't know that there is a way to beat him without bluffing him first."

Sidney lifted his hand to cradle my chin between thumb and forefinger, dragging my gaze back to his. "Then perhaps all those games of brag I played while at ease behind the front, waiting to be called up the line again, weren't for naught." The corners of his lips twitched upward at the feebleness of his joke. Then his voice turned more serious. "We'll get him, Verity. You'll see. You don't have to bluff him alone."

I wrapped my fingers around the skin of his strong wrist where it emerged from his crisp white shirt cuff, staring up at him in gratitude. "Then let's hope my gambit with the envelope back there was worth it, and whatever Max's father decided to write in code is as important as he thought it was."

When we returned to our flat, I was relieved to discover George and Crispin had arrived some thirty minutes earlier without incident. I peered into the study to find George with his shirt sleeves rolled up to the elbows and his dark head covered in tight curls bent over the desk as he worked out the cipher. I knew better than to interrupt him, and from the looks of the pot of tea at his elbow, it appeared Sidney's valet, Nimble, was already seeing to his needs. So I slipped away quietly.

Upon learning it would likely be several hours before we learned anything, Crispin elected to return to the Savoy to rejoin his fiancée. I shook my head fondly at his departing figure. For all his capabilities and strengths, patience was not one of them.

Max joined us soon after, his face drawn and worried. I urged him into the drawing room and asked Nimble to prepare us our own pot of tea. Though he'd only been part of our household for a few weeks, I was already glad to have him. He'd served as my husband's batman during the war, and contrary to his sobriquet, was far from nimble. Much of the time I knew where he was in the flat at all times, for I could hear his clumping footsteps, though I knew he tried to walk softly.

At first, this attribute drove our widowed housekeeper, Mrs. Sadie Yarrow, to distraction, but quickly she came to appreciate it. As a woman of somewhat of a nervous disposition, who hated to be snuck up on, she needn't worry about that ever happening with Nimble. Once she looked beyond his large size and the scars blistering the left side of his face near his hairline and his partially missing left ear, and was able to appreciate his reserve and kindness, they'd seemed to settle into a mutual regard for each other. A few days earlier I'd even overheard Mrs. Yarrow teasing Nimble for letting his hair grow too long, and offering to cut it for him.

But Mrs. Yarrow left at the end of each day, returning to her own residence, where I'd long suspected she cared for someone else. From the beginning of her service, I'd promised her I would not pry. I valued my own secrets too highly to ever interfere in someone else's without need. Though I admitted to an intense curiosity about whom she returned to each night, whether it was someone elderly, an invalided soldier, or perhaps even a child.

Once Nimble had returned with the tea, I prepared a cup for Max before pouring my own. I normally preferred something a bit stronger at this hour, but after all the champagne I'd drunk at the Savoy, I decided it would be better to keep some semblance of my wits about me for whatever that coded letter contained.

"I take it your discussion with Livia did not go well," I said as I sank down onto the opposite end of the emeraldine sofa.

Max lifted his gaze from the spot he'd been staring at in our Aubusson rug for several minutes. "No, she wasn't pleased." He almost seemed surprised to find the cup of tea in his hands, but then he lifted it to take a drink.

My mother believed that tea was the remedy to all ailments, and while I didn't entirely agree with her, I recognized how soothing a familiar ritual or taste could be to the senses. I'd employed the trick often enough during my time in the occupied territories when my nerves were strung too tight and my fear threatened to overwhelm me. Though then I often had to settle for the poor substitutes the Belgians and French living under occupation had to endure, things like roasted oat chaff and pea shells.

"I imagine it was a shock," I coaxed gently, for he was visibly troubled, and I didn't think it was purely his apprehension over the contents of his father's letter.

He nodded. "She didn't like hearing about the part our father played in the smuggling. Or the suggestion that he might have been poisoned." He huffed a humorless laugh. "Rang a reverberating peal over my head at the mere suggestion."

I offered him a commiserating smile, able to empathize with both of them. After all, not so many weeks earlier I'd dreaded telling Max that we suspected his father might have been murdered, dreaded his reaction. None of it was easy to hear.

"But then . . . once she'd calmed down . . ." He seemed to struggle with his words. "She . . . she said Father must have known."

Sidney turned from where he stood, gazing through the tall Georgian windows down at the square below, smoking one of his specially blended Turkish cigarettes. His gaze met mine as Max continued to speak.

"She said he'd acted oddly during the weeks preceding his death. That after he died she'd ascribed it to his declining health. His valet had said he'd been complaining of chest pains, and so she'd chosen to believe it was just another symptom."

"How was he acting oddly?" I said as he took another fortifying sip of tea.

"She said he seemed anxious, unsettled. That he started refusing invitations to dinners and events, something our father had always thrived on. He even summoned her to London all the way from the Isle of Wight, partly she now believes to give her the letter she gave me tonight. That he told her no less than three times not to reveal to anyone that he'd given it to her. That it was to be a surprise for my twenty-ninth birthday and he wanted me to have it even if he wasn't around to give it to me. That he didn't want it spoiled."

"That didn't seem strange to her earlier?" Sidney questioned, crossing the room to join us.

He shrugged one shoulder. "We were used to following Father's directives, no matter how inane they seemed. Livia in particular. He wouldn't brook disobedience." His mouth twisted sourly. "He often overlooked and discounted her in favor of me, his heir."

Something that wasn't uncommon among the aristocracy. After all, what good were daughters but to form dynastic alliances and breed the next generation?

"Your sister seems like a very intelligent, level-headed person," I remarked, considering everything Max had told us. "You trust her impressions?"

"I do," he affirmed.

"Then I find it rather telling. After all, my impression of the late Earl of Ryde was as a confident, commanding personality. He was not intimidated easily, or pushed around."

Max nodded in confirmation.

"And yet in his last weeks she describes him as anxious and unsettled. That he seemed to closet himself away." I glanced at Sidney to see if he was following. "Perhaps hoping to restrict access to his person."

"To prevent someone from harming or killing him," Sidney added, finishing my thought.

We all knew that "someone" was Ardmore, but since he preferred to utilize others to perform his dirty work, it was difficult to tell who had actually posed a threat.

"So you think he *did* know?" Max asked.

"It seems like he at least suspected it. Why else write that letter in code and give it to your sister with such strict instructions," I pointed out.

His features seemed to harden as he brooded over this.

Sidney drummed his fingers against the arm of the chintz

bergère chair across from us. "Have you spoken with your father's valet?"

Max shook his head. "Not since he was released from my employ a few weeks after Father's death."

"Perhaps you should," Sidney prompted. "He might know more than he realizes."

That is, if he's still alive, I thought cynically. Ardmore had a ruthless proficiency at tidying up loose ends.

Max inhaled a tight breath. "You're right. I should track him down."

The door to the drawing room opened, and we all swiveled eagerly in our seats to discover if it was George come to tell us he'd cracked the code. Unfortunately, it was only Nimble asking if we needed another pot of tea or the ice in the bucket on the drinks tray on the sideboard refreshed. Once I declined and thanked him, we settled in to wait.

The hours ticked slowly by, each one stretching our already taut nerves further. At two o'clock, I considered offering George the use of our guest bedchamber, but I knew him. He would want the task completed. And if he couldn't keep his eyes open to do so, he would come tell me so himself.

So I made myself comfortable in the corner of the sofa, dozing in and out while Sidney and Max smoked and talked near the window they'd cracked open. As the night wore on, the sounds of the traffic below began to thin until at times the shush of the wind and the ticking of the clock were all that accompanied the low rumble of their voices. That they were able to find so much to discuss did not surprise me, but the amount of cigarettes Max burned through did. In the past, Max had seemed an infrequent smoker at best. Sidney was the one some months past I'd chided for smoking too much, and I'd noticed he'd taken my request to heart, halving his previous intake. However, in the space of several hours, Max had puffed through one fag after another, even if otherwise he seemed perfectly calm.

When George finally appeared in the doorway to the drawing room, it seemed to take all of us a moment to register that
fact. I blinked wide my tired eyes and sat upright as Max hurried across the chamber toward him.

"Did you decode it?" he asked George, his eyes eagerly
darting back and forth from his face to the papers in his hand.

George nodded, passing him what I presumed to be the
decrypted text. The look on his face when he turned to look
at me was resigned and grim, giving the caramel skin he'd
inherited from his Indian grandmother a slightly sallow cast.
My muscles tightened with anticipation and dread. Whatever
that letter said, it wasn't meaningless.

CHAPTER 11

George dropped into the chair nearest the door, rubbing his forehead with thumb and forefinger, while Sidney sank down beside me on the sofa. I tried not to watch Max's face as he read, but it was impossible. Not that his expression gave much away. His frantic pacing back and forth, on the other hand, proved distracting.

When he finished, he halted midstride. His shoulders slumped and he stared ahead of him blankly, struggling to either comprehend or accept the letter's contents.

"What does it say?" I asked, unable to contain my concern or curiosity a moment longer.

He looked up at me and then Sidney for several moments with the same stunned expression before crossing the room to hand me the decrypted text. My husband leaned close, wrapping his arm around my lower back as he read over my shoulder.

Maximus,

If you're reading this and you don't know what it's about, then the worst has already happened. My papers have been cleared out and I did not survive long enough to speak to you about it myself. Your sister knows nothing of what I'm about to say, and I prefer it should remain that way. I entrusted this letter to her because it was the only way I could see of ensuring it would reach you in due time. All other avenues were vulnerable, and so I took this precaution.

Though it pains me to admit, I have done something terrible and, worst of all, foolish. I pride myself on my wisdom, on my keen insight, but in this I have been deceived. I dare not put the specifics down on paper, even in code, lest I incriminate myself and taint our venerated title needlessly, or leave you open to attack. Speak to the men on Wight who I relied upon during the war. You know of who I speak. They will explain the matter to you, at least so far as they know it.

What they do not know is the other gentlemen involved in the enterprise. Lord Rockham is an imbecile. It's no use speaking to him for he was duped more thoroughly than I was, and even believed wholeheartedly in the success of our aims. But Lord Ardmore is another matter, and the person from whom you have the most to fear. If I am dead, it is by his hand. He is a Cassius, and no friend to our rule of law.

I am aware that these sound like the ramblings of a doddering old man, but I dare not speak straightforwardly for fear this should fall into his hands. I tried to draw him out, and in this I was partially successful, but he has grown suspicious of me, and I know it is only a matter of time before he acts. I fear I do not have time to complete what I have started, so I have hid what evidence I possess.

I am sorry to pass this burden to you, but I do not know who else I can trust. Hopefully with the passage of time, any suspicions he may have about what you know will have faded. You know of my keenest obsession, and I pray you were listening when I lectured about them and not just indulging the whims of your old man. Think back to your tenth birthday. Return to the place I took you. Retrace our steps.

But above all else, do not reveal this to Ardmore. Do not

even let him know you have it. Or else I fear he will stop at
nothing to get it.

I looked up to find Max seated on the sofa across from
us, his head sunken over his shoulders as he leaned forward,
bracing his elbows on his knees.

"Well," I murmured, uncertain what to say into the tense
silence that had fallen. "I suppose this confirms some of our
suspicions." In a vague, dithering way. Almost maddeningly
so. "Do you remember where your father took you on your
tenth birthday?"

Max's gaze shifted forward slightly to stare at my feet as he
nodded. "His obsession was . . ." He broke off to eye George.

"You can trust him," I told him with confidence. "Not just
with the code. With everything."

Max seemed to weigh and assess George. Normally I
would have expected George to fidget through such an examination, but fatigue seemed to have blunted his social ti-
midity. The look on his face said that he didn't give a damn
whether Max found him trustworthy or not.

"His obsession was with Roman antiquities," Max continued, pushing himself upright with a visible effort, as if he'd
shouldered a heavy load. "Of which there are a number of
sites on the Isle of Wight. But on my tenth birthday he took
me to the remains of a villa found at Brading."

"Then we must go there," I declared.

"It appears so."

None of the men seemed very keen on the prospect. "I recognize it's the middle of the night, and I fully empathize with
the shock this must be to Max, but why are you all looking so
glum? Not five hours ago, we had no way of moving forward
in our investigation of Ardmore, and this has just fallen into
our laps."

"Yes, and Ardmore knows it," Sidney snapped. "Not the

exact contents perhaps, but he can deduce them. Especially after that ploy you made with the envelope."

I scowled. "That *ploy* with the envelope is all that kept Ardmore's man from following George and attempting to steal the letter from him rather than me."

George stiffened in his seat, not having heard me explain to Max how my handbag had been snatched outside the Savoy.

Sidney's eyes flashed. "The point is Ardmore knows we have something now. And he's going to be tracking us, trying to get it back."

"He was already surveilling us. The fact that one of his men was at the Savoy watching us proves that. So this changes almost nothing. Max's father never anticipated our involvement." I gestured between me and Sidney. "Or that, together with his son, we'd already figured out much of what he was alluding to."

"Just as he didn't anticipate Rockham being *dead*. His murder manipulated by Ardmore, as well."

"Kent, Verity, please," Max interjected. "Can we just pause for a moment?" His gray eyes pleaded with us as he scraped a hand back through his dark blond hair. "My father has all but confirmed that he was probably murdered. I know we suspected it. That we've been hypothesizing about it for weeks. But . . . to hear him say he anticipated it . . ." He broke off, turning to stare into the fire crackling in the hearth. "It's a lot to absorb."

My cheeks stung, chastened for my callousness. "I'm sorry, Max," I said softly.

He waved my apology aside, but did not turn away from the flames.

I sank back into the sofa, prepared to hold my tongue until he was ready. Sidney draped his arm around my shoulders, and while I turned to meet his glower with one of my own, I was content to let him leave his arm there.

I scrutinized the decryption of the late earl's letter still clutched in my hand, wondering at his choice of words. He spoke of being fooled, and derided Rockham as an imbecile. It seemed he would have us believe he didn't know what was actually going on, or that he didn't believe in the scheme, only that he was supporting it to draw Ardmore out, but was this true? Had he really held altruistic motives, or was he merely trying to save face in the aftermath? The letter was written to his son, after all.

I studied Max's furrowed brow and the tight line of his mouth, curious whether he also wrestled with this question. I supposed time would tell.

"Why did he have to be so bloody vague?" he grumbled, revealing both his grief and irritation over the contents of the letter. He gestured toward the paper in my lap. "Why this runaround? Why not just tell us what he knows, what he's hidden?"

"He was obviously panicked," I replied. "If he thought Ardmore might have him killed at any moment, he couldn't have been in a calm frame of mind."

"Yes, but this was no hastily dashed-off missive. He translated the bloody thing into code, for heaven's sake."

I had to concede he was right. It did appear to be a stark contradiction.

"Was your father normally this . . ." Sidney seemed to fumble for the right word, one that wouldn't be insulting.

Max scoffed. "Melodramatic? Theatrical?"

"You said it, not me."

He exhaled a heavy sigh in acknowledgment, raking his hand back through his hair again. "Yes and no."

"What does that mean?" I asked, hoping for clarification.

"Yes, he could be somewhat of a showman, but not usually in such an overblown way."

"Do you think your father wrote it?" George piped up to say. "Was it his handwriting?"

Max appeared to contemplate the matter for the briefest of moments before nodding. "Yes, it's his handwriting. His way of wording things, as well. And he physically handed it to my sister. I don't see how it could have been written by anyone else but him."

I folded the decrypted text inside the original letter. "Then I suppose we won't be able to understand why he chose to be so secretive until we discover what he's hidden. He must have felt it was important. Otherwise, why go to such trouble? And why fear for his life?"

We all fell silent, ruminating on this somberly. I couldn't help but feel this was about a great deal more than smuggled opium. That whatever the late Earl of Ryde had uncovered was far more serious, and far more dangerous.

"Do you have somewhere you can hide this?" I asked Max, holding up the pages. "Somewhere you're certain it won't be stolen or destroyed. Or do you want me to keep it?"

His gaze dipped to the letter, eyeing it almost as he would a snake. "You hide it."

I nodded. "When do you want to leave for the Isle of Wight?"

Max named a time near midday.

"Then we'll meet you at the station." I half expected Sidney to object, but he said nothing.

"Do you wish me to come?" George's expression plainly communicated that he did not want to.

"Not if you can explain which code the earl used." I gambled that, if whatever Max's father had hidden was also encrypted, it would use either the same code or something similar.

George and I conferred, and then he and Max departed, agreeing to share a cab, lest someone under Ardmore's sway be waiting to ambush them. Sidney closed and locked the door as I retreated to our bedchamber. Once I was certain the drapes were drawn tight, I tipped my vanity bench over and began to pry loose one of the legs. I heard my husband enter the room and pause to watch over my shoulder as I rolled the letter and decryption into a tight tube and then slid it into the thin bored hole in the wood. Then I affixed the leg back in place, using the sole of my shoe to hammer it back into its slot.

After tipping the bench back over onto its legs, I glanced over my shoulder at him, curious what he was thinking. But contrary to the disapproval I'd expected to see, his eyes seemed to glint with approbation.

"Are the other legs similarly contrived?"

I shrugged, rising to my feet to sit on the bench. "Maybe." I decided there was no reason to tell him about my other hiding spots. Not if he wasn't going to reveal where he'd hidden my bracelet for five years.

His lips curled in a brief smile in the reflection of the mirror as I removed my jewelry, almost as if he knew exactly what I was thinking. He reached up to undo his bow tie and then sank down on the edge of the bed to remove his shoes. "You do realize that we are going to be followed to the Isle of Wight? Ardmore is never going to willingly let us out of his sight now."

"Yes." I slid one earring from my ear. "And so we are going to pay very close attention to everyone who boards the train and the ferry with us. Ardmore's men are good, but no one is invisible. Frankly, I'm tired of not knowing their faces. There will be but a few people traveling onto the island from the train, and the next time we see one of those faces, we'll recognize them."

Sidney paused in the middle of removing his cuff links, his gaze sharpening as he watched me in the mirror. "You are enjoying this."

I frowned.

"This game of cat and mouse. This test of your wits."

I pulled my jeweled headband from my hair, fluffing my flattened tendrils as I considered his words. "I don't *enjoy* it. Enjoy is too strong a word. But I suppose I do like the element of challenge. The chance to stretch myself beyond something as frivolous as learning the latest dance step." I swiveled in my seat to face him. "Don't you?"

Rather than answer, he crossed toward me, lifting his hands to cup my jaw between them. "Just don't forget, this match of wits is every bit as deadly as the war. If we're correct about everything, and thus far we have been, then Ardmore has arranged the murder of at least a dozen people. Perhaps more. If he didn't suffer any qualms about killing the late Earl of Ryde when he got too close to the truth, what makes you think he won't do the same to you?"

I clasped my hands over top of his. "I know. Believe me, darling. I suffer no delusions where Ardmore is concerned." Though, in truthfulness, I was more concerned with his striking out at those I loved than me. It seemed like just the sort of thing a man like him would do, recognizing that I feared an attack on those I cared for more than on myself.

Sidney drew me to my feet and wrapped his strong arms around me. I went willingly, pressing my face to his chest, where his heart beat a steady rhythm against my cheek. Inhaling deeply, I smelled the starch of his shirt, the warmth of his skin, and his spicy cologne.

"I know you are more than capable, Verity." He bent his head, pressing his lips to my temple. "But that doesn't stop me from worrying, or from wanting to protect you in every way I can." He trailed his fingers through my hair, pulling it back from my face. "Maybe I should have given you a pocket pistol for your birthday instead of a bracelet."

I smiled. "There's always our anniversary."

Sidney chuckled. "True. It is only thirteen days away, and I *have* been struggling to find the perfect gift."

I lifted my head to coo up at him. "Have our initials carved inside a heart on the palm grip and I'll be the envy of all the ladies in Mayfair."

"Be careful what you wish for," he teased. "I know an engraver who would swoon at such a romantic gesture. He'd probably add a few flowers and a cupid's arrow for good measure."

"As long as he's compensated fairly."

Sidney threw his head back and laughed. It was a gesture I saw so infrequently that I flushed with pleasure at being the one to cause it. I gasped as he swung me up into his arms.

"Who knew I married such a minx," he drawled in a deep voice before pressing his lips to mine and lowering me to the bed.

"Admit it. You love it," I murmured breathlessly as he hovered over me.

"Oh, I do." He pressed his open mouth to my neck, making me arch my back in delight. "Be as brazen as you like, dear wife. So long as it's with me."

And I took his words to heart.

I had just finished breakfast and was in the middle of issuing instructions to Sadie when the telephone rang. Though I'd only gotten a little over four hours of sleep, I was still energized and alert. After all, during my time behind enemy lines during the war I'd adapted to the habit of snatching rest whenever and wherever I could, and making do with what I had. It had been rare for me to manage a full night's sleep, and even rarer to slumber in a proper bed, let alone the plush, comfortable one in our bedchamber with my husband by my side to keep me warm.

Sadie rushed off to answer it while I continued sorting through the contents of my wardrobe, deciding what to pack. When I turned to find her hovering in the doorway, seeming hesitant to speak, I felt a pulse of apprehension as to who was on the other line and what news they might bear. Perhaps we should have insisted Max and George remain here last night.

"It's . . . your mother, ma'am."

My shoulders sank, my nerves melting into irritation, for if Sadie had been unsettled by my mother's voice, it meant only one thing. Sidney peered out at me from the adjoining washroom, where he was adjusting his tie, a sympathetic glint in his eyes.

"Will you pack the things on the bed for me?" I told Sadie, striding from the room and down the corridor to where the telephone sat on the bureau in the front hall. Staring at my reflection in the mirror that hung above it, I inhaled a calming breath before picking up the mouthpiece. "Good morning, Mother."

"Good heavens! What took you so long? Were you still abed at this hour?"

Given the fact it was only half past nine and much of society slept until noon or later, I found this comment to be annoying, but fortunately I could ignore it in favor of the truth. "Of course not, Mother. I've been awake for over an hour."

She harrumphed as if she didn't believe this.

"Did you need something? Because I'm—"

"Your aunt Ernestine telephoned," she interrupted in a stern voice. "She was very upset. She said you couldn't wait to be rid of her."

I gazed up at the ceiling, seeking patience. "That's not true, Mother. I stayed at Littlemote for over three days, and Sidney has promised to do what he can to convince the War Office to reimburse her for the damages as swiftly as possible."

"Yes, but she says you all but dismissed the matter of the thefts, as if hundreds of thousands of pounds mean nothing."

"Cousin Reg knows about the forgeries and thefts. I can't be held responsible for the fact that Aunt Ernestine doesn't want to face the truth about them."

My mother fell silent, sifting through the ramifications of that statement.

"If that's all, then . . ."

"But she says one of her servants was killed while you were there, and you departed as if the death was of little consequence. That she'd taken to her bed, her weak heart struggling to cope from the shock, and still you left her."

"The police were handling the matter," I bit out. "There was nothing for me to do. Unless you wished for us to interfere in such a sordid business?" My mother had already castigated me for my involvement in the few investigations the press had gotten wind of and reported in the papers, so I was calling her bluff, so to speak. The last thing she wanted was for me to be mixed up with another murder, though she granted my husband far more leeway.

"Verity Alice, what has come over you," she gasped. "Of course, I don't mean anything so ghoulish. But you could have sat by your aunt's side, guided her through such a tragedy. Honestly, sometimes I think you've abandoned all sense. You've certainly abandoned your sense of duty and propriety, sacrificing you family obligations in favor of . . . of carousing and drinking and . . . and who knows what other improprieties."

At this, my temper—which I'd already been struggling to maintain—exploded. "You haven't the slightest idea about my obligations and responsibilities! You haven't an inkling . . ." I broke off, grinding my teeth in frustration. For Mother knew nothing of the real nature of my war work—none of my family did—and even if she did, she wouldn't understand it. In her eyes, I'd been living it up in London, working a minor secretarial job at an import-export business delivering supplies to the troops, while my husband fought at the front.

"Such a frivolous waste," she continued as if I'd never spoken. "Ignoring all the sacrifice. What the men returning must think."

"Oh, they understand, Mother. Far better than you do." I turned so that I could see into the drawing room, and gazed longingly at the sideboard across the room, wishing for a drink, as I did during most of my conversations with my mother. "Come to London. Come see the men missing arms and legs, and sporting scars or tin masks. Come meet the veterans selling chewing gum on the street corners because they're no longer able to do the work they did before the war. It's not as if we could ever forget."

"And you think I can?! Every time I look at your brother Rob's photograph . . ." She hiccupped on a sob. "I remember. I remember it all."

I closed my eyes against her words.

"How you never came home. How you *still* haven't come home. How you practically refuse to say his name."

I couldn't, I wouldn't talk about this. Not with my mother. Not when she clearly didn't understand.

"What does Aunt Ernestine expect me to do?" I asked, forcing the words out past the tightness in my chest.

"Verity!" Mother gasped.

"Are her nerves recovered?"

"When I think what a sweet, sweet brother he was to you . . ."

The rest of her words were smothered and then my father spoke. He sounded weary. "Verity, I know your aunt can be a trifle high-strung and demanding, but will you please look in on her again. She's claiming her maid's sister has been detained for the crime, and the entire staff is at loose ends."

So they'd arrested Mrs. Green. That must mean they had enough evidence to prove foul play. My mind began turning over possibilities of what they'd uncovered.

"If you could find a way to set her mind at ease."

I smothered a sigh of resignation, for when my father made a request, it was actually an order. There was no refusing him. "I'll see what I can do."

"Thank you, Ver. Oh, and many happy returns on your birthday. I know my felicitations are a few days late." There was a mumble of Mother speaking in the background. "Your mother says a parcel should be arriving for you either today or tomorrow. Apparently, your brother Tim neglected to take it to the post office for her when he was supposed to."

That sounded like my younger brother. He'd been rather bumbling and forgetful before the war, and evidently two years in the army hadn't changed that.

"I'll tell our housekeeper to watch for it."

"Oh, and, Verity," my mother interjected. "Please do come home for Christmas this year. Everyone will be here for the first time since before the war. Well, everyone but Rob. And you've yet to meet Freddy's sweet baby, Ruth."

My hands tightened around the telephone, the wood biting into my palms. "We'll try," I managed to reply.

My mother exhaled in exasperation. "There's no try about it. You will or you won't."

"We'll try," I repeated, unwilling to commit to anything. Not when the very idea of stepping foot in Upper Wensleydale made my stomach pitch with dread.

"Verity, you'll come," Father informed me, choosing to interfere when normally he stayed out of such matters. "Or I'll sell Ruby to the knacker yard."

"You wouldn't," I protested. Ruby had been my favorite pony growing up, and even though she must have been close to twenty years old, surely she had many good years left.

"Try me."

Hearing the finality in his tone, my words stuck in my throat. Why was he forcing this? Why now?

"Verity," he added more gently. "It's time."

Tears built at the back of my eyes, that he realized, that he knew why I hadn't returned. I turned away from my reflection, the pain shimmering in my eyes too raw. Even though I felt it, acutely, seeing it somehow made it worse, for I could no longer continue lying to myself that I was hiding it successfully.

"All right," I rasped, telling myself that just because I agreed to it didn't mean I couldn't change my mind. Yet another lie I could clutch to myself.

CHAPTER 12

I stood with my hands braced on the bureau for some minutes after I'd ended the call with my parents, struggling to stuff the memories and emotions I'd buried since Rob's death back down inside me and stomp on the lid. I stood there long enough that Sidney came looking for me. The look in his eyes told me he'd overheard much of my conversation, but my gaze must have been forbidding enough that he chose not to pursue the subject that still smarted like an open wound.

"So we're headed back to Littlemote?"

I pushed away from the bureau. "Briefly." I turned to stare at the door to our flat, planting my hands on my hips. "But I don't want Max traveling down to Wight without someone watching his back. Which of our neighbors do you think would be least put out with me for asking to use their telephone?"

Given the fact that photographers and reporters followed us about, sometimes camping outside our building, a number of our fellow tenants were none too pleased with us.

"You think our telephones are tapped?" Sidney asked, reading between the lines.

I arched my eyebrows. "You don't?"

He conceded this with a dip of his head. "Who are you going to telephone?"

I was surprised he even needed to ask. "Who do you think?"

His mouth curled upward sardonically at one corner. I'd known he would be irked, but there was really no other option.

"Given what we know about Ardmore's ruthlessness, it has to be someone highly capable. And before you suggest Crispin, you know he's far too impatient." Not to mention partially deaf.

Sidney's expression didn't lighten, but I could tell he'd accepted my decision. "Don't knock on Mrs. Carter's door unless you want your conversation relayed to the *Telegraph*. I'm almost certain she's profiting from our celebrity."

This did not surprise me. For all her punctilious airs, it was evident by the notorious gossips she called friends that she relished a good chin-wag.

"And I would also avoid the Webbs. One of the photographers snapped a picture of Mr. Webb's business associate departing the building late at night while Mr. Webb was out of town." The glint in his eyes suggested this associate had been doing more than simply sipping tea with Mrs. Webb.

"What of Mrs. Pimlico?"

He voiced no objection to the older widow who lived across the hall. The fact that she sometimes became confused worked to my benefit, for even if she did overhear some of my conversation she might not be believed. I felt slightly remorseful for misleading her by telling her our telephone wasn't working correctly, but it was all to a good purpose.

I'd never used the number I was about to connect to. Officially, I wasn't supposed to have it. But when I'd still worked for the Secret Service I'd had access to it and memorized it. I'd told myself I would use it only in case of emergency, but that wasn't strictly true. Our past was complicated.

I smiled at Mrs. Pimlico, who turned to look at me from

the next room while I waited for him to answer. In truth, I wasn't even certain he held lodgings at the address. He might have moved.

"Hullo," the smooth male voice on the other line said, and my muscles relaxed in relief.

"Erik," I replied brightly, using the code name Captain Alec Xavier had utilized as a staff officer in the German Army, having infiltrated their ranks years before war was declared. "I'm glad I caught you."

"Why am I not surprised you have this number," he murmured in amusement, clearly recognizing my voice.

"The telephone in our flat was malfunctioning, so I'm using one of our neighbors'."

There was a slight hesitation before he responded, letting me know he understood why I was really using another line, but he should still watch what he said. "Oh, is it? Then this must be serious."

"I need you to have someone meet a friend at Waterloo Station at 11:05 and see him safely home. You'll recall Ernest. You met him once at the WO," I informed him, hoping to jog his memory of his encounter with Max at the War Office some months before. I knew my words weren't terribly cryptic. If Ardmore had tapped the line from the building or bribed the switchboard operators to listen, he would still be able to deduce what I was saying, but at least I wouldn't alarm Mrs. Pimlico. "I planned to do so myself, but something has come up."

"I see. And the CX?"

C's secretary, Kathleen Silvernickel, must have already relayed the request I'd made in code two days prior, asking for any and all information they had on Ardmore's past.

"Bring it with you if you can, but keep your wits about you," I cautioned. "I had an encounter with a pickpocket just yesterday."

Out of the corner of my eye, I saw Mrs. Pimlico turn to

look at me. Ostensibly she was watering her flowers, but I knew she was listening, and that my mention of pickpockets would pique her interest. But I couldn't think of any other way of getting my point across to Alec that wouldn't alarm her more.

"I trust he came out the worst for wear." I could hear the speculation in his voice.

"He didn't get what he was after."

"Well, that's something. I'll see what I can do." He paused and then added, "Is there a message I can relay to Ernest?"

I'd already considered this, worried the missive I intended to ask Nimble to deliver to Max would not reach him in time. "Tell him to save me an 8-14-23-8-14-23," I said, risking the use of a shorthand numerical code a number of us in the service had utilized when necessary to spell out the word *pom-pom*. Mrs. Pimlico's brow furrowed in consternation, but then she shook her head and carried on with her watering.

"And he'll know what this means?" Alec asked doubtfully, letting me know he'd been able to decipher my code correctly.

I couldn't help but smile, remembering the first time Max and I had met, and the streamers his niece had affixed to the hood ornament of his Rolls-Royce. "Yes."

"Then leave it in my hands."

"Thank you."

"Being you, I expect there's an interesting story behind all this," he replied wryly.

"There is."

"Then you can tell me all about it over a drink the next time we meet."

I agreed before ringing off, hoping I wasn't making a promise I shouldn't keep.

I thanked Mrs. Pimlico for the use of her telephone and chatted with her about her plants for a moment before excusing myself.

About an hour later, Sidney and I set off not by train, but

in his Pierce-Arrow, motoring west. In a little less than three hours we once again drove up to the imposing edifice of Littlemote House, looking stolid and gloomy under the lowering skies. My aunt did not rush out to greet us this time, but Miles ushered us into the Elizabethan Room, where she sat waiting with her skirt spread wide over the gold chintz fabric of a settee. She made quite the regal, affronted picture, especially with her neck arched so that she could stare down her nose at us.

Though I'd felt nothing but irritation at her moments before for diverting our plans, I couldn't halt the twinge of pity that stirred in me seeing her seated in such a manner. She must truly feel vulnerable if she'd adopted such a contentious posture. Here she was, desperately grasping at anything she could control while her world turned upside down and spun out of her control.

"This wasn't my doing," Reg murmured, having entered the room behind us.

I turned to see his furious scowl. "It's all right," I assured him. The last thing this meeting needed was to start off with a confrontation.

Tucking his walking stick under his arm, he reached out to grip my elbow lightly as I began to stride forward, an acknowledgment of the alterations to the room our presence may have wrought. I guided him toward the wingback chair he seemed to favor before crossing to my aunt and bending to press a kiss to her cheek. "Good afternoon, Aunt Ernestine. That tea gown looks lovely on you."

She glanced down at the navy-blue brushed silk. "Thank you, my dear." She hesitated a moment before adding, "Your uncle also seemed to like me in it best."

I could imagine why. It did make her appear quite formidable—every inch a baronet's wife. Her armor, so to speak. But she had no need of it. Not with me anyway, and I knew Sidney would follow my lead. He pressed a kiss to her cheek as well before retreating to the other wingback chair.

"Now, what is this about Mrs. Green being arrested for her husband's murder?" I declared as I removed my gloves and hat, and laid them on the table next to the settee with my handbag. "Have the police already uncovered enough evidence to do so?"

"They seem to think so, but I am not convinced," she replied.

"Only because Miss Musselwhite isn't," Reg protested.

"Well, Miss Musselwhite would know, wouldn't she? Mrs. Green is her sister."

"And so her opinion is biased."

"Why isn't she convinced?" I raised my voice to ask, then had a better thought. "May we speak with her?"

My aunt considered this request and then nodded. "Sidney, if you would?"

My husband was already striding across the room to pull the tassel to summon Miles, and when he appeared, directed him to send Miss Musselwhite to us.

I crossed my arms over my torso to clutch the opposite elbow with each hand, wishing the fire in the hearth burned a little brighter and warmer. "Have the police revealed how they think Mr. Green was killed?"

My aunt leaned toward where I sat on the opposite end of the settee, her face starkly earnest. "Poison."

"They found cigarette butts soaking in a jar in their kitchen." Reg's voice rang with contempt. "Mrs. Green *claimed* she was making insecticide for her garden."

I frowned. "They believe he was poisoned by nicotine?" Surely the tests that must be conducted to determine such a thing were not finished yet, so they must be basing such a conclusion on other evidence. And yet . . .

"Why does that bother you?" Sidney asked as he rejoined us.

"Well, I thought nicotine poisoning was supposed to cause stomach upset." My gaze shifted to Reg. "But we never found any vomit or other evidence of gastric troubles."

"Maybe it doesn't do so in everyone," my cousin pointed out. "Or maybe the evidence was elsewhere. After all, we didn't search the entire park or the route he would have taken from his home in the village."

Except, surely he would have recognized something was wrong. If he'd begun vomiting or cramping on his way to Littlemote, other symptoms also would have occurred. So why had he continued on?

It was possible he'd come from even deeper in the park, staggering away from the evidence of his gastrointestinal distress. But wouldn't we still have smelled the evidence on him, perhaps faint, but noticeable? A dribble on his shirt or a foul scent about his mouth.

"Is that the only evidence they have against her?" I asked.

Reg scoffed. "That, and her screaming at him like a harpy for all the village to see."

But yelling didn't equate to murdering. "What of the object in Mr. Green's hand? And the earth that was disturbed? Have the police explained about those?"

"Not to us," my aunt replied as the door opened and Miss Musselwhite appeared, hovering in the doorway.

"You wished to see me?" she asked, clasping her hands tightly before her.

"Come closer, Miss Musselwhite. Don't make me shout." Aunt Ernestine's voice might have been crisp, but it was evident she felt some affection for her maid, horrified though she might have been to know that it showed. "Now, Mr. and Mrs. Kent would like to ask you some questions about your sister."

Having risen from his chair, Sidney gestured for her to take it while he fetched from across the room a Hepplewhite chair from the table used for card-playing and carried it closer.

"Oh," she murmured uncertainly, perching on the very edge of the chair's cushion. "What do you want to know?"

Though she was slightly taller than average, her sparse frame and muted coloring made her seem smaller. She was no great beauty, but she was also far from homely, merely unremarkable. But to be fair, that might have been the result of her uniform, which consisted of a gray floral print gown covered in a white apron, with a white lace cap on her head. The gray and white washed out everything but her guinea-gold hair. Given the fact that most lady's maids were allowed to wear simple dresses or cast-offs from their mistresses, I couldn't help but wonder whether my aunt had insisted on this bland attire or Miss Musselwhite had chosen it herself.

"We understand your sister has been arrested for her husband's murder. That must be incredibly distressing," I began sympathetically. "What's been done with the children?"

"My . . . my aunt is caring for them."

I nodded, relieved to hear they were somewhere safe. "But you don't believe your sister did it?"

"No, I . . . I don't." Her voice grew firmer with each word, perhaps recognizing we were not there to patronize her. "My sister and her husband had their problems, but she would *never* have killed him. She loved him."

Reg snorted. "She had a funny way of showing it."

Miss Musselwhite's lips pursed and a telling crease formed between her brows when she looked at my cousin, one that seemed to indicate some deeper emotion she was trying to hide. I suspected she didn't like him very much, but one didn't openly display aversion for one's employer, or one's employer's son.

"Yes, they fought a great deal." She sighed. "And rather openly. But that's because she loved him so desperately." She strained forward in her seat as if to make us understand. "Don't you see? She was *terrified* of losing him. So it simply can't be her. It can't!"

"I can appreciate why you believe that," I replied gently. "But it was evident from your sister's behavior the morning after that she had been drinking the night her husband died."

Her eyes dropped to her lap, her face flushing.

"As I understand it, she does so often. And liquor can make people behave in ways they never would otherwise."

I'd thought Miss Musselwhite was struggling to contain her embarrassment, either on behalf of her sister or their family. But when she lifted her gaze from where she'd clasped her hands together, the knuckles turning white, I realized the color in her cheeks wasn't due to shame but anger.

"Yes, my sister drank too much," she bit out. "And yes, she yelled at her husband. But it was out of fear, not hatred. Frank understood that. He understood *all* of it. The war was too much for Tilly. She couldn't cope with his being gone for so long, and being in so much danger. Eventually the distraction of caring for their children wasn't enough." Her eyes flashed. "If Frank can see it, if Frank can comprehend, then why should it be anyone else's business?!"

"Because Frank Green is now dead," Reg stated flatly before I could say something more diplomatic.

Aunt Ernestine scowled at him, little good it did since he couldn't see her.

"You are right," Sidney told Miss Musselwhite, though he seemed to be directing his voice at Reg, for the tone was similar to what he must have utilized in the trenches to keep his men in line. "Her drinking and their arguments are not necessarily an indication of strife in the marriage, or a motive for murder." His voice moderated. "And the police must recognize this, as well. So what of these cigarette butts they found soaking in water? Is it true she made insecticide from them?"

"Yes, she learned the trick from our mother." She shrugged. "Why pay for the nicotine solution when you can make it for free from your husband's discarded cigarette butts? She

always had a jar on the shelf above her sink, where she collected the butts until she had enough to make the repellent."

"What does she do with them during winter?" my aunt
asked.

"Store them, I presume, like Mother. Until spring."

I looked toward the window, contemplating the overcast
sky. I imagined there was just enough time left in the growing
season that Mrs. Green would be able to use another batch.
Except . . . if she'd used that batch to poison her husband,
then how were there more soaking in the jar? I supposed they
could have been the same ones, but why keep them? Why not
throw them in the fire and destroy any evidence you'd made
the insecticide? There was always the possibility she had ex-
cess, but it seemed like a strange thing to do—preparing or
keeping a second batch after poisoning your husband with
the first.

"What did she do during the war?" Sidney pondered,
seemingly in idle curiosity. "While Mr. Green was gone."

Miss Musselwhite turned to study his face, perhaps surprised he'd asked. "Mr. Plank was kind enough to collect his
butts for her. Even gathered some from the airmen, I believe,
because Tilly always had more than enough."

Then Mr. Plank was aware of her insecticide recipe. For
that matter, much of the village probably was, as well. Any of
them could have used the same method to poison Mr. Green.

That is, if nicotine was the culprit.

"Do the police have any other evidence against your sister?" I asked, feeling uneasy about this revelation.

She shook her head. "Not that they've shared with me."

I considered asking her about the item clutched in her
brother-in-law's dead hand and the disturbed ground, but I
doubted she knew. I looked at my aunt, wondering how far
she expected me to pursue this, whether I was about to tread
where I shouldn't.

"If not your sister, then who do *you* think killed Mr. Green?" I questioned.

Miss Musselwhite turned timorous. "Oh, I . . . I don't know."

"Oh, come. You must have some suspicion."

She shook her head.

I exhaled wearily. "Miss Musselwhite, I recognize why you're hesitant to point the finger at someone else, but the best way you can help your sister is by helping us to understand why someone else would wish your brother-in-law dead."

Her gaze flicked nervously between her employer and her son before settling on a spot on the bare floor several feet in front of her. "Frank was also working for the airfield, helping to maintain their grounds."

"What?!" my aunt demanded, making her maid wince. "How? When?"

"On his days off. And . . ." She hunched her shoulders. "In the early morning or late afternoon when he was less likely to be missed here."

In other words, he'd been working for the airfield while he was still supposed to be working at Littlemote—collecting two wages.

My aunt harrumphed, drawing herself upright in outrage. "And you knew about this?"

Miss Musselwhite nodded, her head still lowered in shame. "I told him he had to stop. That it was dishonest. But he said he had Tilly and the children to think about."

"How did Mr. Green travel back and forth to the airfield?" I asked, ignoring Aunt Ernestine's continued exclamations of indignation in favor of a more pressing matter.

Her gaze lifted to meet mine through her pale lashes, clearly understanding why I was asking. "Through the west park, over the bridge that spans the river to connect the airfield with Littlemote. He made repairs and improvements to it about a year ago."

The same way Minnie Spanswick had been able to rendezvous with her airman.

"Then your brother-in-law often passed through the western portion of the estate park," I clarified. "Which might explain what he was doing there in the early hours of Monday morning."

Except the old stablemaster, Mr. Plank, had said Mr. Green avoided the area, especially during the evening. If he worked at the airfield in the late afternoon, I didn't see how he could avoid passing through the west park in the evening, especially during autumn and winter. Unless he'd been lying. Unless his talk of shadows and ghosts had all been for show, to keep others from venturing there.

"You think his death might have something to do with the airfield, then?" Sidney asked Miss Musselwhite.

"I . . . I don't know," she demurred. "But if he was coming from there, perhaps?"

I turned to see cold rain now splattered against the windows. Obviously we wouldn't be traveling on to the Isle of Wight that day. Not when we had so many answers to uncover, and the weather was being uncooperative. I could only hope Max was enjoying an uneventful journey under the watchful eye of one of Alec's associates, and the explanations to our questions about Mr. Green's murder presented themselves swiftly. For resolved or not, Sidney and I were departing the following afternoon. We couldn't afford to wait any longer than that to pursue the answer to the late Earl of Ryde's riddle. Not with Ardmore's men possibly hot on our tails.

CHAPTER 13

For all that my aunt claimed she wished me to handle the matter, she persisted to meddle. I had decided the first thing to be done was to speak with those members of the staff I thought might hold any answers for us, and I'd explained how they might be more willing to speak candidly without their employer looking over our shoulders, but my aunt still tried to demand she be present for their interviews. Only Reg's plea for her assistance convinced her to retire from the Elizabethan Room before the maid Opal arrived. I cast a grateful look his way before recalling he couldn't see it.

Opal edged into the room, wringing her apron before her. I beckoned her closer, and she scurried across the room before stopping abruptly to dip an awkward curtsey.

"Please, have a seat," I said, gesturing toward the chair Miss Musselwhite had vacated, while Sidney sat next to me on the settee.

She eyed it with misgiving, before slowly sitting and then sliding back so that her toes barely touched the floor. I'd forgotten how petite the girl was, and how great a fright the discovery of Mr. Green's body had given her. Dark circles ringed the eyes gazing warily up at us through long lashes.

"This is my husband, Mr. Kent," I told her, hoping she might perk up at the sight of his dark good looks, and I was not disappointed. A welcome flush of color rose in her cheeks. "We'd like to ask you a few questions. Do you think you can help us?"

She studied me a moment and then nodded.

"Monday morning when you were sent to find Mr. Green, you said someone told you to look in the west garden. That he'd been making repairs to the ha-ha there."

She swallowed and nodded again. "Yes, ma'am. Harry told me. He's the chauffeur."

"But when you got to the west garden, Mr. Green wasn't there."

"No, ma'am. But I . . . I *thought* I saw someone in the distance, walking between the trees in the park. I thought it might be him, so I shouted. But he didn't seem to hear me. So I followed him, and that's when . . . when . . ."

"Yes," I replied, sparing her the necessity of saying the words. That's when she'd found Mr. Green's body. "But I thought you didn't like going into the west park?"

"Oh, that's only at night."

"I see."

"The ghosts don't haunt the park during the daytime," she assured us.

Sidney stilled at this pronouncement, and though I knew if I looked at him I wouldn't be able to see any trace of cynicism, I could practically feel it rolling off him in waves.

I recrossed my ankles and leaned toward her. "Then you're certain the person you saw walking away from you was Mr. Green?"

Her shoulders hunched and her head sank downward rather like a turtle retreating into her shell. "Well, I *thought* I saw someone. I . . . I thought it was Mr. Green. But I don't know. Maybe I was wrong."

I suspected this reticence and uncertainty was the work of the police. For she'd not wavered over the facts the morning she'd found Mr. Green's body. Whatever Inspector Titcomb had said to her, however forcefully he had questioned her on this point, had clearly unsettled her.

"Could it have been someone else?" I coaxed gently. "Another estate worker or an airman, for instance?"

Her head lifted slightly. "I suppose it could have been someone else." Her brow furrowed, and then alarm widened her eyes. "You don't think . . . ? Could it have been the *murderer*?" The last was gasped on a thread of sound.

"Let's not get ahead of ourselves," I hastened to reassure her. "What did this person look like? Why did you think it was Mr. Green?"

"I . . . I only saw their back. It was just a glimpse. And I was looking for Mr. Green, so I just assumed . . ." Her voice tightened with panic.

"But it looked like a man?" I interrupted.

"Yes."

"What was he wearing?"

Her eyes darted left and right as if she was searching her memory. "I don't know. I can't remember. A dark coat and pants, maybe." Her eyes widened. "I don't know."

Considering the fact that Mr. Green had been wearing a drab coat and rough umber trousers, this description wasn't very reassuring. But then, I'd already suspected he'd been dead for some time when she found him, so if she *had* seen someone in the woods, it couldn't have been Mr. Green.

As to that, her fear seemed genuine. Unless she was as good an actress as the errant maid Minnie hoped to be—and I strongly doubted it—then she wasn't lying about what she'd seen. But just to be sure.

"Were you telling the truth when you said you'd never met up with any of the airmen at the edge of the estate? Not like Minnie used to."

Her chin dipped. "I didn't want to say so in front of Agnes, but I did go once. On my day off. But it was before sunset, and I . . . I didn't fancy the chap Minnie's beau introduced me to." She crossed her arms over her chest. "He was dodgy."

"What do you mean?" I asked, my curiosity piqued.

"I don't know how to put it into words, but he gave me a funny feeling in the pit of my stomach. And my mum told me whenever a fellow did that it was best to steer clear of him."

I couldn't argue with that. It was sound advice.

"So you've never been back?"

She shook her head.

I turned to Sidney, and seeing he had nothing to add, dismissed the girl. But once she'd disappeared through the doorway, he found his words soon enough.

"A ghost?" he asked, his voice ringing with skepticism.

"Yes, apparently a number of the staff and surrounding villagers believe that the airfield was built on some ancient burial tomb—a barrow, or what have you—and the souls they disturbed now haunt the grounds." I drummed my fingers on my thigh, still ruminating on the airmen Opal had mentioned. When Sidney did not speak again, but instead sat staring at me in derisive disbelief, I turned to scowl at him. "Oh, don't be so disdainful. Local superstitions can have remarkable power over people. Sometimes it's not always a matter of what's true, but what people perceive to be so."

I sank wearily back against the cushions behind me. "Now, whether these ghosts hold any bearing on Mr. Green's death or not, I don't know. I doubt it. However, the rumors surrounding Froxfield are evidently quite pervasive. I asked Goldy about them, and he was well aware of the tale."

Sidney shifted so that his shoulder brushed against mine. "Well, what say we gather some more logical facts?"

I gazed up at him sideways. "Divide and conquer?" Thus far it had proved the most efficient and effective manner of gathering information.

"I'll go see what I can find out from the police, and whether my war credentials convince them to cooperate."

Given Detective Inspector Titcomb's reaction to my attempts to assist him in the glade where Mr. Green's body had been found, I knew he had a much better chance of learning anything than I did. "Then I think I shall pay a visit to Dr. Razey. Perhaps he'll share some of the police surgeon's findings with me." He'd seemed a reasonable man when I met him when he'd come to give my aunt her injection. As I understood it, he was great friends with the local police surgeon, who would have examined Mr. Green's corpse, and often consulted with him on medical matters.

"Oh, I'm quite certain you can convince him to share the police surgeon's findings." A teasing glint lit his eyes, reminding me he had also met Dr. Razey and witnessed his reaction to me. Though Dr. Razey hadn't stammered precisely, he had seemed rather flummoxed by my presence and overly solicitous.

I made a face. "Oh, stop. I am not going to flirt or turn coy with the man simply to gain information."

"I never supposed you would. I predict that any such ploys on your part are entirely unnecessary." The amused curl of his lips told me he was enjoying teasing me about the physician's interest in me far too much.

"He is rather endearingly courteous." I arched my chin. "Perhaps I'll run away with him."

He laughed. "Please, Ver. If you didn't leave me for Ryde or Xavier, you aren't going to leave me for Dr. Razey."

"Odious man," I retorted, pushing him to the side and rising to my feet.

However, Sidney snagged me around the waist, dragging me back down onto his lap before tipping me back so that he could gaze down into my face. "Come now. It's not my fault you fell in love with me."

I opened my mouth to make some withering remark, but he stopped it with a kiss. One that at first I refused to participate in, but then found I was helpless not to reciprocate. Not when his fingers trailed over the skin at the back of my neck and his lips caressed mine with such supple warmth. His teeth nipped my bottom lip and I gasped, nipping his back. And then I buried my fingers in his hair and gave myself over to the heat of his mouth and the artful dance of his tongue against mine.

When he pulled back, I discovered that all trace of amusement had vanished from his eyes to be replaced with an intensity that seemed to suck all the air from my lungs, making it difficult to draw breath evenly.

"And I thank God every day that you did," he murmured, his calloused thumb trailing over my cheekbone.

I exhaled raggedly and tightened my grip on his hair, pulling him back into the kiss.

Dr. Razey's home and practice were located in a tidy red-brick house in a quiet street between the church and the town hall in Hungerford. Sidney waited long enough to be certain I was invited in before speeding off in his Pierce-Arrow toward the constabulary. Dr. Razey's housekeeper, who couldn't have been a day under sixty, possessed round, rosy cheeks and twinkling eyes beneath a mop of white hair restrained in a bun. She ushered me into the parlor to wait while Dr. Razey finished his consultation with another patient.

My eyes widened at the unique art decorating the walls and side tables. Finely carved tribal masks hung beside brilliantly colored feathered headdresses, while beautifully weaved baskets rubbed elbows with ancient-looking ceramic sculptures. It was more than my mind could absorb in one single glance, and I was still taking it all in when Dr. Razey bustled through the doorway, his face wreathed in a smile.

"Mrs. Kent, what a pleasant surprise." He paused, acknowledging my rapt gaze. "Yes, it is quite impressive, isn't it? It all belongs to my predecessor, Dr. Maslen, of course. As did this house. But he asked if I would look after his collection for him when I took over his practice and residence. He's off to South America again, you know. To the Amazon. It's his true passion. And now that he's retired, he has more time for it."

I nodded and he chuckled in recognition of this somewhat long-winded response.

"In any case, I haven't had the wherewithal yet to redecorate or to even attempt to package all this away. The locals are already used to it, so much of the time I forget how exotic it all is." He grinned. "Except in situations like this. But I thought you and your husband had returned to London." He turned as if searching for Sidney.

"We had. But given recent developments, my aunt asked us to return."

"Oh, yes." Some of the brightness dimmed from his eyes as he assessed my features, seeming to deduce the reason for my visit. "Why don't you come into my office?" He gestured for me to proceed him, and then held open a door across the small corridor for me before closing it. "Please, have a seat."

I settled into the gently worn ladderback chair before his desk, suspecting from the patina of the wood it had cradled decades, if not centuries of bottoms. There was something comforting in that knowledge. Or perhaps it was my surroundings, for Dr. Razey's office was far from cold and clinical. While the parlor still bore the marks of his predecessor, I somehow knew this space had been made over into his own. The usual certificates and licenses graced walls painted the softest shade of mint green, while the furniture was gracefully worn, like what one would normally find in an old aristocratic home. Cabinets lined one wall, with vials neatly arranged in rows behind the glass, and an examination table stood in the corner, its buttery leather draped in a crisp cloth. The clutter of paperwork was tidied into stacks on a side-

board behind him, leaving only a leather blotter on the surface of the desk between us.

As Dr. Razey sank into the worn calfskin chair behind his
desk, the leather creaking with age, I decided the space suited
him. He certainly presented himself as a neat and efficient
man. His brown hair was parted and combed, his clothes
pressed and starched. I judged his age to be about thirty,
which meant he'd likely been in the thick of it during the
war. I would not have been surprised to hear he'd served with
the Royal Army Medical Corp alongside my oldest brother,
Freddy. That might have accounted for the orderliness. But
there was also a depth of warmth and kindness that gleamed
in his dark eyes and tamed the chill that so often accompanied such trimness. I suspected he'd been quite popular with
his patients at the front, and just as much so with the female
residents of Hungerford.

He clasped his hands together and rested them on the desk
before him. "I heard that Mrs. Green had been detained."
His eyes radiated sympathy.

"Yes, her sister, Miss Musselwhite, is distraught. Which
means my aunt is unsettled, as well. They're both convinced
she didn't do it."

A vee formed between his brows. "I understand they found
a nicotine concoction in her home."

"Yes, one that her sister insists she uses as an insecticide,
and has done so for more than a decade." I paused, searching his troubled expression. "It was nicotine poisoning, then,
that killed him?"

"The police won't know that for certain until the toxicology of the samples the police surgeon collected can be tested,
but it is a possibility."

I narrowed my eyes in contemplation. "I thought that nicotine poisoning caused stomach upset. Vomiting and such?"

"Yes, well, usually. Though not always. I understand there
wasn't any evidence of such gastrointestinal distress found

near the body, but it could have occurred elsewhere." He hesitated, as if debating whether to say more. "I can tell you there was very little in his stomach at the time of his death."

Which meant that either he hadn't eaten in some time or he had heaved it back up. But which was it?

"Dr. Winslow thought that was indicative," Dr. Razey added about his police surgeon colleague, but the tone of his voice suggested he himself was not as convinced.

"I suppose there's no doubt Mr. Green was poisoned?"

He nodded once. "He died of respiratory failure, but it was not a natural death. His heart showed no signs of damage. He had no lung conditions or known illnesses. He'd suffered no injuries to his spine or chest." He tilted his head to the side. "He did have an inflamed liver, but that seemed irrelevant to the cause of death." He spread his hands wide. "Which left us with the conclusion the respiratory failure was induced."

I turned my head to gaze out the window at a boy trotting past with a dog following at his heels. The paper and twine package tucked under his arm suggested he was delivering a cut of meat from the butcher. "If the poison was nicotine, how long after he ingested it would it have begun to take effect?"

"Perhaps thirty minutes."

"How long before he died?"

I couldn't tell if my question had shocked him, even as solemnly as I asked it, or if he was merely hesitant to discuss such a thing with a gently-reared woman, but it took a few seconds for him to answer. "It may have taken several hours."

I swallowed, envisioning the agony Mr. Green must have been in. Then, it was entirely possible he could have eaten the poison with his dinner—or at a pub or other establishment he might have visited that evening—vomited on the roadside on his way to Littlemote, and expired in its west park. But once he'd become ill, why hadn't he turned back or sought help? I knew men could be stubborn about such things, but I could only imagine the pain must have been excruciating.

Then another thought occurred to me. A vague remembrance of one of my mother's friends telling us how her gardener had nearly killed himself by spilling insecticide on his skin. "Must the nicotine be ingested? Could it be absorbed through the skin or by an injection or something?"

"Poisoning can occur by skin absorption," he confirmed. "Also inhalation." His gaze dipped to the desk in front of him, seemingly finished with his statement, but I could tell by the slight pursing of his mouth that he had more to say. The question was whether he would share it with me. Recognizing he was a conscientious person, I knew better than to try to verbally impel him. Instead, I waited for him to lift his gaze again to meet mine, communicating with my eyes that I could be trusted.

He cleared his throat, reaching out to straighten the already square blotter. "It's funny you should mention an injection." His gaze darted up toward me before dropping again to the blotter. "Dr. Winslow noticed a prick in the skin of Mr. Green's neck behind his right ear. He dismissed it as a superficial injury, but I wondered if it might have been made by the needle of a syringe." He frowned. "Except nicotine isn't injected."

I sat taller, remembering the small smear of blood I'd noted on Mr. Green's neck in the glade. "What of another poison? Are there other toxins that induce respiratory failure that *can* be injected?"

"Yes, dozens." He shook his head. "But the police found Mrs. Green's nicotine concoction. They say she has ample motive. And unless the toxicology tests show differently, the most likely conclusion is that Mr. Green died from nicotine poisoning."

I understood what he was saying. I even understood why

the police had detained Mrs. Green. More often than not the simplest explanation was the right one. But if they were wrong, that meant the real culprit had already been given days to clean up after themselves.

Dr. Razey and I chatted for a few more minutes about my aunt and the upcoming commemoration of the anniversary of the armistice until I saw Sidney's distinctive carmine-red roadster pull up outside. He stood next to his motorcar, holding the door open for me as rain dripped from the brim of his hat while I thanked the doctor. Seeing Sidney's cheeky grin as he raised his hand to wave at the physician, I glowered at him.

"He was nothing but professional," I snapped at my husband as he joined me inside the Pierce-Arrow.

"Oh, I'm certain," he drawled knowingly.

I rolled my eyes. "What did you discover at the constabulary? Did Inspector Titcomb share anything with you?"

"He did not."

I exhaled a breath of exasperated disappointment. "Well, I wasn't expecting he would tell you much."

"But his constable did."

I turned to Sidney in surprise, just in time to see a smug smile curl his lips. "How did you manage that?"

"When the inspector sent me on my way with a terse, but polite 'go to hell' . . ."

"He didn't actually say that, did he?"

"Well, no. But that's what he meant." He expertly weaved through a narrow passage between two brick buildings and back out to the road leading to Littlemote. "In any case, I'd noticed how that young constable . . . Jones, I believe was his name. I'd noticed how his eyes lit up when I'd introduced myself. I gathered he was slightly too young to have served. He hadn't lost that starry-eyed naïveté," he muttered wryly. "So I decided to avail myself of the deep overhang along the southern side of the building, and no sooner had I lit one of my fags than he came shuffling around the corner."

"What did he say?"

"Not much. Not before the inspector hollered at him to finish his break. But my cigarette managed to loosen his tongue enough for him to tell me that they managed to track most of Mr. Green's movements the evening before his death."

I turned to him eagerly. "And?"

He glanced at me out of the corner of his eye. "And it's not good for Mrs. Green. Their neighbor saw him leave their house around nine thirty, and several more people say they spotted him striding through town toward the road leading to Littlemote at correlating times. He never stopped at a pub or visited another home. At least, none between the Greens' house and the outskirts of town."

I frowned out the rain-splattered window. "Didn't any of them think it was odd for him to do such a thing?"

"I asked the very same question, but apparently it wasn't uncommon to see Mr. Green out walking at night. For that matter, I gather it's not uncommon to see any of the local veterans doing so."

The hollow note in Sidney's voice reminded me he understood precisely why they did so. There were some nights when I woke to find him wearing a hole in the carpet in our drawing room, or staring broodingly into the darkness. London's streets were filled with many such night-walkers, trying to outpace whatever demons, whatever nightmares from the war still held them in their grip.

"What about the evidence the police have collected?" I asked into the tense silence that had fallen. "Did he tell you what Mr. Green was clutching in his palm?"

"No, but he started to tell me about the disturbed ground when the inspector yelled for him. Said there was more than one spot where the soil had been turned over."

I frowned in confusion, wondering why someone would do such a thing, be it Mr. Green or someone else. I began to ask him just that question and then stopped, realizing he wouldn't know the answer any more than I did. "We need to take another look at that glade."

"I agree. But not today." He gestured toward the wind- screen where the electric wiper was struggling to keep up with the steady drumbeat of rain.

I had no intention of arguing with him. Not when what little light there was had already begun to bleed from the sky.

"What of you?" His mouth curled into a grin. "What did Dr. Razey have to say?"

Ignoring the teasing tone of his voice, I relayed what I'd learned about nicotine poisoning, the state of Mr. Green's body, and the discovery of the puncture wound in the corpse's neck.

"You suspect another poison," he surmised as he navigated past the overgrown gatehouse.

"Truthfully?" I sighed. "I don't know what to suspect." I drummed my fingers against my leg as I stared out at the pop- lar trees. "But you must admit that puncture wound is odd."

"And its placement."

"But why would someone inject him with poison? Why not simply shoot him or bash him over the head?" Poisoning Mr. Green in such a manner seemed a rather complicated and roundabout way for the killer to achieve his or her aims.

"Perhaps they didn't have access to a gun, or know how to properly use it. Maybe they were worried they couldn't over- power him or sneak up on him unawares."

"And they did have access to poison and a syringe, and took the chance of being able to get close enough to him to administer the dose without him noticing?"

He tilted his head, conceding my point. Bashing a person over the head took much less finesse, and could be accom- plished at a greater distance, than jabbing them in the neck and then pushing the plunger of a syringe. Sidney gave the engine a gun as we crested the rise and Littlemote House came into view.

"The only logical reason I can think of that the killer would have chosen poison is to distance themselves from the crime. For if the police believe the poison was administered elsewhere, then they're going to pay less attention to the place where the victim actually died."

"I can think of one other," he replied ruefully. "They *wanted* his wife to take the blame."

CHAPTER 14

I reached down to grip the seat as he swung the motorcar to the right, pulling into the enclosed estate yard rather than driving around the circle to the grand entrance. We passed through a pair of brick gate piers with cornices and ball finials to the pitted yard around which a number of buildings ranged, including the carriage house, stables, laundry, and game larder. Sidney drew the Pierce-Arrow to a stop just outside the carriage house, from which my aunt's chauffeur emerged, donning his cap.

There wasn't time to remark on my husband's last statement as the chauffeur opened my door to help me alight, but that didn't mean I wasn't thinking about it. For why would someone wish to frame Mrs. Green? Who hated her that much?

Or was it purely a matter of expedience? For if Mrs. Green was the person most likely to fall under suspicion of her husband's murder because of her conduct, perhaps the killer was merely taking advantage of the circumstances. If so, their ploy had worked thus far. But what if the poison was discovered not to be nicotine? What then?

Rather than approach the house, I turned my steps toward the stables, trusting Sidney would follow. I paused just inside the door, allowing the scents of hay and old wood to fill my nostrils before advancing toward the harness room. The gray mare lifted her head drowsily before snuffling and returning to her bag of oats.

I found Mr. Plank seated in the single chair with his feet propped on one of the battered trunks and one eye propped open to regard who had approached. Yet more evidence that he hadn't the least care for his employer's opinion of him.

"I wondered when ye was gonna come see me," he remarked in his rasping voice. "And I see ye've brought yer 'usband wi' ye this time."

I looked over my shoulder at Sidney. "Yes, he proves to be useful some of the time."

Sidney's lip curled upward at one corner. "I endeavor to please."

Mr. Plank chuckled, lowering his feet. "Come in then. Come in." He eyed Sidney with mischief. "Can I interest ye in a draught o' scrumpy?"

"Don't be fooled," I warned my husband as I removed my gloves. "That cider could down a sailor."

"You forget, I'm from Devonshire," Sidney reminded me. "I'm well aware of the unsuspecting wallop a good glass of cider can have." He accepted the glass of scrumpy from Mr. Plank, who watched him as he took an experimental sip with nary a flinch at the dry bite. He nodded his head in appreciation. "Nice."

I could tell this simple compliment had earned him the old stablemaster's tentative approval. He turned to offer me a glass, but I declined. Fatigue from the too few hours of sleep the night before and the day's discoveries dragged at my bones. Two sips of scrumpy and I would be nodding off. It was also the reason I remained on my feet rather than take the chair Mr. Plank vacated for me.

"You know why we're here?" I asked as he sank down on the battered trunk with his own glass of the golden liquid.

He nodded as he swallowed. "My nephew arrested Mrs. Green, but Miss Musselwhite doesn't believe she did it."

"Succinctly put." I studied his weathered appearance. "But what do you think?"

Leaning back, he surprised me by setting the remainder of his glass on the table at his elbow and scrunching his face as if to give the matter some thought. "I think there must be some sort o' evidence against the missus, or else my nephew would ne'er have arrested 'er. But . . ." He held up a finger. "That doesn't mean 'e's done lookin'." His gaze met mine levelly. "Titcomb may act quickly, but 'e doesn't rest on 'is laurels."

"That's good to hear," I replied, reassured somewhat by this assertion. Though I wasn't sure precisely what this assurance of his diligence meant. That the inspector would be searching hard for more evidence to convict Mrs. Green, or exploring all other avenues and potential suspects. "Did you know Mr. Green was also working for the airfield?"

Mr. Plank reached up to scratch his beard, his gaze turning speculative. "Was 'e now?"

"You didn't know?" Sidney queried, perching on the corner of the desk behind me as he sipped from his glass. He seemed to be weighing the other man's response as much as I was.

"Well, I suppose I had my suspicions," he admitted. "At times 'e wasn't the easiest man to find. But then the estate is large, and there's only the one o' him to tend it."

"You told me he avoided the west park, particularly in the late afternoon and evening," I reminded him. "That he claimed that the fading light played tricks on his eyes."

His scraggly brows formed a vee between his eyes. "That 'e did. It would appear 'e lied. For I presume that's how yer tellin' me 'e moved back and forth from the estate to the airfield."

"I am," I confirmed.

He nodded and then frowned. "Don't know why 'e had to do such a thing. A man's business is his own. I wouldn't o' said anything."

Given his affront, I elected not to voice the obvious. That Mr. Green had lied about the ghosts so that no one would go looking for him in the west gardens or park at that hour of the day, so they wouldn't catch him coming or going to his second job.

"Other than its abuttal to the airfield, and the rumors of ghosts, is there anything else noteworthy about the west park?" I prodded, hoping to draw him out of his unhappy ruminations.

But he shook his head, clearly troubled by this new revelation about Mr. Green.

Sidney and I soon excused ourselves, picking our way across the estate yard through the rainy twilight and into the chill back corridors of the manor. Shadows cloaked the passageway.

"What I don't understand," he declared as he shook the water from his coat. "Is why Mr. Green returned here at ten, ten thirty at night? Why was he in the west park? He couldn't have been on his way to do some work at the airfield."

I matched my tone of voice to his, pitched low so that no one farther along the corridor could overhear us. "If he was poisoned with nicotine before he left his home, as the police believe, then he wouldn't have lived much later than midnight." I frowned in thought, wondering what all duties the late man-of-all-work had undertaken. "Could he have been checking or setting traps of some kind?"

"At that hour?" Sidney's expression was skeptical. "I doubt it."

And yet, Mr. Green must have been there for some reason.

"Perhaps we'll have a better idea what he was doing once we examine the glade tomorrow." I removed my broad-brimmed hat, shaking out my bobbed tresses. "But first, I think I should try to find out what Mrs. Green has to say. Perhaps Miss Musselwhite would like to accompany me."

Sidney nodded, recognizing as I did that Mrs. Green's sister had a better chance of convincing Inspector Titcomb to let us speak with her than my going alone. "It will be, what? Three days since her last drink. It won't be pretty."

"I know. But she may be the only person to hold the answers to some of what we don't know." My lips creased into a rueful smile. "That, or incriminate herself."

True to my expectations, Inspector Titcomb was not happy to see us when we filed into his constabulary the following morning. He was even more displeased when Miss Musselwhite requested that she and I be allowed to speak with her sister. But having already thwarted my aunt's protests about our borrowing her maid, the burly inspector's stony stare seemed much less of a challenge.

Until a suspicious glint lit his eye. One that I instinctively did not trust. He nodded to Constable Jones. "Show 'em back to her cell." He arched his chin. "I'll give ye ten minutes, ladies. No more."

Miss Musselwhite thanked him, but I remained silent, still trying to puzzle out the reason for his easy capitulation and the satisfaction he almost seemed to take in it. I turned to catch Sidney's eye as the constable led me and Miss Musselwhite through a door, trusting he would find a way to see us released should Titcomb attempt to incarcerate us.

However, I swiftly discovered imprisonment wasn't the inspector's objective. Not when I could smell it before we'd even turned the corner at the back of the corridor to reach the block of jail cells. Though we'd passed a room with a table and chairs clearly intended for interviews, Titcomb had decided our discussion with Mrs. Green should take place here, where the air was rank with vomit, sweat, and desperation.

The woman was evidently deep in the grips of illness from the denial of alcohol. She lay draped over the single cot in her cell, her skin slick with perspiration and her hair a tangled mess. Her eyes were open, staring up at the ceiling. In fact, the only sign of her being alive was their periodic blinking.

"Tilly," Miss Musselwhite gasped, hurrying over to the bars. She gripped them between her hands, leaning against them and nearly kicking the tray of food that sat untouched on the floor just inside the cell door. "Oh, my dearest. Might I . . . ?" she turned to ask, but the constable had already retreated, presumably to clearer air.

I approached more slowly, watching Mrs. Green as her sister continued to croon to her, fretting over her condition. The knowledge that this could have been me if I'd continued down the path I'd been on before Sidney had returned from the dead was like a punch in the gut.

Mrs. Green rolled her head to the side to look at us, blinking several times as if to clear her vision. "Rhoda, is that really you?"

"Yes, dearest. Oh, what have they done to you? You must be in despair."

But Mrs. Green had but one thing on her mind. "Did you bring me a drink?" she gasped, pushing herself upright and then cringing from the pain. Her sister fell silent. "Please tell me you brought some gin. Or . . . or even some of Frank's whisky."

Miss Musselwhite appeared stunned, and I wondered how much of her sister's absorption with alcohol she'd willfully ignored. "Well, no, Tilly . . ."

"Why not?" The skin across her face tightened. "I need it, Rhoda. Please, you can bring it to me."

She glanced vaguely in the direction where the constable had disappeared. "No, I . . . I don't think I can." She wavered. "But the children are doing well . . ."

"I need it!" Mrs. Green snarled, her face transforming in twisted fury. "You must get it for me, Rhoda. Now!"

Miss Musselwhite's mouth hung open in shock as her sister tried to rise to her feet and then sank back down.

"Go! Go get it for me. Please, Rhoda. Please. I need it." She begged, her ferocity dissolving into pleading as swiftly as it had begun.

"The police won't let her give it to you, Mrs. Green," I said, drawing her gaze for the first time.

She stared at me as if seeing a woman with two heads, and then her shoulders slumped and she began quietly weeping. "But I need it," she sobbed. "I can't do this. I can't." She hiccupped. "Not without Frank. Oh, Frank." Her fingers scrabbled in the sheets beside her, seeming to reach out blindly for something that wasn't there.

My heart ached for her. Yes, in many ways she'd done this to herself, but in other ways she had not. The war, the weight of fear and anxiety, the isolation caused by being forced to hide her struggles from a society that told its citizens to either press on or that they failed their loved ones and their country. All of it had fallen too heavy on her shoulders. To now be facing the painful process of sobering up without her husband and while under arrest for his murder must make it triply agonizing.

But time was ticking away, and if we were ever to uncover the truth and help her, I could not cosset her or tiptoe around the niceties.

"Mrs. Green, did you kill your husband?"

"Mrs. Kent," Miss Musselwhite protested forcibly. "You can't ask that."

"It's a legitimate question." When she would have further protested, I lifted my hand to forestall her.

Mrs. Green sniffed, her brow furrowing briefly in either confusion or pain. "No," she muttered, and then with more force, "No. How could you . . . ?" She broke off, lowering her head again, as if realizing what a foolish question that was. The effort it cost her was evident, but she straightened, holding her head high. "No, I did not."

"Do you know who did?"

She sat staring at me for a moment, her shoulders sinking, and then began to shake her head. She cringed, pressing her hand to her temple. "No."

I studied the dark circles around her eyes, the puffiness of her features, and tried to breathe shallowly through my nose and ignore the nauseating smells. If nothing else, the woman should be offered a way to bathe beyond the means of the tiny sink, and the mess around the toilet should be cleaned. I suspected her sister would do it, if they would let her into the cell.

"Why did your husband leave your home that night? We know you were fighting."

She didn't speak, simply stared dejectedly at her lap.

"Was he often in the habit of returning to Littlemote at night?"

"He was excited," she murmured so softly I strained to hear her. "He . . . he said he'd found something. Something that could fix everything." She made a sound between a sob and a laugh, and then clapped a shaking hand over her mouth as she began to weep. "But I just wanted him to stay home. To stay . . . with us. Not go out there digging every night."

"Digging for what?" I asked as interest stirred inside me. That disturbed ground we'd found near Mr. Green's body. Had he been the one digging? But then, where was his shovel?

However, this question seemed to recall Mrs. Green to her surroundings, and precisely whom she was talking to, because she pressed her hand to her mouth again, rocking back and forth. After all, the land where her husband had been digging belonged to my cousin, as did any property found on it. Was any such property sitting in her home now?

"Mrs. Green, what did he find?"

But all she did was continue to rock.

"Is any of it at your home now? If so, it could be the proof needed to show the police that someone else may have had motive to kill your husband," I coaxed, despite the fact I still wasn't convinced she hadn't.

She looked up at this, her eyes widening as if she'd never considered this. "I don't know. He . . . he never told me." Her hands clenched and unclenched. "I think he knew if I knew what it was and where he put it, I would . . . spend it. But it was to be for my treatment. The hospitals. They're all full of soldiers. None of 'em would take me." Her gaze drifted to the side, staring sightlessly once again at the floor as she clutched her stomach. "But he said, once we had clout, once we had funds, they would treat us differently. They would find me a place."

Miss Musselwhite dabbed at the tears trailing down her cheeks with her handkerchief. "It's true. Frank tried to have her admitted to several different hospitals." She shook her head. "But none of them would take her. They said priority went to the returning soldiers." Her mouth clamped shut before she could utter the thoughts I saw reflected in her eyes. The unkind remarks I suspected some of those hospital administrators had said about Mrs. Green and her weakness. Having heard enough self-righteous condemnation spewed from the mouths of society matrons, I silently thanked her for not sharing those comments.

Before I could ask Mrs. Green any further questions, she suddenly dove for the toilet. Although most of the sounds we could hear were dry heaves, I still turned away. Miss Musselwhite, on the other hand, cried out for Constable Jones, who took longer to appear than I'd expected, as I'd thought he would be listening just around the corner. He swiftly appraised the situation as she demanded he allow her into the cell.

"There's nothin' you can do for 'er," he said, not unkindly.

"I can comfort her," she protested. "I can clean up that mess."

"No," her sister croaked between heaves. "Go!" She flung her hand back at us, shooing us. "I deserve it."

"Tilly, don't say that," she pleaded.

"It's true. Go!"

Constable Jones ushered us out, ignoring Miss Musselwhite's further protests. I wrapped an arm around her shoulders as she wept into her handkerchief, searching out the inspector's gaze as soon as we returned to the front room. It took everything in me to stifle my anger, knowing any display of temper from me would not help Mrs. Green.

"I realize she has been detained on suspicion of murdering her husband, Inspector, but is there not something that can be done for her condition?"

Titcomb surprised me by responding with equal restraint. "We have a woman coming to tend to matters this morning. And I've asked Dr. Razey to look in on her sometime today."

"Which woman?" Miss Musselwhite demanded.

He named someone I was not familiar with, but the maid seemed content with this response, for she nodded.

"Thank you," I told him.

"Of course. We aren't without compassion here, Mrs. Kent," he replied.

If that was true, this was the first indication I'd seen of it, but I chose to bite my tongue rather than see Mrs. Green punished for my cheek.

CHAPTER 15

Sidney helped me to escort Miss Musselwhite from the constabulary and settle her in the rear seat of his motorcar. He gazed at me over her head, a dozen questions reflected in his eyes, but I shook my head minutely, determined to wait to discuss it until Miss Musselwhite was returned to Littlemote House. Though she didn't speak, lost in her own thoughts, her spirits seemed to revive on the drive back to the manor. At least enough that when I turned in my seat to look at her as we pulled to a stop in the estate yard, she was no longer weeping.

"Thank you for accompanying us. I know that can't have been easy."

Her gaze searched mine, stark with pain, and when she spoke, her voice rasped in her throat. "She didn't do it, you know. She couldn't have."

I opened my mouth to respond, but she turned away, reaching for the door handle. I supposed she didn't need one.

I watched her walk away. It was obvious she was under a tremendous strain, and desperate to see her sister's name cleared, but I still had the sense she was keeping something from us. Something important.

Sidney rounded the Pierce-Arrow, opening the door for me, and I fastened the buttons of my Napoleon blue woolen scarf coat with black trim tightly up to my neck against the chill wind. The sun shone bright in the sky, playing hide and seek with the woolly clouds, so rather than enter the house, we turned west into the gardens. Linking arms, we crossed the terrace from one end of the manor to the other, before traversing the raised walk to the west garden lawn and the ha-ha dividing it from the parkland below. While we walked, I explained what Mrs. Green had revealed to us.

"So you think he was digging in the west park?" he surmised as he reached up to grip my waist and help me over the edge of the ha-ha.

"She didn't say so specifically. But where else?"

Though my feet now touched the ground, he didn't release me. A solemnity settled over his features, and I realized he was searching for something in my eyes. "Seeing Mrs. Green in such a state couldn't have been easy for you either."

My gaze dipped to the knot of his striped tie revealed through the gap at the top of his coat, and I reached up to straighten it, though it needed no adjustment.

"I saw the ferocity in your eyes when you returned to the vestibule, though you tried to hide it."

"Yes, well, it was inhumane to leave Mrs. Green in such conditions."

"I saw the distress, too."

I lifted my gaze to meet his.

"The way it haunted you."

I swallowed past the tightness in my throat, stating aloud the truth I wanted to evade. "If you hadn't come back to me when you did, that could have been me." I had certainly been well on the road to making my consumption of gin a relentless compulsion to blot out the pain and memories, to forget the agony of reality.

His dark eyes that shone too often with cynicism softened, and the flecks of silver that had so fascinated me when we first met glinted like stars in the midnight-blue pools of his eyes. I inhaled past the tightness that had taken root in my breast as he lifted his hand to clasp my jaw, brushing his fingers gently back and forth along the skin at the back of my neck.

"Well, I'm not going anywhere ever again." His gaze dipped to my mouth. "Not without you." His lips pressed to mine in a promise, one that left me feeling slightly dizzy from its intensity as he pulled back. So much so that I remained silent as he tucked my arm through his and began striding down the path Reg and I had taken just four short days ago.

If not for the grimness of our task, it would have been a lovely day for an autumn stroll. The bite in the air was countered by the bright sun and our brisk pace. The trees bursted with color, the rich scent of their decaying leaves perfuming the air as they crunched underfoot. Even the yew trees added their splash of brilliance, sporting red berries on their evergreen boughs. While earlier in the week the river had merely burbled, I could hear that the previous day's rains had swelled its banks, strengthening its rumble.

"Do you have any idea what Mr. Green might have uncovered?" Sidney asked as we neared the glade where the man-of-all-work had been found.

"I do, actually."

He turned to me in interest.

"Reg mentioned that a number of old coins have been found about the estate grounds in centuries past. He claimed that some of them were even Roman and Anglo-Saxon."

His brow furrowed. "Wasn't one of the items that went missing from the manor a box of old coins?"

"Indeed, it was. Apparently, all the coins that had been found over the years were simply tossed inside. And while Reg seemed to think their value was negligible, I suspect to a man like Mr. Green their worth was at least the equivalent of several years' wages."

"You think he stole them?"

"I don't know about that," I murmured as I glanced distractedly up at the sky, hearing the approach of an aeroplane. "But Reg mentioned a coin had been found just last year. What if Mr. Green had heard about it, about the other discoveries, and recognized an opportunity when he saw one. Whether he intended to keep the existence of any treasure he found to himself or offer to split the profit with my cousin is up for debate." I halted my steps, looking up again to catch glimpses of a trio of light bombers soaring overhead toward the south, and then turned to face him. "But that metal object he died clutching in his hand . . . I would stake my emerald bracelet that it was a coin."

He lifted his hands to his hips and turned to survey the expanse of the glade. "Your supposition certainly fits with what Constable Jones told me about there being multiple areas of disturbed soil. That sounds to me like a methodical search. So let's find them."

I led Sidney to the spot where Mr. Green's body had been found, and then we began to systematically explore the glade and farther into the park, looking for any signs of disturbance or evidence of human interference. It wasn't long before we located the first clusters of freshly turned earth, as if holes had been dug and then filled back in. It was impossible to tell how deep they were without digging ourselves, but they were each approximately one to two feet in diameter, arranged in a uniform five-by-five grid.

When we stumbled across a second cluster about one hundred yards to the south, laid out in a matching pattern, I realized we weren't dealing with an isolated dig location, but multiple sites. However, the next mound of backfilled earth we found was a single square about four by four feet. Its edges were less precise, its contours jagged.

Searching deeper into the park, we found additional disturbed sites, each one mimicking either the grid pattern or the single large square. I tried to orient them in my mind, to deduce whether there was a discernible pattern to their placement, but the grid patterns seemed haphazard. The larger squares, however, were each located some two feet to the north of a tree. The type of tree varied, but the placement of the disturbed soil was always the same, as if someone was looking for something purely based on those specifications.

The discovery of all these backfilled holes was bizarre and mildly unsettling. Clearly, they'd been taking advantage of the fact my cousin could no longer see, and so rarely ventured into the park, and my aunt never did. How long had this been going on, and just who was involved? I strongly suspected Mr. Green was responsible for at least some of the holes, but was he really to be blamed for all of them?

I stood with my arms crossed, glaring down at one of the holes in frustration, when suddenly the back of my neck prickled in alarm. I lifted my head as the sensation trickled down my spine like an icy drop of water, and then turned to survey the park around us. What had alerted me, I didn't know. I never did. Perhaps it was the harsh cry of a bird, or a barely imperceptible scent on the breeze, or a tremor I somehow sensed. Whatever the reason, my instincts had sprung to life, and they were telling me we were not alone, and we were not safe.

I moved forward, pressing a hand to Sidney's back as he rose from a crouched position where he'd been examining one of the holes. "Don't question me. Just come," I ordered softly, propelling him toward a small copse of beech trees. Once we were standing amidst their shelter, I pivoted slowly, scrutinizing our surroundings, trying to understand what had so unnerved me.

"You sensed it, too, hmm?" Sidney murmured.

I turned to find his gaze scouring the denser tree line that stood between us and the river with the same intensity I felt. In some ways it was a relief to know I wasn't the only one who had intuited trouble, but it also heightened my vigilance.

For if Sidney had detected the same disturbance I did, then later I couldn't convince myself it hadn't happened.

Some moments later, we heard whistling and then the steady rustle of footsteps through the fallen leaves. My husband's hand stole beneath his coat toward the back of his waistline, and then he cursed. "I left my Luger in the Pierce-Arrow," he replied in answer to my questioning look. "I figured it wasn't good form to take a pistol into a constabulary."

Regardless, I'd already begun to breathe a little easier. After all, the person striding toward us obviously wasn't taking any pains not to be heard, and as such, surely they didn't mean us any harm. Perhaps it was their whistling that had so alarmed us in the first place. From far off, its shrillness might have reached our ears and raised our hackles without us recognizing it.

That's what I wanted to believe, in any case, but I couldn't stop my eyes from scanning the trees again, even as the figure of a man in a khaki uniform emerged. The uniform was a holdover from the Royal Flying Corps before it was merged with the Royal Naval Air Service to form the Royal Air Force in early 1918, and didn't appear so very different from what Sidney had worn as an officer in the army. The fellow seemed to be oblivious to our presence, continuing to whistle as he strolled steadily forward in his highly polished boots. From this distance, I couldn't tell the exact rank, but the braid on his sleeve indicated he was an officer of some sort.

He was nearly upon us and yet I was still torn about whether to hide or make ourselves known, when Sidney shifted his feet into a wider stance, making the decision for us. Though subtle, I knew the movement had been a conscious decision. After four years of war, he knew perfectly well how to remain still and silent, for hours on end if necessary.

The officer's stride checked, though he didn't appear particularly startled. "Oh, hullo! Sorry, didn't see you there."

He shifted course, moving toward us. Sidney stepped forward, extending his hand to meet the airman's proffered one. "Captain Lucas Willoughby." He gestured with his head back in the direction he came. "Stationed at Froxfield. At least, for the time being," he added with a broad grin.

Our search had taken us toward the northwest corner of the estate, where Littlemote Park bordered the river and the airfield beyond. I wondered how close we actually were to the river. The sound of its rushing water had quieted to a burble once again, but Reg had told me it broke off into a number of smaller tributaries and irrigation ditches before reaching the boundary with the airfield, dispersing the water flow and narrowing the river.

Rather than release his grip on Sidney's hand, Captain Willoughby tightened it. "I say, you wouldn't happen to be the chap with that dashed fine motorcar, would you? The red one?"

Sidney's lips curled into an artless smile, disarmed by the compliment to his pride and joy. "Yes, that's my Pierce-Arrow."

"A Pierce-Arrow?" He whistled low. "Never seen one first-hand, but I hear they're a real goer. Certainly kept up with my Ninak." His teeth flashed cheekily. "For a time."

So this was the pilot Sidney had raced on our drive to Littlemote a week ago.

"But then you have the advantage of wide-open skies instead of hedgerows and villages," Sidney countered. "I'm Sidney Kent, by the way."

This seemed to make an even greater impression than his ownership of a Pierce-Arrow.

"Really," Captain Willoughby murmured speculatively, surveying him from head to toe. They were nearly equal in height and physicality, though Sidney's was better concealed beneath the crisp lines of his suit. They also both possessed an attractiveness that most females would be drawn to, though

I much preferred Sidney's dark good looks to the captain's sun-bronzed appearance. What hair could be seen below the brim of his hat had the marked appearance of having been bleached blond from the sun, and I couldn't help but wonder how long he'd been stationed at Froxfield. For I doubted he had achieved that level of a tan under the Wiltshire sun. It seemed more likely he'd served in Africa or Palestine.

"A bona fide war hero," he teased, though I thought I detected something deeper in his tone, something sharp and almost mocking.

Sidney wrinkled his nose. "Now, don't start that."

He chuckled. "You heroes are all the same. Eager for us to forget your acts of derring-do. If I ever earned the sobriquet, you can bet I'd be dining on it for decades, and wooing the ladies with my valiant tales." His gaze shifted to me. "But of course, if I had a wife as lovely as yours, I suppose that wouldn't be necessary." He offered me a practiced smile. "Mrs. Kent, I presume."

I offered him my hand and an equally calculated smile. "You presume correctly."

He touched it briefly, bowing at the waist. "I'm absolutely charmed." But although his expression said so, there was something in his eyes that was decidedly less enamored, almost as if he was weighing and probing, though I was determined he should see nothing of my realization of this. "May I also presume you are Lady Popham's niece?"

"Have you met?"

"Once, not long after Littlemote was returned to her." He cringed. "I'm afraid she was not very pleased with us."

"She's still not."

"Yes, well, it's difficult to keep young officers out of trouble. Particularly when they begin to feel the thrill and invincibility that the mastering of flight seems to give you." His voice turned hollow as his gaze trailed away. "Followed by the swift realization that you're not." His eyes shifted to meet Sidney's. "When one can feel one's clock ticking down, it's difficult to be convinced to care for anything beyond the moment."

The two men fell silent, a grave acknowledgment of this.

Then Captain Willoughby turned to address me again. "I told your aunt to file a claim for the damages and she would be reimbursed."

"Yes, we also told her as much," I replied. "But my aunt is not the most forbearing of individuals."

"Then I imagine she hasn't taken Mr. Green's death well." He nodded in the direction of the house. "I understand his sister-in-law works as her maid, and I wanted to pay my respects, but perhaps I shouldn't." His gaze searched mine in question.

"I'm sure Miss Musselwhite would thank you for the kindness, but perhaps not this morning of all times," I replied as tactfully as I could. Her visit to her sister in jail had been distressful enough, and Lady Popham was certain to suffer an attack of the nerves if Captain Willoughby showed up at her door, giving the poor maid even more to contend with.

He nodded, if not precisely in understanding, at least in acceptance.

"You were acquainted with Mr. Green, then?" I prodded.

"Yes, he helped maintain the grounds at the airfield. Not the landing strip, but the fences and the landscaping and such. He always seemed like a good sort." He frowned. "Though I know his wife gave him a great deal of grief. Is it true the police arrested her?"

"I'm afraid so," Sidney replied.

"Well, that's a cold supper," her murmured almost to himself.

I didn't correct his supposition that she was guilty, deciding we might learn more from him if he thought we wholeheartedly believed it, too. "Mr. Green didn't work at the airfield at night, did he?" I asked, hoping to lay to rest that question.

"What?" he murmured in distraction. "No. Sometimes I saw him about in the early morning and other times in the late afternoon." He glanced about him. "So maybe he was making his way to the airfield the morning he died. He often began when the sky was still dark, pacing the fence line to search for any spots that needed repair."

Except Mr. Green had left his home at nine thirty the evening before and never returned, and the backfilled holes scattered across this parkland attested to the fact that something else was going on. I couldn't see how any of that connected to the airfield, except by proximity, and yet, there was something about Captain Willoughby I didn't trust.

Perhaps I was being paranoid, imagining a villain around every corner. But my instincts had gotten me safely through dozens of trips under the electrified fence into occupied Belgium and back, it had seen me through four dangerous murder investigations, and it had alerted me to the fact that Ardmore was a villain even before I had proof of it. I was not about to turn my back on it now. Not when the hairs at the back of my neck still tingled with awareness and my nerves felt on edge.

Sidney, on the other hand, didn't seem to feel any similar qualms. He stood with his hands in his trouser pockets, his shoulders relaxed, as he made a derisive quip. But, of course, he had always been good at concealing what he didn't wish to be seen. "I suppose he didn't see any of the ghosts then?"

Captain Willoughby laughed. "Been listening to the locals, have you?" He shook his head. "No more than anywhere else. And the barrow they're so concerned with lies two hundred feet to the north of the airfield property, in some farmer's field. For heaven's sake, the site was surveyed before anything was ever built over it." For all that he affected good humor, it was clear that this persistent rumor irritated him.

"Then the maids need not quake in fear to come in this direction?" I bantered.

"Do they do that?" he asked in disbelief, and then shook his head at their gullibility.

I'd hoped he might mention Minnie—the absconding maid—who it seemed had rendezvoused with her airman lover nearby numerous times, or even Opal; but either he didn't know about them, or he was intent on keeping the matter to himself.

"Well, it was a pleasure to meet you both. Swing by the airfield sometime if you've the mind for a tour." He flashed us another grin. "I'm sure we can grant the intrepid Kents a tour." He turned to me. "And, please, offer Miss Mussel-white my condolences on her loss. I suppose doubly so," he added after a moment of consideration. For if Mrs. Green was guilty of murder, she'd lost not only her brother-in-law, but also her sister.

"I will."

We watched him for a moment as he strode away, and then Sidney threaded his arm through mine and pulled me away. I didn't resist, particularly when I noted that he'd maneuvered our path so that the copse of beech trees stood between us and the retreating captain. Rather than return to the path we'd taken, he seemed to be aiming for a more wooded stretch deeper into the park. I knew then that he had not been as at ease as he'd appeared to be.

"What just happened?" I finally ventured to ask once the apprehension prickling along my senses had retreated, and the sound of cheerful bird chatter in the trees above soothed away some of my tension.

Sidney stared ahead of us, a vee forming between his brows. "I don't know. But something wasn't right. You sensed it, and I sensed it. And that was a good enough reason for me for us to make a hasty retreat."

I inhaled a deep breath of the crisp air. "Yes, but what was wrong?"

He shook his head. "All I know is the next time we go there, I won't be leaving my Luger in the glove box."

"*Will* we return there?" I asked, perhaps naïvely. "Haven't we learned everything we needed to? Mr. Green and perhaps someone else were searching for something. Probably more Roman coins." I frowned and tugged my collar up higher against the wind. "Besides, if those toxicology tests indicate Mr. Green was killed with nicotine, then it's probable the police have it right and Mrs. Green *did* commit the crime, whether she remembers doing so or not."

"And so you'll be content to leave it at that?" Sidney asked doubtfully.

"If all the evidence points in that direction, then yes."

He pulled me to a stop and turned to gaze down at me. "Cut line, Ver. Do you honestly expect me to swallow that?"

I glared at him imperiously. "You know, I am *trying* to be reasonable, but between my parents, my aunt, and you, it seems you *want* me to get mixed up in this investigation."

This gave him pause, and I could tell he was considering my words. "That isn't fair of us, is it?"

"No, it's not." I turned to the side. "Though, I'm not truly cross at you," I admitted. "At least, not since you tried to discourage me from investigating Emilie's disappearance in July. You've come around remarkably well." It was my family who bemoaned my exploits and hoydenish tendencies, stopping just short of calling me a pert hussy.

He stepped closer. "Yes, but I also know what you really did during the war."

I frowned. "And if my mother and aunt knew, they would be even more horrified. They would both probably suffer a fit of nerves from which they would never recover."

"I'm not sure you give them enough credit."

I arched my eyebrows. "I think I give them *too* much credit."

His eyes gleamed with quiet affection. "Well, frustrating as it is, I know you're not going to allow their opinion— unfavorable or not—to stop you from uncovering the truth."

"That's true," I grudgingly conceded, looking up at the stolid block of Littlemote House just visible in the distance between the trees. The variations in its flint roof glinted in the sun. "But we're unlikely to uncover anything more about the nature of how Mr. Green died until those toxicology tests are completed. And we can't dally here any longer when Max is waiting for us."

"Agreed. I know how anxious you are to discover whatever evidence the late Earl of Ryde was alluding to in his letter."

"And collect it before Ardmore or his men can intercept it," I added gravely.

"Then let's leave for the Isle of Wight now. If we hurry, we just might be able to catch the evening ferry. Your aunt can telephone us when the police know what poison Mr. Green succumbed to."

I began marching toward the house. "And this time, I'll make it clear to Aunt Ernestine that she's to contact us, *not* my parents, if there are further developments or she has need of us."

"Best inform Miles of that, too."

I tossed an arch smile over my shoulder in recognition of the fact that the butler handled making whatever telephone calls my aunt wished to make, before passing her the device. "Good point."

CHAPTER 16

We pulled into the long drive leading up to Nettlestone Hall just as the last colors of sunset began to fade from the horizon, leaving a brilliant inky-blue sky. The canopy of beech trees overhead, their brilliant leaves muted to shades of gray, soon gave way to the wide expanse of the heavens, where the brightest stars had begun to wink through the firmament. Bright white fences bordered the lane, pointing like arrows to the sprawling limestone manor at the end.

"Mind the hounds," I reminded Sidney perhaps unnecessarily, as he'd already begun to apply the brakes to his speeding Pierce-Arrow. Like all good British gentlemen, he possessed a fondness for dogs, and Max's two caramel-coated bloodhounds had quickly wormed their way into his good graces during our last visit.

True to form, shortly after he brought the motorcar to a stop before the manor's spectacular arched entryway, the two hounds came bounding through the door to greet us. I was relieved to see Max following close behind them, his hands tucked into the pockets of his trousers and an amused grin softening his face.

"They've been pacing the floor for the last half hour. Must have somehow sensed you were nearby."

Sidney squatted down to ruffle the ears of one of the dogs

while the other circled back to beg for attention from me. "But of course, you did. Clever old chap."

"We would have been here sooner, but we just missed the earlier ferry," I told Max, arching up on my toes to buss his cheek in greeting before lavishing my attention on the other hound.

"Well, I'm glad you arrived when you did." Our host tossed a teasing glare over his shoulder at the man emerging from house. "I thought Xavier was going to take up permanent residence staring out the windows."

The sight of Alec standing in the shaft of light cast through the open doorway startled me, causing me to momentarily falter in my petting of the smaller hound. I'd not intended for Alec himself to escort Max, or for them to interact. So to find him here, staying in Max's home and gazing at me in that guarded manner, told me beyond a shadow of a doubt, something significant had gone wrong.

"I wasn't searching out the window for *them*," he replied.

And for the second time that day, I felt the hairs on the back of my neck rise as I turned my head to search the darkness settling around us. Out of the corner of my eye, I could see that Sidney had risen to his feet to do likewise.

"Then perhaps we should go inside," he suggested, rounding the motorcar to place a protective hand against the small of my back.

Though disconcerted by Alec's pronouncement, Max recovered quickly. "Yes, please come in." He coaxed the dogs to follow and then led us into the house.

As we passed Alec, he shot me a significant look, one that made Sidney stiffen. I knew my husband couldn't be pleased to be forced into close proximity again with my former colleague. After all, he might have forgiven me for sleeping with Alec once after a fraught mission when I still believed Sidney to be dead, but that did not mean he wished for Alec's continued company. The fact that C had assigned Alec as my handler for the unofficial investigations I'd undertaken for my former chief at the Secret Service was bad enough. But before now, our telephone conversations and clandestine meetings had been, by necessity, brief and usually conducted in an innocuously public setting. This was far more intimate.

Still, I knew my husband trusted me. Or at least, I hoped he did. For I was about to put that to the test.

When Max paused outside the door to the family parlor overlooking the gardens, which I knew he preferred to the formal drawing room at the front of the house, I excused myself, saying I wished to set myself to rights. He directed me toward the cloakroom, and after straightening my appearance and performing the necessary ablutions, I returned to the hall to find Alec waiting for me.

"What happened?" I demanded in a low voice, casting a glance toward the open parlor door, where the rumble of Sidney's and Max's voices could be heard.

"I couldn't find anyone to shadow Ryde under such short notice, so I decided to do so myself."

"Did C know?"

"Yes, and approved it." His dark eyes glinted with unspoken things. "Provisionally."

I bit back a curse, for had I not needed to return to Littlemote, *I* would have been on that train with Max, and Alec wouldn't be standing here. "I'm guessing those conditions got blown to bits, or else you would be back in London. Did Max recognize you?"

One of his eyebrows quirked. "Give me some credit. I stayed well clear of him, while still keeping him in my line of sight." He scowled. "But unfortunately, I didn't know which other men to be wary of until it was too late. A fellow named Basil Scott recognized me, and I him. He worked for Military Intelligence under Charteris and then Cox at Haig's Command in France during the war."

I nodded, trying to follow why the man's name had caused a tightening around his eyes.

"While I've been on desk duty these past few months, C asked me to review a number of files for candidates within the service for potential transfer to the Secret Service, including Scott's." Alec had taken a bullet in his shoulder in July during an investigation when he'd been assisting me and Sidney, and had yet to be cleared for active duty. "And while on the surface it appeared unexceptionable, I uncovered a few discrepancies, and a number of questionable connections and troubling occurrences which appeared to have been swept under the rug." His gaze met mine significantly. "One of those connections was Ardmore."

My stomach tightened. "You think he's working for Ardmore?"

"I *know* he is. He didn't take kindly to C turning him down." His jaw tightened briefly. "He has a temper. And his methods seemed to be cut from Ardmore's cloth."

I swallowed, wondering what precisely that meant. If Alec disapproved of them, they must be ignoble, indeed. "Did he follow you to Wight?"

"Yes, which forced my hand. I couldn't very well leave Ryde undefended. Not with you and C assuring me he was a critical asset. And not when I couldn't be certain how much Scott knew. So I used that ridiculous code word you gave me." His eyes glinted provocatively as a bit of his usual roguish persona showed through. "Thank heavens he knew what it meant."

He was angling for an explanation, but I wasn't going to give it to him.

"I imagine it helped that Max had met you in the War Office and already knew that we were friends and former colleagues."

His lips twisted. "Yes, well, in my opinion, he's a bit too trusting. But I will say he's been jolly decent not demanding an explanation from me or expecting me to tell him more than I can."

I glanced toward the parlor again, unable to disagree with this assessment. Max *was* too trusting. But then, Xavier and I had spent at least part of the war behind enemy lines, where lies and deceit were necessary for survival, and trust was a dangerous commodity. Even Sidney's ability to trust had been shaken, not only by the destructive, foolhardy orders of his higher command, but also the betrayal of some of his closest friends and fellow officers. So in all likelihood, our perceptions were the ones that were skewed. But in this dangerous game of cat and mouse with Ardmore, none of us could risk letting our guards down. Not when the consequences had already proved deadly.

"Well, don't make the assumption that just because he hasn't demanded an explanation means he hasn't already figured much of it out. He knows we worked together in Belgium, and that I've been in touch with C. I'm sure he realizes your following him down here on my behalf means you're in the thick of it." I crossed my arms over my chest, trying to stifle the growing agitation I felt. "And Ardmore must know now, too. That you're helping me." I lifted my gaze, not bothering to smother my next curse. "Blast it all! He's probably already deduced that C is helping me, as well."

"I'm not sure I'd go that far." But the way his eyes cut to the side once again, avoiding my gaze, told me he was as tense as I was. "After all, Ardmore is no fool. He must realize we have him under surveillance. Just as he's had you and Kent being watched."

I struggled not to flinch at this blunt statement. Until two days ago, I hadn't been certain Ardmore was having us watched. But apparently Alec—and C—had known for some time.

"Perhaps he'll believe we merely noticed his interest in Ryde, and so sought him out to discover why."

"Oh, balderdash, Alec! Don't start lying to me now." I turned away, scraping a hand over my face, and then stared up at the painting before me of the defeat of the Spanish Armada half hidden by shadow. "He knows we worked together in Brussels." He'd even gone so far to allude to it in a snide, insinuating way, though I knew there was no way he could have known the truth about what happened. Alec was no tale-teller. And neither was Sidney.

"And if he had harbored any uncertainty about us working together now, my showing up here this evening will seal the deal on that." I turned to face him. "Or am I just imagining that you believe they have the manor under surveillance even now? That the dogs' excitement earlier wasn't due to the anticipation of our arrival, but because Ardmore's men might have ventured closer to the manor?"

"Dash it all, Verity. You never let me dither around the point, do you? Not even when it's for your own good."

"How could that be for my own good?"

His gaze bored into mine. "Because I know what's going on in that brain of yours. You're blaming yourself for blowing my cover. For showing your hand, per se, to Ardmore." He shook his head. "Don't do it, love. It's likely he already knew anyway."

I scowled up at him, hating that he'd recognized the guilt and frustration roiling inside me. That my request for his help had outed him, and possibly my connection with C. That Ardmore should be two steps ahead of us at every turn.

But before I could form a response, I heard Max's voice growing louder. Recognizing our time was up, I arched my chin, telling him this discussion wasn't over, and then brushed by him to stride across the hall toward the parlor.

"Ah, here you are," Max declared, meeting me as I entered. He passed me a gin rickey. "Kent was just telling me about the murder of that gardener at your aunt's estate. Do you think his wife really did it?"

"Early days," I replied as my gaze met Sidney's across the room. It was guarded, and I did my best to let him see the gratitude shining in my eyes for distracting Max while I spoke with Alec. Sidney's eyes slid to the side to peer over my shoulder, and I assumed Alec had entered the room, for that inscrutable mask Sidney donned so often fell back into place.

I crossed the room to stand beside him before the great stone hearth, the warmth of the crackling fire driving some of the chill from my bones. From the items strewn across the tables—glasses half filled with spirits, ashtrays sprinkled with cigarette butts, and even a book turned over open to mark its page—I could tell this was the room Max and Alec had occupied before our arrival. Which made it even more likely the dogs' restlessness was not due to some sixth sense about the time of our arrival, but something else. I surveyed the tall windows looking out over the terrace and the night-shrouded garden beyond, wondering how thick the glass was and how close one needed to be to see inside.

Not wanting to take any chances, I moved forward as non-chalantly as possible to close the heavy pigeon-blue drapes while Alec and Sidney greeted each other. However, Max was not fooled.

"You think we're being watched. Even now," he murmured in a low voice that nevertheless carried to the other men as he came to help me.

"I don't know," I replied, matching his solemn tone. "But I think from this point forward, it would be best to assume we're always being watched."

Though I hadn't meant to flatten the mood, the truth had to be acknowledged. In truth, my comment didn't seem to faze Alec or even Sidney all that much. I knew both men had already been vigilant, to varying degrees. But Max's brow furrowed in a way that made me suspect he was struggling to acclimate to this fact.

Once the formalities had been completed, and everyone

was settled before the fire with their chosen libations, a tray of crudités and sandwiches ordered from the kitchen for me and Sidney, who had not eaten dinner, I decided it was best to leap to the heart of the matter.

"Tell us about the train," I leaned forward to tell Max. It was a rather broad request for information, but as yet I didn't know how much Max knew about Alec, or how much Alec was comfortable telling him. "Oh, and many happy returns, by the way," I added more gently, having recalled that today was his birthday at some point during our drive down from Littlemote.

Max's regard softened, and he dipped his head once in thanks. Then he sank deeper into his cream upholstered bergère chair, a match to the one Alec occupied while Sidney and I perched side by side on the floral print sofa. "From my point of view, it was a rather uneventful journey. There were one or two men who caught my eye as suspicious, but neither of them boarded the ferry at Portsmouth." Max regarded Alec. "However, Xavier here may have a different tale to tell."

Alec's lips quirked in good humor at the wry tone of his host's voice. I'd warned him Max was not unobservant. "There were three men on board the train who were following Ryde. Two boarded the ferry to Wight."

These definitive pronouncements startled Max, for his shoulders twitched upward and his eyes flared wide.

Seeing this, Alec elaborated, "They're well trained. I'd wager all of them worked for some branch of military or naval intelligence at some point."

"So Ardmore is recruiting from within the ranks, so to speak," Sidney remarked, draping his arm across the back of the sofa behind me and propping one bent leg over the other knee.

"It would appear so. And as such, we have no idea what precisely he's telling them."

"He may be painting us the villains of this piece," I expounded.

Alec's mouth flattened into a grim line. "Yes, in fact, I think it very likely."

If so, who knew how far these men would go to stop us. After all, I'd discovered love and pride—be it of people or country—and avenging those ideals were far greater motivators than money or power. And it was far easier to compromise one's morals when the motives seemed to justify them.

"Have you ventured to the site your father mentioned?" I asked Max.

He shook his head. "No, I thought it better to wait for reinforcements, so to speak."

I nodded, relieved to hear this. For once we tipped our hand in that direction, we couldn't afford to leave without the evidence the late Earl of Ryde had declared he'd hidden.

"But I did speak with the men who helped load the *Zebrina*. Xavier and I tracked them down at a pub in Ventnor. It seemed less suspicious that way."

I'd almost forgotten Max's father had mentioned them in his letter. Several weeks earlier, the two men had been the ones to confirm that the late earl had employed them to load casks of wrecked goods onto the ill-fated flat-bottomed schooner, and that the illicit goods were supposedly bound for the Irish rebels. Or so they claimed the earl had told them.

"Did they have anything more to tell you?" I prodded when Max didn't elaborate, but instead reached inside his coat for his cigarette holder.

"They confirmed again that they loaded the opium," he replied while lighting his fag. Then he took a long drag before exhaling a stream of smoke. "But that's not all they loaded. They said there was a crate that was not part of the wrecked goods. That it was stamped with the words PROPERTY OF THE CORPS OF ROYAL ENGINEERS.

Sidney and I shared a look of mutual astonishment.

"Could they tell you anything more about it?" Sidney asked.

Max's face was pale and rather grim. "Nothing except the fact that it was heavy."

I stared down at the ice circling in my drink, trying to fight back a rising sense of alarm. "That must have been what your father was referring to when he said he'd been deceived," I said calmly, though I felt anything but. I lifted my gaze to meet Max's. "Do you have any guesses as to what the crate contained?"

"Well, if the contents were truly from the Royal Engineers, it could be any number of things."

Any number of *horrible* things. After all, the Corps of Royal Engineers didn't just include the sappers who had dug tunnels under the German trenches to plant explosive mines. They weren't just in charge of fortifications, artillery maintenance, transportation, logistics, and communication. They were also responsible for the British forces' experimental technology and weapons development.

"Perhaps," Alec weighed in. "But somehow I doubt with it being smuggled out of Britain under the cover of night that it was full of wrenches or telephone wire."

"A weapon, then," Sidney stated, for all the world as if we were discussing blends of tea and not a deadly armament. But his brooding gaze made it clear he understood the stakes. "Something that could be used against the Irish rebels."

"That, or *by* them."

We all turned to Alec in query.

"I've been thinking about that opium." He squinted, staring into the hearth. "It's pure speculation at this point. We can't know precisely what happened to it after it was intercepted from the *Zebrina* crew. Whether it was taken to Ireland, or sold elsewhere, or dumped in the sea. But the testimony of the sole surviving crewman leads us to believe that whoever stole the cargo and killed the remainder of the crew was Irish, based on their vocabulary." His gaze shifted to meet mine. "We also know that the Irish rebels are desperate for weapons after the bulk of theirs were confiscated following the Easter Rebellion. So what if that opium was traded for weapons?" He turned to Max as his mouth opened in protest. "I'm not suggesting the late earl knew about it, or even Rockham for that matter. But what if Ardmore tricked them?"

We all fell silent, considering his suggestion, and the unsettling ramifications.

Max was the first to speak. "Given the amount of opium we know the *Zebrina* took on board, they could have traded it for a large amount of guns."

"And it might also explain its relation to the box from the Royal Engineers," I added hesitantly. If they were arming themselves for a future revolt, a revolt which was already under way, then weapons of any kind would be greatly desired.

But all of this hinged on one critical point, which Sidney voiced.

"Is Ardmore sympathetic to the Irish?"

"Ostensibly, no. He seems, like most of the Anglo-Irish aristocracy, to abhor the idea of home rule or concessions to the Irish of any kind. But privately, I'm not so certain." Alec's gaze cut to mine again before returning to my husband. "As I understand it, his mother was Irish, the daughter of an Irish banker. And he spent more of his childhood in his maternal grandparents' home than at his father's estate near Cork."

"Then he might be more sympathetic to the Irish than he first seems," I surmised, recognizing he was sharing information from the CX report I'd requested on Ardmore, if the barest outline of it. "Or he might not." I frowned. "There's a big difference between feeling empathy toward someone and committing treason by supplying weapons to them for their rebellion."

Alec acknowledged this by tipping his head to the side.

Max pushed to his feet to refill his glass from the sideboard. "Whatever the truth, hopefully my father lays it all out succinctly in whatever we find he's hidden for me tomorrow."

That would be wonderful, but somehow I didn't think it would be so easy. And from Max's strained expression, neither did he.

"We need to be prepared for opposition tomorrow." Alec's voice was serious, but the glint in his eyes told me he might actually be looking forward to such a thing. "I don't know about the rest of you, but I intend to be armed."

"Do you think these men will resort to that?" Max questioned as he returned to his chair.

"They're under Ardmore's direction." Alec narrowed his eyes at the rug before him. "I don't put anything past them."

Which was a sobering reminder of all we were potentially up against. It left all of us a little lost for words.

On that somber note, a footman appeared in the doorway bearing the tray of food, and soon any plans for the next day were set aside for more pleasant conversation while we ate. But in the back of my mind I couldn't help but ruminate on the fact that this wasn't the first time I'd been left with the impression that there was some history between Alec and Lord Ardmore of which I was unaware. Twice before he'd made comments that seemed to imply he had personal knowledge of Ardmore's duplicity and the menace he posed. In working with Alec in the past, I'd found him to be almost too sangfroid in the face of danger, and at times downright reckless, despite the fact that he'd waltzed among the enemy daily in his role as a German officer. And yet, Ardmore seemed to unnerve him more.

I was still contemplating this when I excused myself a short time later. The past two days had been long ones, and I suspected I would need my full wits about me to tackle whatever the next day brought. The sympathetic gaze Max turned my way also made me suspect I looked in need of rest, and one look at myself in the mirror in the bedchamber Sidney and I would share confirmed it. Dark circles ringed my eyes, and my complexion was paler than normal.

I removed my jewelry and set it on the vanity table before turning to gaze longingly at the bed and the pair of silk pajamas one of the maids had laid out for me. But there was one more task to be completed before I could slide beneath the sheets. I buttoned the coat of my navy-blue traveling ensemble to my neck against the chill of the evening. Then I pulled the heavy drapes closed over the doors behind me before I slipped out onto the balcony, which ran across the length of the back of the manor.

Leaning against the railing, I gazed out over the rambling gardens. Clouds had rolled in from the west, blocking much of the light from the moon and the stars, and rendering everything a flat gray. I wondered if Ardmore's men were still out there, watching us. In the inky blackness under the balcony, I trusted they couldn't see me.

But the flare of the cigarette tip in the darkness to my left was another matter.

CHAPTER 17

"Are you *trying* to give them something to shoot at," I drawled in annoyance as Alec moved toward me.

"Oh, I doubt assassination is on their agenda. At least, not until they've recovered precisely what we're after. And they can't do that until tomorrow." He paused to lean against the railing beside me, flashing me his blinding smile. "It's good to see you, Ver."

Fortunately, Alec's suave charm had never had the same effect on me as it seemed to have on other women. The sole time I had allowed him to tumble me into bed had not been because of his allure or even his attractive features, but because I had recognized in him, deep down, the same war-weary, disconsolate soul I possessed. That, and we'd just escaped the Germans and near death by the skin of our teeth.

"Your report on Ardmore. I know it must have contained more information than that little bit you shared in the parlor. Does he have strong connections to Ireland?"

"Straight to business, is it? No kiss for my cheek like you gave Ryde."

"He and I don't have the same history we do."

"True."

I crossed my arms over my chest. "And you'd likely turn your head at the last moment just to cause trouble."

The corner of his lips quirked and a curious light lit his

eyes. "I probably would, at that," he muttered in a low voice. When I didn't respond, he took one last drag from his fag before pitching it into the gravel below.

"Yes, Ardmore has connections in Ireland. Stronger than it appears at even a second or third glance." He turned his head to stare out into the darkness. "He owns businesses in a number of industries throughout Ireland. Oh, not in his name. But we've discovered he's owner, or part-owner all the same. Has his hands in a number of their banks, as well."

"I knew there must be further reason for you to suspect him of supplying the Irish rebels with weapons," I replied.

He drummed the railing with his fingers, as if his anger or agitation couldn't be contained. "To the casual outsider, it might seem that a downturn in fortunes for the British would be detrimental to his interests. But I can't also help but wonder whether he's biding his time, wagering that an independent Ireland will mean greater profits for his businesses in the long run. Especially if the men at the top, de Valera and Griffith and Collins and such, knew of his private support during the rebellion."

"But wouldn't they wish for his public support? Wouldn't that be more beneficial?"

"No, they're shrewd. Shrewder than most in our government give them credit for." His lips curled derisively. "Sir Basil Thomson and his cronies are playing a bumbling game with the Irish, and it's going to come back to haunt them," he remarked, referring to the newly created Director of Intelligence at the Home Office, overseeing all the intelligence agencies, including C at the Secret Service. I was no fan of Thomson or his maneuverings, and neither was he a fan of me. And the fact that he was friends with Ardmore and Major Davis—the man who was second in command to C and my greatest adversary within the Secret Service—did not help matters.

"*If* Ardmore is working for the Irish rebels," Alec continued. "Then they understand he's far more beneficial to them as a man on the inside, so to speak. He's part of the Director of Intelligence's inner circle, for Pete's sake," he cursed, using far stronger language. He drew a deep breath into his lungs, so that the next words he spoke were calmer. "In truth, I wonder if he's not playing both sides, intending to benefit from the conflict whichever direction it swings." Hunching over, he rested his elbows on the railing and clasped his hands before him. "The Irish may be aware of this, and willing to accept such terms because they have no other choice." He shook his head. "But the British haven't got a clue."

"Except us," I interjected, surprised to realize Ardmore's guile bothered him as much as me.

"And the late Earl of Ryde. And look where that got him."

It was a sobering thought.

I lowered my hands to rest them on the railing as I turned to stand beside him, our shoulders several inches apart. The salty scent of the sea carried on the chill breeze, along with the smoke from one of the chimneys. "Was there anything else in the report I should be aware of?"

"If you want greater detail, you'll have to wait until we return to London. It was too risky to bring it here."

I recognized that now.

"We can meet in a secure location, and I'll let you read it in entirety."

I studied his profile, the tension in his jaw. Alec might have been the best agent I knew, capable of shifting personas with ease and concealing his thoughts from even the most astute individual, but he wasn't inhuman. He might affect a relaxed pose, but frustration and anxiety were difficult to obscure completely. My shoulders were my telling spot, and for Alec, I knew it was his jaw that more often than not gave him away.

"What happened between you and Ardmore?" When he didn't reply, I pressed my point. "It's obvious there's some history between you. I've never heard you speak of anyone like you do him. Not even that horrid oberst who nearly had you arrested."

Because of me. Because the German oberst—the equivalent of a British colonel—had taken a fancy to me during an assignment where I was posing as Alec's mistress in order to help him copy and smuggle out a German codebook, which led the oberst to take a critical interest in Alec. A month later I was secreting Alec out of Belgium before he could be detained and tortured, and ultimately executed.

He seemed to wrestle with himself, making me wonder whether the information was classified, but my last sentiment provoked him to speak. "When I was stationed in Brussels with the Germans, I saw Ardmore's name mentioned in a report."

I stiffened, not having expected this answer.

He straightened from his slouch. "It was not something I was supposed to have access to, so my glimpse of it was brief, but I knew the title was a British one, and so I knew it was important that I get a closer look. Given the type of report it was, if the Germans were mentioning a British lord—one that, at the time, I was unaware of—then it meant one of two things. Either he was being watched, or he was providing information."

"What did you discover?" I asked as a sick feeling of dread filled me, eclipsing my shock.

He shook his head, his jaw clenching. "I tried to get a better look. Risked my neck to do so. But I stole the wrong dossier." His gaze shifted to meet mine. "That was why I was outed. I didn't flee to that safe house because of the oberst—though I suppose he might have been closing in on me, as well—but because the dossier I took was missed, and I was under suspicion. Given the hostile atmosphere in the German Army during the collapse in the late summer of 1918, I knew I would soon be arrested."

I stared at him in disbelief, almost more surprised by this than I was that Ardmore had been mentioned in a German report.

Alec reached out to grip my hand where it rested on the railing. "I *told* you that you weren't to blame." His mouth compressed into a tight line. "I suppose I should have tried harder when you guided me out of Belgium into Holland to make you understand."

My breath tightened and my cheeks flushed as the bitterness in his gaze and the hollowness of his tone communicated what he was referring to. "Alec, I . . . I didn't sleep with you out of guilt." I scowled, irritation overriding some of my discomfiture as I pulled my hand from his. "Honestly, I'm insulted you would think so."

The look he gave me then was difficult to read, but apparently he wasn't done making disconcerting comments. "Then why did you?"

"It's complicated," I snapped, wondering why he was dredging this up now. I flung my hand out toward the bedchamber I shared with Sidney. "And in any case, it no longer matters."

But I could see that it did. At least, to Alec. And *that*, perhaps, surprised me most of all. I had never seen this side to the carefree, roguish charmer, but now I had to wonder if it had been there all along. Whether he was that good at hiding it, or if I simply hadn't wanted to see it.

I pulled the collar of my coat higher around my neck, desperate to change the subject. "So you never found out why Ardmore was mentioned in that report?"

Alec turned to stare out over the garden again, his mask of indifference smoothing back into place. "No, but I was questioned extensively upon my return to London."

I'd expected as much. After all, he'd spent six or more years within the German ranks, having been implanted in Germany some years before the conflict began, and so possessed a great deal of information that he might not have been able to convey in his regular debriefing reports written in code and smuggled out of Belgium. However, I could tell there was more he wasn't saying. "About the Germans' logistics?"

"Yes, but I meant about my decision to cut and run."

I frowned. "I . . . I didn't know there was any debate over that. We had intercepted German reports conveying that your identity had been compromised. That's why I went in after you."

"Yes, well, there were some who accused me of losing my nerve. They suggested I could have bluffed my way out of any trouble, as I'd done before." He glanced sideways at me. "One of them was Ardmore."

It was all I could do not to gasp out loud. "That bastard!"

"Yes, quite," he bit out. "Fortunately, in the end, there were more voices commending me than maligning me, and my record stood for itself. Your report and those intercepted from the Germans also helped."

"Did you tell them about Ardmore's name being mentioned in that German report?"

"No, because I could see which way the wind was blowing. It was obvious they would have ascribed it to German Intelligence uncovering Ardmore's position with Naval Intelligence, and I had nothing to prove that wasn't the case. I decided it would be better to keep the information under my hat, so to speak. And C agreed when I debriefed him later privately."

Which explained some of the chief's mistrust of Ardmore, though not all. But C had always reveled in secrets. I doubted he would ever reveal all he knew. Not even to his successor.

"Now, I understand," I told Alec. He'd suspected Ardmore of treason long before I had, and had already tangled with him, if briefly. Which only made me more concerned that his role in helping us had been exposed. "This Basil Scott fellow. How dangerous is he?" I asked quietly, recalling that he'd mentioned suspicious coincidences and troubling occurrences in his record.

"Let's put it this way. If there was a situation, embarrassing or unprovable, in which the powers that be would rather have seen it swept under the rug, Major Scott was their man."

Though he didn't say the word, I could read between the lines. It sent a chill down my spine. "You're saying he was an assassin?"

"More or less."

And he'd been assigned to follow Max here. To what exact purpose, I couldn't say, but my imagination was more than ready to fill in the blank.

I exhaled a taut breath. "Then we all need to be armed tomorrow." I narrowed my eyes in determination. "And we need some type of diversion."

"It will have to be impressive to fool someone like Scott."

"Maybe," I replied, backing away from the balustrade, a plan already forming in my mind. "But maybe not."

"You're not going to tell me," he protested, a note of teasing entering his tone.

"Not tonight."

He exhaled in an exaggerated manner. "Women. Always leading one on."

I laughed softly as I opened the door to my bedchamber and stepped inside, closing it carefully behind me before sliding through the part in the drapes to emit as little light as possible to the outside.

It was the wrong way to enter, particularly as Sidney sat in a chair near the hearth directly in front of me. It might have been better had I sported a scowl, one to match his brooding stare as he blew out a stream of smoke from his cigarette, watching me slink inside.

For a moment, I felt a prick of shame, as if I'd wronged him all over again. But then it was overridden by a surge of anger that he should make me feel that way. "Oh, don't look at me like that," I replied as lightly as I could manage. "You know I was merely getting the full report from him on Ardmore and his men."

"Quite the cozy debriefing," he sneered.

"We could hardly stand ten feet apart if we didn't wish

to be overheard," I replied as I unfastened the belt and then began to undo the buttons down the center of my coat.

"Perhaps, but I don't believe he needed to hold your hand while he did so."

I faltered. Of course, Sidney would peer out at us at the one moment that could be construed as intimate. "He was trying to soften the blow of something shocking he told me," I retorted, resuming my disrobing. "And as you'll have noticed, I pulled away quickly enough."

"Seems like it could have been quicker."

I turned to glare at him, planting my hands on my hips. "Why are you questioning me? I thought we'd moved past this."

He exhaled another stream of smoke. "It's difficult to move past anything when you stumble across the man who slept with your wife holding her hand."

"Let's not forget the part where you allowed her to believe you were *dead* for fifteen months," I countered. "That's an important distinction."

"I'm aware," he practically growled, as he pushed to his feet, pitching his cigarette butt in the fireplace.

"Were you or were you not perfectly aware that I was going to be speaking to Alec privately when I retired from the parlor?"

"I had a hunch."

"Of course, you did," I said, refusing to let him play coy. "Because I *expected* you to know. Expected you to know and trust me doing so." I searched his face for any sign of yielding. "Was I wrong? Do you *not* trust me?"

He halted a foot in front of me, his eyes scouring my features. "You're not wrong, Ver. I *do* trust you." His brow crinkled. "It's Xavier I don't trust."

I sighed. "There's nothing between us, you know."

He lifted his hand to touch my face, murmuring almost resignedly. "Ah, but there is, Ver."

I stiffened.

"Not like there is between us," he amended. "But it's there all the same." His gaze when he lifted it from where he had been watching his fingers trace the skin of my cheek wasn't accusing, but rather melancholy.

It caused an answering ache in my chest, for I was beginning to understand what he meant. Just as I'd had to accept that there were things I could never understand about Sidney's service in the trenches, things that Max and Sidney could apprehend without saying a word, the same could be said of me and Alec. My time as a Secret Service agent, the cumulative months spent living among the enemy in the German-occupied territories had irrevocably changed me. And while Alec's clandestine role had been decidedly different, it still gave him insight into me that Sidney would never have, and vice versa.

I pressed my hand over top of his where it cradled my cheek and stepped into his embrace, laying my head against his shoulder. He'd removed his coat and tie, and I could feel the heat of him radiating through his shirt and smell the musk of his cologne. Somehow it seemed that for every step we took toward each other, for every secret we shared, every complication we laid to rest another rose to replace it, forcing us to continually pivot and shift, and sometimes hurdle the impediments that lay between us to reach each other.

"I already know your answer, but I have to ask it anyway." His hand tipped my head back so he could look down into my eyes as I waited for him to speak. "Will you remain here tomorrow?"

"No," I replied simply, already seeing in his eyes that he was reconciled to my involvement, though I could understand his protective instinct.

"Then, I want you to carry the spare pistol I asked to borrow from Ryde."

I couldn't halt the gentle smile curling my lips.

"What's so amusing?"

I shook my head. "The three of you. The fact that none of you are balking at my carrying a weapon when most gentlemen would be shocked and appalled at merely the suggestion."

"Well, you did tell me you know how to fire one."

"I do," I confirmed, smothering the ache that arose from the memory of my brother Rob teaching me to do so. His last brotherly act before he died.

"Then it seems more practical to give you one than not."

I laughed at his furrowed brow. "I'm not criticizing," I told him, pressing my thumb into the shallow cleft in his chin. "I'm grateful."

His expression softened. "Well, I know you're dashed capable, darling. Just do me one favor."

I arched my eyebrows in query.

"Stay close by my side."

I decided that was a reasonable request, so I began to nod, only to bite my lip in hesitation. "First, let me tell you my plan for a diversion."

The following morning, promptly at nine o'clock, Max and I hurried out onto the drive, waving at Sidney and Alec standing in the entryway behind us. We climbed into Max's pale yellow Rolls-Royce, which had already been stuffed with blankets and a hamper filled with food, and set off bowling up the lane. With the men wearing Norfolk jackets in varying tweeds and I a coordinating Donegal tweed suit, we were the picture of the upper class off for a bit of autumn sport and leisure.

However, about two miles down the road, in the direction of St. Helens, Max looked over his shoulder to the space between the two seats where his chauffeur-mechanic hunched down. "Get ready," he told him, allowing the man just enough time to climb into the rear seat behind him before he turned the next corner and then screeched to a halt. We all scrambled from the motorcar, Max and I darted behind a shed near the verge of the road, while the chauffeur climbed behind the driving wheel and set off again at a spanking pace.

Max and I held our breath, waiting to see if Ardmore's men had taken the bait. Several minutes seemed to tick by, though it was likely less than thirty seconds, and then a Vauxhall roared by.

Max and I shared a triumphant grin. We'd suspected Ardmore's instructions to his men had been to follow Max, with perhaps the added caveat that I was to be monitored. So we'd gambled that most, if not all, of Ardmore's men would follow us—believing the picnic supplies our sole attempt at a distraction—rather than Sidney and Alec when they departed Nettlestone Hall in the Pierce-Arrow ten minutes later. On the chance Ardmore's men had two motorcars at their disposal, we'd also concocted another foil. But first Max and I had a short distance to cover.

Once the Vauxhall had disappeared from sight, Max lifted the motorbike from its position leaned against the shed and started the motor, before throwing his leg over the side.

"You do know how to drive one of these, don't you?" I shouted into his ear, perhaps a bit belatedly as he helped me to clamber up behind him.

"Of course."

Once my arms were firmly wrapped around his waist, he pressed down on the throttle, sending us shooting forward and calling into question his assertion. However, once he pulled out onto the road, my confidence in his abilities increased. We drove a couple hundred yards in the direction the motorcars had gone before turning off on a narrower track that led through the woods. This lane was far bumpier than the road, and I pressed tighter to his back, lest I be thrown off. The wind whipped past us, threatening to dislodge my Torin-style side cap, but the extra hairpins I'd used held fast.

When finally we reached another road, we zipped onward to the north, before pulling into the space between a barn and a house. Secreting ourselves and the bike behind the far end, we didn't have long to wait before Sidney's Pierce-Arrow came flying down the road. Breaking hard, he pulled into the gap, concealing the motorcar from the road. Max and I waited once again, peering around the corner at Sidney and Alec seated in the front seat of the roadster. Alec's face was split by a wide grin, and I could tell from the quirk of Sidney's lips that he was also enjoying himself.

Time ticked by, and I was about to suggest that Ardmore's men must not have had the use of another car, when a scrappy-looking Rover suddenly puttered by, its engine gears grinding. Whether it was one of Ardmore's men behind the wheel or simply a resident of the Isle of Wight, we couldn't tell, but I felt another surge of victory as it disappeared down the road. Max and I scrambled into the rear seat of the Pierce-Arrow, and Sidney reversed out of the gap before roaring back down the road in the direction they'd come and then making a sharp right. Max assured us that this lane would connect to a road that ran south and directly through the village of Brading.

The forests and fields of golden crops we barreled by, ripe for harvesting, would have been a peaceful sight if not for the anxiety and anticipation churning inside me. The others seemed to be similarly affected, particularly Max, for they all fell silent as we slowed to pass through Brading. Max had already explained that the remains of the Roman villa lay near the southern edge of the small village.

"The turn should be just after this crossroads," he instructed Sidney. The pole at the corner was covered in more than half a dozen directional signs. To the right lay Knighton and Alverstone, to the left Culver Down and RAF Bembridge, to the south Sandown and the villa.

Sidney located the turn easily enough, and we began bumping down a rough lane. If we had to make a quick getaway, it would be rather difficult. But then our pursuers would be experiencing the same struggle, and I had reservations that the Rover would even hold together over such ruts.

At the end of the lane stood a wooden structure somewhat crudely enclosed with a sloped roof. In many ways it resembled a barn more than anything.

"Most of the remains of the villa are kept under the cover of that building. The mosaics are easily damaged by weathering, particularly in Britain's climate," Max explained as we climbed from the motorcar. He stood with his hands on his hips, surveying the site, his brow furrowed in intense concentration.

"Do you have any idea where your father would have hidden . . . whatever he's hidden?" I asked.

"I don't. But . . . he said to retrace my steps. So I'll try to remember them as best I can."

Considering the fact his tenth birthday had been nineteen years before, that would be no small feat.

He offered me his arm, which I took before glancing over my shoulder to see that Sidney and Alec followed. We entered the covered structure first, strolling through the floorplan of the villa and over the impressive tiled mosaics fitted into the floor. I admit to becoming distracted at a number of places, awed by the Romans' craftsmanship and designs. Animals, geometric patterns, ancient myths, and even a strange cockerel-headed man leapt to life among the dust and dirt of time.

As I stood gazing down at the fragments of surviving mosaics, a memory stirred at the back of my brain. One of me, my brothers, and my cousins playing in the west garden at Littlemote as children. Thomas had wanted to play explorers, and the aim of our expedition was to locate some sort of Roman remains. There had been an argument between the boys over exactly what type. Some of them wanted it to be a coliseum where gladiators had fought, while others wanted it to be a circus for chariot races. However, Thomas had been adamant it had to be a villa.

I couldn't recall now why, only his obstinate face as he went toe to toe with my oldest brother, Freddy, over the matter. It had dissolved into a fight, as my brothers, cousins, and their friends were all wont to do at that age. So I'm not certain we even played at explorers at all. Though I did remember Thomas had given Freddy a cracking black eye.

Of course, Thomas was as temperamental as all the boys, and as the oldest and heir to his baronet father, determined to get his way in all things, but I had to wonder if there was something more to his insistence that the ruins we discovered be a villa. Was he merely being obstinate for obstinacy's sake, or had he known something the rest of us hadn't? It might explain the number of Roman coins found in the grounds nearby. Perhaps even the Anglo-Saxon ones as well, if they had known of and utilized any Roman remains they'd discovered there. Maybe Reg would know. I resolved to telephone him later and turned to focus my attention on the structure covering the site, scouring our surroundings for any worthy hiding places.

Meanwhile, the men examined the stone walls, searching for cracks and breaks in the mortar where the late earl might have concealed something. All while trying to avoid drawing the interest of the handful of other tourists. However, it became all too apparent that Max's father would not have chosen to hide his evidence within such a heavily trafficked area. Not without being certain that someone else would not have stumbled across it unwittingly. So we abandoned the covered shelter in favor of pacing the outer features of the villa. Here luck was with us.

As we stepped out onto the lawn, pausing to gain our bearings as the wind swept across the fields surrounding us already stripped of their harvest, an older man came striding toward us. "I say, Lord Ryde, is that you?"

"Mr. Oglander," Max replied, offering the white-haired gentleman his hand. "It's good to see you."

"And you as well, my good man. It's been some time since I've seen you round this part of the island." His face creased into a good-natured smile. "But I see you have guests. Brought them to see the villa, have you? Well, I would be happy to give you a personal tour." By this, I took it to mean Mr. Oglander was perhaps a curator of sorts, or maybe he simply owned the land on which the villa rested.

"I would like nothing more," Max replied politely. "But unfortunately we are contending with a rather pressing matter." He paused for a brief second, his sharp eyes appraising the other man. "But you might be able to help."

"Of course, what can I do for you?"

"You were a friend of my father's."

"Well, yes, I suppose you could say I had the honor," he replied, almost preening at the compliment. "The late earl was very knowledgeable about his Roman antiquities." He rocked back on his heels. "We enjoyed many an hour of enjoyable discourse on the topic.

"And he visited the villa often?"

"Oh, yes. Four or five times a year. He seemed to like to come with the change of the seasons."

"Do you recall the last time he visited? It would have been a short time before his death."

He nodded his head. "Yes, it was about a year ago, I believe." He turned to survey the site. "Yes, I remember, they were just beginning to cut down the—" His words broke off as he inhaled a swift breath. "Oh, but how neglectful of me. Of course! I know why you're here."

CHAPTER 18

Max blinked in surprise as Mr. Oglander began to search through his pockets, of which he seemed to have many. "You do?"

"Yes!"

My heart quickened at his eager assurance.

"Now . . . where did I put . . . ? Aha!" He extracted a leather pocketbook from the inside of his coat. "I knew I had it," he declared, opening it to begin leafing through its contents. "Your father gave this to me in the strictest confidence. Asked me to keep it on my person at all times. That you would come to retrieve it from me in about a year's time." His fingers finally hit upon the item he was searching for, extracting a folded sheet of paper.

My hopes deflated at the sight of the thin letter. Another clue? For this could not be the cache of evidence we'd hoped for.

Max took the paper from him. "Did he leave any instructions with it?"

"Only that I was to give it to you when you came looking for it." He frowned. "Should I know more?"

He assured his father's friend that he should not and then promised to pay him another visit soon to explain, before hustling us away. We retreated to Sidney's Pierce-Arrow, somewhat more deflated than when we'd arrived. Rather than turn the starter, Sidney swiveled in his seat to join the rest of us in watching Max unfold the letter.

Max cursed. "It's another code."

"May I see it?" I asked softly.

He passed it to me before turning away, fuming in silence.

The paper was wrinkled and worn from being carried inside Mr. Oglander's pocketbook for a year, but the writing had been scrawled in a dark pen, making it perfectly legible. Though it appeared to be nonsense, I could discern the block formation of the text.

"It appears to be the same code as his previous letter, or one very similar," I informed them. "And since George told me how he decrypted the other, I should be able to decipher this one rather quickly. I just need a pencil and paper and a few moments' quiet."

"Back to Nettlestone, then?" Sidney queried of us.

When Max didn't reply, instead continuing to glare out the window, I made the decision for him. "Yes."

Sidney cast one more glance at Max before nodding.

I could empathize with Max's frustration, for I felt it, too. His bloody-minded father might have been worried about whatever evidence he'd collected falling into the wrong hands—namely, Ardmore's—but this dashed quest he'd sent us on was placing us in even more danger. After all, we weren't knights seeking the Holy Grail. And unlike Arthur's knights, we didn't even have the benefit of knowing precisely *what* lay at the end of this search.

But voicing my aggravation would not help Max. Not when he was likely feeling double the exasperation I was. So I remained silent, tucking the letter we'd retrieved into the pocket of my coat for safekeeping.

We returned to Nettlestone Hall in what I suspected was record time, but perhaps my sense of distance had been skewed by the roundabout route we'd taken to the villa in the first place. There was no sign of Ardmore's men, but we all knew they were about someplace. Now that we'd pricked their pride by foiling them, there was the risk that they might be more volatile than before. So, taking no chances, Sidney pulled the Pierce-Arrow as close to the door as he could safely manage, and we all exited on the near side of the motorcar.

Once inside without incident, I retreated to my bedchamber to begin work on the cipher while the men retired to the parlor. I set my handbag, the Webley pistol Max had loaned me still tucked inside, on the desk before removing my gloves and hat and tossing them on the bed. Then I got to work on the code.

Though not precisely the same cipher as the birthday letter to Max, it was a slight variation and, not being a lengthy note, easy to render into plain text. I sat reading the four lines over and over, trying to decide what the devil the old earl was referring to. It appeared to be a poem of some kind, or a riddle. But not one that I could comprehend.

Pushing back my chair, I rose from my seat to take the paper down to the parlor, when I saw movement from the corner of my eye. I shifted to the side, just as an object swung down at my head, narrowly missing me as it crashed into the chair with a loud *thwack*.

Twirling away from my attacker, I reset my balance before striking out with a knee to the man's groin. However, he was too quick, swiveling to the side, so that it glanced off his thigh. I struck upward with the flat of my palm toward his nose, but he pulled me into his body, redirecting the impact to the center of his chest. His greater bulk easily drove me back toward the bed, where he forced me down into the bedding, pressing against my windpipe with his forearm.

Had there been a hard surface against my back, I would have lost consciousness in a matter of seconds. But the yielding mattress both saved me and prolonged the torture as I gasped for air, tugging futilely at his arm. He had the greater leverage, and I had no hope of dislodging him, even as I bucked beneath him with all my might. Flinging out my arm, I scrabbled for something to fight back with, encountering nothing but the leather of my gloves and the wool of my hat.

All the while, his crystalline-blue eyes laughed down at me, his face twisted into a sneer of delight, and I realized I'd seen him before. Not in London or any place in England, but at a temporary brigade headquarters west of Bailleul. This, then, must be Basil Scott. The same Captain Scott—now Major—I had tangled with after delivering that message to General Bishop. They were one and the same.

"I'm not supposed to kill you," he hissed, leaning close enough that his breath washed over my skin. It smelled of onions and American cigarettes, but in doing so, his body had shifted just a fraction, relieving some of the pressure on my trachea. His eyes glinted. "But then, no one is here to stop me, are they, my little traitor?"

Terror shot through me at the realization he might be right. The box or paperweight intended for my head that he'd smashed into the chair might not have been loud enough for anyone to hear. And the cipher had been so swiftly decoded, it was unlikely Sidney would be coming up yet to check on me.

I swept my hand over the bed again beside me, wishing I'd dropped my handbag here, too. Then something pricked my thumb. Clawing with my fingers, I dragged my hat closer, wrestling to extract the hat pin I'd stuck into the side as spots began to dance before my eyes. Once I'd wrangled it free, I struck out with savageness, driving it into the side of his face.

He howled in pain, releasing his hold on me as he lifted his hand to his face and cursed me foully. I rolled, toppling him off the bed before scrambling away from him toward the desk. I nearly stumbled to my knees as I gulped great gasps of air, trying to steady myself as my head whirled from being deprived of oxygen for so long. Yanking the pistol from my handbag, I turned to aim it at Scott, who was struggling to rise to his feet. Blood oozed through the fingers of the hand he clutched over his cheek.

"Stop!" I ordered hoarsely before lowering the gun and firing a shot into the floorboards. I trusted the loud bang would bring the men running. With the pistol once again trained on Scott, I leaned my weight against the desk. "You're the one working for a traitor," I panted.

My words seemed to have no effect on him. In fact, if possible, his eyes only filled with more venom. Though, I didn't miss the way they darted toward the paper at my feet. Keeping the gun pointed at him, I bent my knees to retrieve the decoded message and then grabbed the original from the desk. Experience had taught me how quickly the tables could be turned, so before I could change my mind, I sidestepped toward the hearth, tossing the papers into the fire.

It was then that Scott exploded up from his position, hurling my gloves at me, which must have fallen to the floor with him when we rolled. I flinched, giving him the time he needed to strike out with a blow to my side. I fell to the floor, but rather than attack me, he scrabbled for the papers in the fireplace, apparently remembering his real reason for being here. Lifting the pistol from my position on the floor, I fired into the burning hearth once and then again.

Scott pulled back his hands, hunching as the striking bullets sprayed ashes. His head jerked around at the sound of pounding footsteps approaching down the hall, and he dashed toward the French doors. I hesitated in taking another shot directly at him with the Webley from such an awkward position, not wanting to kill him when we needed him alive for questioning. But by the time I'd sat up on my knees, he was already through the door.

Sidney burst through the door first, followed by the others. "He's on the terrace," I puffed, pointing toward the open door.

Alec set off in pursuit, while Max darted back out into the hall, presumably intending to cut him off from a different direction. Sidney knelt beside me, his frantic gaze taking inventory of my ragged appearance and the blood splattering my tweed suit.

"It's not mine," I told him.

His gaze lifted to the smear of blood Scott had left behind on the door frame, the red handprint stark against the white paint. When it returned to mine, I could see an almost savage light glinting in his eyes. Taking the pistol from my unresisting fingers, he pulled me to him and I buried my face in his starched collar. He held me close, almost uncomfortably so, but when he began to loosen his hold, I clutched him even tighter, and he squeezed me close again.

Several moments passed before I realized I was shaking. "We . . . we sh-should help the others," I croaked.

"They can handle it," Sidney stated firmly, gripping my shoulders to take better stock of my appearance. His gaze riveted on my throat, which ached every time I swallowed. I could tell from the tormented look in his eyes that it must already be beginning to bruise. "Bloody hell! I should have stayed here with you."

"We couldn't have known . . ."

"We should have suspected," he snapped.

I couldn't dispute that, for I was already berating myself for not suspecting Ardmore's men to make such a move. I should have been better prepared.

"What happened?" Sidney asked more gently as he helped me to rise to my feet and then perch on the edge of the bed. But before I could answer, Alec returned through the French door.

"He got away," Alec panted. "Had his cohort waiting in a motorcar on the other side of the stables." His gaze skimmed over me from head to toe. "How's Verity?"

"I'm fine," I replied tersely, lest the men start talking about me as if I wasn't there. "Just a little shaken. Where's Max?"

"Here," Max replied, emerging in the doorway behind Alec. "I was hoping I'd be able to cut him off, but their motorcar was parked closer to the barns than I believed they would dare." He scraped a hand through his dark blond hair, echoing the same frustration it was clear Alec felt. "What happened?"

"I was just coming to show you all the deciphered note when I saw a movement out of the corner of my eye." I nodded toward the pewter candlestick laying on the floor by the desk. "I dodged just in time to avoid that, and then struck out with a kick and a punch of my own. But he overpowered me." My gaze met Alec's as my hand lifted almost unconsciously to my neck. "It was Scott."

"Who's Scott?" Sidney demanded.

"Major Basil Scott. Former Military Intelligence," Alec replied. "He worked for Charteris and then Cox out of Haig's headquarters."

And unbeknownst to me until now, apparently we'd met before.

"Fortunately, I was able to reach one of my hat pins and fend him off."

"Is *that* where he got that nasty gouge down the side of his face," Alec drawled, a vicious smile curling his lips as he shared a look with Max. "He's going to need stitches."

However, Max's thoughts were focused on something else. He strode toward the desk, fanning out the blank papers scattered over the top. "What of my father's letter? Did he get it?"

"No, I . . . I burned it. Along with the translation," I replied. He turned to stare at me in astonishment. "I figured that was better than allowing him to get his hands on them."

"Do . . . do you remember what it said?"

"Oh! Oh, yes," I said, realizing why he was still so stunned.

"I have an excellent memory. Though, perhaps I should write it down again, lest I forget, so we can all memorize it." Moreover, my throat hurt, and I didn't think I could keep repeating myself ad nauseam.

I returned to the desk and began copying out the translation. When I was finished, I sat back, letting the men read over my shoulder.

> On land where Boadicea may have trod, and earth
>   once met the sea,
> Stands a sullen fortress proud, above waves that reach
>   the knee.
> At the point where sails tip the tall tower, with thy
>   back against the flint,
> Beneath the rubble lies a tale so troubled, the wide sky
>   reflects its tint.

Alec was the first to speak, and he didn't spare his words. "Was your father barmy?"

"No," Max replied shortly and then sighed. "Maybe."

"Boadicea was from Norfolk, wasn't she?" I asked, ignoring the aspersions Alec had cast about the late earl in favor of figuring out the riddle.

"Yes, but she and her army also came south to ransack London, remember," Sidney said.

"Yes, but where the 'land once met the sea' seems to imply somewhere near the coast."

"Except England's current coast isn't the same as it was in Roman times," Max pointed out. "And there are almost a dozen Saxon shore forts, stretching from the north shore of Norfolk to Portchester Castle across the Solent, built to defend Roman Britain from marauding Saxons. Much like the Martello towers of the late eighteenth and early nineteenth century were meant to defend the British shore from a French invasion."

"Could it be Portchester?" I asked, since it was so close to our current location.

Max considered the possibility and shook his head. "I don't think Boadicea ever trod in Hampshire."

Alec pivoted to lean his hip against the desk. "Do you have a map of these Saxon shore forts?"

"I'm sure my father did. He has quite an extensive collection of books on Roman Britain in his library." Max turned to stride toward the door, with Alec close at his heels.

I rose to follow, only to feel Sidney's hands fall on my shoulders. "We'll join you in a minute," he called after them before turning me to look up at him. "Are you sure you don't want to lie down? After all, you were just attacked."

I scowled. "If our situations were reversed, would *you* want to lie down?" I countered, hating that my voice sounded so hoarse.

His lips curled into a humorless smile. "No." His hands ran down my shoulders and trailed over my arms to grip my hands. "Then is there anything else I can do?"

I exhaled wearily, realizing he was trying to help. "Have some tea brought to the library." My nose wrinkled as I caught sight of the blood splattered across my coat. "I'll join you after I change." I could only hope someone among Max's staff would have a knack for removing bloodstains.

His gaze trailed toward the French doors. "Why don't I wait with you?"

My stomach quavered at the reminder of what had happened the last time I was alone in this room, perhaps proving I wasn't quite recovered from the encounter after all. "Yes, that's a good idea."

In short order, I had changed into a white voile blouse with pale green collar and cuffs and a navy-blue botany serge skirt, and brushed my bobbed hair, all while avoiding gazing too closely at the dark bruises rising on the skin across my neck and collarbone. After swiping a bit of rose-pink stain across my lips in almost a defiant gesture, I tucked the paper with the decoded text in my pocket and joined Sidney where he stood gazing out the window at the midday sun streaming light over the garden. He stubbed out his cigarette in a pewter ashtray on a nearby table and then turned toward me.

Whatever he saw in my face brought a look of such tender regard to his eyes that I felt my fragile poise begin to crumble.

"Please, don't," I whispered brokenly.

I could read in his eyes that he wanted to pull me into his arms, which would have shattered me completely, but instead he mastered himself for my sake. "All right." His gaze dipped to my mouth. "Who is it you're wearing this for?" he murmured archly as his hand lifted to touch my chin. "It's a dashed nuisance, if you ask me. Makes it difficult to hide what one has been doing, and depending on the shade, with whom." He tilted his head in speculation. "I've changed my mind. I do like it."

I frowned. "You aren't still harping on about Alec, are you? Or Max, for that matter?"

"You seem to have left a trail of broken hearts downstairs."

I glared at him, refusing to respond to that quip, and swiveled to stomp out of the room. However, his arm gripped me from behind, pulling me back toward him. He stared down into my eyes, smiling softly, and I felt my affront begin to melt away. Especially after he leaned forward to press a kiss to my forehead.

"You did that on purpose," I murmured as he threaded my arm through his.

"Did I?" he replied vaguely, and I knew I was right.

I leaned my head on his shoulder as we went in search of the library.

We found it on the ground floor adjacent to the parlor. The door stood wide, emitting the sound of voices and the creak of wood and metal from the ladder Max had climbed to reach the upper shelves. The walls of the room were covered from floor to ceiling with bookshelves in rich oak, save for a fireplace and two tall windows along the outer wall, where cozy nooks had been created, perfect for curling up on a chilly autumn day. The space near the fireplace boasted a pair of wingback chairs, while directly in front of us stood a long table, currently spilling over with maps and two stacks of books. Alec bent over one of these maps, his finger trailing over the surface.

"Here it is," Max exclaimed before descending the ladder, the book already open in his hand.

"Read off the locations of the shore forts, and I'll mark them on the map." Alec flicked a glance up at us. "Kent, come help me."

"Right, starting in northern Norfolk, then. Near the Wash, at Brancaster," Max began, and then rattled off eight more locations, including Portchester.

I poured myself a cup of tea from the pot Sidney had rung for from our bedroom to request it be brought here, and then trailed behind the men as they moved on to mark the forts farther south in Kent and Sussex, looking up only when Max listed Pevensey Castle. I'd forgotten one stood close to our cottage near Seaford. Ignoring their chatter, I refocused my attention on the two forts located in Norfolk and the one in Essex, deciding those were the places that Boadicea was most likely to have set foot.

I frowned. Though, even at that, the timing would have been wrong. If I recalled correctly, the Saxon shore forts hadn't been built until several hundred years after Boadicea's death. But perhaps I was being too literal. After all, she could have trod on the land the forts would eventually be built on. I sighed, kneading my temples with thumb and forefinger, before leaning back over the map.

"How deep is the Wash?" Alec queried, referring to the

broad estuary at the junction of Lincolnshire, Cambridge-shire, and Norfolk bordered by low-lying, marshy fenland, which sometimes sat underwater and sometimes above.

"I should say it varies depending on the tides and your location," Max replied.

"And I daresay, it's altered a great deal over nearly two thousand years." Sidney rounded the table to gaze down at the bay on the map. "Places like that always do." He tapped his finger against the spot where they'd marked the fort at Brancaster. "But parts of it are rather shallow."

"Then, could that be what the late earl was referring to when he wrote about 'waves that reach the knee'?" Alec crossed his arms over his chest, his eyes narrowing in thought. "Haven't they used windmills to drain part of the Wash?"

Max straightened. "You're right. That could be Father's 'sails.'"

I shook my head. "I don't think so." My voice emerged as little more than a croak, forcing me to clear my throat.

"Why? It makes sense, Verity," Alec countered.

"I agree." I pointed to the part of the map I'd been staring at. "Until you see that the second fort, Burgh Castle, over-looks the River *Waveney*." I emphasized the syllables in a way to highlight the earl's play on words.

The men all craned forward to see.

"And Burgh Castle lies in the fens of the Norfolk Broads, which also boast windmills."

"You're right," Alec concurred. "It must be Burgh Castle."

Max looked over his shoulder at the windows. "Then should we set out for Norfolk after luncheon?"

I opened my mouth to agree, but Sidney spoke first.

"After the excitement of this morning, I don't think an afternoon of rest would be remiss. The fort can wait until tomorrow."

Max's gaze darted toward me and then back. "Of course."

"That's not necessary," I replied. "I'm perfectly capable

of travel." This wasn't strictly true, as I was just becoming aware of a number of aches and pains all over my body, and I was beginning to question whether I would be able to swallow anything but soup for the midday meal.

"All the same, we'll set out at first light," Sidney declared, rather high-handedly, in my opinion. But as the other men weren't objecting, there was nothing I could do but relent.

"Has everyone memorized this?" I held up the paper where we'd written the verse, passing it to Max when he asked for it. "Burn it when you're done." I gestured toward the table. "And best fold up that map and put it away, as well as these books." I trusted that if Ardmore's men expended the effort to break into Nettlestone Hall again, they wouldn't take the time to rifle the library shelves.

No, it was far more likely they would bide their time, waiting to strike when we had more information to steal. After all, Ardmore had sent them after us, first and foremost, to recover whatever evidence the late earl had hidden. Though after Scott's vicious attack, I didn't trust them not to use whatever means necessary to achieve their objective, including murder, no matter what Ardmore's directives had been.

CHAPTER 19

I bolted upright, gasping for air, as my eyes searched the darkness.

"Shhh, it's all right, darling. You're safe."

Even without my husband's low voice crooning in my ear, his strong arm wrapping around me, the gray outline of the bed and the commode pushed against the opposite wall would have recalled me to the fact that I was sleeping at an inn in Colchester. But the haze of my dream still clung to me, so much so that if I turned my head I feared I would find myself back on that muddy road outside Bailleul. The smell of blood and earth and explosives still filled my nostrils and clung to the sweat of my skin.

Sidney pulled me close, and while at first I resisted, struggling to return to the present, I soon sank into his embrace. Burying my head in his chest and wrapping my arms around his torso, I allowed him to comfort me, even though he seldom allowed me to return the favor.

Usually, he was the one who suffered from nightmares, his mind replaying the horrors of the war. During bad stretches, sometimes nightly. But rather than endure or indulge in my efforts to soothe him, he preferred to pace our darkened drawing room alone.

I suspected he was the one who actually woke me from my terror, for he rarely, if ever, slept deeply, his mind too attuned to the potential for trouble. Many of the returning soldiers were that way, hypervigilant, as if at any moment they might have to fight for their lives. Which was why when I'd jerked awake, he was already alert and attempting to soothe me.

"The same as last night?" he asked, stroking his fingers through my hair. There was no need to reply, for the answer was obvious. "Replaying Scott's attack?"

At this I exhaled a ragged breath, deciding to be honest. "Not exactly."

"Then what is it?"

I didn't speak, uncertain I wanted to share what was haunting me, whether I wanted to try to put it into words. Wouldn't that make the memory more real? Though, I supposed that was hardly possible. My dreams already felt like I was reliving that moment.

"Verity, talk to me," he murmured softly, coaxing me to look up at him. "We promised to share more with each other."

"Yes, because you're so good at that," I muttered, my nerves frayed.

He smiled humorlessly. "You're right. I'm not. So lead by example."

I huffed in aggravation. He knew I would have a hard time refuting that request. For I did want him to share more, and if I didn't do so, how could I expect him to?

I leaned my head against his shoulder. "I don't know why . . . or perhaps I do," I amended. It did no good to lie. "But I keep dreaming about an incident during the war." Calling it an "incident" was a bit of a misnomer, as it was far more serious than that, but sometimes it was easier to dissemble. "I had orders to deliver a critical message to one of the commanding officers in the thick of the fighting near Ypres. C couldn't trust it to anyone else, for it involved someone from Military Intelligence embedded among the general's staff. So I posed as a French woman fleeing from the Germans' advance."

"When was this?" he asked.

I hesitated before stammering my response. "Late April." I swallowed. "1918."

A month after his reported death.

He stiffened. "Weren't you given leave?"

"A few days." I swallowed again. "I refused any more. I . . . I couldn't handle being alone in our flat. Or anywhere else." My chest tightened, making it difficult to draw breath at the remembrance of those dark days. I'd been drowning in grief, and the only way I could pull myself out was work. "I needed the distraction. It was all I could . . ."

His arms tightened around me. "It's all right, Ver. You don't have to explain. I understand."

I sank against him, wishing in that moment I could stay precisely where I was, within the circle of his arms, and never leave. I inhaled a deep breath, gathering up the threads of my story and my courage. "I delivered my message, and the officer asked one of his subordinates to ensure I made it back to the rear safely. But when we were only twenty yards from the shelter, he suddenly turned on me, demanding to know why I was there. I was trying to fend him off, when suddenly the earth upended around us and we were thrown apart."

Sidney grabbed my upper arms, pulling me back so that he could see into my eyes.

"A . . . a shell had dropped on us."

"Good God, Verity!"

"Hit the shelter square on. Everyone inside was, of course, killed. I believed the chap who attacked me was, too. I-I didn't have a chance to check. I had to take cover."

Sidney's wide eyes scoured my face. "You could have been killed!"

"Yes," I replied. "But at the time, I hadn't really cared."

Anguish tore at his features and he pulled me against him, burying his head in my hair. I could feel his heart beating very fast, and when he spoke again his words were fierce. "Don't ever do that again. Do you hear me, Ver?"

"Yes." It seemed an easy promise to make since the peace treaty was signed. It also didn't escape me the irony of his panic at my experiencing one such incident, when I'd had to endure three and a half long years of knowing he'd narrowly escaped a similar fate as the officers in that dugout dozens, if not hundreds of times.

He exhaled as if in relief, pressing his lips to my forehead for a few more minutes. "Why do you think you're dreaming about that now?"

I lifted my head. "Because the man who attacked me, the one I thought was killed, was Basil Scott."

Sidney's head reared back in shock.

"Quite. At the time I wondered if he might be the member of the general's staff who was sharing intelligence with the Germans. But once the shelling had stopped, I was evacuated back to the rear with the other injured, and I lost track of him. I briefed C on the matter, and he said he'd look into it. A week later I was back in Holland."

"Is that why he attacked you so viciously? Because he thought you could expose him?"

"Maybe." I frowned. "But he was ferocious when he called me a traitor. I could see in his eyes that he believed it, too."

"Maybe Ardmore has him thoroughly convinced."

I dipped my head, willing to concede that.

"Do you think it's related to all of this?"

"I don't know. I don't see how. It's probably just the sight of him again combined with the memory of all that choking dust and rubble thrown on top of me." But I couldn't help the nagging sensation that it was something more. And that something more had as much to do with triggering these nightmares as Scott.

He leaned forward to press his lips to mine. "Don't fret, Ver. We'll figure it out."

I appreciated his vote of confidence and his note of solidarity, but if anyone was ever going to figure it out, it was me and me alone. But not tonight. So I pulled his lips back to mine, striving to forget the rest. At least, temporarily.

I wasn't certain precisely what I expected to find the next day when the Roman fort at Burgh Castle came into view, but it was not this massive, formidable structure. Perhaps it was because all the Roman remains I'd visited in the past were short, and rather insubstantial. Much like the villa at Brading, they'd been excavated from beneath centuries of dirt and rubble, what walls that existed having been destroyed or carted away over the ages for use in other construction. Not so with Burgh Castle.

As we climbed from the Pierce-Arrow and began to wade through the calf-high grass toward it, I realized it still stood to approximately the same height as it had been built, towering over our heads fifteen feet. Its craggy stone and mortar surface still clung together with surprising strength and heft, most of the original terra-cotta tile and flint facings having been stolen over the years. Six rounded bastions protruded from the walls like great fists pounding into the earth, a stolid mass against the endless blue sky.

We paced the length of the walls, searching for the sails of the windmill the late Earl of Ryde's clue had mentioned. As we rounded the northeast corner, I couldn't stop myself from reaching out to touch the structure, its surface feeling alternately sharp and gritty beneath my fingers as I trailed them over the stone. Walking forward a few more feet, the windmill suddenly came into view across the wide expanse where the River Waveney and the River Yare joined. Its black body and white sails formed a stark contrast to the sea of marshy green and yellow fenland beyond.

I paused to stare out at the scene before me, reminded of the landscape south of Rotterdam, Holland. Of the flat expanse of water and sky and reeds, and the soft, wooden creak of the windmills as they turned. I'd traveled those waterways often enough during the war, back and forth from British Intelligence's Rotterdam Station to the border with Belgium. Even the scent of brine and marshy sediment was the same, and the sharp bite of the wind.

"'*At the point where sails tip the tall tower,*'" Max quoted, shifting left and right until he found the right vantage where the windmill's sail touched the bastion as it spun. "Here, maybe."

"Was your father about the same height as you?" Sidney asked.

"Give or take an inch or two."

"But what does he mean by '*with thy back against the flint*'?" Alec queried.

We all turned almost as one to look at the wall. Most of the flint was gone, but here and there a few neatly squared-off pieces still clung to the surface.

"That's a fairly large bit," I pointed out. "Perhaps you're to angle your body so your back is to it."

Max did so, facing almost due north toward a line of stubby trees. "Now what? Do we dig here? Or is there supposed to be some rubble?" He stared down at the overgrown grasses surrounding his feet and the packed earth beneath. It certainly didn't look as if that spot had been disturbed in some time. But appearances could be deceiving.

While the men debated, I tucked my hands in the pockets of my fur-trimmed coat and paced off in the direction Max was facing, wondering if perhaps the answer could be found among the waving grasses. In any case, I needed a moment to myself. Though our drive this morning had been considerably shorter than the day before, having stayed in an inn in Colchester the night before, my body still ached from the hours of driving. The men had seemed determined to make some sort of land speed record, and I'd hardly felt able to complain. Not if I didn't want to find myself deposited at our flat in London as we buzzed through.

Though I didn't want to admit it, I'd been badly shaken by Scott's attack. I supposed it was ridiculous to think Sidney hadn't noticed. Not after I'd woken from nightmares, gasping for air, the past two nights.

The wind stung my cheeks and whipped the curled ends of my hair about my face and neck where they trailed beneath by raspberry cloche hat, but I welcomed the cold. Anything was preferable to the morose fog I felt like I was wandering in. The prospect of finally uncovering the evidence that would prove Ardmore's deception should have excited me, but somehow I knew that wasn't what we were going to find. Not in this desolate, wind-driven place. The late Earl of Ryde would never have cached it in a place such as this.

Perhaps it was my suddenly pessimistic outlook talking, but I couldn't shake the unsettling feeling that we were missing something. Something critical. And yet, I didn't have the foggiest idea what. Max's sister and even that curator Oglander had seemed perfectly earnest. We'd decoded and followed the clues, but there was a broader picture I felt we were missing. Something Ardmore had not.

I lowered my head to sweep the ground with my gaze, determined to find this clue at least. Maybe it would offer a wider perspective. I strolled back and forth in an arc around the spot where Max was now digging with the shovel we'd brought with us from Nettlestone Hall. So absorbed in my thoughts was I that I nearly tripped over the very thing I was looking for. Buried among the grasses sat a jagged rock. I crouched down and began to pull the blades from the ground around it, tossing them to the side. What I discovered there made my heart trip in anticipation.

"Sidney," I shouted. "Max. All of you. Come here!" I continued ripping up the grass until one of them stood over me, and was not surprised when I looked up to find that it was my husband. "Look."

His eyes widened at the sight of the jagged piece of flint,

its waxy pale gray surface appearing almost shiny as the sun-light refracted off it. Max and Alec's reactions were similarly astounded.

"This must be it," Alec said, taking the shovel from Max. He leveraged the flint away from the spot and then began to dig. It wasn't long before we heard the sound of the spade striking something metal.

Max knelt in the grass, scraping away the dirt with his hands to reveal a tin box that had once held Dunlop golf balls. He extracted it from the earth and carefully opened the lid. Nestled inside were a letter and a metal key. The sight of the second object gave me more hope than the first, though I supposed the letter was supposed to direct us to what the key opened.

Alec was less impressed.

"Was your father one of those gentlemen who tormented house guests by making them play parlor games?" he demanded of Max. His dark pomaded hair had fallen over his forehead as he shoveled, and though he'd tried to set it to rights several times, it was now more disheveled than ever.

"No, he despised them."

Alec scoffed. "Could have fooled me." He began to shovel the dirt back into the hole, nearly splattering Max with soil in the process. "Maybe he was one of those secretly contrary fellows, deriding the things he loved most."

Max ignored him in favor of unfolding the letter.

"It's probably in code, too."

Alec was right, but then all of us expected it to be. However, leaning over Max's shoulder I could see this cipher wasn't written in neat blocks like the other two. He'd changed his formula.

"Why don't we retire to somewhere a bit more comfortable," Sidney said, turning his collar up against the wind. "No sense standing around out here now that we've found it."

Alec tapped down the hole and we returned to the Pierce-

Arrow. Max and Alec sat conferring over the paper in the rear seat as Sidney drove us back onto the rough road. Because of the fenland surrounding the River Waveney, we had to swing north through the village of Burgh Castle with its round-tower church to link up with the road traveling south.

As we left the village proper, Max leaned forward to ask me to take a look at the letter. I accepted it from him, though my attention had already been snagged by some familiar-looking buildings in the distance.

"I wonder what that is," I murmured.

"Probably the aerodrome," Alec said. "Heard it was decommissioned a few months ago, along with a few dozen more. Now, I guess the buildings will just sit and rot."

I frowned at the dashboard in front of me. That was the second airfield we'd encountered near a set of Roman remains where the late earl had left us a clue, for I recalled seeing the sign for RAF Bembridge when we were driving to the villa at Brading. Perhaps it was merely a coincidence, but it seemed an odd one at that. How many airfields could there really be constructed within a mile or two from sites of known Roman remains, and yet he'd chosen two of them?

Sidney glanced at me, having evidently noticed my uncharacteristic silence, even if the others had not.

"Max, are you aware of your father's movements in the weeks before he died?" I asked.

Max leaned forward again. "Some of them. Why?"

"Did he go on any trips? I mean . . ." I paused, trying to put my thoughts into words. "If he concealed his letters and that key at these places, then . . . he must have visited them at some point, right?" I swiveled in my seat to look back at him. "But how would he have done so without arousing Ardmore's suspicion?"

Max opened his mouth to respond and then closed it, sinking back in stunned silence.

Alec's dark eyes glinted appreciatively. "Do *you* have a notion?"

"Well, what if he went on some sort of inspection tour of airfields or some such thing," I posited. "After all, both Brading Villa and Burgh Castle have airfields near them. Could that be the connection?"

"I don't know," Max replied. "But I can find out."

I turned forward again in my seat, gazing at the coded message. "Maybe if we knew where he'd been, that might save us time in figuring out where these clues are leading us." I tried to focus my attention on the letters before me, but instead I kept seeing in my mind another airfield. One that might, in fact, also sit next to a site of Roman remains.

But that was impossible, I argued with myself. The incidents at Littlemote and this tiresome treasure hunt Max's father had sent us on could not be linked. Surely, after the unlikely merging of our last two investigations I was merely jumping at happenstances. Ardmore could not possibly have his hands in every pie.

Whatever the case, it was more important than ever that I telephone Reg like I'd planned to days ago and ask him whether any Roman remains had ever been found at Littlemote. If nothing else, maybe he could allay that fear.

I had just convinced myself to set aside that worry for the moment and begun to consider the possible permutations of this new letter's code, when Sidney spoke.

"Everyone, look sharp." His jaw hardened as he gazed into the rearview mirror. "Looks like we've got company." The rest of us turned to see a familiar Vauxhall bearing down on us from behind at a terrific speed.

My stomach dipped. The Pierce-Arrow was already bowling along at a spanking pace, but with the poor state of the road and the marshy ground bordering both sides, Sidney couldn't safely accelerate any faster. That is, until the other motorcar suddenly surged forward and rammed us from behind.

I gasped in alarm as Sidney cursed, fighting to keep the roadster on the road. When the other vehicle nudged forward to slam into us again, he growled, "Oh, no, you don't." We shot forward, outpacing the Vauxhall, though the wheels rattled dangerously over the rough road.

CHAPTER 20

"You have the most rotten luck with your Pierce-Arrows."

I turned to glare over my shoulder at Alec for this ill-timed quip. It was true, Sidney's last Pierce-Arrow had been destroyed during the course of our investigation in Belgium, but now was not the time to remind him of it.

"How on earth did they catch up with us?" Max wondered aloud. "*None* of us saw them following us. So how are they here now?"

I had no answer to that, and it seemed neither did Alec. Sidney was too busy trying to keep us on the road and his rear bumper away from the other motorcar.

I breathed a little easier once the ground on either side of us hardened into firm earth. Now, at least if we careened off the road, it wouldn't be into a boggy water-filled ditch but barley fields. But while Sidney was able to keep three motorcar lengths between us, Ardmore's men also weren't giving up. I gripped the seat beneath me, praying the motorcar wouldn't hit a rock or divot that would send us careening out of control. As excellent a driver as Sidney was, at these speeds even the smallest mistake could be catastrophic.

Then Max said a word I did not want to hear. "Is that a gun?"

The crack of the gunshot that followed was answer enough. Sidney cursed roundly before snapping at us. "Heads

down. Hold on." At this command, he abruptly eased off
the pedal. So much so, that the Vauxhall was forced to brake
hard, lest they slam into us. But just before the vehicles might
have collided, Sidney shot forward again, his tires below us
spitting gravel. This gained us another half dozen motorcar
lengths and ended the gunfire. At least, temporarily. Whether
this was because our pursuers had dropped the pistol or were
wary of more tricks, I didn't know, but Sidney wasn't taking any chances. As we approached the next crossroads, he
seemed to perk up and then made a sharp right turn.

"Have you got a plan, Kent?" Alec asked unhelpfully from
the rear seat.

But rather than bark at him as I expected, Sidney responded calmly. "I recognize where we are. A chum of mine
owns Ravenham Hall, and we used to spend hours racing
motorcars around the property."

"How old were you?" I demanded.

He darted an innocent look at me. "Fourteen. I know the
estate and the roads around it like the back of my hand." He
narrowed his eyes in anticipation. "And I know just where
we're going to lose them." His fingers drummed the driving
wheel. "As long as the gates are open."

I only hoped he remembered that whatever motorcars they
had been driving thirteen years ago would be nothing compared to his Pierce-Arrow. But perhaps he was counting on
that.

We zoomed across the flat landscape and through a series
of shallow curves before making a tight left turn, the motorcar's wheels squealing. Several hundred yards down the road
lined with trees and hedges, we passed a large, weathered
barn before making another sharp turn. A short distance
farther the gates to Ravenham Hall loomed before us. Fortunately, they were open, and we roared past the entrance
pillars and into their leafy park.

I swiveled in my seat, half expecting Ardmore's men to

balk at entering a gentleman's estate uninvited. If they even braked, I couldn't tell, apparently intent on forcing us off the road at all costs. But Sidney was determined not to let that happen. I could see it in his eyes. And while I was clutching the seat beneath me, my insides tied in knots, he was in his element. His shoulders relaxed and a roguish grin even touched his lips.

He bore left at the fork in the drive, taking us away from the main approach to the manor. A series of outbuildings appeared on the left, each grander than most people's homes, though they were just stables and barns. At the end of the row, he darted off on a narrower track to the left, and soon we were flying through a tunnel of trees. With each turn, he gained a little distance from the Vauxhall, whose driver obviously possessed less skill or less nerve, for Sidney nearly sent the Pierce-Arrow careening out of control. However, he seemed to know just when the roadster had reached its limit of capability, riding that edge.

We zipped through a series of curves, forming almost two figure eights, and then shot over a hill to see sky and then water. I gasped, fearing Sidney had misjudged and was about to send the Pierce-Arrow sliding into the pond, but he swung the rear end around just in time, spraying water and pebbles with her rear tires. We sped alongside the pond for a few hundred yards, just long enough to see that the Vauxhall carrying Ardmore's men had not been so lucky, plowing headlong into the water.

Alec let up a shout of laughter just as Sidney swerved back under the cover of the forest. In a few minutes, he'd returned the Pierce-Arrow to the main drive and driven us out the rear gates of the estate.

"Good show, old man," Alec praised, slapping him on the back. "If ever I've need of a getaway driver, I know who to call."

I giggled, partly from nerves and partly from the absurdity

of the statement. "This hardly seems the time to start planning to rob banks."

"Maybe not, but it can't be any more dangerous than tagging along on exploits with you."

"Ardmore does seem remarkably determined to kill you," Sidney bit out, his hands tightening again around the driving wheel.

"Actually, I think it's the opposite."

He eyed me in confusion.

"When Scott was—" I broke off, unwilling to finish that statement. "He said that Ardmore told them not to harm me. I think, in this, Scott may be pursuing his own agenda."

Sidney's gaze met mine briefly, before returning to the road, but I had easily read what he was thinking. He was thinking of the nightmare I'd shared, my memory of that missive I'd delivered and Basil Scott attacking me before a shell explosion sent us flying apart. I knew, because I was thinking of it, too.

We stopped near midday at Bury St. Edmunds to dine at a hotel standing in the shadow of the cathedral. It was a respectable establishment, and after washing my hands and face and setting my hair to rights, I asked to use their telephone. The clerk pointed me toward a booth along the wall near the door. I stepped inside and was soon connected to Littlemote House.

"Miles, this is Verity Kent," I told the butler when he answered. "Could you please bring my cousin to the phone?"

"Of course, Mrs. Kent." He hesitated. "But did you not wish to speak with your aunt?"

"No, it's my cousin I want," I replied.

"Of course. One moment, please."

While waiting, I puzzled over why Miles had asked such a thing. It seemed an odd correction for him to venture, and I'd never seen him treat Reg as more than capable.

It wasn't long before Reg's voice came drawling over the line. "Why, Verity, you've quite shocked Mother by remembering that I do know which part of a telephone to speak into."

"Harassing you, is she?"

"Only when I get called away from the dinner table instead of her. Makes her feel very unimportant."

"Don't be a cad," I told him. "But as it happens, I needed you in particular. Do you recall that time we were playing explorers in the west garden and your brother gave Freddy a black eye because he wouldn't agree with him?"

He chuckled. "I'd forgotten that. But why bring that up now, love?"

"Because Thomas was being so particular that day that we unearth a Roman *villa* rather than a coliseum, or circus, or any old thing. I know he was generally quite annoying about having his way, but it seemed an odd choice for him to take such a strong stance on, and it got me thinking. Were there any Roman remains ever found around Littlemote?"

He hummed in thought. "Can't say that I remember hearing about any, but that doesn't mean there weren't. Do you want me to see if I can find out?"

"Yes, please. That would be extremely helpful." I turned to see Sidney striding into the lobby. He'd been outside bemoaning his dented bumper. I waved at him before holding up a finger to let him know I'd be another minute.

"Of course, you could always ask yourself when you come back down."

"Come back down?" I replied in confusion. "But I'm not certain—"

"Surely you are? We felt certain you'd come as soon as you received Mother's message."

"What message?"

"The one she left at your flat this morning. Didn't you get it?"

"I'm not at my flat. In fact, I'm not even in London at the moment. What's happened?"

"That maid. The one who went missing. She's been found."

My nerves tightened, somehow knowing hers was not going to be a happy ending. "Where?"

"In a shallow grave near the river. She'd been murdered."

My head sank back and I stared up at the dusty ceiling of the booth. And here we'd all thought the girl had run off to London to become an actress. "When was she found?"

"Late yesterday by some boys fishing in the river. Apparently the swell of rain we had last week washed away some of the dirt covering her." He broke off before adding, "The locals have sent for Scotland Yard."

"As they should." Two murders in the same area within the span of a month was definitely sufficient cause to call London.

"But Chief Inspector Titcomb says he still thinks Mrs. Green is the culprit."

"Does he have any reason to do so?"

"Other than pure obstinacy?" he remarked dryly.

"Yes, that."

"He thinks the maid was having an affair with Mr. Green."

"Good grief."

"Apparently she was stepping out with someone, and he's determined to believe it was our man-of-all-work. That Mrs. Green found out and killed the little maid, and then possibly forced her husband to help her cover it up."

I scowled at the almost merry tone of my cousin's voice. "Reg, you are not enjoying this, are you?"

He cleared his throat before replying. "Sorry, cuz. I suppose I forgot for a moment we were speaking of real people and not some ridiculous melodrama at the pictures."

"No harm done. Tell your mother we'll be there just as soon as we can."

"You're not in London?"

"No, Norfolk." I peered around me. "Or is this Suffolk?" I sighed. "We're on our way back to London, and there are a few things we must take care of first. It will probably be late before we can make it to Littlemote."

"Scratch that," he ordered. "I don't know what you've been up to, Ver, but you sound done in. Sleep in your own bed tonight, and we'll see you in the morning."

"You're certain?" I asked, rather looking forward to resting my head against my own pillow at least for one night.

"The dead maid certainly isn't going anywhere."

It was a crude way to put it, but I took his meaning all the same.

"Thanks, Reg."

"Sure, doll."

I rang off and went to tell Sidney the happy news. Another body had been found at Littlemote, but with any luck, the Scotland Yard inspector assigned to investigate would have more of an imagination than Inspector Titcomb, and feel a greater haste in seeing those toxicology tests run.

We delivered Max, along with the key and coded message, to his town house in Mayfair, and Alec shadowed him. They both had their orders. Max was to uncover his father's movements during the weeks and possibly months before his death, and Alec was to mount guard over him and help to locate the late earl's valet so they could question him. Meanwhile, Sidney and I set out for the Albany, where I knew George rented a set of rooms.

I was relieved to find my friend seated before his fire, reading a book, a pipe between his teeth. Part of me had feared Ardmore or his men would get to him before we could, recognizing we might have need of an expert codebreaker. I had tried figuring out the cipher to Max's father's latest letter on our drive from Norfolk, and quickly recognized it was beyond my meager skills. Given more time, I was sure I might be able to decrypt it, but George would be infinitely faster.

After a quick recitation of recent events, he willingly packed a bag and came with us to Max's town house, where I knew he would be safer working than at his far-too-accessible rooms at the Albany. I felt a lingering urge to round up all of my friends and cohorts and take them to Ryde House, but then I wondered if that would simply be playing into Ardmore's hands. If he meant all of us harm, if the latest attempts on our lives hadn't been merely the impulses of the men he'd hired, then I didn't wish to make it easier for him to strike a fatal blow by having them all gathered in one place. Given the half dozen murders we already knew he'd sanctioned, I didn't discount the vile man's capability of committing any heinous act.

Sidney and I were both quiet as we returned to our flat in Berkeley Square. The long days and restless nights had taken their toll, and I wanted nothing more than to retire to my bedchamber and remain there until the morning, but there was much to be done before we set out for Littlemote. Regardless, I knew my mind would never let me sleep for long. It was too busy turning over all the facts we knew and reexamining the questions we didn't. Not to mention my recurring nightmare of what had happened along the road to Bailleul.

Sidney set our bags down next to the bureau in the entry while I removed my hat and gloves and fluffed my hair in the mirror. His valet Nimble wandered in to greet us, and as usual I could hear his clumping approach before I saw him.

"Take our luggage into the bedchamber, if you please. And best start repacking them," Sidney added wearily. "We'll be off again at first light."

"Yes, cap'n," he replied, addressing him as he had when he served as his batman during the war. Sidney had told him numerous times he was merely a mister now, but Nimble persisted in this form of address all the same. It was a peculiar bit of stubbornness from a man who otherwise seemed incredibly compliant.

As such, when he stood his ground, instead of bending to pick up the bags, I looked at him in question. But his gaze was trained on something over my shoulder, and I turned to see our housekeeper, Sadie Yarrow, standing in the opening to the corridor that led to the dining room and kitchen. She wrung the hem of her apron in her hands, at first seeming to dry them and then to buff them to a pristine finish. It was clear that something had unnerved her, and just as clear from the quiet challenge in Nimble's eyes that he expected her to tell us about it.

"Y-you had a caller while you were gone," she stammered, looking up at me through the fringe of her heavily lashed doe eyes. "A Lord Ardmore."

I struggled not to show my shock, for I knew it would only alarm Sadie more, but I was not very successful.

She hunched her shoulders, making her already tiny frame even smaller. "I-I tried to tell him you weren't at home, but h-he pushed his way past me."

"Barreled over her, more like," Nimble grumbled. "Him and his man." His large hands clenched at his sides, and the scar blistering the left side of his face near his hairline stood out white against his pink skin, telling me how much he was repressing his anger. "They musta waited until I left, off to purchase more starch and laundry soap, knowing they could intimidate Mrs. Yarrow." He turned to Sidney. "Found his man in the bedchamber when I returned." He nodded at Sadie. "And his lordship out here bullying Mrs. Yarrow."

"I'm sorry," she mumbled tearfully. "I didn't know what to do, and . . ."

"There's no cause for apology," I told her, pressing a hand

to her shoulder as she dabbed at her eyes with her apron. "Had I even dreamed that foul man would come here, I would have warned you. And Nimble."

"Did they take anything, as far as you can tell?" Sidney asked his valet while Sadie only seemed to weep harder.

"Not that I could tell. But then he scurried out right fast when he caught sight of me." He rolled his broad shoulders. "There are *some* advantages to bein' this size."

"Whatever he said to you must have been perfectly terrible," I said, trying to empathize with Sadie.

She nodded jerkily.

"Will you tell me what it was?"

She sniffed and hiccupped. "It . . . it wasn't just what he said. He . . . he tried to . . . to . . ."

"He was tryin' to blackmail her," Nimble finished for her, his glower promising Ardmore retribution for upsetting Sadie so.

As relieved as I was to discover Nimble harbored quite a chivalrous and protective streak, I was more concerned with our maid. For I had long suspected she was hiding something. Something that, with all my own secrets, I'd been content not to pry into. But if Ardmore had been attempting to blackmail her, then he must have uncovered it, and I didn't know what that meant for her if he followed through on his threats.

"Come with me to the kitchen," I urged her, knowing this conversation would be easier conducted without the men listening.

She went with me willingly, with the look of a woman going to the gallows. It made my nerves tighten with dread at what she might have been keeping from me. I sat her down at the kitchen table and then sank into the seat across from her. Late sunlight filtered through the floral curtains, falling across her drawn features.

"I know I promised you I wouldn't pry into your personal affairs."

Her shoulders tensed.

"But if Lord Ardmore is attempting to blackmail you, then I can only assume he discovered something you wish to remain hidden. That he threatened to reveal it if you didn't tell him what he wanted to know about me and Mr. Kent."

Her eyes flickered like a frightened animal.

"Am I right? Was he asking you to spy on us?"

She nodded, just the barest movement of her head.

I cursed Ardmore for the piker he was, intimidating someone as meek as Sadie, simply to get to me. That was lower than low. And I wasn't about to let him get away with it.

"We can help you," I assured her. "But I'm afraid in order to figure out how to foil him, I need you to tell me what he threatened to reveal."

Her hands shook as she lifted them to the edge of the table. She laid them flat against the wood, staring intently at them as if they somehow held the answers.

"I hate that it's come to this. I truly do. But without knowing how he's threatened you, there isn't much we can do short of whisking you away from here."

She looked up in distress.

"And I know you don't want that," I continued carefully, wondering if she realized how much she'd just exposed. "I know you go home to someone every night. Someone that perhaps relies on you to care for them."

"H-how do you know that?"

"It's a logical deduction. I know you value being allowed to live out. That without that perk, you might resign your post." I studied her skittish demeanor. "Am I right?"

Her brow furrowed, perhaps refusing to confirm this in words, though her silence spoke volumes.

I reached across the table to take one of her hands. "Please, Mrs. Yarrow. Let us help you." I could feel her trembling as she considered my offer.

But then she shook her head, pulling her hand away. "No.

No," she repeated. "He didn't actually say . . . outright . . ." She broke off, seeming short of breath. "Maybe he doesn't know."

"And if he does?" I asked softly.

"Then . . . then . . ." She rocked back and forth. "I don't know. But my secrets are mine! You . . . you promised that."

"You're right. I can't make you tell me. I *won't* make you tell me," I spoke calmly, hoping to soothe her agitation. "Perhaps Nimble's interruption will make Lord Ardmore change his mind. After all, he must expect that Nimble has told us. And so anything you might relay to him will automatically be suspect to manipulation by me." My gaze searched her wary one. "Did he tell you how to get in touch with him?"

She sniffled and shook her head. "He didn't get that far."

I turned toward the window, wondering how much of his bullying of Sadie was real and how much for effect. After all, I already suspected him of tapping our telephone. Perhaps his attempt at blackmailing Sadie was merely a ploy to unsettle me, to make me question everyone around me and wonder who was his eyes and ears.

"Then we'll hope for the best." I laced my voice with a hint of steel. "But if he should contact you again, if he should make further threats, I want you to promise you will tell me."

She began to nod, but I wanted to hear her say it.

"Promise me."

"I promise," she whispered.

I figured that was as good an answer as I was going to get. Whatever Sadie was hiding, she was desperate to keep it, and that made me uneasy. I wanted to believe she would honor her promise to me, but I couldn't be certain. Not when Ardmore had already proven to be a master manipulator and blackmailer. I would have to ask Nimble to keep an eye on her.

I pushed to my feet to leave the kitchen when she stopped me. "He left you a message," she murmured. "In an envelope. I set it next to the telephone."

I dipped my head once before retreating. I wasn't actually surprised by this discovery. In fact, I'd initially suspected it when Sadie first told us of Ardmore's visit. But there was a sour taste at the back of my mouth as I approached the entry bureau, one that told me I was not going to like the contents of this missive, whatever they were.

I found it easily enough, and was surprised by the swirling cursive letters. I'd expected something more hastily scrawled, not this dramatic flourish. Sliding the vellum paper from the envelope, I unfolded it to read six words.

Berkeley Square Garden, Sunset. Come alone.

CHAPTER 21

I frowned. A swift glance at the ormolu clock told me it was half past four, and on this mid-autumn day the sun would already be setting around five o'clock. How on earth could he have known I would return in time to meet him? Perhaps we'd detoured toward Littlemote, perhaps we'd cracked the code and moved on to the next drop, what then? Or maybe he'd intended to wait in the garden at the center of our square every evening until I returned. Though that seemed a tremendous waste of time.

I could hear the murmur of Sidney's and Nimble's voices coming from the bedchamber at the far end of the flat, and joined them. "Nimble, when did Lord Ardmore call here?"

He turned toward me attentively. "Just this morning, madam." His gaze dipped toward the letter in my hand, perhaps surmising whom it was from. Sidney certainly seemed to have guessed if the black scowl he directed at the page was any indication.

"Thank you. That will be all," I said, dismissing him.

He looked to Sidney for confirmation and then exited, closing the door behind him.

"Who the devil is that from?" my husband queried once we were alone.

"Aptly worded," I quipped. "But first, has anything been taken?"

"Not that I can tell." His expression turned wry. "Though, I may not be aware of all your hiding places."

Ignoring this, I strode toward my vanity bench. "What of Max's father's letter?"

"I didn't want to check while Nimble was in the room, but the bench doesn't appear to have been tampered with."

I nodded, deciding I would check it myself once I showed Sidney Ardmore's message.

"The devil you are!" he exclaimed as I knelt to flip over the bench and carefully began to remove the appropriate leg. "You are *not* meeting him alone!"

"Of course, I'm not," I replied, darting an annoyed look over my shoulder at him. "Why else do you think I showed it to you?"

These words seemed to tame the fury leaping in his eyes. "But you mean to go?"

I grunted as the leg came loose, and then reached into the drawer of my vanity table for a pair of tweezers to extract the rolled paper from the hollow of the leg. "*We* are going to go. I don't see how we cannot. I want to know what else the bounder is up to besides frightening my maid and ordering his men to run us off the road." Having confirmed the paper was, indeed, Max's father's birthday letter and not some decoy, I slid it back into place. "It's here."

"I thought you didn't believe Ardmore gave those orders."

"I can change my mind," I retorted, replacing the leg on the bench and standing to stomp it back into position.

"Allow me."

I backed away to sit on the edge of the bed while he drove the wood home with two solid kicks. Picking up the letter from where he'd tossed it aside, I stared down at the words with some misgiving. Not that I thought Ardmore would have us murdered in the middle of Mayfair, just steps from our flat, or that he would try to physically harm us, but whatever reason he wished to meet with me, it could not be good. Not for us.

Glancing up, I noted that the painting of bluebells that hung across from our bed was tilted askew. "I suppose it's a lucky thing I was trained not to keep any written documentation if it could be avoided. No letters, no codes, no notes."

Sidney followed my gaze to the wall, and moved to straighten the frame.

"I know there were other agents who ignored this edict, but I always thought they did so to their own detriment." How many times had the German Secret Police apprehended a subject because of carelessness—a report tucked under a mattress here, a suspicious list concealed behind a drainpipe there. Whenever possible, memory was safer.

He sank down on the bed beside me. "Yes, well, be that as it may, it sounds to me like you've frustrated Ardmore. And that could make him dangerous."

"It's not as if he's about to assassinate us in the middle of the street," I argued.

He flashed me a look of irritation. "I never said he would. Such a method wouldn't be Machiavellian enough for him. He's more likely to stage an opium overdose or send us careening off a cliff in the Pierce-Arrow."

I started. "What of the . . . ?"

"Rufus is taking a look at her."

Rufus was employed as sort of our man-of-all-work, performing the duties of mechanic, chauffeur, and any other eventualities that might arise outside our flat.

Sidney removed a cigarette from his case, tapping it against the battered silver as he ruminated. "I told him the old girl had to be ready by morning. Not sure much can be done for the bumper in the meantime." His gaze narrowed on my fatigue-shadowed eyes. "You truly mean to go through with this?"

I glowered at the swirling pattern of the rug below my feet. "We need to know what he knows. And I'd like to hear what sort of misdirection he's going to try to fob off on us."

Sidney's eyes dipped to the high collar of my leaf-green traveling suit. "I've got a few things I'd like to say to him myself."

I lifted my hand self-consciously, knowing the bruising along my neck and collarbone was terrific at this point. "So long as you don't start a brawl. You're unlikely to come out the winner if Ardmore has his henchmen lingering about."

He pushed to his feet. "All the same, take that pistol Ryde loaned you."

"I planned to."

"Then if you're determined in this, we'd best be on our way."

In short order, we exited our building, crossed the street, and entered the gardens through the north gate in the iron railing that surrounded the green space. For once no reporters or photographers were lingering about, wondering why we'd been missing from our usual nightly haunts. They must not have caught wind of our latest exploits. Or Ardmore had paid them to leave.

The tall plane trees that dominated the square had burst into glorious color, their oranges and yellows bright against the purple sky. Though the sun hadn't yet set, it was hidden behind the tall buildings to the west, which cast their long shadows over the grass. We cut straight across the gravel path that ran down the center, mindful of those around us. A number of people still lingered in the gardens, strolling the oblong circuit of the square and relaxing on the benches spaced here and there. Regardless, it was not difficult to pick out Ardmore's men. They did nothing to draw attention to themselves, having been too well trained for that, but I knew their tricks all the same.

We approached the weathered pump house with its Chinese-style roof at the center of the gardens, and to the left I spied Ardmore, seated alone on a bench beneath the overarching limbs of perhaps one of the oldest trees—its trunk was so wide. He didn't look up as we drew near, instead continuing to read whatever story had captured his interest in the newspaper opened before him. His walking stick was propped between his legs. A fashionable accoutrement, to be sure, but I also suspected it doubled as a weapon, the same as it had for gentlemen in the last century.

When he looked up, I could tell that he had been aware of our approach all along.

"Ah, Mrs. Kent," he declared smoothly as I sat down on the bench beside him without waiting for an invitation. "And Mr. Kent." He cocked his head in amusement. "Why am I not surprised you insisted on accompanying her?"

Sidney arched a single eyebrow. "Because I'm no fool."

"Yes, well, if you suspected me of wanting to harm your charming wife, I'm afraid, then, you are. I have no such intentions."

"Tell that to the bruises around her neck."

I hadn't intended to reveal as much, and cast a quelling glare at Sidney, lest he give anything more away.

"Ah, yes. And so we come to the reason why I asked you here." He turned to look at me with his brilliant mossy-green eyes. "I'm afraid I must apologize to you, Mrs. Kent."

Of all the things I'd expected him to say, this was not one of them. I narrowed my eyes in suspicion.

"Major Scott and his cohorts were under strict orders that you should not come to harm, but it appears he elected to take matters into his own hands." His gaze dipped to my collar. "So to speak."

Given the fact that in the past Ardmore had always been careful never to admit anything outright, I stifled the bemusement and anger simmering inside me and instead latched on to his revelation. "So you admit you sent him to follow Lord Ryde?"

"Come now. That's no surprise to you. Yes, I sent him to monitor the situation." His jaw briefly tightened, hinting at his own fury. "*Not* interfere." He crossed his legs, brushing an invisible piece of lint from his trousers as I continued to stare at him in vexed disbelief. "I wished to warn you, for Major Scott is no longer acting under my orders." His eyes searched mine, avid curiosity glinting in their depths. "He seems to have a personal vendetta against you, Mrs. Kent." That he didn't know precisely why was obvious, just as the fact he was asking me to divulge this information without blatantly doing so.

Sidney and I shared a speaking look, both of us thinking of the nightmare I'd shared, the shelling outside of Bailleul. Why would Scott hold a vendetta against me for that? I could understand his wanting to silence me before I revealed whatever damaging information he thought I held on him, but not a vendetta.

Scott's presence in General Bishop's temporary HQ and his attack on me had already been documented and reported to C. Bishop had called him by name, and I was sure he'd been tracked down. If that had been enough to prove he was the traitor within Bishop's staff, he would have been arrested by now.

Or did Scott fear I would remember something new, something I'd forgotten in the chaos of the shelling? Was that why I continued to relive it every night? *Was* I trying to remember something? Something that happened before the shell struck, or perhaps after, for surely it wasn't the explosion itself. That had been the fault of a German shell, and heaven knew, neither sides' artillery was that skilled with their aim. One had to merely look at the pockmarked craters of No Man's Land and the incidence of death by friendly fire from one's own artillery to realize that.

Pushing aside those ruminations, I focused on Ardmore. "If he's no longer acting under your orders, why don't you simply recall him?"

"I'm afraid it's not as easy as that." He turned to stare off into the distance, his hands quiescent in his lap. "You see, he already knows the targets where you are most likely to appear."

That he turned to look at me then, when I was struggling to mask my shock, was a move of pure calculation. Just as the comment that had elicited such a reaction had been. The very corners of his lips had curled upward in almost a feline smile. If he was claiming he already knew which places we were most likely to turn up, then either he had deduced the late earl's pattern before we had or he was lying. But based on the fact that we'd already been puzzled by his men's swift appearance in Norfolk when we'd felt certain we weren't followed, I had a sinking suspicion it was the former.

There was a third option, of course. That Ardmore had been manipulating this quest from the very beginning, sending us on a fool's errand. But he'd spoken of multiple targets, not a single path. Of course, that might just as easily be another bit of maneuvering to convince us to continue to play his game.

"Do you honestly expect me to believe any of this?" I retorted scornfully once a couple strolling past us had passed out of hearing. "From the beginning, men in your employ have been trying to steal the information we've uncovered. And I seriously doubt you limited the latitude of their methods."

He pressed a hand to his chest in mock insult. "Mrs. Kent, you wound me. Why, what joy would I derive from hearing of your being strangled?" His gaze dipped to my neck again. "Especially when our game has only just begun, and you've already proven to be so diverting."

I bristled at this patronizing comment even as my breath tightened at the memory of Scott's arm pressed against my neck.

"Careful, Ardmore," Sidney growled in warning. "Your men might stop me from killing you, but I doubt they could move fast enough to prevent me from drawing your cork."

Ardmore cast him a withering glare. "Such violence, Mr. Kent. Really."

"Oh, yes, I forgot. You hire others to do your dirty work for you."

"Or blackmail them into it," I sneered, thinking of Ada and Flossie from our previous inquiry, and now Sadie.

Ardmore chose not to respond to these accusations, instead returning to the topic he wished to pursue. "As for *stealing* your information, I don't need it."

My mouth twisted in mocking disbelief, but he was not to be drawn.

"Ryde, the silly fool"—he chuckled—"didn't know a thing of importance. And what he did will never connect to me." He pushed to his feet, tucking his newspaper under his arm. "Now, I've done what I can to warn you. It's your choice whether to heed it." He paused, casting me one last glittering look over his shoulder. "But I do hope you won't turn into a muttonhead like so many others and prove me wrong." With this last elusive comment, he strode away with nary a trace of wariness, even though he was turning his back on my enraged husband.

Sidney withheld the urge to do some sort of violence to him, even though the world would undoubtedly prove to be a safer place were his candle snuffed. Instead, he plopped down on the bench beside me, his muscles flexing in frustration. A few minutes passed in which we both said nothing, merely stared off into the falling twilight, both considering the ramifications of his words.

"Do you believe him?" he murmured, breaking the silence.

"I don't want to," I bit out, and then sighed. "But there is a great deal of merit in much of what he said."

Sidney turned his head sideways to look at me. "And that's the danger, isn't it?"

"Yes."

For that was where Ardmore excelled—in artifice and deception. He was a cunning manipulator, making people question even those things they knew beyond a shadow of a doubt to be true, and exploiting people's best and worst natures to convince them to do things they would never have dreamed themselves capable of.

"Then, we're nowhere, except more twisted than before," he replied, letting his head fall back to stare morosely up at the rustling leaves above.

I agreed, though I couldn't halt the feeling that Ardmore had been more honest than I wished.

It being a Monday, I groaned in remembrance that it was Etta Lorraine's night off. As such, neither she nor her beau, Goldy—who was the person I was really after—would set foot in Grafton Galleries. Which meant Sidney and I had to wait until midnight—when Rector's would be in full swing—for our friends to make an appearance.

Located in a cellar in Tottenham Court Road, Rector's was one of the more popular after-hours nightclubs, and its atmosphere was even less restrained. The band sported firemen's helmets, and I'd heard there were whiskey decanters in the gentlemen's cloakroom. The owner of Rector's was forever trying to lure Etta away from Grafton's, and tonight she actually seemed to be encouraging his efforts. She sat back in her gold fringe gown, twirling the end of her long pearl necklace, with a coy smile playing across her mouth as she listened to his patter. If not for the fact that her eyes kept cutting across the room toward Goldy, where he danced with a pert blond, I might have thought she was serious.

Her cinnamon-brown eyes lifted to meet mine, and she all but shooed the man away. "You make a tempting offer, but I shall need some time to think it over. But you can scrounge up a drink for my friend Verity, here, can't you?"

He turned to look at me, smiling wide in recognition. "But, of course. Whatever you like, Mrs. Kent."

I thanked him and requested a gin rickey, before sliding into the chair he'd vacated.

"I shall have a waiter bring it to you *tout de suite*," he murmured with a significant look at Etta, who nodded her head in appreciation. He'd obviously thrown in the French at the end to impress her, since she frequently peppered her speech with phrases and endearments in that language, a habit developed courtesy of her mother, who had been born in Martinique.

When he had gone, she slid her cocktail across to me. "I know you won't mind me saying this, but you look done in, *ma petite*. Best drink this now."

I demurred. "I'm all right."

She arched her eyebrows. "I would ask if you've been dipping too deep in the hard stuff, but I know you can't abide it. And if that stud of a husband of yours was the reason for your lack of sleep, I know you'd be looking a lot happier. So it must be something far less pleasant."

I smiled tightly. "A new investigation."

"And does this one have anything to do with Ardmore?" she lowered her voice to ask.

"Partially."

She shook her head regretfully. "I'm afraid I haven't caught wind of anything in that quarter. Nothing beyond the politics you can read in the papers."

"Actually, I came here to talk to Goldy. I've an aeronautics question for him."

Her shoulders stiffened and a scowl momentarily wrinkled her nose.

I leaned forward, reaching across the table to touch her hand. "Etta, what is it? Did you two have a spat?"

She shook her head, sending her pearl grapevine earrings swinging. "It's nothing, sugar."

"It's not nothing," I protested. "I saw the way you kept darting glances at him."

Though she strove to hide it, I could tell she was suppressing some strong emotion.

"I forgot how dashed observant you are," she retorted, not meeting my eyes. She huffed. "Yes, we had a spat, as you called it. Not that we haven't had the same spat before."

"What was it about?'

She lifted her hand to fiddle with her pearls again. "Oh, just that his mother has been pressuring him to settle down."

My chest tightened in realization.

"He's supposed to find himself a nice, suitable girl, and I"— she flourished her hand over the mocha skin of her arm—"am not."

I hated seeing the pain in my friend's eyes, hated knowing this was the way much of the world saw her. Truthfully, before we'd met during the war, I'm not sure I would have given it another thought either. But Etta and a few other of my acquaintances had shown me how wrong it was to judge and dismiss someone because of the color of their skin. I'd believed Goldy was different, too, but maybe I was wrong.

"What does Goldy say?" I asked softly.

Her voice was brittle. "He doesn't wish to dwell on such unpleasantness. He doesn't know why we can't simply go on as we are."

The waiter chose that moment to approach our table, handing me my drink before slipping off to deliver the other cocktails on his tray. I took a sip, hoping to wash away some of the bitter taste of disappointment. "Then he's a coward," I stated firmly.

Her gaze lifted to meet mine. "Oh, no, honey. He just doesn't want to face reality."

I frowned, surprised by her willingness to defend him.

"Sugar, you know it can't be. It's simply not how the world works." She picked up her own drink, staring down into its contents. "We can wish it was different all we like, but that doesn't change it."

I understood what she was saying, but it angered me all the same. "Just because the world works that way, doesn't mean it's right," I argued.

She scrutinized me and whatever she saw flashing in my eyes made her jaw tighten. "Don't go off on a crusade for me, Verity. And for Pete's sake, don't say anything to Goldy. I can fight my own battles, make my own decisions. I don't need you fighting them for me."

I swallowed the urge to snap back at her, to tell her she was wrong, because she wasn't. This *was* her battle, and her decision. If she didn't want my interference, then I had to respect that, no matter how it rankled. After all, for all my empathy, I could never truly know, could never truly understand her position.

"Then what *do* you need from me?" I calmed myself enough to ask.

She reached across to clasp my hand. "Just this, *bébé*. Just this." Her nose wrinkled as she took a drink. "And a sip of your gin." She shuddered. "This one has grown watery."

I summoned a smile and passed her my glass.

A few moments later, Sidney wandered over, smoking one of his Turkish cigarettes. I listened with amusement as Etta flirted with my husband in that outrageous way of hers until Goldy finally joined us.

"Verity, darling," he proclaimed as he pressed a kiss to my cheek. "You've taken to these new fashions, as well." His gaze dipped to the stunning amount of calves and ankles the gold-beaded hem of my gown revealed. My silk stockings being sheer, they shimmered in the light cast by the chandeliers above. "Though, I must say, you certainly have the gams for it."

I shook my head at this comment, knowing full well he'd been observing Sidney and Etta's banter, and this bit of inappropriate flattery had been prompted by jealousy.

My husband seemed to recognize this as well, though that

didn't stop him from gibing, "Goldy." He tapped him under the chin. "Let's keep our eyes up here."

"Darling, Verity has a question about aeronautics," Etta told him with only the barest trace of rancor in her voice.

"Of course," he sank into the chair next to mine, his eyes shining earnestly. "What do you want to know?"

"If Goldy's about to launch into a discussion of aeroplanes, I think we'd be better off dancing," Sidney teased, knowing full well I'd just introduced his friend's favorite topic.

Etta laughed, taking his hand. "Gladly."

"Forget these philistines," Goldy replied with a broad grin. "What is it you need?"

"It's not so much about aeronautics as a particular airman."

"Oh?"

"A Captain Lucas Willoughby."

This might have seemed a shot in the dark that Goldy would know of the fellow, but the number of casualties among our flyboys had been so horrific that more often than not there was some familiarity among their ranks. And when one's officers largely came from the same class of public school upbringing, they were even more likely to be acquainted.

"Willoughby." His brow furrowed in thought. "Willoughby, you say?" He turned to watch the dancers foxtrotting across the floor. "Young fellow?"

"More of an age with you and Sidney."

"Oh! I think I know the chap," he exclaimed. "Blondhaired fellow. Bit puffed up."

"That sounds like him."

He sat back, scratching his chin with his unscarred hand. "I didn't remember him at first because he was with the Royal Naval Air Service before they were merged into the Royal Air Force. Had an impressive number of aces."

I opened my mouth to argue that the Captain Willoughby I was referring to must have been part of the Royal Flying

Corps before they and the RNAS were joined to form the RAF, for Willoughby's uniform had been that of an officer in the RFC, but then I hesitated. Not all of the RAF personnel had been fitted with new uniforms after the amalgamation. For one, there was a war on, and no time for such niceties when their original uniforms were perfectly adequate. For another, the new pale blue uniform was exceedingly unpopular, and since then had already been redesigned. But should a former RNAS officer choose to switch uniforms, it would have been to the current RAF form of dress, not an old RFC uniform. And yet, Captain Willoughby—if he was the same man—had purposely switched to an RFC officer's uniform.

It was tempting to think Goldy and I were speaking of two different men, but I suddenly felt very certain we were not. Not if Willoughby had a connection to the person I suspected he did. Then it would make perfect sense that he would switch to an RFC uniform in order to mislead any outsiders, including us.

Goldy had been watching my face as I worked through these ramifications. "Does that help?"

"Yes. Yes, it does," I shifted in my seat to face him more fully. "Now, tell me everything you know about him?"

CHAPTER 22

"So you've finally decided to grace us with your presence," my aunt declared in greeting as Miles admitted us to Littlemote House. Her hands clasped before her and her nose arched in the air, she appeared every inch the offended lady. Whether that offense was at our not hopping into Sidney's Pierce-Arrow and motoring down here the moment she telephoned or at my not asking to speak to her on the telephone yesterday, I couldn't say. Likely both.

I leaned in to buss her cheek, still feeling a bit bleary from falling asleep during our drive. "We came as quickly as we could, Aunt Ernestine."

She harrumphed in disbelief, but her expression softened as she examined my countenance. Her gaze slid over my figure in speculation. I knew I didn't look my best, the short nights of interrupted sleep from nightmares having taken their toll, but my high-necked blouse and rosewood travel coat covered my bruises. Whatever thought had entered her head, for once she didn't voice it. "I'm sure you wish to step into the cloakroom and set yourself to rights. But I must tell you first that Scotland Yard is here." She leaned forward, whispering the last as if someone might overhear us. "They insisted on questioning Miss Musselwhite, though I cannot imagine why."

"Because she's Mrs. Green's sister," I replied evenly, removing my gloves.

My aunt fairly quivered with indignation. "Yes, well, I'm unhappy with this Chief Inspector Thoreau all the same."

I shared a speaking look with Sidney. "Thoreau, you say?" We had encountered the Scotland Yard man just weeks earlier during the investigation into Lord Rockham's murder, and I suddenly felt a sense of deep relief to know the sharp, efficient inspector was taking over the inquiries into both murders here.

"Yes, civil enough man. Seems respectable," she admitted begrudgingly. "But I don't appreciate having my home and servants invaded, all the same."

"He's merely doing his job," I told her. "And the easier you make it for him, the sooner he'll be on his way."

She sniffed. "I suppose one must set an example."

"Precisely. Now, allow me to repair myself, and then show us where you've allowed Chief Inspector Thoreau to conduct his interviews."

I was not surprised to discover the room he'd been given was not the most hospitable. The room smelled of must and mold, no doubt courtesy of the water stains marring one wall, and the furniture within was worn and in desperate need of new upholstery. However, given the more squalid conditions under which a Scotland Yard inspector must sometimes conduct his investigations, I suspected Thoreau was not one to quibble over such minor discomforts.

We reached the chamber just as Miss Musselwhite bustled out, her head down and her arms tight by her sides. She gasped as she nearly collided with Sidney.

"Oh, I beg your pardon." Her fretful gaze lightened at the sight of us. "Oh, Mr. and Mrs. Kent. Lady Popham said you were returning."

"How is your sister?" I asked her gently.

She blinked rapidly, her lashes sparkling with tears. "Not . . . not good."

I offered her a sympathetic smile. "Is Dr. Razey looking after her?"

Her brow darkened with anger as she glanced over her shoulder at the inspector, who had risen to his feet at the sound of our voices. "As much as he's allowed."

I met Thoreau's gaze, finding it remarkably unruffled given the discovery of our interference in yet another of his inquiries. But then, maybe he'd already known. "I believe my aunt is looking for you," I told the maid.

"Of course," she murmured, her eyes searching mine before she skittered away.

I entered the room, glancing to the left at the sergeant seated against the wall, a notebook and pencil in his hands for taking notes. I recalled that during my previous interaction with Thoreau, he'd preferred to have his subordinates sit behind those he was questioning, so that the witness or suspect would not be distracted by their scribbling.

Chief Inspector Thoreau strode forward, his coal-black eyes twinkling with something akin to regret. "Mr. and Mrs. Kent, I would like to say it's a pleasure . . ."

"But under the circumstances, it's not," I replied for him without any rancor.

He shook Sidney's hand and then gestured to the threadbare sofa. "Care to enlighten me how you got mixed up in this affair?"

"Aunt Ernestine invited us down to look into some other matters for her, namely, the damage the RAF officers wrought to some of the rooms."

He folded his tall frame into the narrow club chair across from us, his eyes glinting in understanding that what my aunt was truly after was Sidney's influence.

"There was no suspicion of murder when we arrived. Minnie Spanswick, the maid whose body I understand was found two days past, was already missing at that time, but everyone seemed to think she'd run off to London to pursue a career as an actress. Apparently, it was all she ever talked of."

"Who told you this?"

"Miles, and the other two housemaids—Opal and Agnes. And my aunt also informed me that when she'd contacted Minnie's parents they weren't in the least concerned."

His eyebrows arched, making me wonder if he'd been told something different by Minnie's family.

"Opal mentioned something similar. She said something about her not getting along with her stepmother, and it having been only a matter of time before she struck out on her own."

"Don't forget her beau," my husband interjected as he removed a cigarette from his case, before tipping the case toward the inspector to offer him one.

He declined.

"Yes, Opal also mentioned that Minnie had been meeting an officer from the airfield. That they met frequently at the place along the river where Froxfield adjoins the west park." I inhaled a deep breath scented with the aromatic smoke from Sidney's Turkish cigarettes, grateful for anything to mask the damp and must permeating the room. "I've heard the local police have been attempting to pin the maid's murder on Mrs. Green with some nonsense about her husband having had an affair with Minnie, but I'd like to know what evidence they have to suggest such a thing."

"Miss Musselwhite complained of the same thing," Thoreau admitted, crossing one long leg over the other, before straightening the fall of his crisp suit. "She claims there's no way her brother-in-law would ever have cheated on her sister, especially not with someone like the victim."

"Given what I've heard of Minnie, I doubt she would have ever become enamored of a man like Mr. Green either. She was more interested in actors and celebrities. A brave RAF flyboy sounds more in her line." My eyes fell to the side as guilt began to fill me that I hadn't looked into her disappearance more fully. "Truthfully, I thought maybe Minnie's flyboy had helped set her up in London. And I'd wondered if she might be responsible for the few small items that have gone missing from Littlemote House. Whether she'd stolen them to help fund her new life. I suppose such an assumption wasn't fair to her, was it?"

"Well, I wouldn't go so far as that."

I eyed the inspector in keen interest.

He clasped his hands before him, his olive-skinned features tightening in deliberation. "A number of . . . incompatible items were found with the victim's body," he eventually admitted. "Items that seemed beyond the means of a housemaid."

I leaned toward him. "Such as?"

"An ivory calling card case and a porcelain shepherdess figurine."

I straightened. "Those are among the missing items. As well as a vase, a gold letter opener, and a box of old coins. The butler has the full list. But I take it those other things were not found?"

He shook his head. "I'm afraid not."

I frowned. "What of Minnie's baggage? As I understand it, she took all of her possessions with her."

"That has not been located either."

I sank back, puzzling over this new discovery.

Sidney leaned over to stub out his cigarette in a pewter ashtray. "That's why the local police suspected Minnie of having a beau, and of it being Mr. Green, isn't it? Because of the case and the figurine."

He nodded. "They believed someone had given them to her, and the likeliest explanation was that it was Mr. Green."

"Don't you mean the neatest?" I scoffed.

He did not dispute this.

I shifted on the lumpy cushion, trying to dredge up some empathy for Titcomb and his constables. Presumably most of them had known Minnie. It couldn't have been easy to be confronted with her body after four weeks of decay.

"She was buried near the riverbank, I hear?" With an ivory calling card case and a porcelain figurine in her pockets, but none of her other belongings. That seemed rather odd to me.

"In her maid uniform?"

"No, a pale blue dress and a brown coat," Thoreau explained.

"Poisoned?"

"No."

This made me perk up, for I'd simply presumed this was the case when the local police had made such a connection between the two bodies.

"The victim was stabbed in the abdomen by a long, narrow blade."

This changed things significantly, and my sluggish mind scrambled to find purchase as I blinked at the inspector. "That would have made a considerable mess."

"Quite."

Sidney seemed much struck by this, as well. Poisoning was a cool and removed crime, but a stabbing was visceral and immediate, an act in which the assailant literally had their victim's blood on their hands. "Where do you suspect it happened?"

Thoreau's gaze cut toward his sergeant. "We don't know yet, but we're going to begin with Minnie's room. I've given it a precursory search, but I've got some men coming down from London to fingerprint the room and search for any traces of blood. *If* the attack happened there, the culprit cleaned up the blood remarkably well. Either way, we shall know who has been in that room."

"As long as they didn't wear gloves or wipe down the surfaces they touched," Sidney countered.

The inspector tilted his head in acknowledgment. "But most criminals do not think to do such things. And someone packed up the victim's possessions and removed them if she didn't do so herself."

That was true. Which raised the question again, where were they? If they weren't buried with the body, then they must be hidden somewhere, or already destroyed. That had to be considered, as well. But how? When?

I stared somberly across the room at a water spot in the silk wallpaper that bore a striking resemblance to the profile of a unicorn, wishing I'd tried harder to search for Minnie. It was true, no one who had known her seemed to have raised any alarm about her being missing. I could hardly be blamed for that. But nonetheless, I still felt that I'd let the poor girl down. I'd been so eager to write her off and return to what I'd deemed a more important matter—exposing Ardmore—that I'd not done a thorough job. In fact, I'd been distracted and exerting only a halfhearted effort at best in regard to every aspect of the investigation I'd conducted here at Littlemote. How much had I missed because of that? How shoddy had my deductions been?

"As I understand it, the victim was noticed missing sometime around midday on September twenty-first," Thoreau said, his keen eyes assessing me.

I swallowed my own sense of blame, determined to help in whatever way I could now. "Yes, as far as I understand, most of the staff were off duty so that they might attend church services in the village. When they gathered for luncheon, Minnie was not present, and later when she still didn't show up for duty, her room was checked and it was found emptied of all her belongings."

"Did you ask about her at the railway station?"

I shook my head. "I never got that far." I shrugged futilely. "As I said before, no one seemed very concerned that she was missing. No one but Opal, that is," I added for the sake of honesty. "But even she admitted that it was probable Minnie *had* run off to London. I considered asking in Hungerford at the train station, but it seemed just as likely that her officer from the airfield might have driven her."

"The police wouldn't have done much more," Thoreau told me kindly. "Not if there was no genuine alarm about her disappearance or signs of foul play."

I appreciated his effort to assuage my guilt, but I knew from experience it would not be appeased until we'd at least brought the truth to light and her killer to justice.

"Then, I'll certainly want to speak with this Opal next, and then the rest of the staff," Thoreau told his sergeant, who pushed to his feet, going in search of the butler to request these people be sent to him. "We'll need to discover their movements, as well as who may have seen the victim last."

"What of the toxicology tests being run for Mr. Green?" I asked as the younger policeman stepped from the room. "Have the results come back?"

"Not yet, but these things take time," he assured me, relieving my worries that the local police had botched the matter.

"As I understand it, a mark was found on the back of the neck," I ventured carefully, deciding it would be best not to mention my speaking to Dr. Razey, lest I get him into trouble. "One that might have been made with a needle."

Thoreau's eyebrows shot skyward. "I am, as ever, impressed by your ability to come by such information," he remarked wryly.

"I believe the word you're looking for is annoyed, not impressed," Sidney chimed in, reclining deeper in the couch, though in truth it was rather difficult not to slump entirely, as the back of it sagged.

He shook his head resignedly, accustomed to our bedeviling him. "I suppose I should cease being surprised. You convince *me* to talk, after all."

I grinned back at him unrepentantly.

He gave a single bark of laughter, but was too canny to commit to more than the basics. "I've reviewed the autopsy report and will bear all evidence in mind."

I nodded, content that Thoreau would leave no stone unturned. He was, after all, like his name said, very thorough, and in these circumstances, I found that fact comforting.

"Now, then, before Sergeant Crosswire returns." He glanced at the door, his gaze turning shrewd. "Is there anything else I should know about this investigation? Or am I to believe you're only here at your aunt's behest?"

Sidney and I shared a look of mutual guilelessness. Though my conscience smarted to mislead the inspector, I was not at liberty to explain anything I knew about Ardmore, or the late Earl of Ryde, or any of my suspicions that Froxfield and Littlemote might be the location alluded to in one of his riddles. Perhaps even the final one. Thoreau might be with Scotland Yard. He might be a proven ally. He might even suspect my connection to British Intelligence. But he was not a member of the Secret Service or a chosen former asset.

"I'm not sure what you mean," I replied disingenuously.

His mouth pursed as if he'd tasted something sour—like my lie—and I didn't think for a moment that he believed me. "If you say so."

Fortunately, at that moment, we were interrupted by the return of the sergeant, who gestured for a distraught-looking Opal to enter the room. The slight, young maid shrank into herself as she inched forward. At the sight of me, her eyes widened in alarm, and then she scowled as if it was my fault she was being called in to speak with the Scotland Yard inspector.

"Please, have a seat," Thoreau told her, and then introduced himself. I was faintly surprised when Inspector Thoreau did not insist we leave as he conducted his interviews, as he had in London, but perhaps distance from his disapproving superiors and our glaring involvement in the investigation up to this point had decided him in our favor.

She plunked down on the club chair he'd indicated before darting another look at us. The dark smudges that had been under her eyes during out last interview with her were still there, and if possible her complexion was even more pallid. However, contrary to last time, her fatigue had made her testy. "I don't know what they told you, but I don't have anything to do with Minnie's death. Or . . . or Mr. Green's. I've already told the police everything I know."

"No one is accusing you of anything," Thoreau said in a soothing voice. "Nor are we disputing what you said. But I'm afraid I do need you to go over it again for me. It's standard procedure." When still she didn't relent, he tried a different tact. "And I have a strong suspicion you may be able to help me. Will you do that?"

Her shoulders lowered a fraction, and then she nodded.

Thoreau offered her a small smile, one that transformed his face into something quite handsome, and Opal seemed helpless not to smile back.

"Now, let us speak of Miss Minnie Spanswick first. I understand she was a fellow maid, and a friend, at that. I'm sorry for your loss."

She softened even further under this gentle handling, even beginning to sniffle. "Thank you. Yes, I suppose you could call her my friend."

"Tell me about her." He allowed her to ramble on for a few minutes about her friend, and I could practically see his mind culling through the information for any vital details. When it became obvious that much of it was useless, he redirected her. "I understand that Minnie was stepping out with someone from the airfield. An officer?"

At this, Opal's gaze shifted to meet mine and then back. "Yes, she thought it was serious. I don't know about him."

"You met him?"

She fidgeted in her seat. "Yes, once."

"Do you know his name? Can you describe him?"

"Captain Willoughby. She called him Lucas."

I had to resist the strong urge to look at Sidney, somehow having expected this answer.

"He was tall and tan, with blond hair and a thin mustache."

Something he must have recently shaved, for he'd not had one when we'd met him in the west park.

I was now gladder than ever that I'd spoken to Alec that morning before we left London and asked him to look into this Captain Lucas Willoughby, lately of the Royal Naval Air Service and currently part of the RAF. I wanted to know everything there was to know about the fellow.

"Do . . . is that who you think killed her?" Opal gasped, her hands pressing tightly to her rib cage.

"We don't think anything at this point," Thoreau told her. "We're merely gathering information."

"Oh, yes, I see. It's only . . . he was ever so nice, and handsome," she claimed ingenuously, as if amiability couldn't be feigned and the level of a person's attractiveness was an accurate judge of their potential to commit murder. "It was the other one who gave me a funny feeling in my stomach."

"The other one?"

"His officer friend. Said his name was Smith." She shook her head. "I didn't like him at *all*."

What Thoreau actually thought of all this, I couldn't tell, but his expression appeared absorbed. "Did Captain Willoughby or his officer friend ever visit Littlemote House?"

She frowned, considering this. "I don't think so. She always met him at the bridge connecting the airfield to the park."

"And the day she went missing, can you recall what happened? What did you do when you woke?" he elaborated in answer to her furrowed brow.

"I performed my normal tasks: dusting and sweeping the drawing room—"

"Yes," he interrupted her before we were subjected to a litany of chores. "And then?"

"And then I ate breakfast and cleaned myself up for church."

"Did Miss Spanswick attend church?"

"No." Opal scrunched her nose. "She claimed she was getting a head cold like Miss Musselwhite, but I knew she was lying."

"Then you saw her that morning? Miss Spanswick?"

"Oh, yes. She dallied through her normal tasks, as usual. I had to help her finish. And she seemed fine at breakfast. I thought she simply wanted to sleep."

"Is that the last time you saw her?"

Opal's countenance lowered, her irritation dissolving. "Yes, she didn't join us for luncheon. And when Mr. Miles sent me to fetch her from her room, I discovered she was gone, and all her things, too." Her eyes filled with tears. "I know the others thought she'd run off to London, but I *knew* she wouldn't have done so without saying goodbye."

It was true, she had voiced some objection to this theory, though not as strong as that, and she'd come around to accept the others' assumption easily enough. But, of course, memory has a way of twisting itself, and vague ruminations suddenly manifest into unbearable intuitions.

"What did you think happened to her?" Thoreau asked.

"I . . . I don't know. But *something*." I noticed she'd abandoned the ghost theory she'd handed me and Sidney, or perhaps had wisely deduced that the Scotland Yard inspector would not give it credence.

Thoreau uncrossed his legs and then recrossed them in the opposite direction before folding his hands together in his lap. "You mentioned Miss Musselwhite. That she was ill. Did she remain at Littlemote, as well?"

Opal nodded in sympathy. "Had a right nasty cold. Didn't even come to breakfast."

Then Miss Musselwhite might have heard something of

Minnie's movements and possibly those of her killer while the others were gone. At least, she might be able to tell us whether Minnie packed her things herself.

Thoreau seemed content with her evidence, for he turned to the other murder. "Now, Mr. Green."

Her head bowed, as if frightened of what he would say next.

"I have read your statement, which I understand Inspector Titcomb pressed you on considerably." The corners of his eyes tightened in disapproval. "I will not make you recount it again unless you wish to amend it."

Her entire body seemed to exhale in relief. "Thank you," she murmured with a trembling voice. So agonized was the tone, it made me want to do a particular violence to Inspector Titcomb.

"I merely have one question," Thoreau stated calmly. "And do not tax yourself to remember it, but do you recall the clothing that the person you saw was wearing?"

She lifted a shaking hand to her forehead. "I don't know. Gray maybe. Or beige."

The last time we'd spoken with her, she'd told me and Sidney that she'd thought they were wearing black. But I didn't think she was lying. Rather, I thought she'd been pressed so hard on the importance of that single fact that she was desperate to answer. Sadly, if she *had* noted such a thing, the truth was now lost in a haze of suggestion.

"And it was a man?"

"Y-yes?" she whispered uncertainly.

Thoreau offered her a gentle smile. "Thank you. You may go." He nodded at his sergeant to assist her as she struggled to her feet and then staggered toward the door.

I didn't voice my suspicions regarding Titcomb's interrogation of Opal, trusting Thoreau to handle it in his own way.

CHAPTER 23

Any comments on Opal's testimony were suspended by the appearance of Miles in the open doorway. "Chief Inspector, there are two men from London asking for you."

"Good, good," he declared, rising to his feet to stride toward the door.

I deduced this would be his fingerprint expert and someone to analyze the prospective murder scene.

The butler's gaze shifted to meet mine. "Madam, telephone call for you from Lord Ryde."

At the proclamation of this name, Thoreau cast me a speculative look over his shoulder.

"Excellent." I bustled across the room, eager to hear what was happening up in London. I trusted Sidney would follow me or not, as he wished.

Miles led me to an alcove just off the great hall where a telephone had been installed. It wasn't precisely the most private of locations, but it would do.

"Max, darling. What news?"

"George cracked the code, and as we suspected, it was another riddle."

I gripped the earpiece tighter. "Was?"

He chuckled. "Turns out your friend George is handy in more ways than one. He's got a friend who's a Roman scholar."

This did not surprise me given the fact George had been a mathematics professor before Naval Intelligence had plucked him out to work for their codebreaking department. I suspected this Roman scholar was a member of a university's faculty.

"They puzzled it out together, and they feel certain the code is directing us to Pevensey Castle."

My spine straightened. "Isn't that another of the Saxon shore forts?"

"Indeed. In eastern Sussex."

"It's not far from our cottage, actually," I remarked absently while my brain was busily pondering the ramifications.

"Is it?"

"I've been there. It's not always easy to distinguish the Roman remains from the later Norman and medieval work." I worried my lower lip with my teeth for a moment. "The site is relatively deserted." The perfect place for Scott and the rest of Ardmore's men who were in league with him, be it at Ardmore or Scott's behest, to strike at us again.

I wondered why the late earl had picked Pevensey, or Burgh Castle, for that matter. Yes, they were Saxon shore forts, but the Brading villa had not been. Was the only connection between them the RAF airfields positioned nearby? For RAF Eastbourne was relatively close to Pevensey, as was RAF Polegate, an airship station for anti-submarine patrols.

"I've been there as well," Max replied. "Father helped finance an excavation at Pevensey about a decade ago."

Then perhaps that helped explain why Ryde had chosen it.

"But you'd never been to Burgh Castle?"

"No, I'd never even set foot in Norfolk. Except for a house party I attended once near Mundford," he amended. "But that's on the other side of the county."

I tilted my head, contemplating the portrait of one of the Pophams' dour ancestors hanging on the wall opposite, their mouths bracketed and their eyes filled with sour disapproval.

Gazing at it provoked the urge to stick my tongue out at it like a child. Or to behave in a manner that would give the ancestor something to actually disapprove of. Perhaps it was lucky Sidney hadn't joined me in the great hall.

I still didn't understand precisely what connected all of these sites, or how Ardmore had anticipated them. I had my hunches, but I was looking for confirmation. Otherwise, we were just darting across the country, chasing a series of vague clues, and stumbling into precarious situations. Scott had already proven himself to be volatile and willing to take risks. I didn't trust that the next attack wouldn't be so reckless that it was beyond us to thwart or control it.

"Verity, are you still there?" Max asked after I'd allowed the silence to stretch too long.

"Yes, I'm here." I offered Miss Musselwhite a tight smile as she bustled by, carrying a freshly pressed garment.

"What do you think we should do? Should Xavier and I head down there?"

"Have you had any leads on working out Lord Ryde's schedule during those last few weeks?" Out of the corner of my eye, I saw the maid break stride, her quick, sharp footsteps faltering. It was a subtle misstep, one that could easily have been attributed to a stumble, except for the fact that as she resumed her pace, she turned her head as if to look back at me before hurrying on.

"I've been sorting through everything we put into storage from Father's office. His latest agenda is packed in one of the boxes. And I've also managed to track down his valet. I've arranged to speak with him in the morning."

"Good," I replied, having listened with only half an ear. "Then let's wait until after you've spoken to him before we make any moves."

"You've thought of something." He sounded hopeful.

"Maybe," I hedged, not wanting to give him false hope. "It's too soon to say." I frowned in the direction Miss Musselwhite had gone, wishing I knew exactly what that stumble had meant.

"All right. I've trusted you this far, Verity. I'll trust you a little more."

The warm regard that filled his voice pulled me back to attention, making my chest tighten with answering affection. I sank my head back against the wall, cradling the wooden candlestick mouthpiece closer to me. "Thank you, Max."

I heard another voice in the background.

"Xavier wants to speak to you, so I'll pass the telephone to him. But expect to hear from me tomorrow before midday."

There was muffled movement and then a pause before Alec's low drawl transmitted over the wires. "So that's the way the wind blows if we could ever cut Kent out of the picture."

I suppressed a huff of weary aggravation. I'd known it was only a matter of time before he deduced something by observing all of us together. "Why must you always stir the pot?"

"It's not that I have anything against the chap. He's quite the upstanding fellow. But I would have thought he might be too upright for you."

"And what is that supposed to mean?" I snapped, knowing he was deliberately provoking me. He always *had* enjoyed sparring.

"Certainly not an insult to you. But you know how those old admirable types are. They bore one to tears after a while."

I closed my eyes, refusing to debate with Alec the merits of Max's ability to hold my attention, especially when he was bordering into purely fictitious territory. "Xavier."

"Oh, ho. Back to my surname, is it? I must really be in trouble."

There was a bite to this jest I had not anticipated, and I realized in some bizarre way I had hurt him. Though, what on earth I was supposed to do about it, I didn't know. I was married to *Sidney*. I loved *Sidney*. I was not going to apologize for it, let alone contemplate or discuss who my second choice in a partner would be.

But all the same, I deliberately gentled my voice, allowing some of my worry to creep through. "Alec, have you seen any of Ardmore's men lurking about?"

He didn't respond at first, and I could only think I must have caught him off guard. When he did, the taunting tone had disappeared to be replaced with one of mutual concern. "No, I haven't."

"None?"

"None, and to be perfectly honest, I find that to be unsettling. For either the men who are watching us are better than the last crop, or . . ."

"Or?" I prodded when he didn't continue.

"Or they're not watching us."

The implication was clear. Or they were watching me. Me and Sidney.

"Yes, I'd thought of that," I admitted. "But we're taking precautions. The Scotland Yard inspector who's here is a friend. Of sorts," I amended. "He's an ally. So we're not alone." I exhaled a tight breath. "Anything on Willoughby yet?"

"No, but I should hear back from a colleague shortly. Actually, I should probably ring off in case he's trying to telephone."

"Then I'll say goodbye. But, Alec . . ."

"Yes?"

Though there were hundreds of words I wanted to say, instead I settled on just five. "Be careful. All of you." Whether he realized it or not, I'd placed as much trust in him as Max did me, for I was counting on him to keep Max and George safe. I wouldn't have passed that responsibility on to just anyone.

"I will."

Before I could analyze the tone and the slight catch in his voice, he'd hung up.

I set the telephone down and slowly made my way through the house to rejoin the others. But as I was passing the library, a voice called out, addressing me by name.

I smiled. "Reg, you amaze me." I stopped to gaze at him across the large table, where he sat with a number of books stacked around him. "I was walking across carpet and you still realized it was me from the type of shoes I wear?"

His unseeing eyes lifted vaguely in my direction, and the corners of his lips lifted all too briefly. "More your tread. You have a rather light, slightly bounding way of walking. One I believe Mother would declare was a shade too boisterous for a genteel woman."

I laughed. "Heavens! I feel like I've been psychoanalyzed by one of those Freudian fellows. And all by my manner of walking."

"You can learn a lot about a person simply by listening to the way they move." He nodded toward the door. "That Scotland Yard inspector, for instance. He was quite aggravated a few minutes ago when he strode past here."

"Really?" I wondered what that meant about his initial findings in Minnie's room.

Reg's mouth flattened into a thin line. "It might explain why he insisted on pulling my valet away from me for questioning when I had need of him."

I regarded the pages of the book currently open before the chair next to his. "Searching for information about Littlemote's possible Roman villa?"

"And having a dashed time of it without the use of my eyes." He gestured at the bookshelves covering three walls of the room around him. "We have thousands of books, but only three of them are in Braille. So instead I have to rely on others to read to me what I wish to know."

He simmered with frustration, and I couldn't blame him. Had I been in his shoes, I would have felt the same way. And yet I knew if I offered to remove the task from him, it would only make it worse. So instead, I pulled out the chair across from him and sat down. "Tell me what you've uncovered so far."

He blew out a breath. "Well, Mr. Plank, the stablemaster, told me about an excavation that he recalled his grandfather telling him about. One that had taken place in his grandfather's *grandfather's* day."

"So, what?" I quickly did the math. "The early eighteenth century?"

"As near as we could figure, yes. His grandfather claimed that a spectacular mosaic was uncovered, part of the remains of a Roman villa. That a replica of the mosaic was even embroidered on a tapestry. But for *some* reason the mosaic and the remains of the villa were reburied, and the exact location lost to time," his voice snapped with renewed annoyance.

"It must have been to protect it," I told him. "Mosaics that are exposed to the elements—sun, wind, rain, cold—crack, fade, and deteriorate." I'd learned as much from seeing the mosaics under cover at Brading.

"Be that as it may, the fact that the site was lost is baffling to me. Wouldn't a plow be just as destructive?"

"Of course, it would," I remarked in a quelling voice. "And if this tale of Mr. Plank's is true, then it seems inexcusable to me, as well. But surely he must have had some vague idea of the location."

His teeth flashed in a toothy grin. "Why, haven't you guessed, dear cousin? The west park."

I could tell he'd enjoyed delivering that bit of news, though his aggravation still shone through.

He slapped the table. "Now, if I could just confirm it."

I turned to glance at the charred section of rug in the far corner, courtesy of the airmen. I wondered why Mr. Plank hadn't mentioned the Roman villa when I'd asked him if there was anything else noteworthy about the west park. Unless it had slipped his mind. After all, if the excavation had taken place some two hundred years ago, it was unlikely to be in his immediate thoughts. "What about the tapestry he mentioned?"

"I've asked Mr. Miles to try to locate it among the attics, but I haven't much hope of finding it."

I reached across the table to squeeze his hand. "Well, thank you, nonetheless. I know this may come to nothing, but it also might be the exact clue we're looking for."

"I don't see it." He tipped his head back, the lines at the edge of his mouth softening. "But maybe I'm not supposed to."

I wished I could tell him more, but I couldn't. I thought that might make him angry, but instead his entire face broke into a smile.

"I'll take that as a yes, then. You are a puzzle, Ver. A good one."

"Thank you, Reg."

He waved off my gratitude. "Now, go on. Here comes Hatter."

I turned toward the door, but it was several moments later before his bespectacled valet ambled into the room.

Reg's smile remained at my incredulous silence.

"A cat, that's what you are," I pronounced.

He laughed. "I shall let you know when we uncover something."

Much of the afternoon was spent in a series of long and tedious interviews with the various members of my aunt's staff. As I squirmed in my seat for perhaps the tenth time, trying to find a comfortable position, I wondered at Thoreau's whip-straight posture. Perhaps his chair happened to be better padded than this sagging sofa, but somehow I doubted it. Maybe learning to sit for hours in a lumpy chair had been part of his police training.

Sidney, on the other hand, had always had the remarkable ability of making himself comfortable anywhere. I imagined that had served him well during the war, and I was grateful for it. But just in that moment I couldn't help casting an aggrieved scowl his way. At this look, he arched his eyebrows in query, but I turned away, shoving a threadbare pillow behind my back.

He leaned closer to murmur in my ear in a low voice as I was trying to listen to the chauffeur's responses to the questions put to him. "I would offer to let you sit on my lap, but somehow I think that would be distracting to the others."

I cast him a quelling look out of the corner of my eye, though it did nothing to wipe the arch smile lingering about his mouth. However, the chauffeur's next words succeeded where I hadn't.

"Aye, Mr. Green was verra interested in Mr. Kent's arrival. Said he wished to speak wi' him, but he left before he had the chance. And by the time he returned . . ." He shrugged. "It was too late."

This was the first we'd heard of Mr. Green taking any interest in us. But why? Was it because of our celebrity and Sidney's being placed on a pedestal as a war hero? Somehow I didn't think that was right. Unless he was interested in Sidney's status as a war hero for another reason.

Thoreau seemed to be mulling through these same implications. "Did he tell you *why* he wished to speak with him?"

The lean, tawny-haired driver shrugged again before answering in his Scottish brogue. "I dinna ken if there was a reason. Though he did seem particularly keen on it." He fingered the brim of the cap resting in his lap, seeming to choose his words with care. "Mr. Green kept to himself. He wasna rude or unkind, he just dinna like to jabber. 'Cept sometimes to Mr. Plank." He smiled reflexively. "But then he wasna doin' much o' the talkin'."

I grinned in acknowledgment of the stablemaster's garrulousness.

"Oh, and sometimes you'd see him speakin' to his sister-in-law, Miss Musselwhite. But I gather that was family business."

I'd wondered how close Miss Musselwhite was to Mr. Green. Given Mrs. Green's worrying predilection to alcohol, as the chauffeur alluded to, it would have been a wonder if they hadn't sought each other's support in dealing with it.

"What of the other maids?" Thoreau slid the question in smoothly. "Did he ever interact with any of them?"

The chauffeur shook his head, answering much like the rest of the staff. "Nay. What would he have to say to them?"

Everyone's general consensus that he hadn't had much interaction with any of the housemaids, including Minnie, seemed to put paid to the suggestion that he and Minnie had been conducting an affair, or that Mrs. Green would have any reason to suspect such a thing. Most of the staff also seemed to have alibis for the time of Minnie's disappearance and presumed murder, many of them having attended church together. All but Mr. Plank, Mr. Green, and Miss Musselwhite. But the housekeeper had confirmed that my aunt's maid was suffering from a terrible head cold, and that she'd recommended Miss Musselwhite lie down and rest while she could.

"I'm curious to hear from this Mr. Plank," Thoreau remarked after he'd dismissed the chauffeur. "From what I can gather, he's somewhat of a curmudgeon."

"He is," I confirmed. "But a gentle one, at that. I wonder whether he or Miss Musselwhite saw anything."

"*I'm* wondering if Mr. Green saw anything," Sidney remarked, picking up his cup of tea. "Whether that's what got him killed." He grimaced as he took a sip, for it must have grown cold. "Do you think it's too early for something stronger?" he asked, as he glanced toward the waning light spilling through the eastern-facing windows.

Ignoring the last, I focused on his supposition about Mr. Green. "You know, that does make some sense." I turned to Thoreau. "Did I tell you Miss Musselwhite told us Mr. Green had also been employed by the airfield to help maintain their grounds? Apparently, he'd been flimflamming, as you might say, working there in the early morning and afternoon when he was supposedly doing chores about the estate."

His eyes widened. "Do Lord Reginald and Lady Popham know this?"

"Yes, and as you can imagine, they were none too happy to find out."

"Are you certain they didn't know about this before?"

"My aunt, as I'm sure you've noticed"—I looked about at the dilapidated furniture—"does not allow her displeasure to go unfelt."

His lips quirked.

"And I'm quite sure if a member of her staff had displeased her rather than Scotland Yard, she would have expressed herself directly. As for my cousin . . ."

"He's not under suspicion," Thoreau interjected with a dismissive wave of his hand, and absurdly I felt my hackles rise.

"Why? You don't think a blind person capable of murder?"

His cool, dark eyes assessed me. "Oh, undoubtedly. But if he killed Miss Spanswick, he had an accomplice capable of helping him bury the body and clean up the mess. And I fail to see how he could have administered the poison to Mr. Green, for he was unlikely to prepare or offer him food, or sneak up on him in the forest and plunge a syringe in his neck."

When put like that, I recognized my affront was rather ridiculous, but I couldn't help leaping to Reg's defense. Especially after witnessing how frustrated he was by his inability to read for himself in the library.

"Calm yourself, Ver," Sidney cajoled, wrapping his arm around my shoulders. "I doubt your cousin would appreciate you suggesting him as a murder suspect."

He had a point. I lowered my head.

"I think I must pay a visit to RAF Froxfield this evening," the inspector said. At the sight of a man standing in the doorway—one of his, I presumed—he went to speak with them.

"Don't tell me. You want to try to tag along?" Sidney's voice was wry.

"Actually, no. For one, I doubt Chief Inspector Thoreau would let us," I explained in answer to his look of disbelief. "Or that the RAF would allow us entry, even if you traded on your war hero status."

"And second?" he prodded.

"I'm curious to hear how Captain Willoughby answers his questions without us present." And just as curious to hear whether he offered us the same answers when we questioned him the next day, for I was already making plans for us to speak with him without Scotland Yard listening in.

CHAPTER 24

When Thoreau rejoined us, it was clear the news he'd received was not welcomed. "Not a trace of blood was found in Miss Spanswick's room. But I suppose this doesn't really surprise me, as I've just learned that the housekeeper ordered one of the maids to clean it some days after her departure. She claims it was a shocking mess, with papers and crumbs strewn about." He lit a cigarette, standing before the window to gaze out at the drive. "I don't blame her, but I also can't help but think of the evidence we lost."

"Was Minnie's room normally in such a state?" I asked, rising to my feet to join him. Anything to stretch my muscles and relieve my sore bottom and back.

He nodded, exhaling a stream of smoke. "They all say she was notoriously untidy."

"Then it seems to me she couldn't have been murdered there. For if someone had cleaned up after the fact, wouldn't they have cleared away the rest? How else could they know they'd gathered up all the evidence of their crime?"

"Indeed."

"I would say it also argues that the maid packed her bag herself," Sidney added, sliding his hands in his pockets as he ambled forward. "Wouldn't the killer, in their haste, have taken all of those papers, as well? Not knowing what was important and what wasn't."

"Unless they did, and then replaced them with other paper," Sergeant Crosswire suggested, reminding us of his presence.

"A supposition we cannot test because those papers have long since been disposed of," Thoreau turned to remark. His jaw hardened. "We shall just have to see whether the fingerprints have anything to tell us."

"Anything other than the fact that half the staff have admitted to being inside the victim's room at one time or another," Sidney said. All information willingly and nervously given when Thoreau told them their fingerprints would be required.

"Yes, well, if someone's prints are there that shouldn't be, then perhaps we'll have something."

Someone like her beau, Captain Willoughby. But I thought it unlikely he'd ever set foot in her room. Given the evidence before us, it seemed more probable that Minnie had packed up her belongings while the others were at church and slipped away. Whether she was meeting Captain Willoughby or intent on making her escape alone, we didn't know yet, but someone obviously prevented her from going any farther than the river. They'd murdered her and buried her not far from the spot where it happened. Had the recent rains not uncovered her body, they might have gotten away with it, too.

"I see ye got yourselves on 'er ladyship's bad side."

We all looked up as Mr. Plank flashed us a gap-toothed grin and then hobbled forward in his shambling way.

He gestured to the water-stained walls. "Or has all the manor fallen into this state o' disrepair since the last I seen it?"

"Mr. Plank, I presume." Thoreau moved forward to resume his seat, but the stablemaster waved him back.

"No, stay standin'. There's no need for the formalities with me." His eyes twinkled. "I imagine yer backside's smartin' about now. But I'm sure ye won't mind me takin' a seat." He sank down on the edge of the chair, rubbing his knee. "When ye get to be my age, the joints aren't so well-oiled." The smell of liniment lingered about him, like the type used on horses, and I wondered if he used the same remedy on himself.

"All right, then, Mr. Plank, could you tell us what you can remember about the morning Miss Minnie Spanswick was last seen?"

"I didn't go to church, if that's what ye mean," he declared, leaping straight to the heart of the matter. "Can't stand the way that new vicar rambles on about nonsense as if we've all got time to sit twiddlin' our thumbs. No, I was 'ere. Arrived just after seven, like I always do. Took care o' Miss Marmalade. The mare," he explained. "Saw the others leave, oh"—his gaze lifted to the ceiling as if he was trying to remember—"about nine. Then I had tea with Mr. Green, and—"

"Mr. Green was here then?" The inspector cut in to confirm.

"Yes, shorin' up the foundation o' the gazebo those fool airmen knocked a hole in a year ago. The wall was crumblin' further and 'er ladyship asked 'im to fix it afore it all came tumblin' down."

Then he might have seen something. Seen something and not even known what it meant.

"What of Miss Musselwhite?"

He shook his head. "No, didn't see 'er." He tilted his head. "Usually goes to service wi' the others, but I'm guessin' by your askin' me that she didn't that day."

The corners of Thoreau's lips curled, appreciating this was Mr. Plank's way of showing him that his mind was still sharp even if his body was failing him.

"But I did see Miss Spanswick." That he also knew this was a critical piece of information was clear, for his eyes glinted with satisfaction at being the person to share it. "I'd come up to the kitchen to nab somethin' to eat and I was about to leave when I heard someone comin' down the stairs.

Decided to hide myself and wait to see who it was, and in comes that maid. She be a saucy one. She were actin' all furtive like, lookin' over 'er shoulder as if to be sure she was alone. I understood why when she took a loaf o' bread and a towel full o' tarts from the table where Cook 'ad left 'em to cool. We all knows which food is meant for the master and which for the servants, and yet the minx took them, as cool as you please, and scampered back up the stairs."

"Did she have any baggage with her?" Thoreau asked, his brow furrowed.

"No, but she wasn't wearin' her uniform. She 'ad on some frilly dress and a brown coat and hat."

Then she must have been preparing to leave. Perhaps the bread and tarts were to be provisions. One last thing to tuck inside her baggage before she departed.

"What happened after she went up the stairs?" Thoreau prodded.

Mr. Plank's shoulders slumped, as if he'd expected to draw a more incredulous reaction from us. "I went back to the stables. Stayed there until the others returned."

"Did you see or hear anything else suspicious?"

"No, and Miss Marmalade didn't alert me either."

"Would she have?"

"Oh, yes. Horses 'ave keen senses."

That was true enough, but all that meant was that no one had passed through the estate yard or near the stables. Minnie could have easily exited through any of the doors opening onto the terrace and the gardens beyond, or out the front.

Then I recalled something Mr. Plank had told me during my first visit with him nearly a fortnight ago. "You told me that you stayed on during the war. That you worked for the RFC and later RAF officers living here at the house." I sank down on the edge of the chair Thoreau had inhabited all afternoon, leaning toward the stablemaster. "Did you ever meet a Captain Willoughby?"

He considered my question and then shook his head. "Nay, can't say I recall 'im."

Then he must have come to Froxfield after the war, which fit with what Goldy had told me about his flying for the Navy before the merger, not the Flying Corps.

"What about after the war?" Thoreau interjected. "Did you ever see any airmen hanging about the estate?"

He lifted his chin knowingly. "Yer talkin' about those fellows the maid would meet at the bridge. No, I never saw 'em. Rarely venture that far myself. But Mr. Green used to shake 'is head at 'er. Said she was askin' for trouble. And it looks like she found it."

With his moving back and forth between the airfield and the estate, it wasn't surprising Mr. Green had known about Minnie's relationship with Willoughby, or that he'd disapproved, but at least here was confirmation. And confirmation that Minnie might have known that Mr. Green was working two jobs and cheating Sir Reginald and Lady Popham.

Mr. Plank scratched the whiskers at his chin. "Aye, and there was that other chap. The one Mr. Green was 'elpin'. But he didn't seem to be military. Dressed like a real toff."

I straightened. "When was this?"

"Oh, not long before the war ended. Mr. Green was home on leave for just shy o' a fortnight. Recoverin' from some infection he'd picked up in the trenches. The RAF chaps asked 'im to fix the bridge between the properties that the lower officers used to come and go. I 'spose that's 'ow he met him."

A tingling feeling began at the back of my neck. One I'd felt many times before when it seemed I'd stumbled upon something important. I'd forgotten Mr. Green had been home briefly in the autumn of 1918. That he'd fixed the bridge. Which meant he'd probably met any number of the officers, and possibly any other personnel touring the airfield and its surroundings. What if the late Earl of Ryde had been one of them?"

"How was Mr. Green helping him?" I pressed.

"He never said. But I saw 'em together, pokin' around in the west park." He chuckled. "I thought he was either showin' 'im where the locals were carryin' on about the ghosts bein' near the riverbank or pointin' out the site where the remains o' that Roman villa are likely buried."

The sergeant looked up in surprise from his seat across the room where he'd been taking notes when Mr. Plank mentioned the ghosts, but I was more interested in his allusion to the Roman villa, particularly after he'd failed to mention it before. Perhaps this made up for it.

"What did this gentleman look like?" I knew I was tipping my hand a bit to Thoreau, who turned to look at me in interest at my pursuing this line of questioning. After all, what could a gentleman visiting the estate a year ago have to do with the two murders carried out in the last month? But then he didn't know as much as we did, and we couldn't yet tell him.

"Older chap. Tall. Gray hair. Sharp nose."

All things that could describe Max's father. I sank back, ruminating on this and the possibility that Ryde *had* come here. Until now, I'd wondered if perhaps I was straining to make a connection to the earl's cryptic messages and Ardmore's desire to conceal whatever information they were leading to. If perhaps I wanted it to be so in order to justify my distraction and poor efforts in searching for the maid and solving Mr. Green's murder. After all, it was ridiculous to think Ardmore hid behind every corner, that he had his hand in every strange crime. And yet this seemed to prove I might be right. We would have to wait for confirmation of the earl's schedule from Max, but this seemed to indicate I was not jumping at shadows.

I felt Sidney's gaze resting on me and lifted my eyes to meet it. That he was contemplating much the same thing was evident from the watchfulness of his stance. If Ryde had been here, if Mr. Green's and possibly the maid's deaths were somehow tied up with that, then matters had just become a great deal more complicated and dangerous.

Thoreau posed a few more questions to Mr. Plank about Mr. Green and his death before releasing him and calling in Miss Musselwhite, who hovered in the doorway uncertainly.

"You wanted to see me again?"

The inspector gestured for her to come forward. "Yes, please come in."

We all arranged ourselves in the seats we'd occupied for much of the afternoon, knowing Miss Musselwhite would never be comfortable answering questions with us all standing over her.

"I merely wanted to ask you about the morning Miss Spanswick disappeared," Thoreau prompted.

"Oh, well, of course. Though I'm not sure I can tell you anything."

She was wearing the same drab gray gown and apron, and today it made her look almost sickly. Even her guinea-gold hair had lost its sheen. But I supposed that was understandable. Many people would be shaken by one murder taking place where they lived and worked, let alone two, not to mention the fact her sister had been accused of the crimes.

"I understand you were ill that day."

"Why, yes." She seemed rattled by the fact that he already knew this. "I felt rather miserable, and Mrs. Ford told me I should rest. So I took one of my family's cold remedies. The tincture rather knocks one out."

It very well might, depending on how much alcohol it was dissolved in.

Thoreau dipped his head in understanding. "Then you didn't hear anything from Miss Spanswick?"

She shook her head. "I . . . I'm not even certain I saw her that morning. Maybe she was seated at the breakfast table when I spoke with Mrs. Ford, but I . . . I wasn't really paying attention."

As you wouldn't if you were sick and thinking of nothing but yourself, and completely unaware that one of your fellow servants was about to go missing.

"Had you not taken that remedy, do you think you might have?"

She eyed him warily. "Well, I don't know what you mean, but my room is at the opposite end of the hall from hers. So I doubt it."

"You liked your privacy, then?" Thoreau asked more warmly, trying to set her at ease.

But she wasn't willing to be soothed. "I did. Least I didn't like hearing the housemaids clumping up and down the steps and carrying on at all hours."

"Did you know about Miss Spanswick's officer up at the airfield?"

Here again, she almost seemed to retreat into herself. "I heard rumors."

"But you never saw him yourself?"

She shook her head, but there was a hesitation to it. One that Thoreau also noted, for he arched his eyebrows.

"No, at least . . . I don't think I had," she replied, fumbling to explain herself.

Thoreau studied her carefully, her fidgety manner, her almost cowering posture. "Is there anything else you'd like to tell us? Anything about Miss Spanswick, or Mr. Green, for that matter? Anything you've recalled that might be pertinent?"

"No," she replied, though even *that* seemed to take the form of a question.

His kindly gaze scrutinized her once more, and then Thoreau nodded and told her she could go. She was barely past the threshold when he spoke. "She knows something."

"And it frightens her," I added.

What that could possibly be, we could only guess. But I decided she bore watching, for rare was the person who could resist the urge to return to the source of their distress. When they would be best served to keep quiet and stay away, in their panic most people found themselves irresistibly drawn toward the person or thing they should most stay away from. I suspected Miss Musselwhite would be no different. In fact, I counted on it.

"Why are we here again?" Sidney murmured.

I shushed him, peering up at the darkened terrace from our place concealed behind a line of hedges running north to south along the boundary separating the east garden from the west. The night was still and the sky cloudless, illuminated by a round harvest moon that cast a silvery light over everything. But without the cloud cover, the temperatures had plummeted, making even my fur-lined coat and hat inadequate against the chill. With the heat of my husband's large frame at my back, the wait was bearable, but he was not so content.

"It seems to me, the least you could do is tell me why I'm standing out here freezing." He stamped his feet, glancing about him as he pulled up the collar of his trench coat. "I put up with enough of this sort of thing during the war."

"Wait and see."

He leaned forward to drawl in my ear. "You know, I fancy the staff has a rather cheery fire going in our chamber by now. Perhaps I could . . ."

I pressed my hand to his lips, quieting him as a shadow disengaged from the terrace.

He grumbled something about my not properly appreciating his seduction technique and then fell silent, catching sight of the same thing I had. The shadow solidified into a figure, which pattered lightly down the steps and then hurried across the raised walk toward the west. Without a word, I moved to follow and Sidney kept pace with me, guiding me around a lawn sprinkler when I would have tripped over it.

The figure paused as it reached the ha-ha, and turned to look behind them, perhaps unaware that the bright moonlight illuminated them. I could tell now that I had been right. Miss Musselwhite *was* perturbed, and intent on something. The question was what?

As she leaped down from the ha-ha and set off down the path leading into the west park, I was inclined to believe it had something to do with her brother-in-law. Had *he* known something? Had he told her? Perhaps he'd even concealed it.

In the open park, Sidney and I had to hang back a fair distance so as not to be seen in the moonlight or heard crunching through the fallen leaves underfoot, and once or twice, I feared we'd lost her. But then we picked up her scent again, both literally and figuratively, for she smelled of lavender and vanilla—the bouquet of scents my aunt preferred. It would waft to us faintly on the night breeze, softened by the earthy aromas of the autumn forest. Realizing she was headed deep into the park, I slid my hand into my pocket, grateful for the heft of the Webley pistol tucked there. I had no desire to be taken unawares without a weapon should it be needed.

She was moving in the direction of the airfield, albeit hesitantly, as if perhaps she had not passed this way often, or if ever, at night. I was beginning to wonder if she was making for the airfield itself, when we peered around a tree to find her speaking with two men in a clearing. The first was Captain Willoughby—I recognized him immediately—while the second was unknown to me, though he wore an RFC uniform. From the appearance of her posture, she was wary and not at all comfortable in their presence. When one of them reached out to touch her, she sidestepped, though she seemed careful not to offend and just as careful to keep both of them in her line of sight.

What the devil was she doing with Willoughby?

CHAPTER 25

I had little time to contemplate more than this before one of the men again tried to grab her, more determinedly this time. They were too far away for us to hear what they were saying, and there was no way we could approach and remain concealed. But given the men's evident aggression, I decided there was only one thing to do.

I strode forward, moving swiftly and soundlessly enough to catch the end of what Miss Musselwhite was saying.

". . . don't know where it is. I keep telling you this. I tried looking. . . ." Her desperate voice broke off at the sound of our approach and she whirled to the side. Her wide, frightened eyes fixed on my face above all the others, and I felt the urge to reach out and comfort her.

"Ah, Mr. and Mrs. Kent, how good of you to join us," Captain Willoughby proclaimed as if he were interrupted during clandestine meetings in the woods every evening.

"Captain." I nodded, not bothering to remove my hands from my pockets to greet him properly. I had no intention of stepping any closer to him than I needed to. My gaze shifted to the man standing at his right in question.

If ever a stare could be termed disrespectful, this pucker-mouthed fellow's would be it. It was mocking and insolent, and yet there was a sharp edge I did not trust. "Dodgy" was I believe how Opal described him, and I understood what she meant. Understood why he gave her a funny feeling in the pit of her stomach, as well.

"Allow me to introduce Lieutenant Smith," Willoughby said, confirming my suspicions.

Sidney joined me in scrutinizing his motley uniform, which appeared to be made up of more pieces of army gear than anything else. "Lately of the RFC?" he queried almost scornfully.

"The Royal Fusiliers," he replied, a glint of challenge in his eyes.

Before I could ask why on earth a Royal Fusilier from the army would be detailed to an RAF station after the war, Willoughby caught Miss Musselwhite off guard, wrapping an arm about her waist and pulling her close.

"I'm afraid you interrupted us in the midst of a bit of a lovers' tiff," he declared jocularly.

She turned to look at him, opening her mouth as if to argue, but snapped it shut as he squeezed her even tighter. Obviously it was a warning.

"I was told you had been stepping out with Minnie Spanswick," I contested.

"Minnie?" He laughed. "Good heavens, no. She was a lively girl, and always ready for a bit of fun, but there was nothing serious between us." He nodded at his friend. "Met Lieutenant Smith more often than she did me."

"And half the other chaps up at the airfield, as well," Smith implied with a leer.

"I see," I replied in a clipped tone. The degree of Minnie's promiscuity did not interest me at the moment, though it always infuriated me when men cast aspersions on women they'd been happy to use for their own ends, eager to disregard why they were so desperate for their affections in the first place. What did interest me was why Captain Willoughby was so intent on distancing himself from her.

His mouth twisted in scorn. "Really, Mrs. Kent. You sound

just like that inspector from Scotland Yard who came to see me this evening. I don't know where he, or you, got the notion that I cared for Minnie beyond an evening's fun." He huffed a laugh. "Or had even the slightest notion of setting her up in London." Miss Musselwhite managed to wriggle from his grasp as he shook his head derisively and then sighed. "Look, I'm sorry the poor girl was killed, but I had nothing to do with it." His eyes slid toward the lady's maid. "I doubt anyone at the airfield did."

Miss Musselwhite stepped back from him as if she'd been slapped.

And then Willoughby seemed to turn the screw a little tighter. "Perhaps Mr. Green killed her."

Her hands clenched at her sides, her body practically shaking with the desire to refute this. But most curious of all, she did not.

"Say he did," Sidney agreed doubtfully. "Who killed Mr. Green, then?"

He shrugged. "His wife, maybe. Perhaps she thought they were having an affair."

Back to this again, were we.

I studied his carefree manner, the deliberate casualness of his movements, and felt certain he was not as unaffected by Minnie's death as he seemed. He was lying about something, but at times something shifted in his demeanor that made me wonder if he was telling partial truths.

On the other hand, I had no trouble believing what little Lieutenant Smith had conveyed with his facial expressions. He had not cared one jot for Minnie, and he didn't care if I knew it.

"Well, whatever the state of your relationship with Miss Musselwhite, I suggest you allow us to escort her back to the house now." Sidney's voice brooked no challenge, and Willoughby didn't give it to him.

"Of course. I would be grateful."

The maid stepped forward reluctantly.

"One never knows what might happen in these woods," Willoughby added as we turned to go, and it sounded distinctly like a threat. "They're a dark and haunted place. Or so the locals tell me."

His voice rang with hollow laugher as Sidney and I hurried Miss Musselwhite away. Had it not been for what he viewed as his gentlemanly duty to protect both of us, I suspected my husband would have challenged Willoughby's statement. As it was, I was glad he hadn't. Not when two bodies had already been found in this park.

As if by unspoken agreement, we all walked in silence, attuned to the sound of any pursuit. When the trees around us began to thin, and the hulk of Littlemote House could be seen ahead of us, glinting in the moonlight, I finally ventured to speak.

"Why were you out there? How do you know Captain Willoughby?"

"You heard him," she replied tightly, her voice breaking as she tried to force an air of levity. "We're lovers."

"Please, don't insult us by expecting us to believe such a load of eyewash."

She seemed startled by the vehemence in my voice, and well she should be.

"You are not lovers. And need I remind you, we would not be here investigating now if it were not for your insistence that your sister is innocent of killing her husband. And yet, back there, you allowed Captain Willoughby to baldly state that very thing without a word of denial."

She crossed her arms over her chest and lowered her head as if in shame.

"What hold does he have over you?" I asked more gently.

"Nothing."

"It's obvious he must be threatening you in some way."

"No . . . no, he's not," her voice rose with agitation.

"Then what couldn't you find that he wanted you to?" I asked, referring to the words we'd heard her say as we rushed forward. "Has it anything to do with what your sister claimed Mr. Green found? What he believed would help them."

She shook her head, refusing to answer.

"Miss Musselwhite, we can help you."

But still she wouldn't speak. It made me so frustrated, I wanted to shake her.

"Did you know your brother-in-law wished to speak with me?" Sidney suddenly asked in an even voice.

This, it seemed, had somehow managed to penetrate through her haze of distress, for she stared up at him.

"Before he was killed, he told the chauffeur he was anxious to speak with me on my return. Do you know what it was about?"

It took her a moment to formulate a response, and when she did, it was a simple no. But by the hesitation and inflection, it was obvious that it was a yes. Evidently, she wasn't ready to share the truth, but perhaps by Sidney planting that fact in her brain—that knowledge that Mr. Green had intended to confide something in him—it might work on her in the interim. Maybe then the truth would come to light.

I woke to the sound of screaming. It took me a moment to realize it was my own.

I sank my head into my hands, resting my elbows on my knees as my heart continued to pound. Each beat sent a sickening surge of blood through my veins, making me want to crawl out of my skin. One glance to the side told me Sidney was not in bed with me. Lifting my head, I saw he was seated in the shadows across the room.

I felt ashamed and exposed knowing he'd been sitting there watching me, and then I realized why he hadn't spoken. It was the same reason I hesitated to say anything when he was in the grips of one of his nightmares, or pacing the drawing room, trying to outdistance the memories. Sometimes it was difficult to tell when a dream ended, whether a person was in the present or the past, and if speaking might pull them from it or momentarily force them deeper in.

I'd heard stories of returning soldiers waking in the middle of the night to find themselves choking their wives, convinced that they were the enemy. While Sidney had never done anything like that, I had felt the instinct for violence pulsing through his muscles as he struggled in his sleep. Which was why I'd decided not to question his tendency to leap from bed, to distance himself from me whenever he woke from a nightmare. He was simply doing what he thought best, to protect me, even from himself.

I inhaled a ragged breath, feeling my heart rate begin to slow.

"They're growing worse," he said.

"I know." Though it was the same dream every time, it was growing more intense. "I don't know what to do." My voice rasped as I spoke, raw from shouting. "It's like I'm looking for something."

He rose from his chair. "You already know Scott was there."

"Yes."

"Isn't that it, then?"

I began to search my brain, but I balked at willingly returning to the memory. "I don't think so. If it was, why would it keep getting more vivid?" I pressed a hand to the side of my matted hair. "It's like this itch in my brain, but I just can't scratch it."

"It will come to you."

"Will it?" I looked up as he came to a stop beside the bed. It was then that I noticed he was wearing no shirt, and my chest tightened anew as my eyes became riveted to the scars from his bullet wound—the wound that nearly killed him. Then I became engrossed by something altogether different as the taut definition of the muscles in his abdomen rippled as he climbed into bed beside me. Sidney had always possessed an impressive physique, but war and the trials that followed had whittled away any softness.

"Yes, it has to."

My gaze lifted to his worried one. The implication was clear. If it didn't, I might drive myself mad. I didn't have an answer to that, so I changed the subject.

"Aren't you chilled?" I asked, shivering in the night air as the sweat on my skin cooled.

"Yes, but it helps me think more clearly."

"About?"

His mouth softened into a smile. "Many things." He wrapped his arm around me and pulled me back down into the covers beside him. "None of which I'm going to discuss tonight."

I pressed my hand against his jaw, feeling the dark stubble against my palm, and searched his beloved face. So many secrets, so much pain was locked inside him, and I hadn't the key to release it. I wasn't certain I even had the right. That knowledge constricted my heart.

His smile took on a roguish twist. "Are you in need of a distraction?"

"Yes," I murmured, already feeling my body melting into his as his mouth lowered to my neck.

"Always happy to be of service."

I had respected Chief Inspector Thoreau from the moment I met him in the morning room of the Marquess of Rockham's palatial Grosvenor Square mansion, and my regard and appreciation for his fierce intelligence had only grown over the weeks that followed. But my fondness grew exponentially the moment I walked into the room at the Hungerford Constabulary where Mrs. Green was now being held. Not only was it not the cold, open room divided by steel bars, but it contained some semblance of comfort in the form of thick blankets, a table and chairs, and a separate bathroom. For all that she was accused of killing her husband, in my opinion—and apparently Thoreau's—the evidence thus far was wanting, and her painful period of sobering up punishment enough, at the moment.

I sat across the table from her, relieved to see her gaze was steady and lucid, though she still seemed to be suffering from periods of chills evidenced from the blanket draped around her shoulders that she clutched together before her almost like a shield.

The pleasantries dispensed with, I decided to come straight to the point. "Mrs. Green, do you know who killed your husband?"

She looked up from where she'd been staring at the table between us to shake her head. "No, I wish to God I did!" Her voice broke, and I realized her placidity was a thin façade. That she was struggling not to shatter. "Maybe someone from work?"

"Did he discuss his work at the estate with you?"

"No, not that I remember." She heaved a shamed breath. "Not that I remember much of anything."

"But you did remember he was going back to the estate that night to search for something," I prompted. "You told us he'd found something he thought might help you. Something he might have had to dig to get."

"Yes." Her eyes widened. "He was almost obsessed with it, determined that this would be the way he could set things right. For me. For all of us." She sniffed, tears coming to her eyes.

"Do you know what it was that he found?"

She shook her head, swiping at her cheeks.

"Then do you know where he might have hidden it? Please, it might be important."

"No, I . . . I wish I did. I'm sorry." She began to sob, her head bowed.

I sat quietly with her, not knowing what to say, and yet not wanting to leave her alone. Not when her pain and grief were so immense.

"It's my fault," she gasped. "If I'd been stronger, if I hadn't started drinking, none of this would have happened."

"Mrs. Green, you are not the only woman who picked up a bottle," I told her. "Or the only woman to become lost in it."

She blinked up at me through her tears.

"The world tells us we must be composed, that we must manage it all and manage our fears. That it's on us that the men must rely to bolster them for the war they must fight, and comfort them when they return from it." I inhaled a swift breath, struggling now to contain my own emotions. "But who bolsters *us* for the fight we wage at home against despair? Who comforts *us* when it all becomes too much, or the man who returns to us is not the same as the one who left?" I offered her a tight smile. "There's sympathy for those who mourn the dead, but little left to go around for the rest of us."

She sniffed again, dabbing at her nose with a handkerchief unearthed from somewhere beneath her blanket, but I noticed she *was* listening to me, her eyes bright with interest.

"Don't mistake me. I'm not excusing your drinking. But . . . I understand it." I leaned over the table to be certain she heard me. "You are now well on your way to being sober, and you must find the fight within yourself to stay that way. For your children. For your husband. For yourself. If you wish to honor his memory, let it be in that way."

She nodded. "I will."

I had no idea if she would be able to do it. I had no idea if she would succeed. But in that moment, I believed she meant to try.

I pushed back my chair, preparing to rise, when suddenly she spoke.

"I did think of one thing." She swallowed. "It happened a few months ago. In July, around my birthday." Her hands wrung the handkerchief before her. "I . . . I drank so much one night he almost couldn't revive me. After, he told me he was writing to someone he thought could help. He said he'd helped this person in the past, and with his influence, perhaps he could find me a place in one of the hospitals."

I sat taller.

"I figured it must be someone from the war. An officer maybe." Her brow furrowed in consternation. "But then he never mentioned it again. I don't think he received a response. Or if he did, it wasn't positive."

"Did he tell you the man's name?"

"No." She offered me a grim smile, repeating her earlier words. "Or if he did, I don't remember." She heaved a discouraged sigh. "It's not just my memory, though. Frank was wont to talk in riddles, and in my drunken haze I rarely had the patience to puzzle them out. Like that hiding place you asked me about. He told me once that if you had something to conceal, it was best to do so in a place no one would search. What he meant by that, I haven't the foggiest. But it was merely his way."

She might not have the foggiest, but I had a sneaking suspicion I did.

I thanked her before hastening out to the front room, where Sidney was waiting. Snagging his arm, I practically dragged him from the building, sparing but a moment to offer Constable Jones a cordial wave.

"You've discovered something?" my husband guessed as he opened the door of his Pierce-Arrow for me.

"Several somethings."

"Back to Littlemote, then?" he asked as he climbed in behind the driving wheel.

"Yes, and step on it."

"I thought you didn't like me driving fast," he quizzed me as he pulled away from the constabulary.

"I don't like you driving recklessly. There *is* a difference."

He chuckled. "Who am I to disobey orders?" Once he'd navigated us through the narrow streets of the village, he did precisely as I'd requested, putting his motorcar through its paces. "Now, tell me what you learned."

I explained what Mrs. Green had told me about the letter her husband wrote. "What do you want to bet that letter was to the late Lord Ryde?" I asked, turning in my seat to face him. "The same Lord Ryde who he assisted with something in the autumn of 1918."

"The same Lord Ryde Mr. Plank saw with Mr. Green in the west park," he contributed, catching on to my way of thinking.

"Precisely. He sent that letter, hoping and *hinting* that since he'd done him a favor in the past, perhaps he might return it."

"Not realizing that Lord Ryde was dead." Something that was entirely possible given the fact it occurred during the last weeks of the war, when Mr. Green was already back at the Western Front fighting. The Greens didn't exactly run in aristocratic circles, so he might have never heard that the late earl had passed and the current Lord Ryde was now his son.

"Or that Ardmore was monitoring Ryde's mail for just such a message."

Sidney's eyes darted toward me before returning to the road. "Do you honestly think so?"

"Do you honestly think *not*?"

"He's definitely capable of it," he allowed.

"One thing is for certain, Max never received that letter. For if he had, you can be positive Mr. Green would have received a response." I knew Max well enough to understand that he would never let a kindness go unrewarded, nor would he have callously turned away a plea for his help. "And when we mentioned Littlemote and Mr. Green being killed, he would have spoken up." I glanced distractedly over my shoulder at the motorcar I'd seen parked alongside of the road, but the Pierce-Arrow was traveling too fast around the curve and I dismissed it from my thoughts.

"You're right." His expression was grim as he braked for the turn onto Littlemote's long drive. "Then that could explain why Ardmore's men were here long before we were. They already knew that Lord Ryde had been here. And that he'd had some assistance from Mr. Green, a gardener and man-of-all-work by trade, to do something."

"All it wants is confirmation from Max that his father did, in fact, visit RAF Froxfield in the autumn of 1918, but otherwise all the pieces fit."

"Now the question remains, what on earth did he bury in the west park?"

"And is it still there?"

Sidney frowned. "You don't think it is? What of all those holes we found?"

I faced forward again, narrowing my eyes at the leaves spiraling on the breeze to shower down on the motorcar. "I don't know anything for sure. It's just a hunch. But whatever Mr. Green helped Lord Ryde conceal, I think he may have dug it up again. Wouldn't you, if you suddenly realized there were men searching for it?"

"Then what has he been digging for in the west park?"

"Roman coins."

Sidney's head tipped back in sudden comprehension. "Because of the villa."

"They've been found before. And I suspect that's what he was clutching in his hand when he died."

"So the reason there are two different types of holes is because they were being dug for two different purposes— by Mr. Green searching for coins, and by Ardmore's men searching for . . . well, we don't know precisely what yet."

We rolled past the gatehouse and up the slope toward the house.

"Yes, but I think we might be about to solve that mystery," I said.

"What do you mean?"

"I think I know where Mr. Green may have hid what he dug up. It was something he told his wife that gave me the idea."

"Where?"

But I merely cast him an enigmatic smile. "You'll see."

CHAPTER 26

However, we weren't destined to reach our destination. Not when Miles was waiting for me with a message from Max as I passed him my hat.

I hurried toward the telephone in the alcove situated between the great hall and the corridor leading deeper into the house, removing my gloves as I went. Tucking them in my pocket, I rang up our friend at his town house in London. He answered on the first ring.

"Max, what news?"

"Verity, it's good to hear your voice. I was worried . . ." He broke off. "But never mind that. I spoke to Father's valet."

"Yes?"

"He confirmed what my sister had to tell us. Father *was* unsettled. Even took to sleeping with a pistol in his bedside drawer."

I pressed my hand to my forehead. "Good heavens! Then he *was* worried someone was going to kill him." I looked up at Sidney, who had joined me in the corridor, leaning against the wall near the entry to the alcove.

"It appears so. He took to declining dinner invitations and refused to dine at his club."

And yet he'd still been poisoned. Or so we presumed. I supposed there was no way we would ever know beyond a shadow of a doubt.

I heard Max draw breath, clearly still trying to adjust himself to these facts.

"He also confirmed the schedule I found notated in my father's agenda." He paused, and I knew whatever he said next would be of great importance. "Verity, he *did* go on a tour of a handful of airfields, just as you suspected. And one of them was Froxfield."

My heart kicked in my chest upon hearing confirmation of everything Sidney and I had just speculated on. I nodded at my husband's look of inquiry. "So he was here."

"Yes, and Xavier has more to tell you."

I'd wanted to ask him about Mr. Green's letter, on the off chance he'd simply forgotten about it, but Alec was already speaking over the wires.

"Verity, I've got the information you wanted on that Willoughby chap. You were right. He was with the Royal Naval Air Service. And what's more, he was an intelligence officer."

"Bloody hell," I mumbled, making Sidney's eyebrows arch, not so much in shock—he'd heard me curse before—but alarm. "Willoughby is Naval Intelligence."

"Well, you suspected that, didn't you?" he murmured.

"Yes, but it doesn't make it any more comforting to hear."

"Is Kent there with you?" Alec asked, and I thought I detected strain in his voice.

"Yes."

"Good. Because we haven't seen hide nor hair of Scott here in the past two days, and I took the precaution of sending a man down to Pevensey to investigate the situation, but he hasn't seen him there either." His next words were deathly serious. "I don't like it, Ver. I think he's already at Froxfield, or in the area."

My breath tightened as I recalled the motorcar I'd seen parked along the side of the road, and how distinctive Sidney's Pierce-Arrow was. If that had been Scott, if he'd been looking for proof of our presence at Littlemote, then he'd just received it.

"Ver, are you still there?"

"Yes. Yes, I'm here," I replied, finding my voice.

"Watch your back, Ver. And keep Kent with you at all times. No daring heroics, you hear?"

Being given such a cautionary warning from Alec of all people—the king of daring and reckless impulse—would have been laughable, had I not recognized with chilling certainty how pertinent it was. Lord Ardmore had warned me that Scott was after me, and while I still wasn't certain that wasn't at the cunning lord's behest, that didn't lessen the gravity of the situation. Even my nightmares seemed to be telling me that Scott was a threat I could not ignore.

"Ryde and I are leaving the moment I hang up this phone. We'll be there in three hours. Two, if I can convince him to let me drive."

"Take care," I urged him.

"The same to you."

I replaced the mouthpiece back on the switch hook and turned to face Sidney. The set of his shoulders and the watchfulness of his gaze told me he hadn't missed the apprehension I felt. "They haven't seen Scott in London or Pevensey in the past two days. Which means he's likely already here."

Sidney straightened. "Then we'll have to be extra alert."

I nodded. "Max and Alec are on their way here." I brushed my hands down my charcoal skirt, straightening it. "I suppose I should inform Miles they'll need rooms prepared."

"One moment," Sidney said, wrapping his arm around my waist to pull me to his side. He grasped my chin with his fingers, gazing reassuringly into my eyes. "I'm not going to let anything happen to you."

"I know," I murmured with a forced smile.

But what I really knew was that he might be helpless to prevent it. Just as I knew I might be helpless to prevent harm

coming to him. That's what happened when you loved someone. It made you desperate to protect them, and flounder at
the impossibility of doing so.

Whether he recognized all these things, too, I didn't know,
but the longer he held my gaze with his steady one, the more
grounded I felt. My heartbeat slowed and my nerves unruffled, leaving me more composed than I'd been in days. He
pressed a kiss to my forehead and then released me, though
part of me wished he'd never let go.

I moved toward the Elizabethan Room, intending on tugging the bellpull to summon Miles, when he emerged through
the oak paneled door leading to the servants' stair. "Just the
man I wished to see," I declared. "I have two friends on their
way from London, and they'll each need a bedchamber prepared for them."

He bowed. "Very good, madam. If I may . . ."

I halted in the midst of turning away, waiting for him to
speak.

"I was actually coming to speak with you. Something has
been found in the attics." His gaze shifted to Sidney as he
came to stand beside me. "Something I believe you should
see."

"Of course. Show us the way."

He led us across the hall toward the main staircase with
its panels of ornate wooden carvings. "One of the footmen
was searching for the tapestry Sir Reginald requested be located, when he found it. Miss Spanswick's portmanteau. It
was tucked behind an old painting leaned against the wall."

The butler's tread was slow and even. I doubted his creaking knees could move much faster. But I was suddenly very
anxious to reach the top and had to restrain myself.

"Has Chief Inspector Thoreau been informed?" I asked as
we rounded the steps at the landing. I lifted my gaze to see
Miss Musselwhite standing against the banister at the top, a
pile of garments clutched to her chest as she watched us with

wide eyes. Clearly she had heard what Miles had said. Her eyes blinked rapidly, and then she hurried on.

"Yes, madam. I took the liberty of telephoning the constabulary with a message for him."

We crossed the wide corridor and entered a narrower set of stairs concealed behind another piece of oak paneling. These led upward into a dim space positioned among the eaves. A single tiny window was the only source of natural light in the chilly attic crowded with heaps of boxes and packages, some draped in cloth and some exposed to the light.

A young footman stood along the wall, his back straightening to attention at the sight of us. On the floor beside him sat a battered leather bag.

"Thank you, Robert," the butler said, dismissing him.

He seemed almost reluctant to leave now that the contents were about to be revealed, but dipped his head and followed orders.

I pulled my leather gloves from the pocket of my coat and knelt beside the portmanteau. "Have you looked inside?"

"Only so far as to ascertain it does in fact contain Miss Spanswick's belongings."

I carefully opened the bag and then began to sort through the contents. Wrapped in a towel on top rested the loaf of bread, now grown hard and spotted with mold. I set this aside to rifle through the clothing and was rewarded by the discovery of a small vase, two figurines, and an ornate wooden box that proved to be filled with coins—most of them very old from the looks of them, and some of them still flecked with bits of dirt.

"Are these the items that went missing?" I asked the butler. His mouth puckered in sharp disapproval. "Yes, madam."

However, it was the last item I removed that most interested me. Wound in a dainty floral-print dress near the bottom rested a gold letter opener. Dried blood speckled the cloth, adhering the metal to the cotton. This must be the murder weapon.

The sound of footsteps pounding up the stairs behind us made us all turn. We were soon greeted by the appearance of Inspector Thoreau and his sergeant. The inspector's eyes riveted to the object in my hand. "Well, I suppose that answers one question."

I set down the letter opener in its cloth next to the other objects and backed away so that Thoreau could kneel and have a better look. Miles reviewed everything for him that he'd already told us, and then Thoreau informed him he could go.

The inspector sank back on his heels, his eyes passing over the contents before him, his brow puzzled. When the sound of the butler's footsteps could no longer be heard retreating below, he turned his head to the side to look up at me.

"Perhaps it is merely fortuitous, but I find it rather odd, Mrs. Kent, that your cousin should suddenly request that his servants locate an obscure tapestry for him."

"Actually, that's my fault," I replied.

His brows lifted quizzically.

I recognized an explanation was in order, but I wasn't certain how much I could reveal. "We've been investigating another matter," I began haltingly. "And several circumstances led us to believe there might be a connection to Littlemote."

"I see," he replied brusquely as he pushed to his feet.

"Not to the murders. At least, not at first. Simply the grounds."

His arms crossed over his chest. "But you've since discovered something that makes you think they might be connected to the murders?"

I frowned, disliking the sensation that I was being reproached like a child. "The other investigation involves a connection to sites with Roman remains, and I asked my cousin to look into the matter. I had a vague recollection that there might have been Roman remains uncovered here at some point, and I wanted to know if it was true. Mr. Plank told Reg it was, that his grandfather's grandfather worked in the stables at the time of the discovery. He also said a tapestry had been created of the mosaic that was found. So Reg asked Miles to have the staff search for it while he looked in the records for further proof of the stablemaster's story."

"A fortuitous coincidence, then."

"Yes."

"And what is the connection to these murders?"

I clamped my lips together as I considered what to say, but the look Thoreau fastened on me told me he was not going to back down. He might suspect my connection with the Secret Service, both past and present, and he might be lenient when it came to such matters that I could not share, but he was not going to allow me to conceal information that might be pertinent to his own investigations.

"The object Mr. Green was clutching in his hand when he died. Was it a Roman coin?"

The hard set to his jaw eased a fraction. "Yes."

"I believe he'd been digging in the west park, searching for those for some weeks. That's why he was found there when he was killed."

The look in his eyes did not dispute this, but he pointed out the problems with this theory. "Then where was his shovel and lantern?"

"Taken by the killer, I suppose. Perhaps to confuse the issue."

"And why would he have begun doing so? Purely based on Mr. Plank's story?"

"Because he'd found one before."

Sidney turned to me in surprise, unaware of this information as I'd just remembered it.

"Reg told me a Roman coin had been found just last year, that it had been tossed in with all the others." I nodded at the ornate box at our feet. "I bet it was Mr. Green who did so when he was home on leave last autumn."

"And he merely stumbled across it?" Thoreau queried, his stance softening.

I shared a speaking look with Sidney. "No, he was burying something for someone else near the site where the Roman remains were supposedly found." I wondered if the late Lord Ryde had had better information than even the Pophams currently possessed. If he was counting on the obscurity of the information known to but a few Roman scholars to conceal the object from Ardmore.

"And what is this something he buried?"

But I balked at this, shaking my head. "I can't tell you that."

He glowered at me.

"Or who the *someone* is. He's dead now anyway. Which is part of the reason I think Mr. Green dug the object back up." I scrutinized the contents of Minnie's bag, my brow puckering. "Which is partly what set off this chain of events." A hazy picture was forming. If I could just connect all the dots.

I turned away to pace across the room toward the window. "All the evidence points to the fact that Minnie was our thief, and that she intended to abscond with her ill-gotten goods and make for London. But someone stopped her before she could do so. They killed her, buried her body at the edge of the gardens near the river." I could just make out the spot through the fogged glass where a cobweb stretched across one corner. Whirling about, I surveyed the detritus filling the attic. "And hid her bag up here, where presumably no one would find it for a very long time."

Thoreau accepted all of these suppositions with a single nod. "That would seem to indicate someone who had easy access to the house, but only Miss Musselwhite, Mr. Green, and Mr. Plank were here at the time we assume the victim was murdered. And thus far we've uncovered no viable motives for any of them."

"Do we truly believe that Miss Musselwhite could have dragged the victim's body to the river and buried her?" Sergeant Crosswire ventured to ask.

"No," Thoreau conceded. "Not in the time allotted. And not with the head cold she was suffering from. But she may have had help."

"Her brother-in-law," Sidney supplied gravely. "Who then ended up murdered two weeks later. Dosed with nicotine by his wife or some unknown . . ." He broke off as Thoreau shook his head.

"I've just seen the toxicology results. Mr. Green was not poisoned with nicotine. It was curare."

"Curare," I gasped. "But isn't that rather rare?"

"Yes, from Central and South America. It's not something a person would readily have on hand." His expression was thunderous. "And while in the case of both poisons, death would ultimately result from respiratory failure, the symptoms and other effects to the body are quite different. Though, if no one was around to witness the victim's death, I suppose that could account for the difficulty in diagnosis." Thoreau might be trying to justify the hasty misdiagnosis to me, but I suspected he would not be so kind in his review of the police surgeon and Hungerford constabulary to his superiors.

"Then, has Mrs. Green been released?" I asked.

"She has. We had insufficient evidence to continue to hold her."

I felt a moment's worry about her state of mind, and whether she would be able to resist the temptation to drink now that she had access to it. But it was not my responsibility to keep Mrs. Green sober. That charge fell on her shoulders. I could only hope her neighbors would be willing to help her.

"Miss Musselwhite should be told," I said, knowing she would be relieved to hear it.

He turned to his sergeant. "Ask the butler to have Miss Musselwhite sent to us in that dreadful parlor." Thoreau knelt to begin repacking Minnie's bag as his sergeant hurried off to do as he was bid.

"Then Mr. Green wasn't given the poison with his dinner?" Sidney clarified, reminding us we all had to adjust the time frame of the second murder in our minds.

"No, curare has no effect if it's ingested. It has to be injected into the bloodstream via syringe." He turned to me. "Hence the prick at the back of his neck."

I pressed a hand to my stomach, suddenly recalling something. But was it really possible? The implications were unsettling and bewildering, and yet, it made some sort of bizarre sense.

"Mrs. Kent?" Thoreau prodded, obviously noting my sudden preoccupation.

I inhaled a swift breath and offered him a tight smile. "I just need to powder my nose." A lady's universal euphemism for using the facilities. "I'll meet you in the parlor." I could only hope he would ascribe my odd behavior to a stomach complaint. One glance at Sidney as I brushed past told me he was not so easily fooled. But I wanted to speak with Reg first. I wanted to be sure of my suspicions before I voiced them.

CHAPTER 27

I found my cousin readily enough in the library, waiting impatiently as his valet searched through yet another book of records. His head turned toward the door as I entered. "Still no luck," he told me shortly, his eyes trained vaguely at the wall above my head and his mouth twisted in irritation.

"I'm not here about that," I told him before addressing the valet, who had broken off his search to rise to his feet. "Would you give us a moment?"

He nodded and strode from the room, clearly relieved to have a respite from this tedious task.

"You sound quite serious, Ver," Reg retorted, but then his face lost its derisive appearance. "Has something happened?"

"I need you to answer a few questions." I sank into the chair across from him. "And I want you to do so without your usual scorn and mockery."

He scowled at this request, but then relented with an aggrieved sigh. "What do want to know?"

"Your mother's medicine. Do you know what it is?"

"No. Something Dr. Maslen prescribed for her, and Dr. Razey did not contradict when he took over his patients. I trust they know what they're about."

"It's not curare, is it?"

His brow furrowed. "That stuff used on poison darts in the Amazon?"

"Yes."

"I should think not."

"But am I correct that her medicine is administered by syringe? Is that why she insisted only Miss Musselwhite could do it the day Mr. Green's body was discovered?"

His mind seemed to be grappling with my words, trying to understand why I was asking them. "Yes, she takes an injection once a day, or when it's needed."

I stared down at my hands as the sinking realization began to grip me. Miss Musselwhite had been in the house alone with Minnie when she was killed. She had access to the attics. She had access to a syringe. And she knew that Mr. Green often searched the west park for coins in the dark of night. Where she had gotten the curare from, I didn't know. Neither did I understand why she would have committed either murder. But the facts had to be addressed.

"Why are you asking me these questions?" Reg asked me, uneasiness making his voice sharp. "If you want to know about Mother's health, you should speak to her. Or Miss Musselwhite. She knows all the pertinent details."

"Can you honestly imagine your mother answering any of these questions? She would take great umbrage at my even asking them."

His mouth curled upward at one corner. "True. And harangue Miss Musselwhite to no end if she learned she'd shared them."

I smiled tightly and then let it drop when I remembered he couldn't see it anyway.

"It's no wonder she sneaks out to the terrace every night to have a smoke after Mother goes to bed."

I stilled. "What did you say?"

He faltered, perhaps thrown by my reaction, and then

chuckled incredulously. "Don't tell me you're put off by the idea of a woman smoking?"

"No, the other bit. You said Miss Musselwhite sneaks out to the terrace every night. Who else knows this?"

"Well, no one I suppose. I doubt she even realizes I do. Forgets that just because I can't see her doesn't mean I can't hear her. She has a rather distinctive tread."

She did. I'd recognized it, too. Quick and sharp, like little staccato notes.

"Reg, I need you to think back to the night Mr. Green was killed." I leaned forward anxiously. "Did Miss Musselwhite go out on the terrace?"

His face paled, plainly grasping why I was asking. Why I'd posed all these questions. He swallowed and then nodded. "Yes."

"You're certain?"

"Yes."

"Did you hear her come back in?"

He hesitated and then shook his head. "No, not before I went up to bed."

I sank my head forward for a moment, wrestling with the truth and the weight of all it meant. It hadn't been Ardmore's doing after all. And Mrs. Green was about to face the loss of not only her husband, but her sister, as well.

I pushed to my feet, rounding the table to drop a kiss on Reg's head. "Thank you." Then I tugged on his ear before leaning down to whisper. "Don't ever doubt your worth or ability again."

I turned to go, but his hand reached up to clasp mine where it rested on his shoulder. It lasted only a few seconds, but I recognized what he was saying without words. I slipped away before I could give way to maudlin tears.

Sidney and Chief Inspector Thoreau stood before the window that one of them had forced open, smoking their mutual cigarettes and amicably conversing, when I burst into the room.

"Have you spoken to Miss Musselwhite?"

"No, we're still waiting for Sergeant Crosswire to bring her," Sidney replied. His gaze took in my flushed countenance. "What is it, Ver?"

I crossed the room before murmuring the dreadful words. "She's the one. She's the murderer."

I laid out all the facts I'd learned, including the ones I'd just discovered from Reg. When I'd finished, both men seemed as disturbed by the truth as I was.

"But why? What can her motives have been?" Thoreau ruminated, and I knew he wasn't doubting my interpretation of the facts, merely trying to understand it.

"I'm not sure we'll know until we speak with her. Perhaps she caught Minnie leaving with all those stolen items and tried to stop her. Maybe Minnie turned on her with the letter opener first. I don't know." I clasped my fingers together around one knee. "I have a harder time explaining why she would have killed her brother-in-law, of whom I know she was fond." I glanced sideways at Sidney to see if he was considering the same thing I was. "But perhaps there were other pressures at play."

Captain Willoughby factored into this somehow. I wasn't sure how. But he did. Last night's interaction between them proved it. And Willoughby was the aggressor, not the other way around.

I looked toward the door for about the tenth time. "Shouldn't Sergeant Crosswire have returned by now?"

Thoreau's gaze followed mine. "Yes, I was just thinking the same thing." He rose to his feet to move toward the door when the sergeant suddenly appeared.

His brow was furrowed. "Sorry, sir. But I couldn't locate Miss Musselwhite. Mr. Miles suggested maybe she'd already heard the news and gone to the village."

I sat forward anxiously. "Did you speak to my aunt?"

"Lady Popham is looking for her, too."

Then she hadn't asked permission to go to her sister. An im-
age flashed in my mind of Miss Musselwhite leaning against
the balustrade at the top of the stairs, clutching those garments before her. I sat forward. "She knows. She heard Miles
telling us they'd found Minnie's bag. She knows we know."

"Then she would go to her sister," Thoreau stated.

Maybe. To explain herself. To try to get away. Or would
she go to Willoughby? To try to force him to help her.

"Bring the motorcar around," Thoreau ordered his sergeant before turning to us. "Are you coming?"

"Shouldn't someone stay here in case she turns up?" Sidney asked, his perceptive eyes having already deduced my co-
nundrum.

If Thoreau questioned our willingness to stay behind, he
did so only for a second. "Send word if she appears."

"What are you thinking?" my husband asked as I began to
pace the room.

"I'm trying to decide what Miss Musselwhite would do.
And I suspect it all hinges on *why* she killed her brother-in-
law."

"Maybe she loved him."

"I've already considered that."

"You have?"

"Yes, and it's quite possible she did. In a not strictly sis-
terly sort of way." I shook my head. "But she also loved her
sister. I don't doubt that. And she knew her sister adored her
husband."

"But how did *Mr.* Green feel?" Sidney pointed out with a
lift to his eyebrows.

I paused to look at him. "I don't know. How would you
feel if you'd found yourself in his shoes?"

He slid his hands into his pockets and lifted his gaze to contemplate the tarnished chandelier overhead. "Weary. Guilty.
Anxious to help my wife however I could." He sighed. "But
also frustrated, disappointed, and desperate for some form

of normalcy." His gaze dropped to his feet. "I can't imagine he felt much genuine affection or attraction for his wife after seeing her drunk night after night, and being screamed at day after day for one fault or another."

"But he was so determined to get her accepted to a hospital to address her problem."

"Yes, but that might have been motivated more by guilt than anything else. Guilt for leaving her to fight in the war. Guilt for not being there." He paused. "Guilt for no longer loving her like she wanted him to."

I pressed a hand to my mouth, feeling the ring of truth in his words.

"After all, there's only so much a person can endure before the love they once felt is smothered completely. They might stay. They might soldier on. But it's not out of love. Or not the same kind of love."

"And you think he found this affection, this attraction with Miss Musselwhite?"

He shrugged one shoulder. "Maybe. But it's certain he found stability, and conversation, and compassion."

I inhaled past the tightness in my chest. "Then maybe if Mr. Green did something she couldn't reconcile herself with. Maybe then she could do it."

Sidney crossed toward me, realizing I needed bolstering after all these revelations, and wrapped me in his arms. I allowed myself a moment to revel in his warmth and the familiar scent of the bay rum in his aftershave, and then pushed away, determined to face what was to come.

"Let's go speak to the staff again. Now that we know who our culprit is, they might have more light to shine on the matter."

But once again my plans were interrupted by Miles. He was striding down the corridor toward us as we left the room. A look of consternation etched his face. "Here you are, madam. A message was just delivered for you."

"In the post?" I asked in bafflement as I took the plain white envelope.

"No, he was dressed in uniform. From the airfield, I imagine. And if I do say so, he had a most unpleasant demeanor."

I gazed down at the letter in misgiving. "Did he wait for a response?"

"No, madam. Rode off on a motorbike straightaway."

"Thank you."

He nodded and strode off while we stepped back into the parlor to better utilize the sunlight spilling through the tall windows. There was no seal, no sender, but given the manner in which it was delivered, there were really only a few options. When I slid the paper from the envelope and skimmed to the bottom, the name I most feared leapt out at me.

We have the maid. Bring the package to the barn at the end of the lane opposite the main gate to RAF Froxfield by 14:00 sharp. Come alone. Or else the staff at Littlemote loses one more member.

Major Basil Scott

I lifted my hand to my neck, where the bruises from my last encounter with Major Scott were just beginning to heal, and tinged a shocking palette of colorful shades.

"You are not going alone," Sidney stated firmly.

"I never thought I would," I replied. In my experience, men with ill intentions usually told you to come alone, but they rarely followed through on their threats when you failed to do so. Or if they did, they'd planned to carry them out regardless of whether you complied. No, going alone would be the height of stupidity. "And we're also not taking *the package* with us."

"Not that we know where it is."

Ah, but I was fairly certain I did. I'd simply been distracted from my objective by Max's telephone call and the discovery of Minnie's baggage. But now was not the time to test my theory. Not when Miss Musselwhite was in genuine danger.

"But we can take a decoy," Sidney suggested.

"And hope Scott doesn't know any better than we do precisely what Ryde buried?"

He shrugged. "Do you have a better suggestion?"

"No," I admitted. "But I wish I understood the lay of the land we're heading into."

He frowned. "I do, too. We could be walking, or rather, driving into an ambush."

I looked at the clock on the mantel, hoping it was accurate, and pulled Sidney toward the door. "Come on. We haven't much time, and I want to see if there's a map in the library. It may not have the airfield marked on it, but at least it will give us some idea of the topography."

Five minutes later, we were striding through the great hall with a map in my hand and a box Sidney had scrounged from some storeroom cradled in his arms. My aunt cried out as we neared the entry, hastening after us. "Verity! Verity, what is going on? I can't locate Miss Musselwhite, and the house is all at sixes and sevens."

"I can't stop now, Auntie."

"Verity!" she exclaimed in outrage.

"Miss Musselwhite may be in danger. I must go." I turned to walk backward, seeing her openmouthed stare. "If Chief Inspector Thoreau returns before us, tell him Reg knows where we've gone." It had seemed the best precaution to explain matters as he and his valet helped me locate a map. Then I wheeled about and hurried after Sidney.

The Pierce-Arrow rounded the circle and set off down the drive, her tires spitting crushed stone. We crested the hill and were hurtling downward toward the gatehouse when the sight of another motorcar approaching made Sidney brake hard. I didn't recognize the vehicle, but I did recognize the driver who sat behind the wheel.

"Oh, thank heavens!" I gasped as Sidney pulled to a stop, hailing them.

"Did you not have faith in my ability to make good time?" Alec quipped through the window, evidently having convinced Max to allow him to drive. Likely because this wasn't his pale yellow Rolls-Royce, which was back on the Isle of Wight, but another vehicle.

"Leave the motorcar there and get in," Sidney snapped, having no patience for his bluster. "And bring your pistols."

Alec and Max needed no further encouragement. No sooner had they climbed into the rear seat than Sidney set off again at a cracking pace. We quickly filled them in on the most pertinent details of what we were about to face as we bumped and shuddered over the ruts in the drive. Once we reached the road, the surface smoothed out and I was better able to wrangle the ordnance map and plot the route before us.

"Turn left here," I told Sidney as we approached a side road. "And then left again at the next crossroads."

Alec leaned forward to read over my shoulder. "What are we up against?"

"If I'm judging the position of the airfield correctly, then the barn he speaks of should stand about here," I tapped the map. "The land around it appears relatively level. And there's no way to easily reach it from the rear." I frowned, racking my brain to uncover some flaw, but there simply weren't any. "He chose well," I muttered, delivering the bad news. "There is no way we can make a sneak attack or even creep up on the place without being seen from every angle."

As if in answer to this pronouncement, the droning sound of an approaching aeroplane reached my ears. I turned toward the window, leaning forward to try to see up and behind us, just as Max and Alec did.

"Bloody hell," Sidney cursed as the aeroplane loomed into sight.

If it was Captain Willoughby, and I had no doubt it was,

and he had a mind to shoot or drop a bomb on us, there was nothing we could do to escape it. Not short of careening into the ditch.

Sidney pressed down on the gas pedal, fruitlessly trying to outpace the light bomber just as he'd done on our first trip to Littlemote nearly a fortnight ago. I considered leaning out the window and firing my pistol up at the aeroplane, but what good would that do? The likelihood of my hitting it at that altitude was slim, and the likelihood of the bullet doing any damage almost nil.

I gripped the seat beneath me, bracing as the bomber buzzed nearer. As it roared over us, I held my breath, listening for the familiar whistle of a dropping bomb.

CHAPTER 28

But no telltale whistle came. No thud. And certainly no explosion. The aeroplane followed the road ahead of us and then banked right, away from the airfield looming up on our left. I inhaled sharply, hardly able to believe my eyes. Was it headed toward that weathered stone barn in the distance surrounded by trees? Sidney applied the brakes, watching in rapt fascination along with the rest of us as a projectile suddenly dropped from the Ninak. It disappeared behind the screen of trees, and I braced again, but there was no resulting explosion.

"A dud," Alec guessed.

"Or a practice bomb," Max suggested.

I didn't know which was more likely, but when the aeroplane began to swing around for another pass, I realized he was providing us the distraction we so desperately needed. Sidney seemed to recognize this at the same moment, for he accelerated toward the airfield's front gates and then made a sharp right turn onto the narrow lane. The three of us who were not driving gripped our pistols in preparation as the growl of the bomber's return competed with the rumble of the Pierce-Arrow's engine. The aeroplane dipped toward the barn, and another projectile came hurtling down.

This time we were close enough to see the men positioned outside scatter, diving for cover. When the shell struck the earth with a pronounced thud, sending earth and debris scattering several yards, I knew it for what it was. A practice bomb.

Sidney braked, sending the motorcar's rear wheels careening in the soft gravel before we came to a stop. We threw open the doors and darted after each of the men, shouting directions to each other, before they could recover. Alec cornered one man, easily disarming him, while Sidney and Max took out another.

Keeping low, I crept toward the barn, knowing instinctively that was where Scott would be with Miss Musselwhite. When he appeared suddenly in the doorway, an arm around Miss Musselwhite's neck, holding her in front of him as a shield, I lifted my Webley to point it at him.

"Careful, Mrs. Kent," he fairly spat, raising his own pistol and pressing it into the side of his hostage's abdomen, who gasped. "I don't think you want to do that." His face was pale, the right side sporting an angry scar with fresh stitches from the outer cover of his eye down his cheek to his chin. I tried not to cringe at the evidence of what my hat pin had done, even though he'd deserved it. His gaze flicked toward the men approaching behind me, their footsteps crunching in the dirt and stone. "Though, since you didn't follow my orders, by rights I should shoot her now. But she's proving useful."

His head jerked back, surveying the sky overhead as the aeroplane swung in closer for another pass. I could only hope this time Captain Willoughby would forgo the bombing practice. He roared past, banking sharply, and as I lifted my gaze briefly I could have sworn he saluted.

Perhaps Ardmore truly didn't want me killed. Reluctantly, I had to admit, if we got out of this alive, some of our thanks for that was owed to him and Willoughby. It rankled, but I'd never been one to flinch from the truth. And I wasn't about to start now.

Whatever the case, I knew Willoughby would be long gone by the time we finished here, taking his answers with him.

Focusing all my attention once again on Scott, I could see that he was struggling to regain his self-control. Those practice bombs had shaken him, and I felt an unwelcome pulse of empathy. After all, the shell that had destroyed that dugout outside Bailleul had thrown us both. How many other similar incidences had he survived? How many had his men?

"I suppose that was your doing," he snarled. "I don't know why I ever believed you'd play fair. You didn't before."

I scowled at him in bafflement. The man wasn't making any sense. When before? Surely he didn't blame me for that shell.

I inhaled a deep, even breath, and then another. "What do you want?"

"You." The word was implacable.

"In exchange for Miss Musselwhite?"

Her eyes were closed, her breath sawing in and out of her lungs.

"Yes."

I tilted my head, trying to understand him. "And what do you intend to do to me?"

I heard someone's feet shift behind me and knew without looking that it was Sidney. However, he didn't interfere.

"Turn you in to the authorities." His eyes narrowed. "Make you pay for what you've done." With my life. That's what went unsaid. And what he really intended for me. After all, he seemed to have already tried and convicted me. Why not forgo the justice and move straight to the judgment?

"And what have I done?"

"You know," he snapped, grinding the pistol into Miss Musselwhite's side. She cried out, plainly terrified he would pull the trigger. "You know."

"That shell outside Bailleul?"

"It wasn't a shell."

"Yes, it was," I replied calmly, hoping to talk some sense into him. "It fell from the sky . . ."

He shook his head vehemently.

"It did. I heard the . . ." My words fumbled to a halt, the truth striking me like a punch to the gut. There had been no telltale whistle, no customary shriek of a shell arcing our way. I'd been arguing with Scott and then there was an explosion. "Dear God," I gasped. "It was a bomb." That's why I kept dreaming about it. The general and his staff hadn't been killed by a randomly dropped shell, but by a bomb planted there by someone. When I'd been thrown during the blast and rattled by the subsequent shelling, I'd somehow mixed up or forgotten the details.

"Don't act like you didn't know," Scott sneered, pulling my gaze back to him. "You put it there."

"No." I shook my head. "No, listen to me. I was sent there to warn the general there was a traitor among his staff providing information to the enemy. There were intercepted messages from him as proof."

He narrowed his eyes. "Then why wasn't Military Intelligence given the task of telling him? Why send"—his gaze scoured me up and down, clearly finding me lacking—"you."

I was used to being belittled and discounted simply because I was a woman. Many times, during my more audacious missions, that was precisely why I succeeded. But such words would be wasted on a man like Scott, so I went straight to the truth. "Because we suspected the traitor was connected to Military Intelligence, and so he would be warned."

Having served with Military Intelligence during the war, Scott straightened in affront.

"Given the success of that bomb, it sounds like the information still leaked out to him."

But Scott refused to listen. "*You* planted it. *You* killed six good men." His eyes glittered maniacally. "And now you're going to pay."

In the split second before he shifted his gun, I knew what he was going to do. And when I should have fired my Webley, I hesitated, knowing the aim on the British weapon was rarely true. Had it been a German Luger, I would have had more confidence, but all I had was Max's borrowed Webley, and I didn't want to hit Miss Musselwhite by mistake. Instead my muscles tensed, telling me to move, but it all happened so fast I hadn't the slightest chance of doing so.

The gunshot reverberated through the air, a hammer strike to my senses. But when I expected to be hit, nothing happened. I exhaled a strangled breath, surprised to see it was Scott who was shot, and Miss Musselwhite with him. Not me.

"Sniper," one of the men shouted, and we all dove for the ground.

Renewed alarm surged through my veins. The closest source of cover for me was the barn, so I scrambled forward as fast as I could and crouched on my knees beside where Miss Musselwhite had fallen. One swift glance at Scott showed me he was dead—shot through the heart via Miss Musselwhite's shoulder.

I dragged her deeper into the shelter created by the open barn door. It wasn't the most ideal of covers, but it would have to serve. In any case, the sniper seemed to be finished, for no other shots had been fired, and there had been time to pick off a few more targets.

Untying the apron around Miss Musselwhite's waist, I tore it down the middle and rolled both sides into a pad, positioning one against her wound at the back and pressing the other to her wound in her shoulder, and applied pressure. She was breathing heavily, her eyes wide with pain and terror.

"Try to relax," I told her. "And don't move."

I turned to look about me, seeing that Alec had ventured out from the shrub where he'd dived for cover. When his body remained unmolested, the others began creeping out, one by one.

"Who was that?" Max demanded as he emerged from his hiding place behind the large wheel of an old tractor.

"Lieutenant Smith?" Sidney hazarded to guess, and I had to concede it was also the only suggestion I had. If Willoughby had been the pilot of that aeroplane, it couldn't have been him. Though why Smith had saved me, why he had killed Scott, I couldn't answer. Unless it was simply Ardmore's orders.

I pushed the troubling thought away, as well as the certain knowledge I had just dodged death that day by the slimmest of margins.

"Is Scott dead?" Sidney asked as he approached, leaving Alec and Max to guard the others.

"Yes."

Sidney let out a low whistle as he stood over the body, examining the wound. "Clean shot, too." He considered the shed over his shoulder, which stood some one hundred yards away at an angle to the barn. "And from a considerable distance."

I followed his gaze. "Is that where he shot from?"

"That's my best guess."

"Is he still there?"

As if in answer to this, we heard the sound of a motorbike revving and then a moment later saw it speeding off toward the airfield, a plume of dust rising up behind him.

"Should we go after him?" I queried.

Sidney didn't answer. Perhaps because the answer was obvious. We would never catch up with him now. And in any case, he'd very likely saved my life.

My husband knelt down beside Scott, swiping a hand over his vacant eyes to close them, and then entered the barn. A moment later, he returned with a coarse cloth and draped it over Scott's head and torso.

I studied Miss Musselwhite's face. Her eyes were closed and her facial muscles twitched as if she was fighting to retain any semblance of composure. "Someone has to go for help," I said.

"Ryde," Sidney called. "Take the Pierce-Arrow across to the airfield. Tell them there's been an incident and a woman has been shot. With your title and credentials they should hop to it."

Max conferred briefly with Alec, who had Scott's two cohorts seated on the ground with their backs against a tree trunk, and then raced off toward the motorcar.

"Oh, and tell them to send for Chief Inspector Thoreau at the Hungerford Constabulary," Sidney shouted after him. Max waved his hand, indicating he'd heard, and then slid behind the driving wheel. I wondered precisely how he was going to explain the situation to them, but then decided to leave the matter in his capable hands. We had more pressing concerns.

Miss Musselwhite lay still, the grooves across her forehead etched with discomfort.

"They ambushed you on the way to Hungerford," I said.

She blinked open her eyes, and it took a moment for them to focus on me. "Yes." She licked her lips. "Knocked me off my bicycle."

"You were going to see your sister. Because you realized we knew."

She inhaled a deeper breath, blanching at the pain.

I adjusted my hands, maintaining pressure on Miss Musselwhite's wound. Judging from its location in her right shoulder, I didn't believe she was in critical danger from anything more than too much blood loss. But she didn't seem to be aware of that.

"I want to confess," she gasped. "I want to tell you what happened."

Although I could have remained silent, could have let her pour out her confession believing this might be her last chance, my conscience compelled me to be honest. "You will almost certainly survive this."

Her eyes trailed over my features. "Still. I want to explain."

I nodded. "Go ahead."

She seemed to struggle with where to begin. "I . . . I . . . I killed Minnie." She heaved an agonized breath at the confession, tears filling her eyes. "I didn't mean to. It was an accident."

"What happened?"

She swallowed. "I lied about taking the cold remedy that morning. I was lying in bed, trying to sleep, but I kept hearing Minnie moving around. I did my best to ignore her, until I heard her in the chamber below. Where your aunt is currently sleeping."

"So you went to investigate."

"And found her trying to break into her jewelry case." Her eyes blazed with anger. "I realized she was the thief who'd been stealing the other items about the house, and confronted her. She tried to deny it, but the proof was there in her bag. Then . . . then she turned nasty. Accused me of having an affair with my brother-in-law. Which wasn't true! We only talked. But she said she'd tell my sister so anyway."

"I bet that made you angry."

"Yes, but not angry enough to kill her. She . . . she pushed me and I fell into the bed frame, and then she grabbed her bag and ran out of the house. I chased after her and caught up with her in the west garden. We . . . we tussled and some of the items fell out of her bag. I snatched up the letter opener. I just meant to threaten her with it. But she charged at me, and . . ."

"Impaled herself," I finished for her.

She nodded weakly. "Yes."

"Did Mr. Green see?"

"No, but he came upon us shortly after. I didn't know what to do." Her voice broke in remembered panic. "He told me to pack up her belongings and hide them where no one would find them. Then he tucked a few of the trinkets she'd stolen in her skirts and told me he'd take care of the body while I straightened up inside. He said no one would miss her. That they'd all believe she'd run off to London—she talked about it often enough. And he was right."

"Until the erosions from the recent heavy rains uncovered the body."

Her mouth pulled downward at the corners. "It wasn't just the rains."

"Captain Willoughby?"

She nodded. "Somehow he knew about the body and he told me he would tell the authorities what he knew if I didn't find something for him."

"The package Mr. Green found."

Her eyes widened at the discovery I already knew about it. "Yes."

I shifted my arms again, the muscles growing tired.

Sidney knelt beside me. "Here, let me take a turn."

I willingly gave the duty over to him, knowing his arm strength was greater than mine. Shaking my arms to relieve some of the tension, I leaned closer to examine the cut I'd noticed above her eye. "Tell me about Mr. Green. What did he tell you about the package?" In beginning with a relatively innocuous topic, I hoped we might be able to work our way around to the more troubling one.

"You must know already that he was home on leave last autumn, and while he was repairing the bridge between the west park and the airfield he met Lord Ryde. The late one, anyway." She paused. "I heard you on the telephone."

"I know," I replied.

She licked her lips again and I began to worry about her blood loss.

"He took Frank into his confidence, telling him how critical it was that he hide something for a time, lest it fall into the wrong hands. So Frank helped him bury it in the west park."

"Do you know what that *something* is?"

"No, he refused to tell me. Wouldn't even reveal where he'd buried it. Or where he hid it after he dug it up. But . . . I gathered it was something terrible. This look would come over his face whenever he talked about it. It almost made me frightened to ask."

Sidney's gaze lifted to meet mine, wondering as I was what we were dealing with if a hardened veteran of the worst war the world had ever fought was daunted by it.

"Whatever it was," she continued. "I think he tried to forget about it for a time. At least, he didn't speak of it to me. Not until this summer, when he began to give up hope he would ever find a hospital that could help Tilly. Then he told me he had done a favor for Lord Ryde, that if he wrote to him, maybe he would help." Her brow furrowed. "He waited for weeks for a response. And then one morning I saw him in the garden and he was furious. He said he'd discovered that someone was digging holes in the west park. He assumed whoever was doing it was connected with Lord Ryde because of that letter. But when his temper had cooled, he began to recognize that made little sense. That the letter he'd posted might have been intercepted and inadvertently revealed the secret Lord Ryde had worked so hard to conceal. Once he learned the late Lord Ryde was dead, he became certain of this." She broke off, searching my face. "You're working with his son, aren't you? I heard Mr. Kent say his name."

"Yes," I replied simply, the truth being so much harder to explain.

"Then I wish I knew where Frank hid it. But he never confided it in me. Perhaps he knew I was too weak to keep his secret."

I was not about to be diverted into a discussion of Miss Musselwhite's trustworthiness, or lack thereof. Particularly when I suspected she would have readily given up what others had sacrificed so much to conceal to save her own hide. "So he dug it up and hid it elsewhere to keep it safe," I summarized. "And let me guess, he also found another Roman coin?"

Her eyes closed momentarily in a flicker of pain. "He decided that would be their saving grace."

"Why didn't he take the coins from the box Minnie had stolen?" I asked. "They must have been a sore temptation."

"They were. But he didn't know if they were documented. If the police might come looking for him after he sold them. He decided it was better not to take the chance they could be traced. Instead, he watched Captain Willoughby and Lieutenant Smith probe their holes, and then went in after them to search for more coins. I'm not sure he found many. But he was patient. I know he was trying to decide what to do, who to tell." Her eyes drifted from the sky overhead to Sidney's face. "He . . . he seemed hopeful after your arrival. Asked a lot of questions about you."

A tendril of dark hair had flopped over his forehead above his eyes, which were stark with resignation, realizing what she was hinting around. Mr. Green had decided to confide in Sidney, but he'd been killed before he could do so.

However, I was not going to allow her to pass any of the blame for his death on to my husband, not when he already shouldered so much unwarranted guilt for the deaths of others. Not when she was the person who poisoned him.

"Why did you kill him?" I asked baldly, giving her no room to hide.

She blanched and then inhaled a shaky breath, as if steeling herself. "I didn't want to," she murmured in a soft voice. "I thought we were great friends, you know. Allies. We confided in each other, relied on each other." She swallowed. "But something changed after Minnie was killed. He looked at me differently. And then . . . one night he tried to kiss me. I . . . I told him no. That I couldn't do that. Not to my sister. He grew angry. Really, *really* angry. I've never seen him like that. And then cold and cruel. He froze me out for several days. Until he told me that if I didn't return his affection, he would tell everyone what happened with Minnie and prevent me from seeing my sister." Tears streamed from her eyes, freely flowing down her cheeks. "I was so shocked and hurt. I didn't know what to do. I'd trusted him."

I glanced behind me, seeing a vehicle in the distance driving up the road, dust billowing from beneath its tires.

"I couldn't, I just couldn't do that to my sister." Her words suddenly grew flat and almost distant. I could tell she was growing tired, but this was more than that. It was almost as if she couldn't accept the truth of what she was saying, so she'd closed herself off from it emotionally. "And then I remembered the curare in Dr. Maslen's office. He showed it to me once. He'd brought it back from his trips to South America. Even experimented with it. He'd told me how it worked. So I made an excuse to visit Dr. Razey, and while he was distracted, took the bottle from the cabinet. It was exactly where Dr. Maslen had left it. I couldn't believe how easy it was. I took one of Lady Popham's syringes, and I told Frank to meet me in the west park that night." Her eyes hardened. "I knew he would come. Despite my sister begging him not to. He nearly mauled me when I appeared. And when . . ." She began to falter. "When he was distracted, I plunged it into his neck. At first, it didn't seem to work, and he was furious. I worried I'd done it wrong. But then slowly, slowly it began to take effect." Her voice began to tremble. "At first in his face, and then his neck, and then the rest of his body. Eventually he couldn't move or draw breath, but I could see he was aware, that he was watching me. I left before the end."

I was utterly horrified by what she'd revealed, and much of my empathy was quashed by the fact that her main motivation had been self-preservation. She might profess she did it out of loyalty to her sister, but the truth was she could have revealed what she'd done to Minnie herself, removed the source of Mr. Green's blackmail. The proof lay in the fact that when her sister was accused of the very crime she had committed supposedly out of loyalty to her, she never seemed to have considered confessing to it to save her.

The vehicles were drawing close now, and yet there was one piece still missing from the puzzle, so I began to speak quickly. "You chose to meet Mr. Green in the west park because of the airmen, didn't you? You hoped the blame would fall on them?"

She opened her eyes. "Yes, but they saw me, or they simply knew."

It was likely Willoughby or Smith who had taken the lantern and whatever implements Mr. Green had brought with him. And it was they who Opal had seen in the distance, if she'd seen anyone at all.

"They told me if I didn't bring them the item Frank had taken from the earth before they could find it that they would tell everyone. But I never knew what it was or where it was buried."

So the very extortion she'd thought she'd escaped had come back around to her, merely in a different form.

I shook my head in disgust, turning to address the men hastening forward.

CHAPTER 29

It took several hours of talking to an irate Chief Inspector Thoreau, but he eventually cleared us of any wrongdoing. It took another hour to convince him to leave all mention of the buried package and Scott's particular vendetta against me from his report. Not that I was truly worried. I knew Thoreau understood far more about my secretive work than he wished to, and was far more willing to comply with the necessity to conceal such things than he wanted to believe. But all the same I was grateful, particularly knowing that his superior, the head of CID, was Sir Basil Thomson, who was also the newly appointed Director of Intelligence, and friends with Ardmore.

However, Thoreau proved to be not so compliant when it came to believing this *package* we spoke of was lost. As I said, he understood me too well. So later that evening I happened to lead a party of six through Littlemote House rather than four.

"Where are we going, Ver?" Sidney asked me as we climbed the stairs. "To the attics?"

"No, somewhere much less austere. It's been sitting under our noses from the very beginning."

I turned a corner and then stepped forward to push open a door—one that swung open with the greatest of ease. Sidney and the others stared over my shoulder in incomprehension, and then realization dawned in my husband's eyes. "The master bedchambers."

"Yes," I said, turning to enter the lavish lady's chamber with its rose silk wallpaper and gilded picture frames. "You'll recall it was Mr. Green who claimed that the sticking door was an indication of the structure's warped wood and water damage. Whether there is actually damage or he simply made it up, I'm not qualified to say. But I do believe he chose to use the chambers' vacancy to his own advantage."

"Yes, but he told your aunt to hire an expert to better assess the structure," Sidney countered as he and the others spread out through the room.

"Something he knew my aunt could not afford and so would not do. And with Reg being blind, it was unlikely he would contradict them." I pushed open the door to the dressing room and then strolled on through to the master chamber, having already decided this was the room where the item was most likely stored.

A quick survey of the forest-green walls showed no water stains or other obvious signs of concern, but once again, I was not well-versed in such things. Ornate walnut furnishings filled the space, just as in the lady's chamber, and a thick Aubusson carpet stretched from wall to wall.

"What precisely are we looking for?" Thoreau asked gruffly.

"I'm not exactly certain. But something out of place. It may even be hidden."

"Something like this."

I turned at the sound of Alec's voice as he lifted aside a merlot cloth covering a wooden cask about two feet high— wide and squat. My heart leapt at this proof that I had been right. "Yes, remove the cloth."

He whisked it aside and we all stared down at the barrel.

"Opium?" Thoreau stated perplexedly, for that was what it was labeled.

But I was suspicious. "How do we open it?"

Sergeant Crosswire seemed to have some experience with this, for he stepped forward to handle the task as we all looked on. Once the top was removed, he stepped back to allow the rest of us to peer inside. What met our eyes made the blood drain from my face.

"Is that . . . ?"

"Yes," Sidney replied hollowly.

It was Max who had enough presence of mind to reach inside and lift one of the metal cylinders from the barrel's depths. Three of them had been nestled side by side and padded with hay, each about twenty inches in length and eight inches in diameter. When he turned it face up, we could see the telltale white star marking and read the horrifying word, *Phosgene.*

For a moment, none of us seemed able to speak, too alarming was the discovery. How many of the casks the *Zebrina* had picked up on the Isle of Wight had been opium, and how many had hidden these more sinister contents? And that crate the men on Wight had mentioned, was it a Livens Projector used to hurl these at enemy lines? Had *all* the cargo the *Zebrina* had smuggled out been poison gas, not opium?

It was no wonder Max's father had felt tormented about what he'd done. But what on earth had he intended the phosgene to be used for in the first place? To gas the Irish rebels? The thought was sickening.

And look what had come of it. Though we suspected the gas cylinders had been intercepted by men in the employ of Ardmore, who then killed most of the *Zebrina* crew, we still had no proof of it. I'd expected papers of some kind, a trail of evidence leading straight to Ardmore's door, but all the late Lord Ryde had left us was an even more disturbing puzzle.

Where were the rest of these phosgene cylinders now? And what were they intended for? I briefly considered the possibility that they'd already been utilized, except I'd heard nothing about any gas attacks since the end of the war, and none on British soil.

My gaze lifted to Max's face first, my heart squeezing at the confusion and anguish I saw stamped across his features. Discovering what his father had really been mixed up in could not be easy. Even more so, the realization of what his father had been willing to do. Max had been at the front. He had likely seen what phosgene did to a man—drowning him in the liquid discharged from his own lungs. I'd never witnessed it myself, but I'd read the reports. It was a ghastly way to die.

I turned to Sidney next, seeing the anger flashing in his eyes as he tried to push aside his shock. Easier to be furious than give in to the memories of his time in the trenches. After the first gas attack at Ypres in April 1915, he and his men had faced every day knowing they might be smothered by the enemy with poisonous gas. "Put it back carefully," he told Max unnecessarily, but someone had to break the tense silence.

I studied Alec, whose expression I could not read. "Did you have any suspicions about this?"

He shook his head. "No, if there were ever missing cylinders of phosgene, I was never told about it."

Given the fact that they would have disappeared during the autumn of 1917, in the midst of a brutal war, as smuggled cargo for the *Zebrina*'s doomed voyage, I suspected the fact had been hushed up or brushed aside as faulty accounting.

"Forget that. What in blazes do you intend to do with them?" Thoreau demanded, clearly more unsettled than he wished to appear. I began to wonder how he'd spent his war serving.

After the trouble he'd given us over the incident with Scott and my failure to confide in him earlier, I expected Chief Inspector Thoreau to put up a fight about the disposition of the gas cylinders. I wasn't sure if his ready capitulation was an indication of his trust in me, or an acknowledgment that the matter had taken on a complexity that surpassed his means and would draw the unwanted attention of his glory-hound superior—Sir Basil Thomson. Whatever the case, he gamely allowed us to take the cylinders back with us to London. Where I passed them into Alec's care, relying on him to deliver them to C without incident and explain the matter to him.

Given the alarming nature of our report, I'd hoped C might arrange to meet with me in person, despite the complications that could arise should the discovery of our direct communication be revealed. But it was Alec who I once again met in St. James's Park four days later. The afternoon was blustery and threatened rain, so we and a few other brave souls had the paths all to ourselves.

"C offers his compliments," Alec began as we strolled side by side, hands tucked in our pockets, around the lake speckled with the leaves from the trees ringing it.

I made a noise somewhere between a grunt and a rumble of ascent. The truth was, I was growing distinctly annoyed with C, with all of the Secret Service, even though I had known this was the way it would be. After all, I had been the one to contact C for his unofficial help some three months past.

"Major Scott's men are refusing to talk, of course," Alec said, debriefing me on the dramatis personae from the incident at Littlemote. "And they've secured a rather influential barrister. One who is decidedly beyond their means."

"Hmm, yes. I wonder who is footing the bill," I remarked dryly.

"No trail, of course," Alec added. "Ardmore's too clever for that. But all indications are Scott's men shall get off with little more than a slap to the wrist. Particularly as we were unable to press charges for their more serious crimes without revealing secrets the state would rather we not."

I huddled deeper into my coat. "And let me guess, Captain Willoughby and Lieutenant Smith have both been reassigned. Posts unknown."

"No, one better." His voice was deep with reluctant admiration. "The records show they were never posted to Froxfield at all."

I turned to him in shock. "How on earth . . . ?" I broke off, frustration simmering in my veins. "Aliases?" I guessed.

"Maybe. Though they may not have been necessary."

"Because we never actually saw them at the airfield." It was always in adjacent properties that could have been accessed by other means, or the sky. "But I saw Captain Willoughby flying one of the light bombers."

He shrugged. "Maybe it took off from an adjacent property."

I closed my eyes briefly, unable to believe the deception that had played out right under our noses.

"Though I was able to find out that, as you expected, Lieutenant Smith was never assigned to the RAF. He *was* a Fusilier. A sniper."

I supposed that explained his ability to shoot Major Scott through the heart at such a distance, even through the body of another human. I scowled. And perhaps that strange intuition of danger Sidney and I had both experienced in the west park the morning we first met Captain Willoughby. Had Lieutenant Smith been perched in one of the trees? Would he have shot us? I guessed we might never know.

I exhaled, rolling my head to relieve some of the tension in my neck. "Then we have nothing but a suspicion that Ardmore possesses an unknown quantity of phosgene he intends to use in some unspecified manner at some unidentified location, and yet no way to prove it," I snapped beneath my breath.

"Yes, but it could be worse. At least *we* know."

I glared at Alec, finding the fact that he was trying to cheer me both decidedly unhelpful and annoying. "Yes, and he knows we know. I received a note from him just yesterday expressing his appreciation for finding the gas cylinders, and conveying how fortunate it was they didn't fall into the wrong hands."

He shook his head in astonishment. "That man certainly enjoys goading you." Alec grinned. "But then again, so do I."

I cast him a black look, one that, absurdly, I knew would only please him.

However, the chief problem with Ardmore's missive hadn't been his provoking comments, but the acknowledgment that perhaps *I* should have been the one expressing my gratitude to *him* for stopping Scott from killing me, as well as possibly Sidney, Max, and Alec. If not for Willoughby's aerial daring and Smith's sharp-shooting, I held no illusions the confrontation could have turned out quite differently.

Pushing these uncomfortable thoughts to the back of my mind, I turned the conversation to another disturbing topic. "What of the bomb that killed General Bishop and his staff? Were there any survivors?"

"C assured me the matter would be investigated." He kicked a stray acorn fallen into the path from one of the trees overhead. "I gather there was an investigation of some sort at the time of the incident, but it stalled due to lack of or conflicting evidence."

I assumed that conflicting evidence was my and Scott's contradictory reports. The fact that shells had fallen in the area soon after, and then the army had been forced to retreat farther from the Germans' continued advance had muddied any physical evidence that might have been available.

Though I knew it was useless to blame myself for neglecting to recognize that shelter had been blown up by a bomb and not a shell, that I'd been fortunate enough just to survive and escape any severe injuries, I still couldn't help but mentally castigate myself. I prided myself on my observation skills, and yet in a moment when I'd needed them most, I'd failed to utilize them sufficiently, too distracted by my own grief and self-pity over Sidney's reported death. Though C didn't say so, or perhaps Alec simply hadn't repeated it, I knew the chances now of uncovering the culprit who'd planted and detonated that explosive were slim to none. But that didn't mean I wasn't going to try. After all, C and Alec weren't my only sources of information.

As if recognizing this, Alec tipped his head toward me. "Have a care who you send Ryde to ask information from at the War Office," he advised me. "If your bomber is the same man as that traitor you were warning Bishop of, then he might still be haunting the halls of Whitehall."

I repressed a scowl at his having already anticipated my intentions to ask Max to do just that, perfectly aware of the risks. "Haven't you been cleared for active duty yet?" I groused. From what I could tell his shoulder seemed perfectly healed.

Far from insulted, Alec's expression turned arrogant. "Eager to get rid of me, are you?"

"Like a bad haircut."

He chuckled. "Say what you like, Ver, but I know you'll miss me when I'm gone."

And dash it all, if he wasn't right. I would miss him. And worry for him. For he'd always been too brash for his own good. Given the state of affairs, he was most likely to be sent to Ireland, and who knew what trouble he might get himself into there?

Almost as if to illustrate this point, his attention shifted to the trio of men striding toward us from Downing Street. We had turned onto a side path to stroll toward Horse Guards Road, passing beneath the shade of the trees lining the rim of the park. "Well, I'll be damned. It can't be?" He narrowed his eyes. "But so it is. Now what are they about? It can't be anything good."

"Who?" I asked, trying to tell whether I recognized any of the men, whether I *should* recognize them. But to my eyes they appeared like rather ordinary gentlemen in three-piece suits and dark overcoats. The only thing about them that stood out to me was the fact that the other two seemed to subtly defer to the tall, broad-shouldered man on the right.

Alec glanced at me, and I could tell he was debating whether to speak. "Mark the one on the right well," he finally said. "That's Michael Collins."

I struggled not to react. "You mean, the Irish revolutionary?"

He nodded. "And their Director of Intelligence, from what I hear."

"But I thought no one knew what he looked like?"

"Some of us do," he answered obliquely.

I could only wonder what that meant. "But isn't he wanted by the authorities?" And yet he was here, in the heart of London, walking by the prime minister's lodgings. "Should we follow them?"

"*I* will."

I arched my eyebrows in silent challenge.

"You're too conspicuous, Ver," he replied unrepentantly. "I know in Belgium during the war you ground dirt into your hair and made yourself dowdy to pass by unnoticed, but in your normal garb you're much too arresting. There's no way they wouldn't mark a lovely woman following them about. They've already marked you."

I didn't turn my head to see if this was true, having already recognized the truth in what he said. There were times when attractiveness worked to one's advantage and times when it did not.

We turned left down Horse Guards Road, shadowing them on the opposite side of the street, and I knew he would expect us to separate at the intersection with The Mall if not sooner.

"What of the other two men? Do you know who they are?" I asked, curious how much he knew.

"Liam Tobin and Desmond Fitzgerald."

"Intelligence officers?"

"Of a sort."

I recognized that answer for what it was. I wouldn't hear any more from him about it. The fact he'd revealed what he had was purely because he thought I might need to identify them in the future, and recognize them for what they were. This, more than anything, confirmed to me he was already preparing to go to Ireland, and that he thought I might be headed there as well before the end. It wasn't a possibility I was yet willing to face, still hoping we might foil Ardmore by other means. That his maneuverings didn't involve the Irish rebellion. But what else could it be?

"Sidney and I are going away for a time," I told him as we neared the point of our separation. "At least until after the anniversary of the armistice and all the memorials they've scheduled are passed."

Neither of us wanted to face that milestone in the public spotlight. Some might find meaning and relief in marking the day in the ways that were planned, but for others it was too much. Too raw. Too painful. Too haunting.

Alec understood this without words. "Then I'll wish you safe journeys until we meet again." That he would be gone from London when we returned went unstated, but I inferred it anyway.

I lifted my hand to touch his cheek briefly as we came to a stop near the corner. "Be safe," I told him earnestly, wondering if he had anyone else to tell him so. If he had anyone who worried when he didn't.

His dark eyes burned with an intensity that left me feeling guilty for somehow inspiring it. I walked away swiftly, refusing to look back.

I found Sadie and Nimble in the midst of flurried preparations for our removal to our cottage in Sussex. Though Sadie would remain behind to mind our flat and whatever secrets she was hiding, Nimble would be accompanying us and all our sundry baggage. I had no intention of traveling light this trip. Sadie claimed that Lord Ardmore had not approached her again, and I hoped that our absence from London would convince him blackmailing her for information was a non-starter.

I retreated to our bedchamber, intending to change into my traveling clothes, and discovered Sidney standing in the middle of the room, staring up at the painting of the bluebell wood he'd bought me two days after our wedding. His gaze flicked to me and then back to the artwork, as if there was something he was trying to puzzle out. I moved to stand beside him, wondering what it was he was analyzing so intently, and if it was even related to the painting.

"You told me once," he began softly, "that you considered getting rid of this after you received the telegram informing you that I was missing and presumed dead. That it was too painful to look at because it constantly reminded you of me." His gaze when it shifted to meet mine was searching. "Why didn't you?"

I tilted my head, studying the bright blue flecks of paint, the play of light and shadow. "I suppose because, at first, it was beyond my ability to remove it. I simply didn't have the will." I swallowed the lump forming in my throat at the memory of the dark, fathomless pit of those early days. "And then . . . then the idea of *not* having it there was as painful as the memories it awoke." My voice grew hoarse. "I knew if I moved it, even if I hung something in its place, I would always know what should have been there. And that would hurt more than the initial reminder."

He didn't look at me, and something in his posture told me my touch would not be welcomed at the moment. I understood why when he next spoke.

"Do you think it cowardly of me not to remain in London? To not stand on Whitehall with all the dignitaries for the anniversary commemorations?"

"No, I don't," I told him firmly. "Who made you feel so?"

"Your mother telephoned."

Of course.

"And my uncle Oswald." The Marquess of Treborough. "They don't understand why we don't intend to remain. Why I'm not grateful for the honor." He sank down on the bench at the end of our bed.

"You upheld your honor by fighting for your family and this country for four bloody years," I snapped in fury as I sat beside him. "No one has any right to ask more of you."

"Yes, but it's not as if I can ignore the moment is passing. I'll mark it all the same wherever I am, whether I'm on a stage in front of thousands or sitting on our terrace."

I gazed into his eyes, seeing the despair and bewilderment marked there, and reached for his hand. "It takes just as much courage to mark the moment alone as it does to mark it in front of thousands," I told him, knowing how he both longed for and dreaded it in equal measure. "The only difference is that in front of a crowd you are doing it for them. Alone you are doing it for yourself."

His Adam's apple bobbed up and down as he swallowed. "But I won't be alone?"

I smiled tenderly. "No, wild horses couldn't drag me from your side." My smile slipped away, remembering the hundreds of friends, family, acquaintances, and colleagues I'd lost. Remembering my brother Rob. "I'll need you, too."

He wrapped his arm around me, pulling me to his side. We sat that way for some time, leaning on each other, listening to the sounds of Nimble moving about in the next room. When Sidney finally spoke, it was in a voice that almost sounded normal.

"Your mother wanted to remind us we promised to come for the holidays."

I sighed. "As if I could forget."

"And she wanted to wish us a happy anniversary."

I looked up in surprise. "That was nice of her. Though it's not until tomorrow."

His lips quirked. "I didn't correct her. Especially not when she began thanking us for handling your aunt Ernestine's difficulties. Apparently she's been singing our praises and is traveling to Yorkshire to visit your parents next week."

I eyed him suspiciously. "You mean thanking *you*. My mother would never give me that much credit. Nor would my aunt."

"Yes, well, I told her it was all your doing."

I crossed my arms over my chest. "Which she didn't believe. Probably called you an adorably doting husband."

He didn't contradict this. "At least your cousin fully appreciated the truth."

"That's true," I replied, softening. It had been difficult leaving Reg. Though I swore I would never let so much time pass between visits again, and I'd already honored my promise to him by sending two boxes filled with books written in Braille.

"I know you worry about him out there in Wiltshire with only his mother for company," Sidney said, correctly interpreting my expression. "So I hope you won't mind that I invited him to join us in Sussex."

I turned to him in pleased surprise. "You did?"

"Ryde, as well. We've still got that key of his we found out at Burgh Castle to puzzle out. And your George and Daphne."

I hardly knew what to say.

"It will be a lopsided party, but I don't think they'll mind."

I grasped his face between my hands. "Sidney, I think that's the most wonderful thing!"

"Yes, well, it didn't seem right to let any of them spend the anniversary of the armistice alone. And I knew it would please you."

I pressed a kiss to his lips. "Oh, you are the dearest."

"I suppose you'll want to invite Xavier, too."

"No," I said, trying not to let my worry for him show. "I'm sure he has other plans."

He searched my eyes for a moment. "Does he?"

But I could not, would not say any more.

"Well, in any case, I've warned your friends not to appear on our doorstep until at least All Saints' Day." He pulled me closer, speaking a hair's breadth from my lips. "I've waited five years to spend a wedding anniversary with you, and I will *not* be rushed or interrupted."

"Is that so?"

"Yes, I'm selfish. I want you all to myself. So turn that delightful mind of yours away from all things mysterious and macabre, and focus your thoughts solely on me, for I will not be sidetracked by mayhem or murder."

I laughed. "These things are hardly under my control."

"So you say."

"Well, then I suppose you'll simply have to keep me sufficiently diverted."

A roguish glint lit his eyes at this gauntlet being thrown down, and he set about reminding me of how very diverting he could be.

Don't miss the first book in the
Verity Kent mystery series . . .

THIS SIDE OF MURDER

**The Great War is over, but in this captivating new mystery
from award-winning author Anna Lee Huber, one young
widow discovers the real intrigue has only just begun . . .**

England, 1919. Verity Kent's grief over the loss of her husband pierces anew when she receives a cryptic letter, suggesting her beloved Sidney may have committed treason before
his untimely death. Determined to dull her pain with revelry,
Verity's first impulse is to dismiss the derogatory claim. But
the mystery sender knows too much—including the fact that
during the war Verity worked for the Secret Service, something not even Sidney knew.

Lured to Umbersea Island to attend the engagement party of
one of Sidney's fellow officers, Verity mingles among the men
her husband once fought beside, and discovers dark secrets—
along with a murder clearly meant to conceal them. Relying on little more than a coded letter, the help of a dashing
stranger, and her own sharp instincts, Verity is forced down
a path she never imagined—and comes face to face with the
shattering possibility that her husband may not have been the
man she thought he was. It's a truth that could set her free—
or draw her ever deeper into his deception . . .

CHAPTER 1

You might question whether this is all
a ruse, whether I truly have anything
to reveal. But I know what kind of
work you really did during the war.
I know the secrets you hide. Why
shouldn't I also know your husband's?

June 1919
England

They say when you believe you're about to die your entire life passes before your eyes in a flurry of poignant images, but all I could think of, rather absurdly, was that I should have worn the blue hat. Well, that and that my sister would never forgive me for proving our mother right.

Mother had never approved of Sidney teaching me how to drive his motorcar that last glorious summer before the war. Or of my gadding about London and the English countryside in his prized Pierce-Arrow while he was fighting in France. Or of my decision to keep the sleek little Runabout instead of selling it after a German bullet so callously snatched him from me. In my mother's world of rules and privilege, women—even wealthy widows—did not own motorcars, and they certainly didn't drive them. She'd declared it would be the death of me. And so it might have been, had it not been for the other driver's bizarre bonnet ornament.

Once my motorcar had squealed to a stop, a bare two inches from the fender of the other vehicle, and I'd peeled open my eyes, I could see that the ornament was some sort of pompon. Tassels of bright orange streamers affixed to the Rolls-Royce's more traditional silver lady. When racing down the country roads, I supposed they trailed out behind her like ribbons of flame, but at a standstill they drooped across the grille rather like limp seagrass.

I heard the other driver open his door, and decided it was time to stop ogling his peculiar taste in adornment and apologize. For there was no denying our near collision was my fault. I had been driving much too fast for the winding, shrubbery-lined roads. I was tempted to blame Pinky, but I was the dolt who'd chosen to follow his directions even though I'd known they would be rubbish.

When my childhood friend Beatrice had invited me to visit her and her husband, Pinky, at their home in Winchester, I'd thought it a godsend, sparing me the long drive from London to Poole in one shot. I hadn't seen either of them since before the war, other than a swift bussing of Pinky's cheek as I passed him at the train station one morning, headed back to the front. All in all, it had been a lovely visit despite the evident awkwardness we all felt at Sidney's absence.

In any case, although Pinky was a capital fellow, he'd always been a bit of a dodo. I couldn't help but wonder if he'd survived the war simply by walking in circles—as he'd had me driving—never actually making it to the front.

I adjusted my rather uninspired cream short-brimmed hat over my auburn castle-bobbed tresses and stepped down into the dirt and gravel lane, hoping the mud wouldn't damage my blue kid leather pumps. My gaze traveled over the beautiful pale yellow body of the Rolls-Royce and came to rest on the equally attractive man rounding her bonnet. Dark blond hair curled against the brim of his hat, and when his eyes lifted from the spot where our motorcars nearly touched, I could see they were a soft gray. I was relieved to see they weren't bright with anger. Charming a man out of a high dudgeon had never been my favorite pastime.

One corner of his mouth curled upward in a wry grin. "Well, that was a near thing."

"Only if you're not accustomed to driving in London." I offered him my most disarming smile as I leaned forward to see just how close it had been. "But I do apologize. Clearly, I shouldn't have been in such a rush."

"Oh, I'd say these hedgerows hold some of the blame." He lifted aside his gray tweed coat to slide his hands into his trouser pockets as he nodded toward the offending shrubbery. "It's almost impossible to see around them. Otherwise, I would have seen you coming. It's hard to miss a Pierce-Arrow," he declared, studying the currant-red paint and brass fittings of my motorcar.

"Yes, well, that's very good of you to say so."

"Nonsense. And in any case, there's no harm done."

"Thanks to your colorful bonnet ornament."

He followed my pointed stare to the pompon attached to his silver lady, his wry grin widening in furtive amusement.

"There must be a story behind it."

"It just seemed like it should be there."

"And that's all there is to it?"

He shrugged. "Does there need to be more?"

I tilted my head, trying to read his expression. "I suppose not. Though, I'll own I'm curious where you purchased such a bold piece of frippery."

"Oh, I didn't." His eyes sparkled with mischief. "My niece kindly let me borrow it. Just for this occasion."

I couldn't help but laugh. Had he been one of my London friends I would have accused him of having a jest, but with this man I wasn't certain, and told him so. "I'm not sure if you're quite serious or simply having a pull at me."

"Good." He rocked back on his heels, clearly having enjoyed our exchange.

I shook my head at this teasing remark. He truly was a rather appealing fellow, though there was something in his features—perhaps the knife-blade sharpness of his nose—that kept him from being far too handsome for any woman's good. Which was a blessing, for combined with his artless charm and arresting smile he might have had quite a devastating effect. He still might, given a more susceptible female. Unfortunately, I had far too much experience with charming, attractive men to ever fold so quickly.

I pegged him at being just shy of thirty, and from his manner of speech and cut of clothes, undoubtedly a gentleman. From old money, if I wagered a guess. A well-bred lady can always tell these things. After all, we're taught to sniff out the imposters from the cradle, though it had begun to matter less and less, no matter what my mother and her like said about the nouveau riche.

He pulled a cigarette case from his pocket and offered me one, which I declined, before lighting one for himself. "If I may be so bold . . ." he remarked after taking a drag. "Where precisely were you rushing to?"

"Poole Harbor. There's a boat I'm supposed to meet." I sighed. "And I very much fear I've missed it."

"To Umbersea Island?"

I blinked in surprise. "Why, yes." I paused, considering him. "Are you also . . ."

"On my way to Walter Ponsonby's house party?" He finished for me. "I am. But don't worry. They won't leave without us." He lifted his arm to glance at his wristwatch. "And if they do, we'll make our own way over."

"Well, that's a relief," I replied, feeling anything but. Some of the sparkle from our encounter had dimmed at this discovery. Still, I couldn't let him know that. "Then I suppose if we're going to be spending the weekend together we should introduce ourselves." I extended my hand across the small gap separating our motorcars. "Mrs. Verity Kent."

His grip was warm, even through my cream leather glove, as he clasped my hand for a moment longer than was necessary. "Max Westfield, Earl of Ryde. But, please, call me Ryde. Or Max, even. None of that Lord business." Something flickered in his eyes, and I could tell he was debating whether to say something else. "You wouldn't by chance be Sidney Kent's widow?"

I'm not sure why I was startled. There was no reason to be. After all, I'd just discovered we were both making our way to the same house party. A party thrown by one of Sidney's old war chums. There were bound to be one or two of Sidney's fellow officers attending. Why shouldn't Lord Ryde be one of them?

My eyes dipped briefly to the glow at the end of the fag clasped between Ryde's fingers, before returning to his face. "You knew him?" I remarked as casually as I could manage, determined not to show he'd unsettled me.

"I was his commanding officer." He exhaled a long stream of smoke. "For a short time, anyway." His eyes tightened at the corners. "I'm sorry for your loss. He was a good man," he added gently.

I tried to respond, but found alarmingly that I had to clear my throat before I could get the words out. "Thank you."

It was the standard litany. The standard offer of condolences and expression of gratitude that had been repeated dozens of times since Sidney's death. I'd developed a sort of callus from hearing the words over and over. It prevented them from overly affecting me, from making me remember.

Except, this time was different.

"Did you know Sidney before the war?" I managed to say with what I thought was an admirable amount of aplomb. They were of an age with each other, and both being gentlemen it seemed a safe assumption.

"Yes, Kent was a year behind me at Eton and Oxford. Same as your brother, if I recall. They were chums."

I nodded. "Yes, that's how we met. Sidney came home with Freddy to Yorkshire one school holiday."

"Love at first sight?"

"Goodness, no. At least, not for him. I was all of eleven to his sixteen. And a rather coltish eleven, at that. All elbows and knees."

He grinned. "Well, that didn't last."

I dimpled cheekily. "Why, thank you for noticing. No, Sidney didn't return to Upper Wensleydale for six more years. But by then, of course, things had changed."

My chest tightened at the bittersweet memories, and I turned to stare at the bonnet of my motorcar—Sidney's motorcar—gleaming in the sunshine. I'd known this weekend was going to be difficult. I'd been preparing myself for it as best I could. Truth be told, that's why I'd nearly collided with Lord Ryde. I'd been distracted by my recollections. The ones I'd been ducking since the telegram arrived to inform me of Sidney's death.

I'd gotten rather good at avoiding them. At calculating just how many rags I needed to dance, and how much gin I needed to drink so I could forget, and yet not be too incapacitated to perform my job the following morning. And when I was released from my position after the war, well, then it didn't matter anymore, did it?

But this weekend I couldn't afford the luxury of forgetfulness.

As if sensing the maudlin turn of my thoughts, Ryde reached out to touch my motorcar's rather plain bonnet ornament, at least compared to his. "Kent used to talk about his Pierce-Arrow. Claimed it was the fastest thing on four wheels."

"Yes, he was rather proud of it." I recognized the turn in subject for the kindness it was. He'd sensed my discomfort and was trying to find a gracious way to extricate ourselves from this awkwardness. I should have felt grateful, but I only felt troubled.

I lifted my gaze to meet his, trying to read something in his eyes. "I suppose there wasn't much to talk about in the trenches."

His expression turned guarded. "No, not that we wanted to. Motorcars were just about the safest topic we could find."

I nodded, understanding far more than he was saying. Though, I also couldn't help but wonder if that was a dodge.

Almost reflexively, I found myself searching Ryde for any visible signs of injury. I'd learned swiftly that those soldiers fortunate enough to survive the war still returned wounded in some way, whether it be in body or mind. The unluckiest suffered both.

As if he knew what I was doing, he rolled his left shoulder self-consciously before flicking his fag into the dirt. He ground it out before glancing down the road toward Poole. "I suppose we should be on our way then, lest our fellow guests truly leave us behind to shrift for ourselves."

"It does seem rude to keep them waiting longer than necessary," I admitted, suddenly wishing very much to be away, but not wanting to appear overeager. "Is it much farther?"

"Just over the next rise or two, you should be able to see the town laid out before you."

"That close?"

"Yes, and as I said, I suspect Ponsonby will have told them to wait for us all before departing. He was always considerate about such things."

"You know him well then?" I asked in genuine curiosity.

He shrugged, narrowing his eyes against the glare of the midday sun. "As well as one can know another man serving beside him during war." It was rather an obscure answer. And yet Ponsonby had thought them friendly enough to invite him to his house party to celebrate his recent engagement to be married. Of course, the man had also invited me, a woman he hardly knew, though I assumed that was because of Sidney.

As if sensing my interest and wishing to deflect it from himself, he added, "I know he and Kent were great friends."

"Yes, since Eton. I met Walter once or twice before the war. And, of course, he attended our wedding." One of the numerous hasty ceremonies performed throughout Britain during the months at the start of the war, between Sidney's training and his orders to report to France as a fresh-faced lieutenant. I'd only just turned eighteen and hadn't the slightest idea what was to come. None of us had.

I looked up to find Ryde watching me steadily, as if he knew what I was thinking, for it was what he was thinking, too. It was an odd moment of solidarity under the brilliant June sky, and I would remember it many times in the days to come.

Because who of us ever really knows what's coming? Or what secrets will come back to haunt us in the end? The war might be over, but it still echoed through our lives like an endless roll of thunder.

Connect with U S

Visit us online at
KensingtonBooks.com
to read more from your favorite authors, see books
by series, view reading group guides, and more.

Join us on social media

for sneak peeks, chances to win books and prize packs,
and to share your thoughts with other readers.

facebook.com/kensingtonpublishing
twitter.com/kensingtonbooks

Tell us what you think!

To share your thoughts, submit a review,
or sign up for our eNewsletters, please visit:
KensingtonBooks.com/TellUs.